DANTE ALI█████████████████████y, in 1265. His early poetr█████████████████████oetry that passed from the████████████████████uido Cavalcanti, Dante's███████████████████work was the *Vita Nuova* (█████████████████nce of lyrics, sonnets, and prose narrative describes his love, first earthly, then spiritual, for Beatrice, whom he had first seen as a child of nine, and who had died when Dante was twenty-five.

Dante married around 1285, served Florence in battle, and rose to a position of leadership in the bitter factional politics of that city-state. As one of the city's magistrates, he found it necessary to banish leaders of the so-called "Black" faction, and his friend Cavalcanti, who like Dante was a prominent "White." But after the Blacks seized control of Florence in 1301, Dante himself was tried in absentia and was banished from the city on pain of death. He never returned to Florence.

In exile he wrote *Convivio,* or *Banquet,* a kind of poetic compendium of medieval philosophy, as well as a political treatise, *Monarchia.* He probably began his *Comedy* (later to be called the *Divine Comedy* and consisting of three parts, the *Inferno,* the *Purgatorio,* and the *Paradiso*) around 1307–1308. On a diplomatic mission to Venice in 1321, Dante fell ill and returned to Ravenna, where he died.

"Dante's basic, quintessential clarity has largely been captured, and for the first time in English. . . . At long last, an English Dante which . . . should satisfy Italianists, and medievalists, and readers of poetry."

—Burton Raffel, *The Denver Quarterly*

"Lovers of the English language will be delighted by this eloquently accomplished enterprise."

—*Book Review Digest*

"A miracle. A lesson in the art of translation and a model (an encyclopedia) for poets. The full range and richness of American English is displayed as perhaps never before."

—Charles Simic

The Divine Comedy of
DANTE ALIGHIERI
PURGATORIO

A Verse Translation

with an Introduction
by Allen Mandelbaum

Notes by Laury Magnus, Allen Mandelbaum, and
Andrew Oldcorn, with Daniel Feldman

Drawings by Barry Moser

BANTAM CLASSIC

This translation of the PURGATORIO *is inscribed to*
Irma Brandeis and Helaine Newstead—
as l'altro Guido *had it:*
CHÉ 'N TUTTE GUISE VI DEGGIO LAUDARE

THE DIVINE COMEDY: PURGATORIO
A Bantam Book
PUBLISHING HISTORY
THE DIVINE COMEDY OF DANTE ALIGHIERI, translated by Allen
Mandelbaum, is published in hardcover by the University of California Press:
Volume I, INFERNO (1980); Volume II, PURGATORIO (1981); Volume III,
PARADISO (1982). Of the three separate volumes of commentary under the
general editorship of Allen Mandelbaum, Anthony Oldcorn, and Charles Ross,
Volume I: THE CALIFORNIA LECTURA DANTIS: INFERNO was published
by the University of California Press in 1998. For information, please address
University of California Press, 2223 Fulton St., Berkeley, CA 94720.

Bantam Classic edition / January 1984
Bantam Classic reissue edition / August 2004

Published by
Bantam Dell
A division of Random House, Inc.
New York, New York

ISBN 0-553-21344-X

Manufactured in the United States of America
Published simultaneously in Canada

OPM 28

PURGATORIO

CONTENTS

INTRODUCTION

F OR THE Virgil of Dante's *Purgatorio,* "love is the seed in
you of every virtue/and of all acts deserving punishment"
(XVII, 104–105). To find one same source for all good and all
evil is to insist on the need for the education of desire. The descent through Hell and ascent of the seven terraces of the
Mount of Purgatory are the tale of that education of Dante's
hungering, longing, thirsting will. After those terraces, at the
threshold of the Earthly Paradise, Virgil can assure him:
"Today your hungerings will find their peace / ... My son,
you've seen the temporary fire / and the eternal fire; you have
reached / the place past which my powers cannot see. / I've
brought you here through intellect and art; / from now on, let
your pleasure be your guide; / you're past the steep and past the
narrow paths.... / Await no further word or sign from me: /
your will is free, erect, and whole—to act / against that will
would be to err: therefore / I crown and miter you over yourself" (XXVII, 115–142).

This tale forms part of what Thomas Carlyle called Dante's
"unfathomable heart-song." But in the *Purgatorio,* the song is
sung by a careful cartographer and passionately precise
watcher of the skies, one who contains time and space in the
calculated space and time of his own lines: "Reader, I am not
squandering more rhymes / in order to describe their forms;
since I / must spend elsewhere, I can't be lavish here" (XXIV,
97–99); and then, "If, reader, I had ampler space in which /
to write, I'd sing—though incompletely—that / sweet draught for
which my thirst was limitless; / but since all of the pages pre-
disposed / for this, the second canticle, are full, / the curb of art
will not let me continue" (XXXIII, 136–141).

The space of Dante's island Mountain of Purgatory is in the southern hemisphere of Earth, directly opposite the northern hemisphere's Jerusalem. In that southern hemisphere, the hemisphere of water, it is the only body of land. Souls who will undergo purgation before their entry into Paradise disembark on the shore of the solitary island. Behind them lies their sea-voyage from the mouth of the Tiber, which "always is the place of gathering / for those who do not sink to Acheron" (II, 104–105), under the care of a "helmsman sent from Heaven," in a "boat so light, so quick / that nowhere did the water swallow it" (II, 40–41). Ahead of Dante there lies the writing of the *Purgatorio,* also—by way of likeness—a sea-voyage: "To course across more kindly waters now / my talent's little vessel lifts her sails, / leaving behind herself a sea so cruel" (I, 1–3).

The lower slopes of the island are a waiting place, the Ante-Purgatory (II–IX), where those who delayed their repentance until the end of life must wait longest before they are allowed to enter Purgatory.

Purgatory proper, occupying eighteen cantos of *Purgatorio,* is entered by a gate at the top of a three-step stairway (IX, 76–145) and consists of seven terraces. These are level indentations in the tall mountain; they are joined to each other by stairways carved through the rifted rock, with the ascent growing easier as one moves upward. Each of the terraces punishes a sin; and the hierarchy of sins places the most grievous sins on the lower terraces. In ascending order, the seven terraces punish—remedially—pride, envy, wrath, sloth, avarice (coupled with its counter-sin, prodigality), gluttony, and lust.

The Earthly Paradise occupies the summit of the island mountain and the last, and rather autonomous, six cantos of *Purgatorio* (XXVIII–XXXIII). (Indeed, this mountain may also be called the Mountain of Earthly Paradise, the mountain foreshadowed by the "mountain of delight" that Dante cannot climb in Canto I of the *Inferno*—and it is probably the same peak

Ulysses sees at the end of Canto XXVI of the *Inferno,* the summit in sight of which Ulysses, unaided by grace, shipwrecks.)

Time is charted with equal care: Dante the voyager moves through these three regions of Purgatory in an ascent that most paraphrasts explain as lasting from the morning of Easter Sunday, April 10, 1300, to noon of Wednesday, April 13. Where the *Inferno* begins at night in the "shadowed forest," with the entry into Hell, or, more precisely, to the Ante-Inferno, on the evening of Good Friday (*Inf.* II, 1–3), *Purgatorio* begins shortly before dawn, the entry to Purgatory proper, two hours after dawn, and to the Earthly Paradise at dawn.

But Dante climbs only by day. The first night is spent in that portion of the Ante-Purgatory called the Valley of the Rulers, where men of state who, in life, delayed their repentance through negligence wait (IX); the second night is spent on the fourth terrace, the terrace of sloth, at the end of his climb through the terraces of the four weightier sins, at the threshold of the fifth terrace (XVIII, 143 to XIX, 36). The third night is spent, after Dante's passage through fire on the seventh terrace (this is the "temporary fire," as Hell's fire is the "eternal fire" of XXVII, 127–128), the terrace of the lustful, at the threshold of the Earthly Paradise (XXVII). On each of these equidistant nights, Dante dreams: first the dream of the Eagle (IX, 13–32); then the dream of the Siren and the nameless "alert and saintly" woman, (XIX, 7–33); and finally the dream of Leah, exemplar of the active life, and Rachel, exemplar of the meditative life (XXVII, 91–114).

The movements of heavenly bodies, somewhat clairvoyantly referred to by Virgil but never directly present in Hell, punctuate *Purgatorio* throughout. References play between the southern skies of Purgatory, present *there* for Dante, and our skies, the skies of the northern hemisphere, present to us and to Dante returned from his voyage. Here, in our world, Jerusalem marks the center, and the mouth of the Ganges marks the eastern limit; while the western limit is marked by the Straits of

Gibraltar or, in its stead, either Gades (our Cadiz) or the River Ebro. Reading the hands of his Earth clock, Dante can amplify the hour of sunset in Purgatory thus: "Just as, there where its Maker shed His blood, / the sun shed its first rays, and Ebro lay / beneath high Libra, and the ninth hour's rays / were scorching Ganges' waves; so here, the sun / stood at the point of day's departure . . ." (XXVII, 1–5).

The planets (of which the sun, for Dante, is one), the constellations, the hours—all participate in these recordings.

Sometimes Dante's recordings are direct, even when allegorical, as in the vision of the four stars that symbolize the four "natural" virtues (prudence, justice, fortitude, and temperance). There his most memorable juxtaposition of Purgatorial skies and our skies concludes his first scanning of Purgatory's skies (I, 13–27):

> The gentle hue of oriental sapphire
> in which the sky's serenity was steeped—
> its aspect pure as far as the horizon—
>   brought back my joy in seeing just as soon
> as I had left behind the air of death
> that had afflicted both my sight and breast.
>   The lovely planet that is patroness
> of love made all the eastern heavens glad,
> veiling the Pisces in the train she led.
>   Then I turned to the right, setting my mind
> upon the other pole, and saw four stars
> not seen before except by the first people.
>   Heaven appeared to revel in their flames:
> o northern hemisphere, because you were
> denied that sight, you are a widower!

Sometimes he is obsessively periphrastic; at a pole far from plain style (and Dante experiments with *all* styles), he lets us know that it is 3 p.m., the beginning of vespers, "there" in Purgatory by a likeness that measures the morning span between 6 a.m. and 9 a.m.: "As many as the hours in which the sphere / that's always playing like a child appears / from daybreak to the end of the third hour, / so many were the hours of light still left / before the course of day had reached sunset; / vespers was there; and where we are, midnight" (XV, 1–6).

And at times Dante records the skies not through the movements of stellar bodies but through the motions of the soul, as in the six lines for which Paget Toynbee, in 1900, could total up sixteen translations into English independent of translations forming part of full translations of the *Purgatorio* or the *Comedy:* "It was the hour that turns seafarers' longings / homeward—the hour that makes their hearts grow tender / upon the day they bid sweet friends farewell; / the hour that pierces the new traveler / with love when he has heard, far off, the bell / that seems to mourn the dying of the day" (VIII, 1–6).

The heavens serve not only to measure time there; Dante will also use our skies here as likenesses of what he saw there, most indelibly in reinforcing his first vision of Beatrice in the *Comedy* (XXX, 22–39):

> I have at times seen all the eastern sky
> becoming rose as day began and seen,
> adorned in lovely blue, the rest of heaven;
>   and seen the sun's face rise so veiled that it
> was tempered by the mist and could permit
> the eye to look at length upon it; so,
>   within a cloud of flowers that were cast
> by the angelic hands and then rose up
> and then fell back, outside and in the chariot,
>   a woman showed herself to me; above
> a white veil, she was crowned with olive boughs;
> her cape was green; her dress beneath, flame-red.
>   Within her presence, I had once been used
> to feeling—trembling—wonder, dissolution;
> but that was long ago. Still, though my soul,
>   now she was veiled, could not see her directly,

by way of hidden force that she could move,
I felt the mighty power of old love.

This tight construct of space and time serves as container for a *cantica* less dispersive and digressive than the *Inferno,* with its crowded population and its percussiveness.

Of course, even in *Purgatorio,* Dante can, with *Infern*-al velocity, in thirty lines, examine the nature of attentiveness, refute the Platonic doctrine of the plurality of souls, offer us the vision of a farmer preventing thieves from entering his field, conjure hard ascents and descents in four Italian hilly terrains, and define Virgil as "the guide who gave me hope and was my light" (IV, 1–30).

And he can dart, in his dance of likenesses, from "a fledgling stork" to the "iron of the arrow" touching the "bowstring," to "leavings left on the table"—a likeness of the blood the veins have not drunk up—to seeing the fetus as a "sea-sponge," to invoking "the sun's heat that, when combined / with sap that flows from vines, is then made wine," to summoning "the saturated air," which, reflecting "the rays the sun has sent, / takes rainbow colors as its ornament," and then to conjuring the flame that follows after "the fire whenever fire moves" (with the poet's own pace not unlike the flame's)—justifying, as much as does the combustible thread of exposition along which these flames run, the conclusion: "This is the cause of your astonishment" (XXV, 10–108). The end of the previous canto is not much less various (XXIV, 94–154), as Dante's likenesses move from a horseman who "sometimes gallops out, / leaving behind his troop of riders, so / that he may gain the honor of the first / clash," to "little, eager, empty-headed children / who beg—but he of whom they beg does not / reply, but to provoke their longing, he / holds high, and does not hide, the thing they want," to seeing himself as "a scared young animal," to the red glow of "glass or metal . . . seen within a furnace," to the "breeze of May that—heralding / the dawning of the day—when it is steeped / in flowers and in grass, stirs fragrantly," in a passage that ends by blessing those "whose hungering is always in just measure" but belies that "just measure" with Dante's own measureless hungering for metaphor.

But, generally, the similes of *Purgatorio* share the tighter "curb of art" and sense of rite that rein the actions, rhetoric, spacings, and timings of *Purgatorio:* a gravity, a concentration, that relies on prefatory announcement and alerting, on formal greetings and valedictions, on strategies of stylization and sacralization.

The line of rite begins in the first canto, with its formal pre-announcement by Cato: "Go then; but first / wind a smooth rush around his waist and bathe / his face to wash away all of Hell's stains" (I, 94–96), and then its emblematic etching of a shore where only pliant rushes can grow (I, 100–105):

> *This solitary island, all around*
> *its very base, there where the breakers pound,*
> *bears rushes on its soft and muddy ground.*
> *There is no other plant that lives below:*
> *no plant with leaves or plant that, as it grows,*
> *hardens—and breaks beneath the waves' harsh blows.*

That line of rite continues in the angelic apparition of Canto II, the first of a series (Cantos VIII, IX, XII, XVII, XIX); in the formal entry to Purgatory with its three steps and seven *P*'s (for *peccato,* sin) traced on Dante's forehead; in the astonished shades' repeated recognitions of Dante's having a material body; in the sequence of dreams noted above (Cantos IX, XIX, XXVII), each dream preceded, in the sentence announcing it, by the time of its occurrence, pre-dawn; in the embeddings, within this verbal artifact, of artifacts that include the wall reliefs and pavement reliefs of the first terrace; in the double immersion of Dante, first in Lethe, the classic river of forgetfulness, erasing the memory of misdoing, then with Eunoe, the river of recall, Dante's invention, restoring memory of the good we have done;

in the retinue of Beatrice, with her seven handmaids, four for the "natural" virtues, three for the theological; and in the vast processional in the Earthly Paradise.

That line will be reinforced by two complementary aspects of *Purgatorio:* its more frequent intervals of solitude or shared solitude—of Dante or of what he sees (Cato, Sordello, Matilda)—and the choral sense that makes its terraces, as Francesco D'Ovidio had it, a "colossal monastery," with its hymns and psalms, rapid Biblical and liturgical inserts, its Latin and paraphrases of Latin joined by citation and translations (and a mistranslation) of Virgil, and, twice, by Dante's own Latin inserts.

Rite will also find support in rhetorical symmetries, as in the sequence of thirteen tercets (XII, 25–63) in which four tercets beginning with "I saw" are followed by four beginning with exclamatory "O"'s and four beginning with "it showed," with that sequence followed by a summative thirteenth tercet, where the lines begin, respectively, "I saw," "o," and "it showed": "I saw Troy turned to caverns and to ashes; / o Ilium, your effigy in stone— / it showed you there so squalid, so cast down!" (XII, 61–63).

However sardonically placed it is, even Dante's designation of his long polemic against Italy and Florence as "digression" (VI, 128), his only use of the word in all the *Comedy,* involves some self-conscious sense of transgression and reinforces our sense of art as rite in *Purgatorio.*

For similes that—unlike the staccato, nervous examples cited above—participate in the formal ritual climate, witness the doves (II, 124–132), the sheep moving out of the fold (III, 79–87), even the elaborated street-scene of the dice-players (VI, 1–12), and the corbels (X, 130–135), and the likeness that embraces Virgil and Statius as herdsmen and Dante as goat (XXVII, 76–87):

> *Like goats that, when they grazed, were swift and tameless*
> *along the mountain peaks, but now are sated,*

and rest and ruminate—while the sun blazes—
untroubled, in the shadows, silently,
watched over by the herdsman as he leans
upon his staff and oversees their peace;
or like the herdsman in the open fields,
spending the night beside his quiet flock,
watching to see that no beast drives them off;
such were all three of us at that point—they
were like the herdsmen, I was like the goat;
upon each side of us, high rock walls rose.

If *Purgatorio* is more circumscribed than *Inferno,* it is because of the "immense desire" that it abets and must contain
(IV, 29). Dante's constant intellectual and visual curiosity now
has "natural thirst," the thirst to know and to know that which
grace alone can offer, as its source: "The natural thirst that
never can be quenched / except by water that gives grace—the
draught / the simple woman of Samaria sought— / tormented
me" (XXI, 1–4).

Dante drives and is driven beyond the melancholia of
Virgil's injunction, Virgil's questioning of questing, his reasoning's self-delimiting sadness, its awareness that it can describe
what is but cannot supply the *why* (III, 37–45):

"Confine yourselves, o humans, to the quia;
had you been able to see all, there would
have been no need for Mary to give birth.
You saw the fruitless longing of those men
who would—if reason could—have been content,
those whose desire eternally laments:
I speak of Aristotle and of Plato—
and many others." Here he bent his head
and said no more, remaining with his sorrow.

Dante's need to array thirsts and hungerings and longings is
as "limitless" as his thirst for the waters of Eunoe in the final
canto (XXXIII, 138–139). When Dante receives an answer, he

continues: "I am more hungry now for satisfaction" (XV, 58). His soul tastes "that food which, even as / it quenches hunger, spurs the appetite" (XXXI, 129–130). He is "still goaded by new thirst" (XVIII, 4). Reluctantly, he draws his "unquenchable sponge out of the water" (XX, 3). "A thousand longings burning more than flames" compel his eyes (XXXI, 118). Guido Guinizzelli burns for an answer "in fire and thirst" and lets Dante know that Guinizzelli's fellow shades thirst for that answer "more than / an Indian or Ethiopian / thirsts for cool water" (XXVI, 18–22). When Dante asks the Muses for recompense ("O Virgins, sacrosanct, if I have ever, / for your sake, suffered vigils, cold, and hunger, / great need makes me entreat my recompense": XXIX, 37–39), the hunger seems not only the hunger of indigent exile but the hungering and thirsting of this work.

That force of longing is, of course, only abetted by the nearness now, in Purgatory, of Beatrice, by the ten years of thirst between her death in 1290 and the date of the fictive voyage, and the even longer span between her death and Dante's writing of the *Purgatorio* (XXXII, 1–9):

> *My eyes were so insistent, so intent*
> *on finding satisfaction for their ten-*
> *year thirst that every other sense was spent.*
> *And to each side, my eyes were walled in by*
> *indifference to all else (with its old net,*
> *the holy smile so drew them to itself),*
> *when I was forced to turn my eyes leftward*
> *by those three goddesses because I heard*
> *them warning me: "You stare too fixedly."*

It is this uncontainable desire that presses against the container. So, too, do the ways of envisioning that *Purgatorio* spans. If what Dante sees here is less varied than what he saw in the *Inferno,* his modes of vision are much more various. He sees with the sensual waking eye (both seeing directly and seeing mimetic artifacts), with the "intellect's sharp eyes" (XVIII,

16), with the "shut...eyes" of dream (XVIII, 144–145): and in "ecstatic vision" (XV, 86), he sees images that are impressed upon—or have "rained" into—his "fantasy" and "imagination" (XVII, 13–45). Dante comments on these latter modes as if he were providing us with one aspect of the poetics of his larger fiction through his anatomy of these partial envisionings of fantasy (these "not false errors": XV, 117): "At this, my mind withdrew to the within, / to what imagining might bring; no thing / that came from the without could enter in" (XVII, 22–24). Another direction, another aspect of Dante's poetics, his emphasis on mimetic credibility, is reinforced by the firmness with which he asserts the accuracy of the wall reliefs and pavement reliefs he sees on the first terrace, "carvings / so accurate—not only Polycletus / but even Nature, there, would feel defeated" (X, 31–33): "What master of the brush or of the stylus / had there portrayed such masses, such outlines / as would astonish all discerning minds? / The dead seemed dead and the alive, alive: / I saw, head bent, treading those effigies, / as well as those who'd seen those scenes directly" (XII, 64–69).

Dante will also examine attentively the points of passage between waking vision, sharp thought, random thought, reverie, dream, and fantasy, and the paralimnions of each state (even as he had examined the shoreline of Purgatory):

"I was so drawn from random thought / to thought that, wandering mind, I shut / my eyes, transforming thought on thought to dream" (XVIII, 144–145); "And when this image shattered of itself, / just like a bubble that has lost the water / beneath which it was formed..." (XVII, 31–34); and, "Even as sleep is shattered when new light / strikes suddenly against closed eyes and, once / it's shattered, gleams before it dies completely, / so my imagination fell away" (XVII, 40–43).

In this last passage, "new light" almost becomes an emblem of Dante's own light, a light that is both more abruptly shattering and more darting than the light of Virgil's *Aeneid:* whatever limits Dante sets for himself in the *Purgatorio,* his is a more restless light than Virgil's—a modern light, the light of the "immense desire" that made the need for *Purgatorio*'s "curb of art" so imperative.

In a journey as long as the *Comedy,* with its 14,233 lines and more than 650 similes, our memory not only commits paraphrase; it also misremembers, and dismembers the text through specific but highly selective recall, even as Dante himself—as Gianfranco Contini reminds us—recalls configurations of sound but uses those configurations in drastically altered contexts. Few readers of the *Inferno* will not tally up Francesca, Farinata, Pier della Vigna, Brunetto Latini, Ulysses. Sometimes these tesserae in the mosaic of memory are not personages but extended similes. Sometimes they are bits as swift as "the lightning-flash" of the lizard in *Inf.* XXV, or the plunging fish of *Purg.* XXVI. In edifying the *Purgatorio,* the mosaic of memory draws heavily on the rituals and repetitions noted above, and on the map of space and time that Dante is so careful to trace for the reader-voyager. But groupings of personages found in three divisions of the mountain, Ante-Purgatory, Purgatory proper, and the Earthly Paradise, can also serve as tesserae. (In the case of *Purgatorio,* memory can more easily contain the complete array of characters who speak; even hasty scrutinists can intuit the presence of fewer figures in the round than the *Inferno* presents, and Thomas Bergin's demographic comparison of the three *cantiche* documents their intuition.)

In *Inferno* there was only one principal figure from antiquity other than Virgil: Ulysses, whose insatiable curiosity makes him a kind of counter-figure of Dante. In *Purgatorio,* Statius, another poet of antiquity, will join Virgil as a figure complementing, not countering, Dante. And antiquity also provides the guardian of Purgatory's shores: Cato of Utica (95–46 B.C.).

Pagan and, after Caesar's victories at Pharsalus in 48 B.C. and Thapsus in 46 B.C., a suicide at Utica in Africa, the in-

tractable republican would have been a possible candidate for
Limbo, where his widow Marcia is to be found, or for the
Wood of the Suicides *(Inf.* XIII). But Dante had already, in his
Convivio, glorified "the most holy breast of Cato" (IV, V, 16),
and had asked and answered: "And what earthly man was was
more worthy of signifying God than Cato? Certainly no one"
(IV, XXVIII, 15). And in his *Monarchy* (very possibly composed
after the *Purgatorio),* Dante speaks of "the ineffable sacrifice
of the most intransigent champion of liberty, Marcus Cato...
who showed how great liberty is by preferring to die rather
than to live without it" (II, V, 15). Behind this image of Cato
there lie Book IX of Lucan's *Pharsalia* and Cicero's *De officiis;*
but it is a daring appropriator who, though he himself is a
Christian and a pro-Imperial poet, mobilizes a pagan and an
adversary of Caesar for the guardianship of Purgatory.

Cato hardly belongs to any Purgatorial lodge—of either ancients or moderns. Unlike the shades he superintends, he does
not need the prayers of those still alive, and the cords that link
Forese Donati to his widow Nella (XXIII, 85–93) are hardly
present for Cato in relation to his Marcia (I, 85–90).

But with Casella in Canto II, we meet inhabitants of Purgatory who are more collegial and choral than Cato is. Casella,
like Belacqua in Canto IV, Nino Visconti in Canto VIII, and
Forese Donati in Cantos XXIII–XXIV, is a friend of Dante. And,
as a musician, he joins Sordello (who appears in Cantos
VI–VII–VIII not only as courtier but as fellow-Mantuan of Virgil
and fellow-poet—in the "mother tongues"—of Dante) in the
series of *Purgatorio's* artists that will also include the miniaturist Oderisi of Gubbio (XI, 73–142) and the poets Bonagiunta da
Lucca (XXIV, 19–21 and 34–63), Guido Guinizzelli (XXVI,
16–24 and 72–135), Arnaut Daniel (XXVI, 136–148), and Statius himself—as well as others who are referred to, evoked.

Casella's affection and gentle, enrapturing singing of a setting for one of Dante's own poems had been preceded by

Cato's austerity and is interrupted by Cato's austerity (II, 118–123).

From the music of Casella, we move, in Canto III, to the violent death and dispersed bones of the excommunicate Manfred, the last great hope of the Imperial forces against the Papacy in the 13th century, a hope shattered when Manfred, illegitimate son of Frederick II, was defeated at Benevento in 1266. With the alternations characteristic of these opening cantos, Manfred's bones bathed by rain give way to the languor of Belacqua, whose laziness is not without humor. He asks: "And have you fathomed how / the sun can drive his chariot on your left?" (IV, 119–120), addressing his question to his friend Dante, who had, with such fanatic energy, wondered why the sun was at his left as he faced east. In turn, the listless Belacqua is followed, in the next canto, by three shades who underwent violent deaths.

The death of Jacopo del Cassero (1260–1298), a distinguished warrior and politician, at the hands of Ezzo d'Este's killers was so well-known to Dante's contemporaries that Dante does not even need to name him (V, 64–84).

Buonconte da Montefeltro (born c. 1250), son of Guido da Montefeltro *(Inf.* XXVII), was the leader of the Ghibellines of Arezzo in the battle of Campaldino, fought against the forces of Florence, a battle in which Dante himself probably took part. Buonconte died in that encounter on June 11, 1289, and his body was never found. But where his father, in *Inferno,* was, at the point of death, snatched from St. Francis by a devil, the soul of the son is saved from the devil by an angel. The devil's revenge on Buonconte's body counters the cloudless skies of Purgatory with an inexorable storm-scene in our world (V, 85–129).

Pia, possibly of the Tolomei family of Siena, was killed— hurled down from the balcony of her house—by her husband, Nello, chief magistrate of Volterra and Lucca, who outlived

Dante. She concentrates her tragedy in three lines, but not before she has voiced her own compassion for the weariness of any living body undertaking a journey as arduous as Dante's: "Pray, after your returning to the world, / when, after your long journeying, you've rested / ... may you remember me, who am La Pia; / Siena made—Maremma unmade—me: / he who, when we were wed, gave me his pledge / and then, as nuptial ring, his gem, knows that" (v, 130–136).

After these three (and others who suffered violent deaths but do not speak—or better, who importune Dante but without his referring their words to us), it is the quiet enclave of the Valley of the Rulers that occupies the rest of Ante-Purgatory. We and Dante are introduced to the valley and its inhabitants (identified in the headnote to Canto VII) by Sordello (c. 1200–1269), the most famous of the Italian troubadours, who wrote in Provençal and served as courtier in Italy, Provence, and then again—under Charles of Anjou—in Italy. It is Sordello's greeting of his fellow-Mantuan, Virgil, in Canto VI, 71–75, that spurs Dante's polemical "digression" against Italy and Florence, well-placed in this canto of Sordello, a poet whose own achievements in political and didactic poetry were notable. Sordello's review of the presences in the valley (VII, 91–136) is complemented in the next canto by the direct encounter with a political figure whom Dante knew well, the Guelph Nino Visconti—grandson of the Ugolino of Canto XXXIII of the *Inferno*—who died in 1296, after serving as animator of Guelph Genoa, Florence, and Lucca against Pisa. (Visconti's only daughter, Giovanna, died in poverty in Florence before 1339; in 1300, his widow married Galeazzo Visconti, lord of Milan, who then fell on hard times. The serpent was emblem of the Milanese Visconti, the rooster of the Pisan Visconti: VIII, 67–81.) In that same canto Dante encounters Currado Malaspina, who died in 1294, but whose family offered their hospitality (here repaid) to the exiled Dante in 1306.

In Purgatory proper, Canto X has no new presences; and the next nine cantos assign speaking roles—or amply refer—to nine modern Italian penitents: the Tuscan Aldobrandesco (who died in 1259), lord of Campagnatico and a powerful enemy of Siena, who died in battle near Campagnatico or was killed in bed by assassins hired by the Sienese (XI, 49–72); Oderisi of Gubbio (who died c. 1299), the famous miniaturist, whose place in the terrace of pride is not divorced from Dante's awareness of his own desire for artistic eminence (XI, 73–142); Provenzan Salvani of Siena (c. 1220–1269), a Ghibelline leader, who humbled himself to beg funds for the ransom of a friend who had been captured by Charles of Anjou (XI, 121–142); Sapia of Siena, an aunt of Provenzan (XIII, 100–154); one Ghibelline of Romagna, Guido del Duca (who died after 1249), and one Guelph, Rinieri da Calboli (who died in 1296), joint presences in Canto XIV; Marco Lombardo, a figure of the second half of the 13th century, known for his wisdom primarily from literary sources, not least this Canto XVI; the Abbot of St. Zeno, an abbot of Verona who has never been well identified outside this Canto XVIII; and in Canto XIX, Pope Adrian V, Ottobono Fieschi (born between 1210 and 1215), member of a powerful Genoese family, who was pope for 38 days in 1276, when he died (and since there is little warrant for applying Dante's account to Adrian V but much for its relevance to Adrian IV, pope from 1154 to 1159, Umberto Bosco sees some confusion here in Dante). In Canto XX, Hugh (II) Capet, king of France from 987 to 996 (whom Dante confounds with Hugh II's father, Hugh the Great, as the founder of the dynasty of France), excoriates his successors.

On the remaining terraces of Purgatory (Cantos XXI–XXVII), all the speaking roles other than Virgil's and Dante's are assigned to poets—from three literatures, Latin, Italian, and Provençal—and to an old friend of Dante, Forese Donati, who, though not essentially a poet, had exchanged epistolary poems with Dante.

Statius (c. 45–96 A.D.), to whom Dante, following medieval confusions, assigns Toulouse as birthplace rather than Naples, was the poet of the *Thebaid,* the tale of Thebes from the struggle between Eteocles and Polynices to Theseus' expedition against Creon; and of the *Achilleid,* which was to recount all the tale of Achilles, but was interrupted in the middle of Book II by Statius' death. (Dante probably did not know the *Silvae* of Statius.) With or without previous medieval sources before him, Dante "recruits" Statius to Christianity; and with warrant in Statius' own work, he finds a surrogate and passionate complement for his—Dante's—own adoration of Virgil (XXI, 94–136 and XXII, 64–73). Statius completes the company of poets of antiquity to whom Dante had himself joined in Limbo, in Canto IV of the *Inferno.* The poets of Limbo had included Homer, Virgil, Horace, Ovid, Lucan; and now, Juvenal as well as others are mentioned "retroactively" by Virgil (XXII, 13–14 and 97–108). But the "effective" company to which Dante adds himself has Virgil, Ovid, Lucan, and Statius as its poets. However warm his relations to his Romance predecessors are, it is antiquity he hopes to join or asserts he has joined (even as the vision of the otherworld granted to Dante allows him to join Aeneas and Paul "in a manner most unusual for moderns": XVI, 41–42).

For those Romance predecessors, it is three colloquies in *Purgatorio* that are central. The first is in Canto XXIV (34–63) with Bonagiunta (Orbiciani) da Lucca (c. 1220–death date uncertain), a poet instrumental in introducing the mode of the Sicilian poets to central Italy. The poets whom he sees as having been overarched by the "sweet [or suasive] new manner" of Dante and others are: the "Notary," that is, Jacopo da Lentini, poet and notary at the court of Frederick II, doyen of the Sicilian school, who died c. 1250; and Guittone d'Arezzo, who died in Florence in 1294, the head of the school that may be seen as having worked in modes less harmonious and subtle than those of Cavalcanti and the earlier Dante.

The second colloquy with a Romance poet (XXVI) has as its poet-interlocutor Guido Guinizzelli (probably to be identified with a Guido who was exiled from Bologna in 1274 and died by 1276). Seen by Cavalcanti and Dante as forerunner of their manner, Guinizzelli here also comes down hard on Guittone d'Arezzo (or, better, one may say that Dante, using both Bonagiunta and Guinizzelli, seems to come down strangely—or un-derstandably—too hard on Guittone, a predecessor to whom both he and Guinizzelli are much indebted). He also reap-praises, among the Provençal poets, Giraut de Bornelh (in fact born near Limoges rather than in it: XXVI, 120), who lived be-tween the last half of the twelfth century and the beginning of the thirteenth; for where Dante, in his *De vulgari eloquentia,* had praised Giraut, it is now Arnaut Daniel whom he has Guinizzelli praise as *"il miglior fabbro",* "a better / artisan of the mother tongue—surpassing / all those who wrote their po-ems of love or prose / romances" (XXVI, 116–119).

Arnaut, Dante's third Romance interlocutor, born in the same region as Giraut, was active as poet between 1180 and 1210. However much Guinizzelli may have been used by Dante for "local" anti-Guittone purposes, there is significant freedom from chauvinism in allowing Italian no special privilege among the modern maternal tongues, in assigning the premier post among all writers in the modern tongues to a Provençal (who here, in *Purgatorio,* speaks in Provençal: XXVI, 140–147).

This leaves one Florentine friend requiring a brief note: Forese Donati (XXIII and XXIV). Forese is seen here chiefly as intimate friend of Dante; but his exchange of sonnets with Dante was so intemperate and scurrilous that Dante, recalling that and obviously much more in their years of friendship to-gether, can only feel shame (XXIII, 115–117). But certainly the energies of invective, venom, and execration share place with the energy of love in Dante's descent and ascent.

The remorse of both Forese (who died in 1296)—distant rel-ative of Dante's wife, Gemma Donati—and Dante, and Forese's tenderness with respect to his widow, Nella (XXIII, 85–93) and sister Piccarda (XXIV, 10–16), whom we shall meet in Canto III of *Paradiso,* are followed by his prophecy of the death of his brother, Corso Donati. Corso (c. 1250–1308), one of the most arrogant and violent protagonists of Florentine politics, did not participate directly in the bloody brawl of May Day, 1300, between the White Guelphs ("the party of the woods" of *Inf.* VI, 60–72, and Dante's own party) and the Black Guelphs (Corso's party), but he was the principal conspirator in the Black cabal that followed that brawl. He had conspired from a distance and was condemned to death in contumacy. With the entry of Charles de Valois into Florence in 1301, the exiled Blacks— abetted, as always, by Boniface VIII—regained control of Florence. By April, 1302, more than six hundred Whites were exiled, among them Dante himself. Corso was the chief power in the city after that, and the figure most hated by the banished Whites. But it was the hatred of those within Florence that finally overthrew him in 1308. In flight, he was caught by Catalan mercenaries and may indeed have been killed in the way Dante describes, dragged at the tail of a horse (XXIV, 82–87).

In the Earthly Paradise, Virgil talks no more. Only his smile speaks in XXVIII, 147, and only his eyes speak in XXIX, 55–57. His words concluding Canto XXVII were indeed his valediction, as Dante will see when he turns around to share with Virgil the awesome wonder of re-encountering Beatrice, only to find that Virgil has vanished (XXX, 43–54, where the "ancient mother" is, of course, Eve):

> *I turned around and to my left—just as*
> *a little child, afraid or in distress,*
> *will hurry to its mother—anxiously,*
> > *to say to Virgil: "I am left with less*
> *than one drop of my blood that does not tremble:*
> *I recognize the signs of the old flame."*
> > *But Virgil had deprived us of himself,*
> *Virgil, the gentlest father, Virgil, he*
> *to whom I gave my self for my salvation;*
> > *and even all our ancient mother lost*
> *was not enough to keep my cheeks, though washed*
> *with dew, from darkening again with tears.*

The chief speaker of the Earthly Paradise is Beatrice, the "soul more worthy than I am" of Virgil's account in *Inf.* I, 122.

Born in 1266, the year after Dante's birth, Beatrice is loved by Dante from his boyhood and celebrated by Dante—after her death in 1290—in his *Vita Nuova*. If that is already a saint's life, with Beatrice as implicit incarnation of the divine way of the power of grace, the *Vita Nuova* did not yet contain polemic against the way of self-sufficient reason, a way "distant from the divine" (XXXIII, 85–90); nor was the *Vita Nuova* subject to political imperatives, which here make Beatrice prophesy "a time in which, dispatched by God, a Five / Hundred and Ten and Five will slay the whore / together with that giant who sins with her" (XXXIII, 43–45—and see below for the giant and the whore), where the Roman numerals for five-hundred and ten and five yield D.X.V., probably to be transposed to D.V.X. (leader), and possibly to be identified with a secular political figure, Henry VII—the last Imperial hope of Dante—who descended into Italy in 1311 but died suddenly, at Buonconvento, in 1313.

But it is Beatrice's companion whom Dante meets first in the Earthly Paradise, though he and we learn her name, Matilda, only toward the very end of *Purgatorio* (XXXIII, 119). Identifying Matilda with a historical personage is an attempt that, however assiduously pursued, remains problematic. And no allegorical accounting for her matches the haunting sense of her initial presence under the aegis of namelessness (XXVIII, 34–42 and 52–55):

> I halted, and I set my eyes upon
> the farther bank, to look at the abundant
> variety of newly-flowered boughs;
>   and there, just like a thing that, in appearing
> most suddenly, repels all other thoughts,
> so great is the astonishment it brings,
>   I saw a solitary woman moving,
> singing, and gathering up flower on flower—
> the flowers that colored all of her pathway.

and

As, when she turns, a woman, dancing, keeps
her soles close to the ground and to each other
and scarcely lets one foot precede the other,
so did she turn..........................

The limited population of the Earthly Paradise allows life-space for a procession of emblematic presences, moving behind a standard made up of seven candelabra, or—some would have it—one candelabrum with seven candles. For this procession, one can more easily use the equation words "is" and "are" and "may be" and "represent." In Canto XXIX, 43–150, the seven candelabra may be the seven churches of Asia, with the seven pennants as the seven gifts of the Holy Ghost. The twenty-four elders represent the twenty-four books of the Old Testament; the four animals, the books of the four Evangelists; the chariot, the Church; the griffin—with the head of a lion and body and wings of an eagle—Christ, with his two natures; and of the seven women, the three to the right of the chariot are the three theological virtues (faith, hope, and charity, dressed in white, green, and red) and the four to the left, the four cardinal virtues (prudence, justice, fortitude, and temperance, with prudence having three eyes—to see past, present, and future). The final seven elders represent: the Acts of the Apostles, whose author was St. Luke, a physician; the Epistles of St. Paul, who had urged the faithful to wear "God's armor" and take up "the sword of the spirit, which is the word of God" (Ephesians 6: 11 ff.); the four Epistles of Peter, John, James, and Jude; and Revelation, with an elder "as if in sleep," that is, visionary, and "keen," that is, prophetic.

In Canto XXXII, still other emblematic actors are involved in a tableau of Church history: the eagle, emblem of the Roman Empire, persecutor of the Church from Nero to Diocletian; the fox, emblem of heresy; the dragon, for whom the Anti-Christ is only one of many readings; the giant, probably the dynasty of France; and the whore, the corrupted Church.

In the Earthly Paradise, Virgil vanishes and Statius is silent; and though other emblematic members of the sacred procession do hymn or sing or chant, the only emblems that speak are the seven handmaids. Indeed, through all six cantos of the Earthly Paradise, only women—Beatrice, Matilda, and the handmaids—speak to Dante. Nine female presences—though eight of them dance—do not always reinforce mystery, and certainly not in some of the harsh rebukes leveled by Beatrice; but they certainly do so in the first apparition of Matilda and in the approach to Eunoe, where "the seven ladies halted at the edge / of a dense shadow such as mountains cast / beneath green leaves and black boughs, on cold banks" (XXXIII, 109–111).

Often, in the *Comedy,* Dante's lucidities and relentless analysis and cartography might remind us of an anecdote about Aeschylus, who, when accused of revealing the mysteries, may—like other distracted scribes—have won his acquittal by replying: "I said the first thing that occurred to me—I did not know it was a secret." But some of the rites of Purgatory, not least, the drinking of Eunoe's waters, do mime the mystery of Augustine's *"pacem quietis, pacem sabbati, pacem sine vespera,"* "peace of quiet, sabbath peace, peace that knows no twilight." Here, at least, for the most restless of poets, there is provisional rest before the ascent through Paradise.

Prior to that ascent, Dante sums up and transcends all the many changes rung on the word "new" by the thirteenth-century Italian poets who preceded him and by his own use of "new" in the title of his *Vita Nuova* (just as in his transmutation of Dido's line into his own awareness of Beatrice—"I recognize the signs of the old flame" in XXX, 48—he had offered a summative epigraph for his many uses of *"antico,"* "old"): "Remade, as new trees are / renewed when they bring forth new boughs, I was / pure and prepared to climb unto the stars" (XXXIII, 143–145).

Most of this *Purgatorio* translation was completed in Orta San Giulio and Boulder, Colorado. I thank Luigi Alberti, Luciana

Lamperti, and Carlo Carena, who live, above Orta, in the house that honors the *"cantor de' buccolici carmi,"* for the blessings their presence has brought to me over many years; and Margherita Bogat, whose love of Orta has been *ardor* and *seme* and *favilla*. I am grateful to many colleagues and students who, in Boulder and Denver and on Bellyache Ridge, complemented the skies of Colorado, which indeed *"a li occhi miei ricominciò diletto"* when translating *Inferno* lay behind me. Ruth Hein, as always, edited copy with needling, fruitful care; my son Jonathan lent me his precious skills at a crucial time in revisions, and Ellen E. Martin worked probingly and unstintingly in the preparation of the final drafts. Paul Mariani, Bruce Bassoff, and James Hans were constant sources—not least, through their own work—of the spirit that engenders. Michael Bixler shared his craft and serenity with Barry Moser, Chet Grycz, and me. Laury Magnus—unfailing, invaluable— took soundings and governed the ungovernable sea of rough drafts like a *"celestial nocchier[e]."* Barry Moser, through the fourth volume on which we have worked together, has been both penetrating *fabbro* and buoyant friend, ever *"disposto a salire"* to the next volume.

The Graduate Center   Allen Mandelbaum
of the City University of New York
September, 1981

PURGATORIO

PURGATORIO

CANTO I

Per correr miglior acque alza le vele
   omai la navicella del' mio ingegno,
che lascia dietro a sé mar sì crudele;

   e canterò di quel secondo regno   4
dove l'umano spirito si purga
e di salire al ciel diventa degno.

   Ma qui la morta poesì resurga,   7
o sante Muse, poi che vostro sono;
e qui Calïopè alquanto surga,

   seguitando il mio canto con quel suono   10
di cui le Piche misere sentiro
lo colpo tal, che disperar perdono.

   Dolce color d'orïental zaffiro,   13
che s'accoglieva nel sereno aspetto
del mezzo, puro infino al primo giro,

   a li occhi miei ricominciò diletto,   16
tosto ch'io usci' fuor de l'aura morta
che m'avea contristati li occhi e 'l petto.

   Lo bel pianeto che d'amar conforta   19
faceva tutto rider l'orïente,
velando i Pesci ch'erano in sua scorta.

   I' mi volsi a man destra, e puosi mente   22
a l'altro polo, e vidi quattro stelle
non viste mai fuor ch'a la prima gente.

   Goder pareva 'l ciel di lor fiammelle: 25
oh settentrïonal vedovo sito,
poi che privato se' di mirar quelle!

   Com' io da loro sguardo fui partito,   28
un poco me volgendo a l'altro polo,
là onde 'l Carro già era sparito,

Proem and Invocation. The skies of the Southern Pole before dawn. The four stars. Cato of Utica, custodian of the island Mountain of Purgatory. Cato's queries and Virgil's reply. Instructions by Cato. Virgil bathing Dante's face and, on the shore, girding him with a rush.

To course across more kindly waters now
    my talent's little vessel lifts her sails,
leaving behind herself a sea so cruel;
    and what I sing will be that second kingdom,   4
in which the human soul is cleansed of sin,
becoming worthy of ascent to Heaven.
    But here, since I am yours, o holy Muses,   7
may this poem rise again from Hell's dead realm;
and may Calliope rise somewhat here,
    accompanying my singing with that music   10
whose power struck the poor Pierides
so forcefully that they despaired of pardon.
    The gentle hue of oriental sapphire   13
in which the sky's serenity was steeped—
its aspect pure as far as the horizon—
    brought back my joy in seeing just as soon   16
as I had left behind the air of death
that had afflicted both my sight and breast.
    The lovely planet that is patroness   19
of love made all the eastern heavens glad,
veiling the Pisces in the train she led.
    Then I turned to the right, setting my mind   22
upon the other pole, and saw four stars
not seen before except by the first people.
    Heaven appeared to revel in their flames: 25
o northern hemisphere, because you were
denied that sight, you are a widower!
    After my eyes took leave of those four stars,   28
turning a little toward the other pole,
from which the Wain had disappeared by now,

vidi presso di me un veglio solo,   31
degno di tanta reverenza in vista,
che più non dee a padre alcun figliuolo.

Lunga la barba e di pel bianco mista   34
portava, a' suoi capelli simigliante,
de' quai cadeva al petto doppia lista.

Li raggi de le quattro luci sante   37
fregiavan sì la sua faccia di lume,
ch'i' 'l vedea come 'l sol fosse davante.

"Chi siete voi che contro al cièco fiume   40
fuggita avete la pregione etterna?"
diss' el, movendo quelle oneste piume.

"Chi v'ha guidati, o che vi fu lucerna,   43
uscendo fuor de la profonda notte
che sempre nera fa la valle inferna?

Son le leggi d'abisso così rotte?   46
o è mutato in ciel novo consiglio,
che, dannati, venite a le mie grotte?"

Lo duca mio allor mi diè di piglio,   49
e con parole e con mani e con cenni
reverenti mi fé le gambe e 'l ciglio.

Poscia rispuose lui: "Da me non venni: 52
donna scese del ciel, per li cui prieghi
de la mia compagnia costui sovvenni.

Ma da ch'è tuo voler che più si spieghi   55
di nostra condizion com' ell' è vera,
esser non puote il mio che a te si nieghi.

Questi non vide mai l'ultima sera;   58
ma per la sua follia le fu sì presso,
che molto poco tempo a volger era.

Sì com' io dissi, fui mandato ad esso   61
per lui campare; e non lì era altra via
che questa per la quale i' mi son messo.

Mostrata ho lui tutta la gente ria;   64
e ora intendo mostrar quelli spirti
che purgan sé sotto la tua balìa.

Com' io l'ho tratto, saria lungo a dirti;   67
de l'alto scende virtù che m'aiuta
conducerlo a vederti e a udirti.

I saw a solitary patriarch   31
near me—his aspect worthy of such reverence
that even son to father owes no more.

His beard was long and mixed with white, as were   34
the hairs upon his head; and his hair spread
down to his chest in a divided tress.

The rays of the four holy stars so framed   37
his face with light that in my sight he seemed
like one who is confronted by the sun.

"Who are you—who, against the hidden river,   40
were able to escape the eternal prison?"
he said, moving those venerable plumes.

"Who was your guide? What served you both as lantern 43
when, from the deep night that will always keep
the hellish valley dark, you were set free?

The laws of the abyss—have they been broken?   46
Or has a new, a changed decree in Heaven
let you, though damned, approach my rocky slopes?"

My guide took hold of me decisively;   49
by way of words and hands and other signs,
he made my knees and brow show reverence.

Then he replied: "I do not come through my   52
own self. There was a lady sent from Heaven;
her pleas led me to help and guide this man.

But since your will would have a far more full   55
and accurate account of our condition,
my will cannot withhold what you request.

This man had yet to see his final evening;   58
but, through his folly, little time was left
before he did—he was so close to it.

As I have told you, I was sent to him   61
for his deliverance; the only road
I could have taken was the road I took.

I showed him all the people of perdition;   64
now I intend to show to him those spirits
who, in your care, are bent on expiation.

To tell you how I led him would take long;   67
it is a power descending from above
that helps me guide him here, to see and hear you.

Or ti piaccia gradir la sua venuta: 70
libertà va cercando, ch'è sì cara,
come sa chi per lei vita rifiuta.

Tu 'l sai, ché non ti fu per lei amara   73
in Utica la morte, ove lasciasti
la vesta ch'al gran dì sarà sì chiara.

Non son li editti etterni per noi guasti,   76
ché questi vive e Minòs me non lega;
ma son del cerchio ove son li occhi casti

di Marzia tua, che 'n vista ancor ti priega,   79
o santo petto, che per tua la tegni:
per lo suo amore adunque a noi ti piega.

Lasciane andar per li tuoi sette regni;   82
grazie riporterò di te a lei,
se d'esser mentovato là giù degni."

"Marzïa piacque tanto a li occhi miei   85
mentre ch'i' fu' di là," diss' elli allora,
"che quante grazie volse da me, fei.

Or che di là dal mal fiume dimora,   88
più muover non mi può, per quella legge
che fatta fu quando me n'usci' fora.

Ma se donna del ciel ti move e regge,   91
come tu di', non c'è mestier lusinghe:
bastisi ben che per lei mi richegge.

Va dunque, e fa che tu costui ricinghe   94
d'un giunco schietto e che li lavi 'l viso,
sì ch'ogne sucidume quindi stinghe;

ché non si converria, l'occhio sorpriso   97
d'alcuna nebbia, andar dinanzi al primo
ministro, ch'è di quei di paradiso.

Questa isoletta intorno ad imo ad imo,   100
là giù colà dove la batte l'onda,
porta di giunchi sovra 'l molle limo:

null' altra pianta che facesse fronda   103
o indurasse, vi puote aver vita,
però ch'a le percosse non seconda.

Poscia non sia di qua vostra reddita;   106
lo sol vi mostrerrà, che surge omai,
prendere il monte a più lieve salita."

Now may it please you to approve his coming; 70
he goes in search of liberty—so precious,
as he who gives his life for it must know.

You know it—who, in Utica, found death 73
for freedom was not bitter, when you left
the garb that will be bright on the great day.

Eternal edicts are not broken for us; 76
this man's alive, and I'm not bound by Minos;
but I am from the circle where the chaste

eyes of your Marcia are; and she still prays 79
to you, o holy breast, to keep her as
your own: for her love, then, incline to us.

Allow our journey through your seven realms. 82
I shall thank her for kindness you bestow—
if you would let your name be named below."

"While I was there, within the other world, 85
Marcia so pleased my eyes," he then replied,
"each kindness she required, I satisfied.

Now that she dwells beyond the evil river, 88
she has no power to move me any longer,
such was the law decreed when I was freed.

But if a lady come from Heaven speeds 91
and helps you, as you say, there is no need
of flattery; it is enough, indeed,

to ask me for her sake. Go then; but first 94
wind a smooth rush around his waist and bathe
his face, to wash away all of Hell's stains;

for it would not be seemly to approach 97
with eyes still dimmed by any mists, the first
custodian angel, one from Paradise.

This solitary island, all around 100
its very base, there where the breakers pound,
bears rushes on its soft and muddy ground.

There is no other plant that lives below: 103
no plant with leaves or plant that, as it grows,
hardens—and breaks beneath the waves' harsh blows.

That done, do not return by this same pass; 106
the sun, which rises now, will show you how
this hillside can be climbed more easily."

Così sparì; e io sù mi levai   109
sanza parlare, e tutto mi ritrassi
al duca mio, e li occhi a lui drizzai.

El cominciò: "Figliuol, segui i miei passi: 112
volgianci in dietro, ché di qua dichina
questa pianura a' suoi termini bassi."

L'alba vinceva l'ora mattutina   115
che fuggia innanzi, sì che di lontano
conobbi il tremolar de la marina.

Noi andavam per lo solingo piano   118
com' om che torna a la perduta strada,
che 'nfino ad essa li pare ire in vano.

Quando noi fummo là 've la rugiada   121
pugna col sole, per essere in parte
dove, ad orezza, poco si dirada,

ambo le mani in su l'erbetta sparte   124
soavemente 'l mio maestro pose:
ond' io, che fui accorto di sua arte,

porsi ver' lui le guance lagrimose;   127
ivi mi fece tutto discoverto
quel color che l'inferno mi nascose.

Venimmo poi in sul lito diserto,   130
che mai non vide navicar sue acque
omo, che di tornar sia poscia esperto.

Quivi mi cinse sì com' altrui piacque: 133
oh maraviglia! ché qual elli scelse
l'umile pianta, cotal si rinacque

subitamente là onde l'avelse.   136

With that he vanished; and without a word,   109
I rose and drew in closer to my guide,
and it was on him that I set my eyes.

And he began: "Son, follow in my steps;   112
let us go back; this is the point at which
the plain slopes down to reach its lowest bounds."

Daybreak was vanquishing the dark's last hour,   115
which fled before it; in the distance, I
could recognize the trembling of the sea.

We made our way across the lonely plain,   118
like one returning to a lost pathway,
who, till he finds it, seems to move in vain.

When we had reached the point where dew contends   121
with sun and, under sea winds, in the shade,
wins out because it won't evaporate,

my master gently placed both of his hands—   124
outspread—upon the grass; therefore, aware
of what his gesture and intention were,

I reached and offered him my tear-stained cheeks;   127
and on my cheeks, he totally revealed
the color that Inferno had concealed.

Then we arrived at the deserted shore,   130
which never yet had seen its waters coursed
by any man who journeyed back again.

There, just as pleased another, he girt me.   133
O wonder! Where he plucked the humble plant
that he had chosen, there that plant sprang up

again, identical, immediately.   136

CATO

II·27

CANTO II

Già era 'l sole a l'orizzonte giunto
lo cui meridïan cerchio coverchia
Ierusalèm col suo più alto punto;

   e la notte, che opposita a lui cerchia,   4
uscia di Gange fuor con le Bilance,
che le caggion di man quando soverchia;

   sì che le bianche e le vermiglie guance,   7
là dov' i' era, de la bella Aurora
per troppa etate divenivan rance.

   Noi eravam lunghesso mare ancora,   10
come gente che pensa a suo cammino,
che va col cuore e col corpo dimora.

   Ed ecco, qual, sorpreso dal mattino,   13
per li grossi vapor Marte rosseggia
giù nel ponente sovra 'l suol marino,

   cotal m'apparve, s'io ancor lo veggia,   16
un lume per lo mar venir sì ratto,
che 'l muover suo nessun volar pareggia.

   Dal qual com' io un poco ebbi ritratto   19
l'occhio per domandar lo duca mio,
rividil più lucente e maggior fatto.

   Poi d'ogne lato ad esso m'appario   22
un non sapeva che bianco, e di sotto
a poco a poco un altro a lui uscìo.

   Lo mio maestro ancor non facea motto,   25
mentre che i primi bianchi apparver ali;
allor che ben conobbe il galeotto,

   gridò: "Fa, fa che le ginocchia cali.   28
Ecco l'angel di Dio: piega le mani;
omai vedrai di sì fatti officiali.

Ante-Purgatory. Dawn on the shore of the island mountain. The sudden light upon the sea. The helmsman angel and the boat full of arriving souls. The encounter with Casella, Dante's friend. Casella's singing. Cato's rebuke. The simile of the doves.

By now the sun was crossing the horizon
of the meridian whose highest point
covers Jerusalem; and from the Ganges,

night, circling opposite the sun, was moving   4
together with the Scales that, when the length
of dark defeats the day, desert night's hands;

so that, above the shore that I had reached,   7
the fair Aurora's white and scarlet cheeks
were, as Aurora aged, becoming orange.

We still were by the sea, like those who think   10
about the journey they will undertake,
who go in heart but in the body stay.

And just as Mars, when it is overcome   13
by the invading mists of dawn, glows red
above the waters' plain, low in the west,

so there appeared to me—and may I see it   16
again—a light that crossed the sea: so swift,
there is no flight of bird to equal it.

When, for a moment, I'd withdrawn my eyes   19
that I might ask a question of my guide,
I saw that light again, larger, more bright.

Then, to each side of it, I saw a whiteness,   22
though I did not know what that whiteness was;
below, another whiteness slowly showed.

My master did not say a word before   25
the whitenesses first seen appeared as wings;
but then, when he had recognized the helmsman,

he cried: "Bend, bend your knees: behold the angel   28
of God, and join your hands; from this point on,
this is the kind of minister you'll meet.

Vedi che sdegna li argomenti umani,   31
sì che remo non vuol, né altro velo
che l'ali sue, tra liti sì lontani.

Vedi come l'ha dritte verso 'l cielo,   34
trattando l'aere con l'etterne penne,
che non si mutan come mortal pelo."

Poi, come più e più verso noi venne   37
l'uccel divino, più chiaro appariva;
per che l'occhio da presso nol sostenne,

ma chinail giuso; e quei sen venne a riva   40
con un vasello snelletto e leggero,
tanto che l'acqua nulla ne 'nghiottiva.

Da poppa stava il celestial nocchiero,   43
tal che parea beato per iscripto;
e più di cento spirti entro sediero.

"In exitu Isräel de Aegypto"   46
cantavan tutti insieme ad una voce
con quanto di quel salmo è poscia scripto.

Poi fece il segno lor di santa croce;   49
ond' ei si gittar tutti in su la piaggia:
ed el sen gì, come venne, veloce.

La turba che rimase lì, selvaggia   52
parea del loco, rimirando intorno
come colui che nove cose assaggia.

Da tutte parti saettava il giorno   55
lo sol, ch'avea con le saette conte
di mezzo 'l ciel cacciato Capricorno,

quando la nova gente alzò la fronte   58
ver' noi, dicendo a noi: "Se voi sapete,
mostratene la via di gire al monte."

E Virgilio rispuose: "Voi credete   61
forse che siamo esperti d'esto loco;
ma noi siam peregrin come voi siete.

Dianzi venimmo, innanzi a voi un poco,   64
per altra via, che fu sì aspra e forte,
che lo salire omai ne parrà gioco."

L'anime, che si fuor di me accorte,   67
per lo spirare, ch'i' era ancor vivo,
maravigliando diventaro smorte.

See how much scorn he has for human means;   31
he'd have no other sail than his own wings
and use no oar between such distant shores.

See how he holds his wings, pointing to Heaven,   34
piercing the air with his eternal pinions,
which do not change as mortal plumage does."

Then he—that bird divine—as he drew closer   37
and closer to us, seemed to gain in brightness,
so that my eyes could not endure his nearness,

and I was forced to lower them; and he   40
came on to shore with boat so light, so quick
that nowhere did the water swallow it.

The helmsman sent from Heaven, at the stern,   43
seemed to have blessedness inscribed upon him;
more than a hundred spirits sat within.

"In exitu Isräel de Aegypto,"   46
with what is written after of that psalm,
all of those spirits sang as with one voice.

Then over them he made the holy cross   49
as sign; they flung themselves down on the shore,
and he moved off as he had come—swiftly.

The crowd that he had left along the beach   52
seemed not to know the place; they looked about
like those whose eyes try out things new to them.

Upon all sides the sun shot forth the day;   55
and from mid-heaven its incisive arrows
already had chased Capricorn away,

when those who'd just arrived lifted their heads   58
toward us and said: "Do show us, if you know,
the way by which we can ascend this slope."

And Virgil answered: "You may be convinced   61
that we are quite familiar with this shore;
but we are strangers here, just as you are;

we came but now, a little while before you,   64
though by another path, so difficult
and dense that this ascent seems sport to us."

The souls who, noticing my breathing, sensed   67
that I was still a living being, then,
out of astonishment, turned pale; and just

E come a messagger che porta ulivo   70
tragge la gente per udir novelle,
e di calcar nessun si mostra schivo,

così al viso mio s'affisar quelle   73
anime fortunate tutte quante,
quasi oblïando d'ire a farsi belle.

Io vidi una di lor trarresi avante   76
per abbracciarmi, con si grande affetto,
che mosse me a far lo somigliante.

Ohi ombre vane, fuor che ne l'aspetto!   79
tre volte dietro a lei le mani avvinsi,
e tante mi tornai con esse al petto.

Di maraviglia, credo, mi dipinsi;   82
per che l'ombra sorrise e si ritrasse,
e io, seguendo lei, oltre mi pinsi.

Soavemente disse ch'io posasse;   85
allor conobbi chi era, e pregai
che, per parlarmi, un poco s'arrestasse.

Rispuosemi: "Così com' io t'amai   88
nel mortal corpo, così t'amo sciolta:
però m'arresto; ma tu perché vai?"

"Casella mio, per tornar altra volta   91
là dov' io son, fo io questo vïaggio,"
diss' io; "ma a te com' è tanta ora tolta?"

Ed elli a me: "Nessun m'è fatto oltraggio,   94
se quei che leva quando e cui li piace,
più volte m'ha negato esto passaggio;

ché di giusto voler lo suo si face: 97
veramente da tre mesi elli ha tolto
chi ha voluto intrar, con tutta pace.

Ond' io, ch'era ora a la marina vòlto   100
dove l'acqua di Tevero s'insala,
benignamente fu' da lui ricolto.

A quella foce ha elli or dritta l'ala,   103
però che sempre quivi si ricoglie
qual verso Acheronte non si cala."

E io: "Se nuova legge non ti toglie   106
memoria o uso a l'amoroso canto
che mi solea quetar tutte mie voglie,

as people crowd around a messenger   70
who bears an olive branch, to hear his news,
and no one hesitates to join that crush,

so here those happy spirits—all of them—   73
stared hard at my face, just as if they had
forgotten to proceed to their perfection.

I saw one of those spirits moving forward   76
in order to embrace me—his affection
so great that I was moved to mime his welcome.

O shades—in all except appearance—empty!   79
Three times I clasped my hands behind him and
as often brought them back against my chest.

Dismay, I think, was painted on my face;   82
at this, that shadow smiled as he withdrew;
and I, still seeking him, again advanced.

Gently, he said that I could now stand back;   85
then I knew who he was, and I beseeched
him to remain awhile and talk with me.

He answered: "As I loved you when I was   88
within my mortal flesh, so, freed, I love you:
therefore I stay. But you, why do you journey?"

"My own Casella, to return again   91
to where I am, I journey thus; but why,"
I said, "were you deprived of so much time?"

And he: "No injury is done to me   94
if he who takes up whom—and when—he pleases
has kept me from this crossing many times,

for his own will derives from a just will.   97
And yet, for three months now, he has accepted,
most tranquilly, all those who would embark.

Therefore, I, who had turned then to the shore   100
at which the Tiber's waters mix with salt,
was gathered in by his benevolence.

Straight to that river mouth, he set his wings: 103
that always is the place of gathering
for those who do not sink to Acheron."

And I: "If there's no new law that denies   106
you memory or practice of the songs
of love that used to quiet all my longings,

di ciò ti piaccia consolare alquanto   109
l'anima mia, che, con la sua persona
venendo qui, è affannata tanto!"

"Amor che ne la mente mi ragiona"   112
cominciò elli allor sì dolcemente,
che la dolcezza ancor dentro mi suona.

Lo mio maestro e io e quella gente   115
ch'eran con lui parevan sì contenti,
come a nessun toccasse altro la mente.

Noi eravam tutti fissi e attenti   118
a le sue note; ed ecco il veglio onesto
gridando: "Che è ciò, spiriti lenti?

qual negligenza, quale stare è questo?   121
Correte al monte a spogliarvi lo scoglio
ch'esser non lascia a voi Dio manifesto."

Come quando, cogliendo biado o loglio,   124
li colombi adunati a la pastura,
queti, sanza mostrar l'usato orgoglio,

se cosa appare ond' elli abbian paura,   127
subitamente lasciano star l'esca,
perch' assaliti son da maggior cura;

così vid' io quella masnada fresca   130
lasciar lo canto, e fuggir ver' la costa,
com' om che va, né sa dove rïesca;

né la nostra partita fu men tosta.   133

then may it please you with those songs to solace   109
my soul somewhat; for—having journeyed here
together with my body—it is weary."

"Love that discourses to me in my mind"   112
he then began to sing—and sang so sweetly
that I still hear that sweetness sound in me.

My master, I, and all that company   115
around the singer seemed so satisfied,
as if no other thing might touch our minds.

We all were motionless and fixed upon   118
the notes, when all at once the grave old man
cried out: "What have we here, you laggard spirits?

What negligence, what lingering is this?   121
Quick, to the mountain to cast off the slough
that will not let you see God show Himself!"

Even as doves, assembled where they feed,   124
quietly gathering their grain or weeds,
forgetful of their customary strut,

will, if some thing appears that makes them fear,   127
immediately leave their food behind
because they are assailed by greater care;

so did I see that new-come company—   130
they left the song behind, turned toward the slope,
like those who go and yet do not know where.

And we were no less hasty in departure.   133

CANTO III

Avvegna che la subitana fuga
dispergesse color per la campagna,
rivolti al monte ove ragion ne fruga,
   i' mi ristrinsi a la fida compagna: 4
e come sare' io sanza lui corso?
chi m'avria tratto su per la montagna?
   El mi parea da sé stesso rimorso: 7
o dignitosa coscïenza e netta,
come t'è picciol fallo amaro morso!
   Quando li piedi suoi lasciar la fretta,   10
che l'onestade ad ogn' atto dismaga,
la mente mia, che prima era ristretta,
   lo 'ntento rallargò, sì come vaga,   13
e diedi 'l viso mio incontr' al poggio
che 'nverso 'l ciel più alto si dislaga.
   Lo sol, che dietro fiammeggiava roggio,   16
rotto m'era dinanzi a la figura,
ch'avëa in me de' suoi raggi l'appoggio.
   Io mi volsi dallato con paura   19
d'essere abbandonato, quand' io vidi
solo dinanzi a me la terra oscura;
   e 'l mio conforto: "Perché pur diffidi?"   22
a dir mi cominciò tutto rivolto;
"non credi tu me teco e ch'io ti guidi?
   Vespero è già colà dov'è sepolto   25
lo corpo dentro al quale io facea ombra;
Napoli l'ha, e da Brandizio è tolto.
   Ora, se innanzi a me nulla s'aombra,   28
non ti maravigliar più che d'i cieli
che l'uno a l'altro raggio non ingombra.

Ante-Purgatory. From the shore to the base of the mountain. Dante's fear when his shadow—and no other—appears. Reassurance by Virgil and explanation of the nature of shades. Consideration of the way to ascend the Mountain of Purgatory. The meeting with the souls of the Late-Repentant who were also Excommunicates. Manfred.

B ut while their sudden flight was scattering
those souls across the plain and toward the mountain
where we are racked by rightful punishments,

    I drew in closer to my true companion.   4
For how could I have run ahead without him?
Who could have helped me as I climbed the mountain?

    He seemed like one who's stung by self-reproof;   7
o pure and noble conscience, you in whom
each petty fault becomes a harsh rebuke!

    And when his feet had left off hurrying—   10
for haste denies all acts their dignity—
my mind, which was—before—too focused, grew

    more curious and widened its attention;   13
I set my vision toward the slope that rises
most steeply, up to heaven from the sea.

    Behind my back the sun was flaming red;   16
but there, ahead of me, its light was shattered
because its rays were resting on my body.

    And when I saw the ground was dark in front   19
of me and me alone, afraid that I
had been abandoned, I turned to my side;

    and he, my only comfort, as he turned   22
around, began: "Why must you still mistrust?
Don't you believe that I am with—and guide—you?

    The body from within which I cast shadows   25
is buried where it now is evening: taken
from Brindisi, it now belongs to Naples.

    Thus, if no shadow falls in front of me,   28
do not be more amazed than when you see
the heavens not impede each other's rays.

A sofferir tormenti, caldi e geli   31
simili corpi la Virtù dispone
che, come fa, non vuol ch'a noi si sveli.

Matto è chi spera che nostra ragione   34
possa trascorrer la infinita via
che tiene una sustanza in tre persone.

State contenti, umana gente, al *quia;*   37
ché, se potuto aveste veder tutto,
mestier non era parturir Maria;

e disïar vedeste sanza frutto   40
tai che sarebbe lor disio quetato,
ch'etternalmente è dato lor per lutto:

io dico d'Aristotile e di Plato   43
e di molt' altri"; e qui chinò la fronte,
e più non disse, e rimase turbato.

Noi divenimmo intanto a piè del monte;   46
quivi trovammo la roccia sì erta,
che 'ndarno vi sarien le gambe pronte.

Tra Lerice e Turbìa la più diserta,   49
la più rotta ruina è una scala,
verso di quella, agevole e aperta.

"Or chi sa da qual man la costa cala,"   52
disse 'l maestro mio fermando 'l passo,
"sì che possa salir chi va sanz' ala?"

E mentre ch'e' tenendo 'l viso basso   55
essaminava del cammin la mente,
e io mirava suso intorno al sasso,

da man sinistra m'apparì una gente   58
d'anime, che movieno i piè ver' noi,
e non pareva, sì venïan lente.

"Leva," diss' io, "maestro, li occhi tuoi: 61
ecco di qua chi ne darà consiglio,
se tu da te medesmo aver nol puoi."

Guardò allora, e con libero piglio   64
rispuose: "Andiamo in là, ch'ei vegnon piano;
e tu ferma la spene, dolce figlio."

Ancora era quel popol di lontano,   67
i' dico dopo i nostri mille passi,
quanto un buon gittator trarria con mano,

The Power has disposed such bodiless   31
bodies to suffer torments, heat and cold;
how this is done, He would not have us know.

Foolish is he who hopes our intellect   34
can reach the end of that unending road
only one Substance in three Persons follows.

Confine yourselves, o humans, to the *quia;*   37
had you been able to see all, there would
have been no need for Mary to give birth.

You saw the fruitless longing of those men   40
who would—if reason could—have been content,
those whose desire eternally laments:

I speak of Aristotle and of Plato—   43
and many others." Here he bent his head
and said no more, remaining with his sorrow.

By this time we had reached the mountain's base,   46
discovering a wall of rock so sheer
that even agile legs are useless there.

The loneliest, most jagged promontory   49
that lies between Turbìa and Lerici,
compared with it, provides stairs wide and easy.

"Now who knows where, along this mountainside,"   52
my master, halting, asked, "one finds a rise
where even he who has no wings can climb?"

While he, his eyes upon the ground, consulted   55
his mind, considering what road to take,
and I looked up around the wall of rock,

along the left a band of souls appeared   58
to me to be approaching us—but so
unhurriedly, their movements did not show.

"Lift up your eyes," I told my master; "here   61
are those who can advise us how to go,
if you can find no counsel in yourself."

At this, he looked at them and, less distressed,   64
replied: "Let us go there; their steps are slow;
and you, my gentle son, hold fast to hope."

The distance from that company to us—   67
I mean when we had gone a thousand paces—
was still as far as a fine hurler's toss,

quando si strinser tutti ai duri massi   70
de l'alta ripa, e stetter fermi e stretti
com' a guardar, chi va dubbiando, stassi.

"O ben finiti, o già spiriti eletti,"   73
Virgilio incominciò, "per quella pace
ch'i' credo che per voi tutti s'aspetti,

ditene dove la montagna giace,   76
sì che possibil sia l'andare in suso;
ché perder tempo a chi più sa più spiace."

Come le pecorelle escon del chiuso   79
a una, a due, a tre, e l'altre stanno
timidette atterrando l'occhio e 'l muso;

e ciò che fa la prima, e l'altre fanno,   82
addossandosi a lei, s'ella s'arresta,
semplici e quete, e lo 'mperché non sanno;

sì vid' io muovere a venir la testa   85
di quella mandra fortunata allotta,
pudica in faccia e ne l'andare onesta.

Come color dinanzi vider rotta   88
la luce in terra dal mio destro canto,
sì che l'ombra era da me a la grotta,

restaro, e trasser sé in dietro alquanto,   91
e tutti li altri che venieno appresso,
non sappiendo 'l perché, fenno altrettanto.

"Sanza vostra domanda io vi confesso   94
che questo è corpo uman che voi vedete;
per che 'l lume del sole in terra è fesso.

Non vi maravigliate, ma credete   97
che non sanza virtù che da ciel vegna
cerchi di soverchiar questa parete."

Così 'l maestro; e quella gente degna   100
"Tornate," disse, "intrate innanzi dunque,"
coi dossi de le man faccendo insegna.

E un di loro incominciò: "Chiunque   103
tu se', così andando, volgi 'l viso:
pon mente se di là mi vedesti unque."

Io mi volsi ver' lui e guardail fiso: 106
biondo era e bello e di gentile aspetto,
ma l'un de' cigli un colpo avea diviso.

when they all huddled toward the hard rock wall   70
and, once they'd crowded there, refused to budge,
even as men, when apprehensive, halt.

"O chosen souls, you who have ended well,"   73
Virgil began, "by virtue of that peace
which I believe awaits you all, please tell

us where the slope inclines and can be climbed;   76
for he who best discerns the worth of time
is most distressed whenever time is lost."

Even as sheep that move, first one, then two,   79
then three, out of the fold—the others also
stand, eyes and muzzles lowered, timidly;

and what the first sheep does, the others do,   82
and if it halts, they huddle close behind,
simple and quiet and not knowing why:

so, then, I saw those spirits in the front   85
of that flock favored by good fortune move—
their looks were modest; seemly, slow, their walk.

As soon as these souls saw, upon my right,   88
along the ground, a gap in the sun's light,
where shadow stretched from me to the rock wall,

they stopped and then drew back somewhat; and all   91
who came behind them—though they did not know
why those ahead had halted—also slowed.

"Without your asking, I shall tell you plainly   94
that you are looking at a human body;
that's why the sunlight on the ground is broken.

Don't be astonished; rest assured that he   97
would not attempt to cross this wall without
a force that Heaven sent him as support."

These were my master's words. That worthy band   100
replied: "Come back, and move in our direction,"
and gestured—with backhanded motions—right.

And one of them began: "Whoever you   103
may be, as you move forward, turn and see:
consider if—beyond—you've ever seen me."

I turned to look at him attentively: 106
he was fair-haired and handsome and his aspect
was noble—but one eyebrow had been cleft

Quand' io mi fui umilmente disdetto   109
d'averlo visto mai, el disse: "Or vedi";
e mostrommi una piaga a sommo 'l petto.

Poi sorridendo disse: "Io son Manfredi,   112
nepote di Costanza imperadrice;
ond' io priego che, quando tu riedi,

vadi a mia bella figlia, genitrice   115
de l'onor di Cicilia e d'Aragona,
e dichi 'l vero a lei, s'altro si dice.

Poscia ch'io ebbi rotta la persona   118
di due punte mortali, io mi rendei,
piangendo, a quei che volontier perdona.

Orribil furon li peccati miei;   121
ma la bontà infinita ha sì gran braccia,
che prende ciò che si rivolge a lei.

Se 'l pastor di Cosenza, che a la caccia   124
di me fu messo per Clemente allora,
avesse in Dio ben letta questa faccia,

l'ossa del corpo mio sarieno ancora   127
in co del ponte presso a Benevento,
sotto la guardia de la grave mora.

Or le bagna la pioggia e move il vento   130
di fuor dal regno, quasi lungo 'l Verde,
dov' e' le trasmutò a lume spento.

Per lor maladizion sì non si perde,   133
che non possa tornar, l'etterno amore,
mentre che la speranza ha fior del verde.

Vero è che quale in contumacia more   136
di Santa Chiesa, ancor ch'al fin si penta,
star li convien da questa ripa in fore,

per ognun tempo ch'elli è stato, trenta,   139
in sua presunzïon, se tal decreto
più corto per buon prieghi non diventa.

Vedi oggimai se tu mi puoi far lieto,   142
revelando a la mia buona Costanza
come m'hai visto, e anco esto divieto;

ché qui per quei di là molto s'avanza."   145

by a swordstroke. When I had humbly noted   109
that I had never seen him, he said: "Look
now"—showing me a wound high on his chest.

Then, as he smiled, he told me: "I am Manfred,   112
the grandson of the Empress Constance; thus,
I pray that, when you reach the world again,

you may go to my lovely daughter, mother   115
of kings of Sicily and Aragon—
tell her the truth, lest she's heard something other.

After my body had been shattered by   118
two fatal blows, in tears, I then consigned
myself to Him who willingly forgives.

My sins were ghastly, but the Infinite   121
Goodness has arms so wide that It accepts
who ever would return, imploring It.

And if Cosenza's pastor, who was sent   124
to hunt me down—alive or dead—by Clement,
had understood this facet of God's mercy,

my body's bones would still be there—beneath   127
the custody of the great heap of stones—
near Benevento, at the bridgehead; now

rain bathes my bones, the wind has driven them   130
beyond the Kingdom, near the Verde's banks,
where he transported them with tapers spent.

Despite the Church's curse, there is no one   133
so lost that the eternal love cannot
return—as long as hope shows something green.

But it is true that anyone who dies   136
in contumacy of the Holy Church,
though he repented at the end, must wait

along this shore for thirty times the span   139
he spent in his presumptuousness, unless
that edict is abridged through fitting prayers.

Now see if you, by making known to my   142
kind Constance where you saw my soul and why
delay's decreed for me, can make me happy;

those here—through those beyond—advance more quickly."

MANFRED

BELACQUA

CANTO IV

Quando per dilettanze o ver per doglie,
che alcuna virtù nostra comprenda,
l'anima bene ad essa si raccoglie,
    par ch'a nulla potenza più intenda;   4
e questo è contra quello error che crede
ch'un'anima sovr' altra in noi s'accenda.
    E però, quando s'ode cosa o vede   7
che tegna forte a sé l'anima volta,
vassene 'l tempo e l'uom non se n'avvede;
    ch'altra potenza è quella che l'ascolta,   10
e altra è quella c'ha l'anima intera:
questa è quasi legata e quella è sciolta.
    Di ciò ebb' io esperïenza vera,   13
udendo quello spirto e ammirando;
ché ben cinquanta gradi salito era
    lo sole, e io non m'era accorto, quando   16
venimmo ove quell' anime ad una
gridaro a noi: "Qui è vostro dimando."
    Maggiore aperta molte volte impruna   19
con una forcatella di sue spine
l'uom de la villa quando l'uva imbruna,
    che non era la calla onde salìne   22
lo duca mio, e io appresso, soli,
come da noi la schiera si partìne.
    Vassi in Sanleo e discendesi in Noli,   25
montasi su in Bismantova e 'n Cacume
con esso i piè; ma qui convien ch'om voli;
    dico con l'ale snelle e con le piume   28
del gran disio, di retro a quel condotto
che speranza mi dava e facea lume.

When any of our faculties retains
  a strong impression of delight or pain,
the soul will wholly concentrate on that,

  neglecting any other power it has   4
(and this refutes the error that maintains
that—one above the other—several souls

  can flame in us); and thus, when something seen   7
or heard secures the soul in stringent grip,
time moves and yet we do not notice it.

  The power that perceives the course of time   10
is not the power that captures all the mind;
the former has no force—the latter binds.

  And I confirmed this by experience,   13
hearing that spirit in my wonderment;
for though the sun had fully climbed fifty

  degrees, I had not noticed it, when we   16
came to the point at which in unison
those souls cried out to us: "Here's what you want."

  The farmer, when the grape is darkening,   19
will often stuff a wider opening
with just a little forkful of his thorns,

  than was the gap through which my guide and I,   22
who followed after, climbed, we two alone,
after that company of souls had gone.

  San Leo can be climbed, one can descend   25
to Noli and ascend Cacume and
Bismantova with feet alone, but here

  I had to fly: I mean with rapid wings   28
and pinions of immense desire, behind
the guide who gave me hope and was my light.

Noi salavam per entro 'l sasso rotto,   31
e d'ogne lato ne stringea lo stremo,
e piedi e man volea il suol di sotto.

Poi che noi fummo in su l'orlo suppremo   34
de l'alta ripa, a la scoperta piaggia,
"Maestro mio," diss' io, "che via faremo?"

Ed elli a me: "Nessun tuo passo caggia;   37
pur su al monte dietro a me acquista,
fin che n'appaia alcuna scorta saggia."

Lo sommo er' alto che vincea la vista,   40
e la costa superba più assai
che da mezzo quadrante a centro lista.

Io era lasso, quando cominciai: 43
"O dolce padre, volgiti, e rimira
com' io rimango sol, se non restai."

"Figliuol mio," disse, "infin quivi ti tira,"   46
additandomi un balzo poco in sùe
che da quel lato il poggio tutto gira.

Sì mi spronaron le parole sue,   49
ch'i' mi sforzai carpando appresso lui,
tanto che 'l cinghio sotto i piè mi fue.

A seder ci ponemmo ivi ambedui   52
vòlti a levante ond' eravam saliti,
che suole a riguardar giovare altrui.

Li occhi prima drizzai ai bassi liti;   55
poscia li alzai al sole, e ammirava
che da sinistra n'eravam feriti.

Ben s'avvide il poeta ch'io stava   58
stupido tutto al carro de la luce,
ove tra noi e Aquilone intrava.

Ond' elli a me: "Se Castore e Poluce   61
fossero in compagnia di quello specchio
che sù e giù del suo lume conduce,

tu vedresti il Zodïaco rubecchio   64
ancora a l'Orse più stretto rotare,
se non uscisse fuor del cammin vecchio.

Come ciò sia, se 'l vuoi poter pensare,   67
dentro raccolto, imagina Sïòn
con questo monte in su la terra stare

We made our upward way through rifted rock;   31
along each side the edges pressed on us;
the ground beneath required feet and hands.

When we had reached the upper rim of that   34
steep bank, emerging on the open slope,
I said: "My master, what way shall we take?"

And he to me: "Don't squander any steps;   37
keep climbing up the mountain after me
until we find some expert company."

The summit was so high, my sight fell short;   40
the slope was far more steep than the line drawn
from middle-quadrant to the center point.

I was exhausted when I made this plea: 43
"O gentle father, turn around and see—
I will be left alone unless you halt."

"My son," he said, "draw yourself up to there," 46
while pointing to a somewhat higher terrace,
which circles all the slope along that side.

His words incited me; my body tried;   49
on hands and knees I scrambled after him
until the terrace lay beneath my feet.

There we sat down together, facing east,   52
in the direction from which we had come:
what joy—to look back at a path we've climbed!

My eyes were first set on the shores below,   55
and then I raised them toward the sun; I was
amazed to find it fall upon our left.

And when the poet saw that I was struck   58
with wonder as I watched the chariot
of light passing between the north and us,

he said to me: "Suppose Castor and Pollux   61
were in conjunction with that mirror there,
which takes the light and guides it north and south,

then you would see the reddish zodiac   64
still closer to the Bears as it revolves—
unless it has abandoned its old track.

If you would realize how that should be,   67
then concentrate, imagining this mountain
so placed upon this earth that both Mount Zion

sì, ch'amendue hanno un solo orizzòn   70
e diversi emisperi: onde la strada
che mal non seppe carreggiar Fetòn,

    vedrai come a costui convien che vada   73
da l'un, quando a colui da l'altro fianco,
se lo 'ntelletto tuo ben chiaro bada."

    "Certo, maestro mio," diss'io, "unquanco   76
non vid' io chiaro sì com' io discerno
là dove mio ingegno parea manco,

    che 'l mezzo cerchio del moto superno,   79
che si chiama Equatore in alcun' arte,
e che sempre riman tra 'l sole e 'l verno,

    per la ragion che di', quinci si parte   82
verso settentrïon, quanto li Ebrei
vedevan lui verso la calda parte.

    Ma se a te piace, volontier saprei   85
quanto avemo ad andar; ché 'l poggio sale
più che salir non posson li occhi miei."

    Ed elli a me: "Questa montagna è tale,   88
che sempre al cominciar di sotte è grave;
e quant' om più va sù, e men fa male.

    Però, quand' ella ti parrà soave   91
tanto, che sù andar ti fia leggero
com' a seconda giù andar per nave,

    allor sarai al fin d'esto sentiero;   94
quivi di riposar l'affanno aspetta.
Più non rispondo, e questo so per vero."

    E com' elli ebbe sua parola detta,   97
una voce di presso sonò: "Forse
che di sedere in pria avrai distretta!"

    Al suon di lei ciascun di noi si torse,   100
e vedemmo a mancina un gran petrone,
del qual né io né ei prima s'accorse.

    Là ci traemmo; e ivi eran persone   103
che si stavano a l'ombra dietro al sasso
come l'uom per negghienza a star si pone.

    E un di lor, che mi sembiava lasso,   106
sedeva e abbracciava le ginocchia,
tenendo 'l viso giù tra esse basso.

and it, although in different hemispheres,   70
share one horizon; therefore, you can see,
putting your mind to it attentively,

　　how that same path which Phaethon drove so poorly   73
must pass this mountain on the north, whereas
it skirts Mount Zion on the southern side."

　　I said: "My master, surely I have never—   76
since my intelligence seemed lacking—seen
as clearly as I now can comprehend,

　　that the mid-circle of the heavens' motion   79
(one of the sciences calls it Equator),
which always lies between the sun and winter,

　　as you explained, lies as far north of here   82
as it lies southward of the site from which
the Hebrews, looking toward the tropics, saw it.

　　But if it please you, I should willingly   85
learn just how far it is we still must journey:
the slope climbs higher than my eyes can follow."

　　And he to me: "This mountain's of such sort   88
that climbing it is hardest at the start;
but as we rise, the slope grows less unkind.

　　Therefore, when this slope seems to you so gentle   91
that climbing farther up will be as restful
as traveling downstream by boat, you will

　　be where this pathway ends, and there you can   94
expect to put your weariness to rest.
I say no more, and this I know as truth."

　　And when his words were done, another voice   97
nearby was heard to say: "Perhaps you will
have need to sit before you reach that point!"

　　Hearing that voice, both of us turned around,   100
and to the left we saw a massive boulder,
which neither he nor I—before—had noticed.

　　We made our way toward it and toward the people   103
who lounged behind that boulder in the shade,
as men beset by listlessness will rest.

　　And one of them, who seemed to me exhausted,   106
was sitting with his arms around his knees;
between his knees, he kept his head bent down.

"O dolce segnor mio," diss'io, "adocchia   109
colui che mostra sé più negligente
che se pigrizia fosse sua serocchia."

Allor si volse a noi e puose mente,   112
movendo 'l viso pur su per la coscia,
e disse: "Or va tu sù, che se' valente!"

Conobbi allor chi era, e quella angoscia   115
che m'avacciava un poco ancor la lena,
non m'impedì l'andare a lui; e poscia

ch'a lui fu' giunto, alzò la testa a pena,   118
dicendo: "Hai ben veduto come 'l sole
da l'omero sinistro il carro mena?"

Li atti suoi pigri e le corte parole   121
mosser le labbra mie un poco a riso;
poi cominciai: "Belacqua, a me non dole

di te omai; ma dimmi: perché assiso   124
quiritto se'? attendi tu iscorta,
o pur lo modo usato t'ha' ripriso?"

Ed elli: "O frate, andar in sù che porta?   127
ché non mi lascerebbe ire a' martìri
l'angel di Dio che siede in su la porta.

Prima convien che tanto il ciel m'aggiri   130
di fuor da essa, quanto fece in vita,
per ch'io 'ndugiai al fine i buon sospiri,

se orazïone in prima non m'aita   133
che surga sù di cuor che in grazia viva;
l'altra che val, che 'n ciel non è udita?"

E già il poeta innanzi mi saliva,   136
e dicea: "Vienne omai; vedi ch'è tocco
meridïan dal sole, e a la riva

cuopre la notte già col piè Morrocco."   139

"O my sweet lord," I said, "look carefully   109
at one who shows himself more languid than
he would have been were laziness his sister!"

Then that shade turned toward us attentively,   112
lifting his eyes, but just above his thigh,
and said: "Climb, then, if you're so vigorous!"

Then I knew who he was, and the distress   115
that still was quickening my breath somewhat,
did not prevent my going to him; and

when I had reached him, scarcely lifting up   118
his head, he said: "And have you fathomed how
the sun can drive his chariot on your left?"

The slowness of his movements, his brief words   121
had stirred my lips a little toward a smile;
then I began: "From this time on, Belacqua,

I need not grieve for you; but tell me, why   124
do you sit here? Do you expect a guide?
Or have you fallen into your old ways?"

And he: "O brother, what's the use of climbing?   127
God's angel, he who guards the gate, would not
let me pass through to meet my punishment.

Outside that gate the skies must circle round   130
as many times as they did when I lived—
since I delayed good sighs until the end—

unless, before then, I am helped by prayer   133
that rises from a heart that lives in grace;
what use are other prayers—ignored by Heaven?"

And now the poet climbed ahead, before me,   136
and said: "It's time; see the meridian
touched by the sun; elsewhere, along the Ocean,

night now has set its foot upon Morocco."   139

CANTO V

Io era già da quell' ombre partito,
e seguitava l'orme del mio duca,
quando di retro a me, drizzando 'l dito,

    una gridò: "Ve' che non par che luca   4
lo raggio da sinistra a quel di sotto,
e come vivo par che si conduca!"

    Li occhi rivolsi al suon di questo motto,   7
e vidile guardar per maraviglia
pur me, pur me, e 'l lume ch'era rotto.

    "Perché l'animo tuo tanto s'impiglia,"   10
disse 'l maestro, "che l'andare allenti?
che ti fa ciò che quivi si pispiglia?

    Vien dietro a me, e lascia dir le genti: 13
sta come torre ferma, che non crolla
già mai la cima per soffiar di venti;

    ché sempre l'omo in cui pensier rampolla   16
sovra pensier, da sé dilunga il segno,
perché la foga l'un de l'altro insolla."

    Che potea io ridir, se non "Io vegno"?   19
Dissilo, alquanto del color consperso
che fa l'uom di perdon talvolta degno.

    E 'ntanto per la costa di traverso   22
venivan genti innanzi a noi un poco,
cantando *"Miserere"* a verso a verso.

    Quando s'accorser ch'i' non dava loco   25
per lo mio corpo al trapassar d'i raggi,
mutar lor canto in un "oh!" lungo e roco;

    e due di loro, in forma di messaggi,   28
corsero incontr' a noi e dimandarne:
"Di vostra condizion fatene saggi."

I had already left those shades behind
and followed in the footsteps of my guide
when, there beneath me, pointing at me, one

    shade shouted: "See the second climber climb: 4
the sun seems not to shine on his left side,
and when he walks, he walks like one alive!"

    When I had heard these words, I turned my eyes   7
and saw the shades astonished as they stared
at me—at me, and at the broken light.

    "Why have you let your mind get so entwined,"   10
my master said, "that you have slowed your walk?
Why should you care about what's whispered here?

    Come, follow me, and let these people talk: 13
stand like a sturdy tower that does not shake
its summit though the winds may blast; always

    the man in whom thought thrusts ahead of thought   16
allows the goal he's set to move far off—
the force of one thought saps the other's force."

    Could my reply be other than "I come"?   19
And—somewhat colored by the hue that makes
one sometimes merit grace—I spoke those words.

    Meanwhile, along the slope, crossing our road   22
slightly ahead of us, people approached,
singing the *Miserere* verse by verse.

    When they became aware that I allowed   25
no path for rays of light to cross my body,
they changed their song into a long, hoarse "Oh!"

    And two of them, serving as messengers,   28
hurried to meet us, and those two inquired:
"Please tell us something more of what you are."

E 'l mio maestro: "Voi potete andarne   31
e ritrarre a color che vi mandaro
che 'l corpo di costui è vera carne.

Se per veder la sua ombra restaro,   34
com' io avviso, assai è lor risposto:
fàccianli onore, ed esser può lor caro."

Vapori accesi non vid' io sì tosto   37
di prima notte mai fender sereno,
né, sol calando, nuvole d'agosto,

che color non tornasser suso in meno;   40
e, giunti là, con li altri a noi dier volta,
come schiera che scorre sanza freno.

"Questa gente che preme a noi è molta,   43
e vegnonti a pregar," disse 'l poeta:
"però pur va, e in andando ascolta."

"O anima che vai per esser lìeta   46
con quelle membra con le quai nascesti,"
venian gridando, "un poco il passo queta.

Guarda s'alcun di noi unqua vedesti,   49
sì che di lui di là novella porti:
deh, perché vai? deh, perché non t'arresti?

Noi fummo tutti già per forza morti,   52
e peccatori infino a l'ultima ora;
quivi lume del ciel ne fece accorti,

sì che, pentendo e perdonando, fora   55
di vita uscimmo a Dio pacificati,
che del disio di sé veder n'accora."

E io: "Perché ne' vostri visi guati,   58
non riconosco alcun; ma s'a voi piace
cosa ch'io possa, spiriti ben nati,

voi dite, e io farò per quella pace   61
che, dietro a' piedi di sì fatta guida,
di mondo in mondo cercar mi si face."

E uno incominciò: "Ciascun si fida   64
del beneficio tuo sanza giurarlo,
pur che 'l voler nonpossa non ricida.

Ond' io, che solo innanzi a li altri parlo,   67
ti priego, se mai vedi quel paese
che siede tra Romagna e quel di Carlo,

My master answered them: "You can return   31
and carry this report to those who sent you:
in truth, the body of this man is flesh.

If, as I think, they stopped to see his shadow,   34
that answer is sufficient: let them welcome
him graciously, and that may profit them."

Never did I see kindled vapors rend   37
clear skies at nightfall or the setting sun
cleave August clouds with a rapidity

that matched the time it took those two to speed   40
above; and, there arrived, they with the others
wheeled back, like ranks that run without a rein.

"These people pressing in on us are many;   43
they come beseeching you," the poet said;
"don't stop, but listen as you move ahead."

"O soul who make your way to gladness with   46
the limbs you had at birth, do stay your steps
awhile," they clamored as they came, "to see

if there is any of us whom you knew,   49
that you may carry word of him beyond.
Why do you hurry on? Why don't you stop?

We all were done to death by violence,   52
and we all sinned until our final hour;
then light from Heaven granted understanding,

so that, repenting and forgiving, we   55
came forth from life at peace with God, and He
instilled in us the longing to see Him."

And I: "Although I scrutinize your faces,   58
I recognize no one; but, spirits born
to goodness, if there's anything within

my power that might please you, then—by that   61
same peace which in the steps of such a guide
I seek from world to world—I shall perform it."

And one began: "We all have faith in your   64
good offices without your oath, as long
as lack of power does not curb your will.

Thus I, who speak alone—before the others—   67
beseech you, if you ever see the land
that lies between Romagna and the realm

che tu mi sie di tuoi prieghi cortese   70
in Fano, sì che ben per me s'adori
pur ch'i' possa purgar le gravi offese.

Quindi fu' io; ma li profondi fóri   73
ond' uscì 'l sangue in sul quale io sedea,
fatti mi fuoro in grembo a li Antenori,

là dov' io più sicuro esser credea: 76
quel da Esti il fé far, che m'avea in ira
assai più là che dritto non volea.

Ma s'io fosse fuggito inver' la Mira,   79
quando fu' sovragiunto ad Orïaco,
ancor sarei di là dove si spira.

Corsi al palude, e le cannucce e 'l braco   82
m'impigliar sì ch'i' caddi; e lì vid' io
de le mie vene farsi in terra laco."

Poi disse un altro: "Deh, se quel disio   85
si compia che ti tragge a l'alto monte,
con buona pïetate aiuta il mio!

Io fui di Montefeltro, io son Bonconte;   88
Giovanna o altri non ha di me cura;
per ch'io vo tra costor con bassa fronte."

E io a lui: "Qual forza o qual ventura   91
ti travïò sì fuor di Campaldino,
che non si seppe mai tua sepultura?"

"Oh!" rispuos' elli, "a piè del Casentino   94
traversa un'acqua c'ha nome l'Archiano,
che sovra l'Ermo nasce in Apennino.

Là 've 'l vocabol suo diventa vano,   97
arriva' io forato ne la gola,
fuggendo a piede e sanguinando il piano.

Quivi perdei la vista e la parola;   100
nel nome di Maria fini', e quivi
caddi, e rimase la mia carne sola.

Io dirò vero, e tu 'l ridì tra ' vivi: 103
l'angel di Dio mi prese, e quel d'inferno
gridava: 'O tu del ciel, perché mi privi?

Tu te ne porti di costui l'etterno   106
per una lagrimetta che 'l mi toglie;
ma io farò de l'altro altro governo!'

of Charles, that you be courteous to me, 70
entreating those in Fano to bestow
fair prayers to purge me of my heavy sins.

My home was Fano; but the piercing wounds 73
from which there poured the blood where my life lived—
those I received among Antenor's sons,

there where I thought that I was most secure; 76
for he of Este, hating me far more
than justice warranted, had that deed done.

But had I fled instead toward Mira when 79
they overtook me at Oriaco, then
I should still be beyond, where men draw breath.

I hurried to the marsh. The mud, the reeds 82
entangled me; I fell. And there I saw
a pool, poured from my veins, form on the ground."

Another shade then said: "Ah, so may that 85
desire which draws you up the lofty mountain
be granted, with kind pity help my longing!

I was from Montefeltro, I'm Buonconte; 88
Giovanna and the rest—they all neglect me;
therefore, among these shades, I go in sadness."

And I to him: "What violence or chance 91
so dragged you from the field of Campaldino
that we know nothing of your burial place?"

"Oh," he replied, "across the Casentino 94
there runs a stream called Archiano—born
in the Apennines above the Hermitage.

There, at the place where that stream's name is lost, 97
I came—my throat was pierced—fleeing on foot
and bloodying the plain; and there it was

that I lost sight and speech; and there, as I 100
had finished uttering the name of Mary,
I fell; and there my flesh alone remained.

I'll speak the truth—do you, among the living, 103
retell it: I was taken by God's angel,
but he from Hell cried: 'You from Heaven—why

do you deny me him? For just one tear 106
you carry off his deathless part; but I
shall treat his other part in other wise.'

Ben sai come ne l'aere si raccoglie   109
quell' umido vapor che in acqua riede,
tosto che sale dove 'l freddo il coglie.

Giunse quel mal voler che pur mal chiede   112
con lo 'ntelletto, e mosse il fummo e 'l vento
per la virtù che sua natura diede.

Indi la valle, come 'l dì fu spento,   115
da Pratomagno al gran giogo coperse
di nebbia; e 'l ciel di sopra fece intento,

sì che 'l pregno aere in acqua si converse;   118
la pioggia cadde, e a' fossati venne
di lei ciò che la terra non sofferse;

e come ai rivi grandi si convenne,   121
ver' lo fiume real tanto veloce
si ruinò, che nulla la ritenne.

Lo corpo mio gelato in su la foce   124
trovò l'Archian rubesto; e quel sospinse
ne l'Arno, e sciolse al mio petto la croce

ch'i' fe' di me quando 'l dolor mi vinse;   127
voltòmmi per le ripe e per lo fondo,
poi di sua preda mi coperse e cinse."

"Deh, quando tu sarai tornato al mondo   130
e riposato de la lunga via,"
seguitò 'l terzo spirito al secondo,

"ricorditi di me, che son la Pia;   133
Siena mi fé, disfecemi Maremma:
salsi colui che 'nnanellata pria

disposando m'avea con la sua gemma."   136

You are aware how, in the air, moist vapor   109
will gather and again revert to rain
as soon as it has climbed where cold enfolds.

His evil will, which only seeks out evil,   112
conjoined with intellect; and with the power
his nature grants, he stirred up wind and vapor.

And then, when day was done, he filled the valley   115
from Pratomagno far as the great ridge
with mist; the sky above was saturated.

The dense air was converted into water;   118
rain fell, and then the gullies had to carry
whatever water earth could not receive;

and when that rain was gathered into torrents,   121
it rushed so swiftly toward the royal river
that nothing could contain its turbulence.

The angry Archiano—at its mouth—   124
had found my frozen body; and it thrust
it in the Arno and set loose the cross

that, on my chest, my arms, in pain, had formed.   127
It rolled me on the banks and river bed,
then covered, girded me with its debris."

"Pray, after your returning to the world,   130
when, after your long journeying, you've rested,"
the third soul, following the second, said,

"may you remember me, who am La Pia;   133
Siena made—Maremma unmade—me:
he who, when we were wed, gave me his pledge

and then, as nuptial ring, his gem, knows that."   136

BUONCONTE

VI · 149

CANTO VI

Quando si parte il gioco de la zara,
    colui che perde si riman dolente,
repetendo le volte, e tristo impara;

    con l'altro se ne va tutta la gente;   4
qual va dinanzi, e qual di dietro il prende,
e qual dallato li si reca a mente;

    el non s'arresta, e questo e quello intende;   7
a cui porge la man, più non fa pressa;
e così da la calca si difende.

    Tal era io in quella turba spessa,   10
volgendo a loro, e qua e là, la faccia,
e promettendo mi sciogliea da essa.

    Quiv' era l'Aretin che da le braccia   13
fiere di Ghin di Tacco ebbe la morte,
e l'altro ch'annegò correndo in caccia.

    Quivi pregava con le mani sporte   16
Federigo Novello, e quel da Pisa
che fé parer lo buon Marzucco forte.

    Vidi conte Orso e l'anima divisa   19
dal corpo suo per astio e per inveggia,
com' e' dicea, non per colpa commisa;

    Pier da la Broccia dico; e qui proveggia,   22
mentr' è di qua, la donna di Brabante,
sì che però non sia di peggior greggia.

    Come libero fui da tutte quante   25
quell' ombre che pregar pur ch'altri prieghi,
sì che s'avacci lor divenir sante,

    io cominciai: "El par che tu mi nieghi,   28
o luce mia, espresso in alcun testo
che decreto del cielo orazion pieghi;

Ante-Purgatory. Still the Second Spur. The simile of the gamester. Others who died deaths by violence. The efficacy of prayers for the dead. Virgil and his fellow Mantuan, Sordello. Dante's invective against Italy and Florence.

When dicing's done and players separate,
  the loser's left alone, disconsolate—
rehearsing what he'd thrown, he sadly learns;

  all of the crowd surrounds the one who won—   4
one goes in front, and one tugs at his back,
and at his side one asks to be remembered;

  he does not halt but listens to them all;   7
and when he gives them something, they desist;
and so he can fend off the pressing throng.

  And I, in that persistent pack, was such: 10
this way and that, I turned my face to them
and, making promises, escaped their clutch.

  There was the Aretine who met his death   13
beneath Ghino di Tacco's bestial hands,
and one who drowned when, in pursuit, he ran.

  There, with his outstretched hands, was Federigo   16
Novello, praying, and the Pisan who
made good Marzucco show his fortitude.

  I saw Count Orso, and I saw the soul   19
cleft from its body out of spite and envy—
not, so it said, because it had been guilty—

  I mean Pier de la Brosse (and may the Lady   22
of Brabant, while she's still in this world, watch
her ways—or end among a sadder flock).

  As soon as I was free from all those shades   25
who always pray for others' prayers for them,
so as to reach their blessed state more quickly,

  I started: "O my light, it seems to me   28
that in one passage you deny expressly
that prayer can bend the rule of Heaven, yet

e questa gente prega pur di questo: 31
sarebbe dunque loro speme vana,
o non m'è 'l detto tuo ben manifesto?"

Ed elli a me: "La mia scrittura è piana;   34
e la speranza di costor non falla,
se ben si guarda con la mente sana;

ché cima di giudicio non s'avvalla   37
perché foco d'amor compia in un punto
ciò che de' sodisfar chi qui s'astalla;

e là dov' io fermai cotesto punto,   40
non s'ammendava, per pregar, difetto,
perché 'l priego da Dio era disgiunto.

Veramente a così alto sospetto   43
non ti fermar, se quella nol ti dice
che lume fia tra 'l vero e lo 'ntelletto.

Non so se 'ntendi: io dico di Beatrice;   46
tu la vedrai di sopra, in su la vetta
di questo monte, ridere e felice."

E io: "Segnore, andiamo a maggior fretta,   49
ché già non m'affatico come dianzi,
e vedi omai che 'l poggio l'ombra getta."

"Noi anderem con questo giorno innanzi,"   52
rispuose, "quanto più potremo omai;
ma 'l fatto è d'altra forma che non stanzi.

Prima che sie là sù, tornar vedrai   55
colui che già si cuopre de la costa,
sì che ' suoi raggi tu romper non fai.

Ma vedi là un'anima che, posta   58
sola soletta, inverso noi riguarda:
quella ne 'nsegnerà la via più tosta."

Venimmo a lei: o anima lombarda,   61
come ti stavi altera e disdegnosa
e nel mover de li occhi onesta e tarda!

Ella non ci dicëa alcuna cosa,   64
ma lasciavane gir, solo sguardando
a guisa di leon quando si posa.

Pur Virgilio si trasse a lei, pregando   67
che ne mostrasse la miglior salita;
e quella non rispuose al suo dimando,

these people pray precisely for that end.   31
Is their hope, therefore, only emptiness,
or have I not read clearly what you said?"

    And he to me: "My text is plain enough,   34
and yet their hope is not delusive if
one scrutinizes it with sober wit;

    the peak of justice is not lowered when   37
the fire of love accomplishes in one
instant the expiation owed by all

    who dwell here; for where I asserted this—   40
that prayers could not mend their fault—I spoke
of prayers without a passageway to God.

    But in a quandary so deep, do not   43
conclude with me, but wait for word that she,
the light between your mind and truth, will speak—

    lest you misunderstand, the *she* I mean   46
is Beatrice; upon this mountain's peak,
there you shall see her smiling joyously."

    And I: "Lord, let us move ahead more quickly,   49
for now I am less weary than before;
and—you can see—the slope now casts a shadow."

    "As long as it is day, we'll make as much   52
headway as possible," he answered; "but
our climb won't be as rapid as you thought.

    You will not reach the peak before you see   55
the sun returning: now he hides behind
the hills—you cannot interrupt his light.

    But see—beyond—a soul who is completely   58
apart, and seated, looking toward us; he
will show us where to climb most speedily."

    We came to him. O Lombard soul, what pride   61
and what disdain were in your stance! Your eyes
moved with such dignity, such gravity!

    He said no thing to us but let us pass,   64
his eyes intent upon us only as
a lion watches when it is at rest.

    Yet Virgil made his way to him, appealing   67
to him to show us how we'd best ascend;
and he did not reply to that request,

    ma di nostro paese e de la vita   70
ci 'nchiese; e 'l dolce duca incominciava
"Mantüa...," e l'ombra, tutta in sé romita,

    surse ver' lui del loco ove pria stava,   73
dicendo: "O Mantoano, io son Sordello
de la tua terra!"; e l'un l'altro abbracciava.

    Ahi serva Italia, di dolore ostello,   76
nave sanza nocchiere in gran tempesta,
non donna di provincie, ma bordello!

    Quell' anima gentil fu così presta,   79
sol per lo dolce suon de la sua terra,
di fare al cittadin suo quivi festa;

    e ora in te non stanno sanza guerra   82
li vivi tuoi, e l'un l'altro si rode
di quei ch'un muro e una fossa serra.

    Cerca, misera, intorno da le prode   85
le tue marine, e poi ti guarda in seno,
s'alcuna parte in te di pace gode.

    Che val perché ti racconciasse il freno   88
Iustinïano, se la sella è vòta?
Sanz' esso fora la vergogna meno.

    Ahi gente che dovresti esser devota,   91
e lasciar seder Cesare in la sella,
se bene intendi ciò che Dio ti nota,

    guarda come esta fiera è fatta fella   94
per non esser corretta da li sproni,
poi che ponesti mano a la predella.

    O Alberto tedesco ch'abbandoni   97
costei ch'è fatta indomita e selvaggia,
e dovresti inforcar li suoi arcioni,

    giusto giudicio da le stelle caggia   100
sovra 'l tuo sangue, e sia novo e aperto,
tal che 'l tuo successor temenza n'aggia!

    ch'avete tu e 'l tuo padre sofferto,   103
per cupidigia di costà distretti,
che 'l giardin de lo 'mperio sia diserto.

    Vieni a veder Montecchi e Cappelletti,   106
Monaldi e Filippeschi, uom sanza cura:
color già tristi, e questi con sospetti!

but asked us what our country was and who   70
we were, at which my gentle guide began
"Mantua"—and that spirit, who had been

so solitary, rose from his position,   73
saying: "O Mantuan, I am Sordello,
from your own land!" And each embraced the other.

Ah, abject Italy, you inn of sorrows.   76
you ship without a helmsman in harsh seas,
no queen of provinces but of bordellos!

That noble soul had such enthusiasm: 79
his city's sweet name was enough for him
to welcome—there—his fellow-citizen;

But those who are alive within you now   82
can't live without their warring—even those
whom one same wall and one same moat enclose

gnaw at each other. Squalid Italy,   85
search round your shores and then look inland—see
if any part of you delight in peace.

What use was there in a Justinian's   88
mending your bridle, when the saddle's empty?
Indeed, were there no reins, your shame were less.

Ah you—who if you understood what God   91
ordained, would then attend to things devout
and in the saddle surely would allow

Caesar to sit—see how this beast turns fierce   94
because there are no spurs that would correct it,
since you have laid your hands upon the bit!

O German Albert, you who have abandoned   97
that steed become recalcitrant and savage,
you who should ride astride its saddlebows—

upon your blood may the just judgment of   100
the stars descend with signs so strange and plain
that your successor has to feel its terror!

For both you and your father, in your greed   103
for lands that lay more close at hand, allowed
the garden of the Empire to be gutted.

Come—you who pay no heed—do come and see   106
Montecchi, Cappelletti, sad already,
and, filled with fear, Monaldi, Filippeschi.

Vien, crudel, vieni, e vedi la pressura   109
d'i tuoi gentili, e cura lor magagne;
e vedrai Santafior com' è oscura!

Vieni a veder la tua Roma che piagne   112
vedova e sola, e dì e notte chiama:
"Cesare mio, perché non m'accompagne?"

Vieni a veder la gente quanto s'ama!   115
e se nulla di noi pietà ti move,
a vergognar ti vien de la tua fama.

E se licito m'è, o sommo Giove   118
che fosti in terra per noi crucifisso,
son li giusti occhi tuoi rivolti altrove?

O è preparazion che ne l'abisso   121
del tuo consiglio fai per alcun bene
in tutto de l'accorger nostro scisso?

Ché le città d'Italia tutte piene   124
son di tiranni, e un Marcel diventa
ogne villan che parteggiando viene.

Fiorenza mia, ben puoi esser contenta   127
di questa digression che non ti tocca,
mercé del popol tuo che si argomenta.

Molti han giustizia in cuore, e tardi scocca   130
per non venir sanza consiglio a l'arco;
ma il popol tuo l'ha in sommo de la bocca.

Molti rifiutan lo comune incarco;   133
ma il popol tuo solicito risponde
sanza chiamare, e grida: "I' mi sobbarco!"

Or ti fa lieta, ché tu hai ben onde: 136
tu ricca, tu con pace e tu con senno!
S'io dico 'l ver, l'effetto nol nasconde.

Atene e Lacedemona, che fenno   139
l'antiche leggi e furon sì civili,
fecero al viver bene un picciol cenno

verso di te, che fai tanto sottili   142
provedimenti, ch'a mezzo novembre
non giugne quel che tu d'ottobre fili.

Quante volte, del tempo che rimembre,   145
legge, moneta, officio e costume
hai tu mutato, e rinovate membre!

Come, cruel one, come see the tribulation   109
of your nobility and heal their hurts;
see how disconsolate is Santafior!

Come, see your Rome who, widowed and alone,   112
weeps bitterly; both day and night, she moans:
"My Caesar, why are you not at my side?"

Come, see how much your people love each other!   115
And if no pity for us moves you, may
shame for your own repute move you to act.

And if I am allowed, o highest Jove,   118
to ask: You who on earth were crucified
for us—have You turned elsewhere Your just eyes?

Or are You, in Your judgment's depth, devising   121
a good that we cannot foresee, completely
dissevered from our way of understanding?

For all the towns of Italy are full   124
of tyrants, and each townsman who becomes
a partisan is soon a new Marcellus.

My Florence, you indeed may be content   127
that this digression would leave you exempt:
your people's strivings spare you this lament.

Others have justice in their hearts, and thought   130
is slow to let it fly off from their bow;
but your folk keep it ready—on their lips.

Others refuse the weight of public service;   133
whereas your people—eagerly—respond,
even unasked, and shout: "I'll take it on."

You might be happy now, for you have cause!   136
You with your riches, peace, judiciousness!
If I speak truly, facts won't prove me wrong.

Compared to you, Athens and Lacedaemon,   139
though civil cities, with their ancient laws,
had merely sketched the life of righteousness;

for you devise provisions so ingenious—   142
whatever threads October sees you spin,
when mid-November comes, will be unspun.

How often, in the time you can remember,   145
have you changed laws and coinage, offices
and customs, and revised your citizens!

E se ben ti ricordi e vedi lume,   148
vedrai te somigliante a quella inferma
che non può trovar posa in su le piume,
  ma con dar volta suo dolore scherma.   151

And if your memory has some clarity,   148
then you will see yourself like that sick woman
who finds no rest upon her feather-bed,
    but, turning, tossing, tries to ease her pain.   151

CANTO VII

Poscia che l'accoglienze oneste e liete
   furo iterate tre e quattro volte,
Sordel si trasse, e disse: "Voi, chi siete?"

   "Anzi che a questo monte fosser volte   4
l'anime degne di salire a Dio,
fur l'ossa mie per Ottavian sepolte.

   Io son Virgilio; e per null' altro rio   7
lo ciel perdei che per non aver fé."
Così rispuose allora il duca mio.

   Qual è colui che cosa innanzi sé   10
sùbita vede ond' e' si maraviglia,
che crede e non, dicendo "Ella è... non è...,"

   tal parve quelli; e poi chinò le ciglia,   13
e umilmente ritornò ver' lui,
e abbracciòl là 've 'l minor s'appiglia.

   "O gloria di Latin," disse, "per cui   16
mostrò ciò che potea la lingua nostra,
o pregio etterno del loco ond' io fui,

   qual merito o qual grazia mi ti mostra?   19
S'io son d'udir le tue parole degno,
dimmi se vien d'inferno, e di qual chiostra."

   "Per tutt' i cerchi del dolente regno,"   22
rispuose lui, "son io di qua venuto;
virtù del ciel mi mosse, e con lei vegno.

   Non per far, ma per non fare ho perduto   25
a veder l'alto Sol che tu disiri
e che fu tardi per me conosciuto.

   Luogo è là giù non tristo di martìri,   28
ma di tenebre solo, ove i lamenti
non suonan come guai, ma son sospiri.

Ante-Purgatory. From the Second Spur to the Valley of the Rulers—they too, through negligence, among the Late-Repentant. Rudolph I of Hapsburg; Ottokar II of Bohemia; Phillip III of France; Henry I of Navarre; Peter III of Aragon; Charles I of Anjou; Peter, youngest son of Peter III of Aragon; Henry II of England—all thirteenth-century rulers.

When glad and gracious welcomings had been
    repeated three and four times, then Sordello
drew himself back and asked: "But who are you?"

    "Before the spirits worthy of ascent   4
to God had been directed to this mountain,
my bones were buried by Octavian.

    I am Virgil, and I am deprived of Heaven   7
for no fault other than my lack of faith."
This was the answer given by my guide.

    Even like one who, suddenly, has seen   10
something before him and then, marveling,
does and does not believe, saying, "It is . . .

    is not," so did Sordello seem, and then   13
he bent his brow, returned to Virgil humbly,
and clasped him where the lesser presence clasps.

    He said: "O glory of the Latins, you   16
through whom our tongue revealed its power, you,
eternal honor of my native city,

    what merit or what grace shows you to me?   19
If I deserve to hear your word, then answer:
tell me if you're from Hell and from what cloister."

    "Through every circle of the sorry kingdom,"   22
he answered him, "I journeyed here; a power
from Heaven moved me, and with that, I come.

    Not for the having—but not having—done,   25
I lost the sight that you desire, the Sun—
that high Sun I was late in recognizing.

    There is a place below that only shadows—   28
not torments—have assigned to sadness; there,
lament is not an outcry, but a sigh.

Quivi sto io coi pargoli innocenti   31
dai denti morse de la morte avante
che fosser da l'umana colpa essenti;

quivi sto io con quei che le tre sante   34
virtù non si vestiro, e sanza vizio
conobber l'altre e seguir tutte quante.

Ma se tu sai e puoi, alcuno indizio   37
dà noi per che venir possiam più tosto
là dove purgatorio ha dritto inizio."

Rispuose: "Loco certo non c'è posto;   40
licito m'è andar suso e intorno;
per quanto ir posso, a guida mi t'accosto.

Ma vedi già come dichina il giorno,   43
e andar sù di notte non si puote;
però è buon pensar di bel soggiorno.

Anime sono a destra qua remote;   46
se mi consenti, io ti merrò ad esse,
e non sanza diletto ti fier note."

"Com' è ciò?" fu risposto. "Chi volesse   49
salir di notte, fora elli impedito
d'altrui, o non sarria ché non potesse?"

E 'l buon Sordello in terra fregò 'l dito, 52
dicendo: "Vedi? sola questa riga
non varcheresti dopo 'l sol partito:

non però ch'altra cosa desse briga,   55
che la notturna tenebra, ad ir suso;
quella col nonpoder la voglia intriga.

Ben si poria con lei tornare in giuso   58
e passeggiar la costa intorno errando,
mentre che l'orizzonte il dì tien chiuso."

Allora il mio segnor, quasi ammirando,   61
"Menane," disse, "dunque là 've dici
ch'aver si può diletto dimorando."

Poco allungati c'eravam di lici,   64
quand' io m'accorsi che 'l monte era scemo,
a guisa che i vallon li sceman quici.

"Colà," disse quell' ombra, "n'anderemo   67
dove la costa face di sé grembo;
e là il novo giorno attenderemo."

There I am with the infant innocents, 31
those whom the teeth of death had seized before
they were set free from human sinfulness;

there I am with those souls who were not clothed 34
in the three holy virtues—but who knew
and followed after all the other virtues.

But if you know and you are able to, 37
would you point out the path that leads more quickly
to the true entry point of Purgatory?"

He answered: "No fixed place has been assigned 40
to us; I'm free to range about and climb;
as far as I may go, I'll be your guide.

But see now how the day declines; by night 43
we cannot climb; and therefore it is best
to find some pleasant place where we can rest.

Here to the right are spirits set apart; 46
if you allow me, I shall lead you to them;
and not without delight, you'll come to know them."

"How is that?" he was asked. "Is it that he 49
who tried to climb by night would be impeded
by others, or by his own lack of power?"

And good Sordello, as his finger traced 52
along the ground, said: "Once the sun has set,
then—look—even this line cannot be crossed.

And not that anything except the dark 55
of night prevents your climbing up; it is
the night itself that implicates your will.

Once darkness falls, one can indeed retreat 58
below and wander aimlessly about
the slopes, while the horizon has enclosed

the day." At which my lord, as if in wonder, 61
said: "Lead us then to there where, as you say,
we may derive delight from this night's stay."

We had not gone far off, when I perceived 64
that, just as valleys hollow mountains here
in our world, so that mountain there was hollowed.

That shade said: "It is there that we shall go— 67
to where the slope forms, of itself, a lap;
at that place we'll await the new day's coming."

Tra erto e piano era un sentiero schembo,   70
che ne condusse in fianco de la lacca,
là dove più ch'a mezzo muore il lembo.

Oro e argento fine, cocco e biacca,   73
indaco, legno lucido e sereno,
fresco smeraldo in l'ora che si fiacca,

da l'erba e da li fior, dentr'a quel seno   76
posti, ciascun saria di color vinto,
come dal suo maggiore è vinto il meno.

Non avea pur natura ivi dipinto,   79
ma di soavità di mille odori
vi facea uno incognito e indistinto.

"Salve, Regina" in sul verde e 'n su' fiori   82
quindi seder cantando anime vidi,
che per la valle non parean di fuori.

"Prima che 'l poco sole omai s'annidi,"   85
cominciò 'l Mantoan che ci avea vòlti,
"tra color non vogliate ch'io vi guidi.

Di questo balzo meglio li atti e' volti   88
conoscerete voi di tutti quanti,
che ne la lama giù tra essi accolti.

Colui che più siede alto e fa sembianti   91
d'aver negletto ciò che far dovea,
e che non move bocca a li altrui canti,

Rodolfo imperador fu, che potea   94
sanar le piaghe c'hanno Italia morta,
sì che tardi per altri si ricrea.

L'altro che ne la vista lui conforta,   97
resse la terra dove l'acqua nasce
che Molta in Albia, e Albia in mar ne porta:

Ottacchero ebbe nome, e ne le fasce   100
fu meglio assai che Vincislao suo figlio
barbuto, cui lussuria e ozio pasce.

E quel nasetto che stretto a consiglio   103
par con colui c'ha sì benigno aspetto,
morì fuggendo e disfiorando il giglio:

guardate là come si batte il petto!   106
L'altro vedete c'ha fatto a la guancia
de la sua palma, sospirando, letto.

There was a slanting path, now steep, now flat;   70
it led us to a point beside the valley,
just where its bordering edge had dropped by half.

Gold and fine silver, cochineal, white lead,   73
and Indian lychnite, highly polished, bright,
fresh emerald at the moment it is dampened,

if placed within that valley, all would be   76
defeated by the grass and flowers' colors,
just as the lesser gives way to the greater.

And nature there not only was a painter,   79
but from the sweetness of a thousand odors,
she had derived an unknown, mingled scent.

Upon the green grass and the flowers, I   82
saw seated spirits singing *"Salve, Regina";*
they were not visible from the outside.

"Before the meager sun seeks out its nest,"   85
began the Mantuan who led us here,
"do not ask me to guide you down among them.

From this bank, you'll be better able to   88
make out the acts and features of them all
than if you were to join them in the hollow.

He who is seated highest, with the look   91
of one too lax in what he undertook—
whose mouth, although the rest sing, does not move—

was Emperor Rudolph, one who could have healed   94
the wounds that were the death of Italy,
so that another, later, must restore her.

His neighbor, whose appearance comforts him,   97
governed the land in which are born the waters
the Moldau carries to the Elbe and

the Elbe to the sea: named Ottokar—   100
in swaddling-bands he was more valiant than
his son, the bearded Wenceslaus, who feeds

on wantonness and ease. That small-nosed man,   103
who seems so close in counsel with his kindly
friend, died in flight, deflowering the lily:

see how he beats his breast there! And you see   106
the other shade, who, as he sighs, would rest
his cheek upon his palm as on a bed.

    Padre e suocero son del mal di Francia: 109
sanno la vita sua viziata e lorda,
e quindi viene il duol che sì li lancia.

    Quel che par sì membruto e che s'accorda,   112
cantando, con colui dal maschio naso,
d'ogne valor portò cinta la corda;

    e se re dopo lui fosse rimaso   115
lo giovanetto che retro a lui siede,
ben andava il valor di vaso in vaso,

    che non si puote dir de l'altre rede;   118
Iacomo e Federigo hanno i reami;
del retaggio miglior nessun possiede.

    Rade volte risurge per li rami   121
l'umana probitate; e questo vole
quei che la dà, perché da lui si chiami.

    Anche al nasuto vanno mie parole   124
non men ch'a l'altro, Pier, che con lui canta,
onde Puglia e Proenza già si dole.

    Tant' è del seme suo minor la pianta,   127
quanto, più che Beatrice e Margherita,
Costanza di marito ancor si vanta.

    Vedete il re de la semplice vita   130
seder là solo, Arrigo d'Inghilterra:
questi ha ne' rami suoi migliore uscita.

    Quel che più basso tra costor s'atterra,   133
guardando in suso, è Guiglielmo marchese,
per cui e Allesandria e la sua guerra

    fa pianger Monferrato e Canavese."   136

Father and father-in-law of the pest   109
of France, they know his life—its filth, its vice;
out of that knowledge grows the grief that has
    pierced them. That other, who seems so robust   112
and sings in time with him who has a nose
so manly, wore the cord of every virtue;
    and if the young man seated there behind him   115
had only followed him as king, then valor
might have been poured from vessel unto vessel;
    one cannot say this of his other heirs;   118
his kingdoms now belong to James and Frederick—
but they do not possess his best bequest.
    How seldom human worth ascends from branch   121
to branch, and this is willed by Him who grants
that gift, that one may pray to Him for it!
    My words suggest the large-nosed one no less   124
than they refer to Peter, singing with him,
whose heir brings Puglia and Provence distress:
    the plant is lesser than its seed, just as   127
the man whom Beatrice and Margaret wed
is lesser than the husband Constance has.
    You see the king who led the simple life   130
seated alone: Henry of England—he
has better fortune with his progeny.
    He who is seated lowest on the ground,   133
and looking up, is William the Marquis—
for him, both Alexandria and its war
    make Monferrato and Canavese mourn."   136

VIII · 30

VIII · 100

CANTO VIII

E ra già l'ora che volge il disio
    ai navicanti e 'ntenerisce il core
lo dì c'han detto ai dolci amici addio;

    e che lo novo peregrin d'amore   4
punge, se ode squilla di lontano
che paia il giorno pianger che si more;

    quand' io incominciai a render vano   7
l'udire e a mirare una de l'alme
surta, che l'ascoltar chiedea con mano.

    Ella giunse e levò ambo le palme,   10
ficcando li occhi verso l'orïente,
come dicesse a Dio: "D'altro non calme."

    "Te lucis ante" sì devotamente   13
le uscìo di bocca e con sì dolci note,
che fece me a me uscir di mente;

    e l'altre poi dolcemente e devote   16
seguitar lei per tutto l'inno intero,
avendo li occhi a le superne rote.

    Aguzza qui, lettor, ben li occhi al vero,   19
ché 'l velo è ora ben tanto sottile,
certo che 'l trapassar dentro è leggero.

    Io vidi quello essercito gentile   22
tacito poscia riguardare in sùe,
quasi aspettando, palido e umìle;

    e vidi uscir de l'alto e scender giùe   25
due angeli con due spade affocate,
tronche e private de le punte sue.

    Verdi come fogliette pur mo nate   28
erano in veste, che da verdi penne
percosse traean dietro e ventilate.

Ante-Purgatory. The Valley of the Rulers. Sunset. The two angels. Dante's friend, Nino Visconti. The three stars. The serpent put to flight by the angels. Colloquy with Currado Malaspina.

I t was the hour that turns seafarers' longings
  homeward—the hour that makes their hearts grow tender
upon the day they bid sweet friends farewell;

    the hour that pierces the new traveler   4
with love when he has heard, far off, the bell
that seems to mourn the dying of the day;

    when I began to let my hearing fade   7
and watched one of those souls who, having risen,
had signaled with his hand for our attention.

    He joined his palms and, lifting them, he fixed   10
all his attention on the east, as if
to say to God: "I care for nothing else."

    "Te lucis ante" issued from his lips   13
with such devotion and with notes so sweet
that I was moved to move beyond my mind.

    And then the other spirits followed him—   16
devoutly, gently—through all of that hymn,
their eyes intent on the supernal spheres.

    Here, reader, let your eyes look sharp at truth,   19
for now the veil has grown so very thin—
it is not difficult to pass within.

    I saw that company of noble spirits,   22
silent and looking upward, pale and humble,
as if in expectation; and I saw,

    emerging and descending from above,   25
two angels bearing flaming swords, of which
the blades were broken off, without their tips.

    Their garments, just as green as newborn leaves,   28
were agitated, fanned by their green wings,
and trailed behind them; and one angel came

L'un poco sovra noi a star si venne,   31
o l'altro scese in l'opposita sponda,
sì che la gente in mezzo si contenne.

Ben discernëa in lor la testa bionda;   34
ma ne la faccia l'occhio si smarria,
come virtù ch'a troppo si confonda.

"Ambo vegnon del grembo di Maria,"   37
disse Sordello, "a guardia de la valle,
per lo serpente che verrà vie via."

Ond' io, che non sapeva per qual calle,   40
mi volsi intorno, e stretto m'accostai,
tutto gelato, a le fidate spalle.

E Sordello anco: "Or avvalliamo omai   43
tra le grandi ombre, e parleremo ad esse;
grazïoso fia lor vedervi assai."

Solo tre passi credo ch'i' scendesse,   46
e fui di sotto, e vidi un che mirava
pur me, come conoscer mi volesse.

Temp' era già che l'aere s'annerava,   49
ma non sì che tra li occhi suoi e ' miei
non dichiarisse ciò che pria serrava.

Ver' me si fece, e io ver' lui mi fei: 52
giudice Nin gentil, quanto mi piacque
quando ti vidi non esser tra ' rei!

Nullo bel salutar tra noi si tacque;   55
poi dimandò: "Quant' è che tu venisti
a piè del monte per le lontane acque?"

"Oh!" diss' io lui, "per entro i luoghi tristi   58
venni stamane, e sono in prima vita,
ancor che l'altra, sì andando, acquisti."

E come fu la mia risposta udita,   61
Sordello ed elli in dietro si raccolse
come gente di sùbito smarrita.

L'uno a Virgilio e l'altro a un si volse   64
che sedea lì, gridando: "Sù, Currado!
vieni a veder che Dio per grazia volse."

Poi, vòlto a me: "Per quel singular grado   67
che tu dei a colui che sì nasconde
lo suo primo perché, che non li è guado,

and stood somewhat above us, while the other   31
descended on the opposite embankment,
flanking that company of souls between them.

My eyes made out their blond heads clearly, but   34
my sight was dazzled by their faces—just
like any sense bewildered by excess.

"Both come from Mary's bosom," said Sordello,   37
"to serve as the custodians of the valley
against the serpent that will soon appear."

At this, not knowing where its path might be,   40
frozen with fear, I turned around, pressing
close to the trusty shoulders. And Sordello

continued: "Let us now descend among   43
the great shades in the valley; we shall speak
with them; and seeing you, they will be pleased."

I think that I had taken but three steps   46
to go below, when I saw one who watched
attentively, trying to recognize me.

The hour had now arrived when air grows dark,   49
but not so dark that it deprived my eyes
and his of what—before—they were denied.

He moved toward me, and I advanced toward him.   52
Noble Judge Nino—what delight was mine
when I saw you were not among the damned!

There was no gracious greeting we neglected   55
before he asked me: "When did you arrive,
across long seas, beneath this mountainside?"

I told him, "Oh, by way of the sad regions,   58
I came this morning; I am still within
the first life—although, by this journeying,

I earn the other." When they heard my answer,   61
Sordello and Judge Nino, just behind him,
drew back like people suddenly astonished.

One turned to Virgil, and the other turned   64
and called to one who sat there: "Up, Currado!
Come see what God, out of His grace, has willed!"

Then, when he turned to me: "By that especial   67
gratitude you owe to Him who hides
his primal aim so that no human mind

quando sarai di là da le larghe onde,   70
dì a Giovanna mia che per me chiami
là dove a li 'nnocenti si risponde.

Non credo che la sua madre più m'ami,   73
poscia che trasmutò le bianche bende,
le quai convien che, misera!, ancor brami.

Per lei assai di lieve si comprende   76
quanto in femmina foco d'amor dura,
se l'occhio o 'l tatto spesso non l'accende.

Non le farà sì bella sepultura   79
la vipera che Melanesi accampa,
com' avria fatto il gallo di Gallura."

Così dicea, segnato de la stampa,   82
nel suo aspetto, di quel dritto zelo
che misuratamente in core avvampa.

Li occhi miei ghiotti andavan pur al cielo,   85
pur là dove le stelle son più tarde,
sì come rota più presso a lo stelo.

E 'l duca mio: "Figliuol, che là sù guarde?"   88
E io a lui: "A quelle tre facelle
di che 'l polo di qua tutto quanto arde."

Ond' elli a me: "Le quattro chiare stelle   91
che vedevi staman, son di là basse,
e queste son salite ov' eran quelle."

Com' ei parlava, e Sordello a sé il trasse   94
dicendo: "Vedi là 'l nostro avversaro";
e drizzò il dito perché 'n là guardasse.

Da quella parte onde non ha riparo   97
la picciola vallea, era una biscia,
forse qual diede ad Eva il cibo amaro.

Tra l'erba e ' fior venìa la mala striscia,   100
volgendo ad ora ad or la testa, e 'l dosso
leccando come bestia che si liscia.

Io non vidi, e però dicer non posso,   103
come mosser li astor celestïali;
ma vidi bene e l'uno e l'altro mosso.

Sentendo fender l'aere a le verdi ali,   106
fuggì 'l serpente, e li angeli dier volta,
suso a le poste rivolando iguali.

may find the ford to it, when you return 70
across the wide waves, ask my own Giovanna—
there where the pleas of innocents are answered—

to pray for me. I do not think her mother 73
still loves me: she gave up her white veils—surely,
poor woman, she will wish them back again.

Through her, one understands so easily 76
how brief, in woman, is love's fire—when not
rekindled frequently by eye or touch.

The serpent that assigns the Milanese 79
their camping place will not provide for her
a tomb as fair as would Gallura's rooster."

So Nino spoke; his bearing bore the seal 82
of that unswerving zeal which, though it flames
within the heart, maintains a sense of measure.

My avid eyes were steadfast, staring at 85
that portion of the sky where stars are slower,
even as spokes when they approach the axle.

And my guide: "Son, what are you staring at?" 88
And I replied: "I'm watching those three torches
with which this southern pole is all aflame."

Then he to me: "The four bright stars you saw 91
this morning now are low, beyond the pole,
and where those four stars were, these three now are."

Even as Virgil spoke, Sordello drew 94
him to himself: "See there—our adversary!"
he said; and then he pointed with his finger.

At the unguarded edge of that small valley, 97
there was a serpent—similar, perhaps,
to that which offered Eve the bitter food.

Through grass and flowers the evil streak advanced; 100
from time to time it turned its head and licked
its back, like any beast that preens and sleeks.

I did not see—and therefore cannot say— 103
just how the hawks of heaven made their move,
but I indeed saw both of them in motion.

Hearing the green wings cleave the air, the serpent 106
fled, and the angels wheeled around as each
of them flew upward, back to his high station.

L'ombra che s'era al giudice raccolta   109
quando chiamò, per tutto quello assalto
punto non fu da me guardare sciolta.

"Se la lucerna che ti mena in alto   112
truovi nel tuo arbitrio tanta cera
quant' è mestiere infino al sommo smalto,"

cominciò ella, "se novella vera   115
di Val di Magra o di parte vicina
sai, dillo a me, che già grande là era.

Fui chiamato Currado Malaspina;   118
non son l'antico, ma di lui discesi;
a' miei portai l'amor che qui raffina."

"Oh!" diss' io lui, "per li vostri paesi   121
già mai non fui; ma dove si dimora
per tutta Europa ch'ei non sien palesi?

La fama che la vostra casa onora,   124
grida i segnori e grida la contrada,
sì che ne sa chi non vi fu ancora;

e io vi giuro, s'io di sopra vada,   127
che vostra gente onrata non si sfregia
del pregio de la borsa e de la spada.

Uso e natura sì la privilegia,   130
che, perché il capo reo il mondo torca,
sola va dritta e 'l mal cammin dispregia."

Ed elli: "Or va; che 'l sol non si ricorca   133
sette volte nel letto che 'l Montone
con tutti e quattro i piè cuopre e inforca,

che cotesta cortese oppinïone   136
ti fia chiavata in mezzo de la testa
con maggior chiovi che d'altrui sermone,

se corso di giudicio non s'arresta."   139

The shade who, when the judge had called, had drawn 109
closer to him, through all of that attack,
had not removed his eyes from me one moment.

"So may the lantern that leads you on high 112
discover in your will the wax one needs—
enough for reaching the enameled peak,"

that shade began, "if you have heard true tidings 115
of Val di Magra or the lands nearby,
tell them to me—for there I once was mighty.

Currado Malaspina was my name; 118
I'm not the old Currado, but I am
descended from him: to my own I bore

the love that here is purified." I answered: 121
"never visited your lands; but can
there be a place in all of Europe where

they are not celebrated? Such renown 124
honors your house, acclaims your lords and lands—
even if one has yet to journey there.

And so may I complete my climb, I swear 127
to you: your honored house still claims the prize—
the glory of the purse and of the sword.

Custom and nature privilege it so 130
that, though the evil head contorts the world,
your kin alone walk straight and shun the path

of wickedness." And he: "Be sure of that. 133
The sun will not have rested seven times
within the bed that's covered and held fast

by all the Ram's four feet before this gracious 136
opinion's squarely nailed into your mind
with stouter nails than others' talk provides—

if the divine decree has not been stayed." 139

CANTO IX

La concubina di Titone antico
già s'imbiancava al balco d'orïente,
fuor de le braccia del suo dolce amico;

di gemme la sua fronte era lucente,   4
poste in figura del freddo animale
che con la coda percuote la gente;

e la notte, de' passi con che sale,   7
fatti avea due nel loco ov' eravamo,
e 'l terzo già chinava in giuso l'ale;

quand' io, che meco avea di quel d'Adamo,   10
vinto dal sonno, in su l'erba inchinai
là 've già tutti e cinque sedavamo.

Ne l'ora che comincia i tristi lai   13
la rondinella presso a la mattina,
forse a memoria de' suo' primi guai,

e che la mente nostra, peregrina   16
più da la carne e men da' pensier presa,
a le sue visïon quasi è divina,

in sogno mi parea veder sospesa   19
un'aguglia nel ciel con penne d'oro,
con l'ali aperte e a calare intesa;

ed esser mi parea là dove fuoro   22
abbandonati i suoi da Ganimede,
quando fu ratto al sommo consistoro.

Fra me pensava: "Forse questa fiede   25
pur qui per uso, e forse d'altro loco
disdegna di portarne suso in piede."

Poi mi parea che, poi rotata un poco,   28
terribil come folgor discendesse,
e me rapisse suso infino al foco.

N ow she who shares the bed of old Tithonus,
    abandoning the arms of her sweet lover,
grew white along the eastern balcony;

    the heavens facing her were glittering   4
with gems set in the semblance of the chill
animal that assails men with its tail;

    while night within the valley where we were   7
had moved across two of the steps it climbs,
and now the third step made night's wings incline;

    when I, who bore something of Adam with me,   10
feeling the need for sleep, lay down upon
the grass where now all five of us were seated.

    At that hour close to morning when the swallow   13
begins her melancholy songs, perhaps
in memory of her ancient sufferings,

    when, free to wander farther from the flesh   16
and less held fast by cares, our intellect's
envisionings become almost divine—

    in dream I seemed to see an eagle poised,   19
with golden pinions, in the sky: its wings
were open; it was ready to swoop down.

    And I seemed to be there where Ganymede   22
deserted his own family when he
was snatched up for the high consistory.

    Within myself I thought: "This eagle may   25
be used to hunting only here; its claws
refuse to carry upward any prey

    found elsewhere." Then it seemed to me that, wheeling   28
slightly and terrible as lightning, it
swooped, snatching me up to the fire's orbit.

Ivi parea che ella e io ardesse;   31
e sì lo 'ncendio imaginato cosse,
che convenne che 'l sonno si rompesse.

Non altrimenti Achille si riscosse,   34
li occhi svegliati rivolgendo in giro
e non sappiendo là dove si fosse,

quando la madre da Chirón a Schiro   37
trafuggò lui dormendo in le sue braccia,
là onde poi li Greci il dipartiro;

che mi scoss' io, sì come da la faccia   40
mi fuggì 'l sonno, e diventa' ismorto,
come fa l'uom che, spaventato, agghiaccia.

Dallato m'era solo il mio conforto,   43
e 'l sole er' alto già più che due ore,
e 'l viso m'era a la marina torto.

"Non aver tema," disse il mio segnore;   46
"fatti sicur, ché noi semo a buon punto;
non stringer, ma rallarga ogne vigore.

Tu se' omai al purgatorio giunto: 49
vedi là il balzo che 'l chiude dintorno;
vedi l'entrata là 've par digiunto.

Dianzi, ne l'alba che procede al giorno,   52
quando l'anima tua dentro dormia,
sovra li fiori ond' è là giù addorno

venne una donna, e disse: 'I' son Lucia;   55
lasciatemi pigliar costui che dorme;
sì l'agevolerò per la sua via.'

Sordel rimase e l'altre genti forme;   58
ella ti tolse, e come 'l dì fu chiaro,
sen venne suso; e io per le sue orme.

Qui ti posò, ma pria mi dimostraro   61
li occhi suoi belli quella intrata aperta;
poi ella e 'l sonno ad una se n'andaro."

A guisa d'uom che 'n dubbio si raccerta   64
e che muta in conforto sua paura,
poi che la verità li è discoperta,

mi cambia' io; e come sanza cura   67
vide me 'l duca mio, su per lo balzo
si mosse, e io di rietro inver' l'altura.

And there it seemed that he and I were burning; 31
and this imagined conflagration scorched
me so—I was compelled to break my sleep.

Just like the waking of Achilles when 34
he started up, casting his eyes about him,
not knowing where he was (after his mother

had stolen him, asleep, away from Chiron 37
and in her arms had carried him to Skyros,
the isle the Greeks would—later—make him leave);

such was my starting up, as soon as sleep 40
had left my eyes, and I went pale, as will
a man who, terrified, turns cold as ice.

The only one beside me was my comfort; 43
by now the sun was more than two hours high;
it was the sea to which I turned my eyes.

My lord said: "Have no fear; be confident, 46
for we are well along our way; do not
restrain, but give free rein to, all your strength.

You have already come to Purgatory: 49
see there the rampart wall enclosing it;
see, where that wall is breached, the point of entry.

Before, at dawn that ushers in the day, 52
when soul was sleeping in your body, on
the flowers that adorn the ground below,

a lady came; she said: 'I am Lucia; 55
let me take hold of him who is asleep,
that I may help to speed him on his way.'

Sordello and the other noble spirits 58
stayed there; and she took you, and once the day
was bright, she climbed—I following behind.

And here she set you down, but first her lovely 61
eyes showed that open entryway to me;
then she and sleep together took their leave."

Just like a man in doubt who then grows sure, 64
exchanging fear for confidence, once truth
has been revealed to him, so was I changed;

and when my guide had seen that I was free 67
from hesitation, then he moved, with me
behind him, up the rocks and toward the heights.

Lettor, tu vedi ben com' io innalzo   70
la mia matera, e però con più arte
non ti maravigliar s'io la rincalzo.

Noi ci appressammo, ed eravamo in parte   73
che là dove pareami prima rotto,
pur come un fesso che muro diparte,

vidi una porta, e tre gradi di sotto   76
per gire ad essa, di color diversi,
e un portier ch'ancor non facea motto.

E come l'occhio più e più v'apersi,   79
vidil seder sovra 'l grado sovrano,
tal ne la faccia ch'io non lo soffersi;

e una spada nuda avëa in mano,   82
che reflettëa i raggi sì ver' noi,
ch'io dirizzava spesso il viso in vano.

"Dite costinci: che volete voi?"   85
cominciò elli a dire, "ov' è la scorta?
Guardate che 'l venir sù non vi nòi."

"Donna del ciel, di queste cose accorta,"   88
rispuose 'l mio maestro a lui, "pur dianzi
ne disse: 'Andate là: quivi è la porta.'"

"Ed ella i passi vostri in bene avanzi,"   91
ricominciò il cortese portinaio:
"Venite dunque a' nostri gradi innanzi."

Là ne venimmo; e lo scaglion primaio   94
bianco marmo era sì pulito e terso,
ch'io mi specchiai in esso qual io paio.

Era il secondo tinto più che perso,   97
d'una petrina ruvida e arsiccia,
crepata per lo lungo e per traverso.

Lo terzo, che di sopra s'ammassiccia,   100
porfido mi parea, sì fiammeggiante
come sangue che fuor di vena spiccia.

Sovra questo tenëa ambo le piante   103
l' angel di Dio sedendo in su la soglia
che mi sembiava pietra di diamante.

Per li tre gradi sù di buona voglia   106
mi trasse il duca mio, dicendo: "Chiedi
umilemente che 'l serrame scioglia."

Reader, you can see clearly how I lift   70
my matter; do not wonder, therefore, if
I have to call on more art to sustain it.

Now we were drawing closer; we had reached   73
the part from which—where first I'd seen a breach,
precisely like a gap that cleaves a wall—

I now made out a gate and, there below it,   76
three steps—their colors different—leading to it,
and a custodian who had not yet spoken.

As I looked more and more directly at him,   79
I saw him seated on the upper step—
his face so radiant, I could not bear it;

and in his hand he held a naked sword,   82
which so reflected rays toward us that I,
time and again, tried to sustain that sight

in vain. "Speak out from there; what are you seeking?"   85
so he began to speak. "Where is your escort?
Take care lest you be harmed by climbing here."

My master answered him: "But just before,   88
a lady came from Heaven and, familiar
with these things, told us: 'That's the gate; go there.'"

"And may she speed you on your path of goodness!"   91
the gracious guardian of the gate began
again. "Come forward, therefore, to our stairs."

There we approached, and the first step was white   94
marble, so polished and so clear that I
was mirrored there as I appear in life.

The second step, made out of crumbling rock,   97
rough-textured, scorched, with cracks that ran across
its length and width, was darker than deep purple.

The third, resting above more massively,   100
appeared to me to be of porphyry,
as flaming red as blood that spurts from veins.

And on this upper step, God's angel—seated   103
upon the threshold, which appeared to me
to be of adamant—kept his feet planted.

My guide, with much good will, had me ascend   106
by way of these three steps, enjoining me:
"Do ask him humbly to unbolt the gate."

Divoto mi gittai a' santi piedi;   109
misericordia chiesi e ch'el m'aprisse,
ma tre volte nel petto pria mi diedi.

Sette P ne la fronte mi descrisse   112
col punton de la spada, e "Fa che lavi,
quando se' dentro, queste piaghe" disse.

Cenere, o terra che secca si cavi,   115
d'un color fora col suo vestimento;
e di sotto da quel trasse due chiavi.

L'una era d'oro e l'altra era d'argento;   118
pria con la bianca e poscia con la gialla
fece a la porta sì, ch'i' fu' contento.

"Quandunque l'una d'este chiavi falla,   121
che non si volga dritta per la toppa,"
diss' elli a noi, "non s'apre questa calla.

Più cara è l'una; ma l'altra vuol troppa   124
d'arte e d'ingegno avanti che diserri,
perch' ella è quella che 'l nodo digroppa.

Da Pier le tegno; e dissemi ch'i' erri   127
anzi ad aprir ch'a tenerla serrata,
pur che la gente a' piedi mi s'atterri."

Poi pinse l'uscio a la porta sacrata,   130
dicendo: "Intrate; ma facciovi accorti
che di fuor torna chi 'n dietro si guata."

E quando fuor ne' cardini distorti   133
li spigoli di quella regge sacra,
che di metallo son sonanti e forti,

non rugghiò sì né si mostrò sì acra   136
Tarpëa, come tolto le fu il buono
Metello, per che poi rimase macra.

Io mi rivolsi attento al primo tuono,   139
e *"Te Deum laudamus"* mi parea
udire in voce mista al dolce suono.

Tale imagine a punto mi rendea   142
ciò ch'io udiva, qual prender si suole
quando a cantar con organi si stea;

ch'or sì or no s'intendon le parole.   145

I threw myself devoutly at his holy   109
feet, asking him to open out of mercy;
but first I beat three times upon my breast.

Upon my forehead, he traced seven *P*'s   112
with his sword's point and said: "When you have entered
within, take care to wash away these wounds."

Ashes, or dry earth that has just been quarried,   115
would share one color with his robe, and from
beneath that robe he drew two keys; the one

was made of gold, the other was of silver;   118
first with the white, then with the yellow key,
he plied the gate so as to satisfy me.

"Whenever one of these keys fails, not turning   121
appropriately in the lock," he said
to us, "this gate of entry does not open.

One is more precious, but the other needs   124
much art and skill before it will unlock—
that is the key that must undo the knot.

These I received from Peter; and he taught me   127
rather to err in opening than in keeping
this portal shut—whenever souls pray humbly."

Then he pushed back the panels of the holy   130
gate, saying: "Enter; but I warn you—he
who would look back, returns—again—outside."

And when the panels of that sacred portal,   133
which are of massive and resounding metal,
turned in their hinges, then even Tarpeia

(when good Metellus was removed from it,   136
for which that rock was left impoverished)
did not roar so nor show itself so stubborn.

Hearing that gate resound, I turned, attentive;   139
I seemed to hear, inside, in words that mingled
with gentle music, *"Te Deum laudamus."*

And what I heard gave me the very same   142
impression one is used to getting when
one hears a song accompanied by organ,

and now the words are clear and now are lost.   145

IX · 19

IX ·112

CANTO X

Poi fummo dentro al soglio de la porta
che 'l mal amor de l'anime disusa,
perché fa parer dritta la via torta,

sonando la senti' esser richiusa;   4
e s'io avesse li occhi vòlti ad essa,
qual fora stata al fallo degna scusa?

Noi salavam per una pietra fessa,   7
che si moveva e d'una e d'altra parte,
sì come l'onda che fugge e s'appressa.

"Qui si conviene usare un poco d'arte,"   10
cominciò 'l duca mio, "in accostarsi
or quinci, or quindi al lato che si parte."

E questo fece i nostri passi scarsi,   13
tanto che pria lo scemo de la luna
rigiunse al letto suo per ricorcarsi,

che noi fossimo fuor di quella cruna;   16
ma quando fummo liberi e aperti
sù dove il monte in dietro si rauna,

ïo stancato e amendue incerti   19
di nostra via, restammo in su un piano
solingo più che strade per diserti.

Da la sua sponda, ove confina il vano,   22
al piè de l'alta ripa che pur sale,
misurrebbe in tre volte un corpo umano;

e quanto l'occhio mio potea trar d'ale,   25
or dal sinistro e or dal destro fianco,
questa cornice mi parea cotale.

Là sù non eran mossi i piè nostri anco,   28
quand' io conobbi quella ripa intorno
che dritto di salita aveva manco,

The First Terrace: the Prideful. The hard ascent. The sculptured wall with three examples of humility: the Virgin Mary, David, and Trajan. The Prideful punished by bearing the weight of heavy stones.

When I had crossed the threshold of the gate
    that—since the soul's aberrant love would make
the crooked way seem straight—is seldom used,

  I heard the gate resound and, hearing, knew   4
that it had shut; and if I'd turned toward it,
how could my fault have found a fit excuse?

  Our upward pathway ran between cracked rocks;   7
they seemed to sway in one, then the other part,
just like a wave that flees, then doubles back.

  "Here we shall need some ingenuity,"   10
my guide warned me, "as both of us draw near
this side or that side where the rock wall veers."

  This made our steps so slow and hesitant   13
that the declining moon had reached its bed
to sink back into rest, before we had

  made our way through that needle's eye; but when   16
we were released from it, in open space
above, a place at which the slope retreats,

  I was exhausted; with the two of us   19
uncertain of our way, we halted on
a plateau lonelier than desert paths.

  The distance from its edge, which rims the void,   22
in to the base of the steep slope, which climbs
and climbs, would measure three times one man's body;

  and for as far as my sight took its flight,   25
now to the left, now to the right-hand side,
that terrace seemed to me equally wide.

  There we had yet to let our feet advance   28
when I discovered that the bordering bank—
less sheer than banks of other terraces—

    esser di marmo candido e addorno   31
d'intagli sì, che non pur Policleto,
ma la natura lì avrebbe scorno.

    L'angel che venne in terra col decreto   34
de la molt' anni lagrimata pace,
ch'aperse il ciel del suo lungo divieto,

    dinanzi a noi pareva sì verace   37
quivi intagliato in un atto soave,
che non sembiava imagine che tace.

    Giurato si saria ch'el dicesse *"Ave!"*;   40
perché iv' era imaginata quella
ch'ad aprir l'alto amor volse la chiave;

    e avea in atto impressa esta favella   43
"Ecce ancilla Deï!," propriamente
come figura in cera si suggella.

    "Non tener pur ad un loco la mente,"   46
disse 'l dolce maestro, che m'avea
da quella parte onde 'l cuore ha la gente.

    Per ch'i' mi mossi col viso, e vedea   49
di retro da Maria, da quella costa
onde m'era colui che mi movea,

    un'altra storia ne la roccia imposta;   52
per ch'io varcai Virgilio, e fe'mi presso,
acciò che fosse a li occhi miei disposta.

    Era intagliato lì nel marmo stesso   55
lo carro e ' buoi, traendo l'arca santa,
per che si teme officio non commesso.

    Dinanzi parea gente; e tutta quanta,   58
partita in sette cori, a' due mie' sensi
faceva dir l'un "No," l'altro "Sì, canta."

    Similemente al fummo de li 'ncensi   61
che v'era imaginato, li occhi e 'l naso
e al sì e al no discordi fensi.

    Lì precedeva al benedetto vaso,   64
trescando alzato, l'umile salmista,
e più e men che re era in quel caso.

    Di contra, effïata ad una vista   67
d'un gran palazzo, Micòl ammirava
sì come donna dispettosa e trista.

was of white marble and adorned with carvings   31
so accurate—not only Polycletus
but even Nature, there, would feel defeated.

The angel who reached earth with the decree   34
of that peace which, for many years, had been
invoked with tears, the peace that opened Heaven

after long interdict, appeared before us,   37
his gracious action carved with such precision—
he did not seem to be a silent image.

One would have sworn that he was saying, *"Ave"*;   40
for in that scene there was the effigy
of one who turned the key that had unlocked

the highest love; and in her stance there were   43
impressed these words, *"Ecce ancilla Dei,"*
precisely like a figure stamped in wax.

"Your mind must not attend to just one part,"   46
the gentle master said—he had me on
the side of him where people have their heart.

At this, I turned my face and saw beyond   49
the form of Mary—on the side where stood
the one who guided me—another story

engraved upon the rock; therefore I moved   52
past Virgil and drew close to it, so that
the scene before my eyes was more distinct.

There, carved in that same marble, were the cart   55
and oxen as they drew the sacred ark,
which makes men now fear tasks not in their charge.

People were shown in front; and all that group,   58
divided into seven choirs, made
two of my senses speak—one sense said, "No,"

the other said, "Yes, they do sing"; just so,   61
about the incense smoke shown there, my nose
and eyes contended, too, with *yes* and *no*.

And there the humble psalmist went before   64
the sacred vessel, dancing, lifting up
his robe—he was both less and more than king.

Facing that scene, and shown as at the window   67
of a great palace, Michal watched as would
a woman full of scorn and suffering.

I' mossi i piè del loco dov' io stava,   70
per avvisar da presso un'altra istoria,
che di dietro a Micòl mi biancheggiava.

Quiv' era storïata l'alta gloria   73
del roman principato, il cui valore
mosse Gregorio a la sua gran vittoria;

i' dico di Traiano imperadore;   76
e una vedovella li era al freno,
dì lagrime atteggiata e di dolore.

Intorno a lui parea calcato e pieno   79
di cavalieri, e l'aguglie ne l'oro
sovr' essi in vista al vento si movieno.

La miserella intra tutti costoro   82
pareva dir: "Segnor, fammi vendetta
di mio figliuol ch'è morto, ond' io m'accoro";

ed elli a lei rispondere: "Or aspetta   85
tanto ch'i' torni"; e quella: "Segnor mio,"
come persona in cui dolor s'affretta,

"se tu non torni?"; ed ei: "Chi fia dov' io,   88
la ti farà"; ed ella: "L'altrui bene
a te che fia, se 'l tuo metti in oblio?";

ond' elli: "Or ti conforta; ch'ei convene   91
ch'i' solva il mio dovere anzi ch'i' mova:
giustizia vuole e pietà mi ritene."

Colui che mai non vide cosa nova   94
produsse esto visibile parlare,
novello a noi perché qui non si trova.

Mentr' io mi dilettava di guardare   97
l'imagini di tante umilitadi,
e per lo fabbro loro a veder care,

"Ecco di qua, ma fanno i passi radi,"   100
mormorava il poeta, "molte genti:
questi ne 'nvïeranno a li alti gradi."

Li occhi miei, ch'a mirare eran contenti   103
per veder novitadi ond' e' son vaghi,
volgendosi ver' lui non furon lenti.

Non vo' però, lettor, che tu ti smaghi   106
di buon proponimento per udire
come Dio vuol che 'l debito si paghi.

To look more closely at another carving,   70
which I saw gleaming white beyond Michal,
my feet moved past the point where I had stood.

And there the noble action of a Roman   73
prince was presented—he whose worth had urged
on Gregory to his great victory—

I mean the Emperor Trajan; and a poor   76
widow was near his bridle, and she stood
even as one in tears and sadness would.

Around him, horsemen seemed to press and crowd;   79
above their heads, on golden banners, eagles
were represented, moving in the wind.

Among that crowd, the miserable woman   82
seemed to be saying: "Lord, avenge me for
the slaying of my son—my heart is broken."

And he was answering: "Wait now until   85
I have returned." And she, as one in whom
grief presses urgently: "And, lord, if you

do not return?" And he: "The one who'll be   88
in my place will perform it for you." She:
"What good can others' goodness do for you

if you neglect your own?" He: "Be consoled;   91
my duty shall be done before I go:
so justice asks, so mercy makes me stay."

This was the speech made visible by One   94
within whose sight no thing is new—but we,
who lack its likeness here, find novelty.

While I took much delight in witnessing   97
these effigies of true humility—
dear, too, to see because He was their Maker—

the poet murmured: "See the multitude   100
advancing, though with slow steps, on this side:
they will direct us to the higher stairs."

My eyes, which had been satisfied in seeking   103
new sights—a thing for which they long—did not
delay in turning toward him. But I would

not have you, reader, be deflected from   106
your good resolve by hearing from me now
how God would have us pay the debt we owe.

Non attender la forma del martìre: 109
pensa la succession; pensa ch'al peggio
oltre la gran sentenza non può ire.

Io cominciai: "Maestro, quel ch'io veggio   112
muovere a noi, non mi sembian persone,
e non so che, sì nel veder vaneggio."

Ed elli a me: "La grave condizione   115
di lor tormento a terra li rannicchia,
sì che ' miei occhi pria n'ebber tencione.

Ma guarda fiso là, e disviticchia   118
col viso quel che vien sotto a quei sassi:
già scorger puoi come ciascun si picchia."

O superbi cristian, miseri lassi,   121
che, de la vista de la mente infermi,
fidanza avete ne' retrosi passi,

non v'accorgete voi che noi siam vermi   124
nati a formar l'angelica farfalla,
che vola a la giustizia sanza schermi?

Di che l'animo vostro in alto galla,   127
poi siete quasi antomata in difetto,
sì come vermo in cui formazion falla?

Come per sostentar solaio o tetto,   130
per mensola talvolta una figura
si vede giugner le ginocchia al petto,

la qual fa del non ver vera rancura   133
nascere 'n chi la vede; così fatti
vid' io color, quando puosi ben cura.

Vero è che più e meno eran contratti   136
secondo ch'avien più e meno a dosso;
e qual più paziënza avea ne li atti,

piangendo parea dicer: "Più non posso."   139

Don't dwell upon the form of punishment: 109
consider what comes after that; at worst
it cannot last beyond the final Judgment.

"Master," I said, "what I see moving toward us   112
does not appear to me like people, but
I can't tell what is there—my sight's bewildered."

And he to me: "Whatever makes them suffer   115
their heavy torment bends them to the ground;
at first I was unsure of what they were.

But look intently there, and let your eyes   118
unravel what's beneath those stones: you can
already see what penalty strikes each."

O Christians, arrogant, exhausted, wretched,   121
whose intellects are sick and cannot see,
who place your confidence in backward steps,

do you not know that we are worms and born   124
to form the angelic butterfly that soars,
without defenses, to confront His judgment?

Why does your mind presume to flight when you   127
are still like the imperfect grub, the worm
before it has attained its final form?

Just as one sees at times—as corbel for   130
support of ceiling or of roof—a figure
with knees drawn up into its chest (and this

oppressiveness, unreal, gives rise to real   133
distress in him who watches it): such was
the state of those I saw when I looked hard.

They were indeed bent down—some less, some more— 136
according to the weights their backs now bore;
and even he whose aspect showed most patience,

in tears, appeared to say: "I can no more."   139

CANTO XI

O Padre nostro, che ne' cieli stai,
    non circunscritto, ma per più amore
ch'ai primi effetti di là sù tu hai,

    laudato sia 'l tuo nome e 'l tuo valore   4
da ogne creatura, com' è degno
di render grazie al tuo dolce vapore.

    Vegna ver' noi la pace del tuo regno,   7
ché noi ad essa non potem da noi,
s'ella non vien, con tutto nostro ingegno.

    Come del suo voler li angeli tuoi   10
fan sacrificio a te, cantando *osanna,*
così facciano li uomini de' suoi.

    Dà oggi a noi la cotidiana manna,   13
sanza la qual per questo aspro diserto
a retro va chi più di gir s'affanna.

    E come noi lo mal ch'avem sofferto   16
perdoniamo a ciascuno, e tu perdona
benigno, e non guardar lo nostro merto.

    Nostra virtù che di legger s'adona,   19
non spermentar con l'antico avversaro,
ma libera da lui che sì la sprona.

    Quest' ultima preghiera, segnor caro,   22
già non si fa per noi, ché non bisogna,
ma per color che dietro a noi restaro."

    Così a sé e noi buona ramogna   25
quell' ombre orando, andavan sotto 'l pondo,
simile a quel che talvolta si sogna,

    dispartamente angosciate tutte a tondo   28
e lasse su per la prima cornice,
purgando la caligine del mondo.

Our Father, You who dwell within the heavens—
but are not circumscribed by them—out of
Your greater love for Your first works above,

praised be Your name and Your omnipotence,   4
by every creature, just as it is seemly
to offer thanks to Your sweet effluence.

Your kingdom's peace come unto us, for if   7
it does not come, then though we summon all
our force, we cannot reach it of our selves.

Just as Your angels, as they sing Hosanna,   10
offer their wills to You as sacrifice,
so may men offer up their wills to You.

Give unto us this day the daily manna   13
without which he who labors most to move
ahead through this harsh wilderness falls back.

Even as we forgive all who have done   16
us injury, may You, benevolent,
forgive, and do not judge us by our worth.

Try not our strength, so easily subdued,   19
against the ancient foe, but set it free
from him who goads it to perversity.

This last request we now address to You,   22
dear Lord, not for ourselves—who have no need—
but for the ones whom we have left behind."

Beseeching, thus, good penitence for us   25
and for themselves, those shades moved on beneath
their weights, like those we sometimes bear in dreams—

each in his own degree of suffering   28
but all, exhausted, circling the first terrace,
purging themselves of this world's scoriae.

Se di là sempre ben per noi si dice,   31
di qua che dire e far per lor si puote
da quei c'hanno al voler buona radice?

Ben si de' loro atar lavar le note   34
che portar quinci, sì che, mondi e lievi,
possano uscire a le stellate ruote.

"Deh, se giustizia e pietà vi disgrievi   37
tosto, sì che possiate muover l'ala,
che secondo il disio vostro vi lievi,

mostrate da qual mano inver' la scala   40
si va più corto; e se c'è più d'un varco,
quel ne 'nsegnate che men erto cala;

ché questi che vien meco, per lo 'ncarco   43
de la carne d'Adamo onde si veste,
al montar sù, contra sua voglia, è parco."

Le lor parole, che rendero a queste   46
che dette avea colui cu' io seguiva,
non fur da cui venisser manifeste;

ma fu detto: "A man destra per la riva   49
con noi venite, e troverete il passo
possibile a salir persona viva.

E s'io non fossi impedito dal sasso   52
che la cervice mia superba doma,
onde portar convienmi il viso basso,

cotesti, ch'ancor vive e non si noma,   55
guardere' io, per veder s'i' 'l conosco,
e per farlo pietoso a questa soma.

Io fui latino e nato d'un gran Tosco: 58
Guiglielmo Aldobrandesco fu mio padre;
non so se 'l nome suo già mai fu vosco.

L'antico sangue e l'opere leggiadre   61
d'i miei maggior mi fer sì arrogante,
che, non pensando a la comune madre,

ogn' uomo ebbi in despetto tanto avante,   64
ch'io ne mori', come i Sanesi sanno,
e sallo in Campagnatico ogne fante.

Io sono Omberto; e non pur a me danno   67
superbia fa, ché tutti miei consorti
ha ella tratti seco nel malanno.

If there they pray on our behalf, what can   31
be said and done here on this earth for them
by those whose wills are rooted in true worth?

Indeed we should help them to wash away   34
the stains they carried from this world, so that,
made pure and light, they reach the starry wheels.

"Ah, so may justice and compassion soon   37
unburden you, so that your wings may move
as you desire them to, and uplift you,

show us on which hand lies the shortest path   40
to reach the stairs; if there is more than one
passage, then show us that which is less steep;

for he who comes with me, because he wears   43
the weight of Adam's flesh as dress, despite
his ready will, is slow in his ascent."

These words, which had been spoken by my guide,   46
were answered by still other words we heard;
for though it was not clear who had replied,

an answer came: "Come with us to the right   49
along the wall of rock, and you will find
a pass where even one alive can climb.

And were I not impeded by the stone   52
that, since it has subdued my haughty neck,
compels my eyes to look below, then I

should look at this man who is still alive   55
and nameless, to see if I recognize
him—and to move his pity for my burden.

I was Italian, son of a great Tuscan: 58
my father was Guiglielmo Aldobrandesco;
I do not know if you have heard his name.

The ancient blood and splendid deeds of my   61
forefathers made me so presumptuous
that, without thinking on our common mother,

I scorned all men past measure, and that scorn   64
brought me my death—the Sienese know how,
as does each child in Campagnatico.

I am Omberto; and my arrogance   67
has not harmed me alone, for it has drawn
all of my kin into calamity.

E qui convien ch'io questo peso porti   70
per lei, tanto che a Dio si sodisfaccia,
poi ch'io nol fe' tra ' vivi, qui tra ' morti."

  Ascoltando chinai in giù la faccia;   73
e un di lor, non questi che parlava,
si torse sotto il peso che li 'mpaccia,

  e videmi e conobbemi e chiamava,   76
tenendo li occhi con fatica fisi
a me che tutto chin con loro andava.

  "Oh!" diss' io lui, "non se' tu Oderisi,   79
l'onor d'Agobbio e l'onor di quell' arte
ch'alluminar chiamata è in Parisi?"

  "Frate," diss' elli, "più ridon le carte   82
che pennelleggia Franco Bolognese;
l'onore è tutto or suo, e mio in parte.

  Ben non sare' io stato sì cortese   85
mentre ch'io vissi, per lo gran disio
de l'eccellenza ove mio core intese.

  Di tal superbia qui si paga il fio;   88
e ancor non sarei qui, se non fosse
che, possendo peccar, mi volsi a Dio.

  Oh vana gloria de l'umane posse!   91
com' poco verde in su la cima dura,
se non è giunta da l'etati grosse!

  Credette Cimabue ne la pittura   94
tener lo campo, e ora ha Giotto il grido,
sì che la fama di colui è scura.

  Così ha tolto l'uno a l'altro Guido   97
la gloria de la lingua; e forse è nato
chi l'uno e l'altro caccerà del nido.

  Non è il mondan romore altro ch'un fiato   100
di vento, ch'or vien quinci e or vien quindi,
e muta nome perché muta lato.

  Che voce avrai tu più, se vecchia scindi   103
da te la carne, che se fossi morto
anzi che tu lasciassi il 'pappo' e 'l 'dindi,'

  pria che passin mill' anni? ch'è più corto   106
spazio a l'etterno, ch'un muover di ciglia
al cerchio che più tardi in cielo è torto.

Until God has been satisfied, I bear   70
this burden here among the dead because
I did not bear this load among the living."

My face was lowered as I listened; and   73
one of those souls—not he who'd spoken—twisted
himself beneath the weight that burdened them;

he saw and knew me and called out to me,   76
fixing his eyes on me laboriously
as I, completely hunched, walked on with them.

"Oh," I cried out, "are you not Oderisi,   79
glory of Gubbio, glory of that art
they call illumination now in Paris?"

"Brother," he said, "the pages painted by   82
the brush of Franco Bolognese smile
more brightly: all the glory now is his;

mine, but a part. In truth I would have been   85
less gracious when I lived—so great was that
desire for eminence which drove my heart.

For such pride, here one pays the penalty;   88
and I'd not be here yet, had it not been
that, while I still could sin, I turned to Him.

O empty glory of the powers of humans!   91
How briefly green endures upon the peak—
unless an age of dullness follows it.

In painting Cimabue thought he held   94
the field, and now it's Giotto they acclaim—
the former only keeps a shadowed fame.

So did one Guido, from the other, wrest   97
the glory of our tongue—and he perhaps
is born who will chase both out of the nest.

Worldly renown is nothing other than   100
a breath of wind that blows now here, now there,
and changes name when it has changed its course.

Before a thousand years have passed—a span   103
that, for eternity, is less space than
an eyeblink for the slowest sphere in heaven—

would you find greater glory if you left   106
your flesh when it was old than if your death
had come before your infant words were spent?

Colui che del cammin sì poco piglia   109
dinanzi a me, Toscana sonò tutta;
e ora a pena in Siena sen pispiglia,
    ond' era sire quando fu distrutta   112
la rabbia fiorentina, che superba
fu a quel tempo sì com' ora è putta.
    La vostra nominanza è color d'erba,   115
che viene e va, e quei la discolora
per cui ella esce de la terra acerba."
    E io a lui: "Tuo vero dir m'incora   118
bona umiltà, e gran tumor m'appiani;
ma chi è quei di cui tu parlavi ora?"
    "Quelli è," rispuose, "Provenzan Salvani;   121
ed è qui perché fu presuntüoso
a recar Siena tutta a le sue mani.
    Ito è così e va, sanza riposo,   124
poi che morì; cotal moneta rende
a sodisfar chi è di là troppo oso."
    E io: "Se quello spirito ch'attende,   127
pria che si penta, l'orlo de la vita,
qua giù dimora e qua sù non ascende,
    se buona orazïon lui non aita,   130
prima che passi tempo quanto visse,
come fu la venuta lui largita?"
    "Quando vivea più glorïoso," disse,   133
"liberamente nel Campo di Siena,
ogne vergogna diposta, s'affisse;
    e lì, per trar l'amico suo di pena,   136
ch'e' sostenea ne la prigion di Carlo,
si condusse a tremar per ogne vena.
    Più non dirò, e scuro so che parlo;   139
ma poco tempo andrà, che ' tuoi vicini
faranno sì che tu potrai chiosarlo.
    Quest' opera li tolse quei confini."   142

All Tuscany acclaimed his name—the man   109
who moves so slowly on the path before me,
and now they scarcely whisper of him even

in Siena, where he lorded it when they   112
destroyed the raging mob of Florence—then
as arrogant as now it's prostitute.

Your glory wears the color of the grass   115
that comes and goes; the sun that makes it wither
first drew it from the ground, still green and tender."

And I to him: "Your truthful speech has filled   118
my soul with sound humility, abating
my overswollen pride; but who is he

of whom you spoke now?" "Provenzan Salvani,   121
he answered, "here because—presumptuously—"
he thought his grip could master all Siena.

So he has gone, and so he goes, with no   124
rest since his death; this is the penalty
exacted from those who—there—overreached."

And I: "But if a spirit who awaits   127
the edge of life before repenting must—
unless good prayers help him—stay below

and not ascend here for as long a time   130
as he had spent alive, do tell me how
Salvani's entry here has been allowed."

"When he was living in his greatest glory,"   133
said he, "then of his own free will he set
aside all shame and took his place upon

the Campo of Siena; there, to free   136
his friend from suffering in Charles's prison,
humbling himself, he trembled in each vein.

I say no more; I know I speak obscurely;   139
but soon enough you'll find your neighbor's acts
are such that what I say can be explained.

This deed delivered him from those confines."   142

OMBERTO

ARACHNE

Di pari, come buoi che vanno a giogo,
m'andava io con quell' anima carca,
fin che 'l sofferse il dolce pedagogo.

Ma quando disse: "Lascia lui e varca;   4
ché qui è buono con l'ali e coi remi,
quantunque può, ciascun pinger sua barca";

dritto sì come andar vuolsi rife'mi   7
con la persona, avvegna che i pensieri
mi rimanessero e chinati e scemi.

Io m'era mosso, e seguia volontieri   10
del mio maestro i passi, e amendue
già mostravam com' eravam leggeri;

ed el mi disse: "Volgi li occhi in giùe: 13
buon ti sarà, per tranquillar la via,
veder lo letto de le piante tue."

Come, perché di lor memoria sia,   16
sovra i sepolti le tombe terragne
portan segnato quel ch'elli eran pria,

onde lì molte volte si ripiagne   19
per la puntura de la rimembranza,
che solo a' pïi dà de le calcagne;

sì vid' io lì, ma di miglior sembianza   22
secondo l'artificio, figurato
quanto per via di fuor del monte avanza.

Vedëa colui che fu nobil creato   25
più ch'altra creatura, giù dal cielo
folgoreggiando scender, da l'un lato.

Vedea Brïareo fitto dal telo   28
celestïal giacer, da l'altra parte,
grave a la terra per lo mortal gelo.

A s oxen, yoked, proceed abreast, so I
moved with that burdened soul as long as my
kind pedagogue allowed me to; but when

 he said: "Leave him behind, and go ahead;   4
for here it's fitting that with wings and oars
each urge his boat along with all his force,"

 I drew my body up again, erect—   7
the stance most suitable to man—and yet
the thoughts I thought were still submissive, bent.

 Now I was on my way, and willingly   10
I followed in my teacher's steps, and we
together showed what speed we could command.

 He said to me: "Look downward, for the way 13
will offer you some solace if you pay
attention to the pavement at your feet."

 As, on the lids of pavement tombs, there are 16
stone effigies of what the buried were
before, so that the dead may be remembered;

 and there, when memory—inciting only   19
the pious—has renewed their mourning, men
are often led to shed their tears again;

 so did I see, but carved more skillfully,   22
with greater sense of likeness, effigies
on all the path protruding from the mountain.

 I saw, to one side of the path, one who   25
had been created nobler than all other
beings, falling lightning-like from Heaven.

 I saw, upon the other side, Briareus   28
transfixed by the celestial shaft: he lay,
ponderous, on the ground, in fatal cold.

Vedea Timbreo, vedea Pallade e Marte,   31
armati ancora, intorno al padre loro,
mirar le membra d'i Giganti sparte.

Vedea Nembròt a piè del gran lavoro   34
quasi smarrito, e riguardar le genti
che 'n Sennaàr con lui superbi fuoro.

O Nïobè, con che occhi dolenti   37
vedea io te segnata in su la strada,
tra sette e sette tuoi figliuoli spenti!

O Saùl, come in su la propria spada   40
quivi parevi morto in Gelboè,
che poi non sentì pioggia né rugiada!

O folle Aragne, sì vedea io te   43
già mezza ragna, trista in su li stracci
de l'opera che mal per te si fé.

O Roboàm, già non par che minacci   46
quivi 'l tuo segno; ma pien di spavento
nel porto un carro, canza ch'altri il cacci.

Mostrava ancor lo duro pavimento   49
come Almeon a sua madre fé caro
parer lo sventurato addornamento.

Mostrava come i figli si gittaro   52
sovra Sennacherìb dentro dal tempio,
e come, morto lui, quivi il lasciaro.

Mostrava la ruina e 'l crudo scempio   55
che fé Tamiri, quando disse a Ciro:
"Sangue sitisti, e io di sangue t'empio."

Mostrava come in rotta si fuggiro   58
li Assiri, poi che fu morto Oloferne,
e anche le reliquie del martiro.

Vedeva Troia in cenere e in caverne;   61
o Ilïón, come te basso e vile
mostrava il segno che lì si discerne!

Qual di pennel fu maestro o di stile   64
che ritraesse l'ombre e ' tratti ch'ivi
mirar farieno uno ingegno sottile?

Morti li morti e i vivi parean vivi: 67
non vide mei di me chi vide il vero,
quant' io calcai, fin che chinato givi.

I saw Thymbraeus, I saw Mars and Pallas,   31
still armed, as they surrounded Jove, their father,
gazing upon the Giants' scattered limbs.

I saw bewildered Nimrod at the foot   34
of his great labor; watching him were those
of Shinar who had shared his arrogance.

O Niobe, what tears afflicted me   37
when, on that path, I saw your effigy
among your slaughtered children, seven and seven!

O Saul, you were portrayed there as one who   40
had died on his own sword, upon Gilboa,
which never after knew the rain, the dew!

O mad Arachne, I saw you already   43
half spider, wretched on the ragged remnants
of work that you had wrought to your own hurt!

O Rehoboam, you whose effigy   46
seems not to menace there, and yet you flee
by chariot, terrified, though none pursues!

It also showed—that pavement of hard stone—   49
how much Alcmaeon made his mother pay:
the cost of the ill-omened ornament.

It showed the children of Sennacherib   52
as they assailed their father in the temple,
then left him, dead, behind them as they fled.

It showed the slaughter and the devastation   55
wrought by Tomyris when she taunted Cyrus:
"You thirsted after blood; with blood I fill you."

It showed the rout of the Assyrians,   58
sent reeling after Holofernes' death,
and also showed his body—what was left.

I saw Troy turned to caverns and to ashes;   61
o Ilium, your effigy in stone—
it showed you there so squalid, so cast down!

What master of the brush or of the stylus   64
had there portrayed such masses, such outlines
as would astonish all discerning minds?

The dead seemed dead and the alive, alive: 67
I saw, head bent, treading those effigies,
as well as those who'd seen those scenes directly.

Or superbite, e via col viso altero,   70
figliuoli d'Eva, e non chinate il volto
sì che veggiate il vostro mal sentero!

Più era già per noi del monte vòlto   73
e del cammin del sole assai più speso
che non stimava l'animo non sciolto,

quando colui che sempre innanzi atteso   76
andava, cominciò: "Drizza la testa;
non è più tempo di gir sì sospeso.

Vedi colà un angel che s'appresta   79
per venir verso noi; vedi che torna
dal servigio del dì l'ancella sesta.

Di reverenza il viso e li atti addorna,   82
sì che i diletti lo 'nvïarci in suso;
pensa che questo dì mai non raggiorna!"

Io era ben del suo ammonir uso   85
pur di non perder tempo, sì che 'n quella
materia non potea parlarmi chiuso.

A noi venìa la creatura bella,   88
biancovestito e ne la faccia quale
par tremolando mattutina stella.

Le braccia aperse, e indi aperse l'ale;   91
disse: "Venite: qui son presso i gradi,
e agevolemente omai si sale.

A questo invito vegnon molto radi: 94
o gente umana, per volar sù nata,
perché a poco vento così cadi?"

Menocci ove la roccia era tagliata;   97
quivi mi batté l'ali per la fronte;
poi mi promise sicura l'andata.

Come a man destra, per salire al monte   100
dove siede la chiesa che soggioga
la ben guidata sopra Rubaconte,

si rompe del montar l'ardita foga   103
per le scalee che si fero ad etade
ch'era sicuro il quaderno e la doga;

così s'allenta la ripa che cade   106
quivi ben ratta da l'altro girone;
ma quinci e quindi l'alta pietra rade.

Now, sons of Eve, persist in arrogance,   70
in haughty stance, do not let your eyes bend,
lest you be forced to see your evil path!

We now had circled round more of the mountain   73
and much more of the sun's course had been crossed
than I, my mind absorbed, had gauged, when he

who always looked ahead insistently,   76
as he advanced, began: "Lift up your eyes;
it's time to set these images aside.

See there an angel hurrying to meet us,   79
and also see the sixth of the handmaidens
returning from her service to the day.

Adorn your face and acts with reverence,   82
that he be pleased to send us higher. Remember—
today will never know another dawn."

I was so used to his insistent warnings   85
against the loss of time; concerning that,
his words to me could hardly be obscure.

That handsome creature came toward us; his clothes   88
were white, and in his aspect he seemed like
the trembling star that rises in the morning.

He opened wide his arms, then spread his wings;   91
he said: "Approach: the steps are close at hand;
from this point on one can climb easily.

This invitation's answered by so few: 94
o humankind, born for the upward flight,
why are you driven back by wind so slight?"

He led us to a cleft within the rock,   97
and then he struck my forehead with his wing;
that done, he promised me safe journeying.

As on the right, when one ascends the hill   100
where—over Rubaconte's bridge—there stands
the church that dominates the well-ruled city,

the daring slope of the ascent is broken   103
by steps that were constructed in an age
when record books and measures could be trusted,

so was the slope that plummets there so steeply   106
down from the other ring made easier;
but on this side and that, high rock encroaches.

Noi volgendo ivi le nostre persone,   109
"Beati pauperes spiritu!" voci
cantaron sì, che nol diria sermone.

Ahi quanto son diverse quelle foci   112
da l'infernali! ché quivi per canti
s'entra, e là giù per lamenti feroci.

Già montavam su per li scaglion santi,   115
ed esser mi parea troppo più lieve
che per lo pian non mi parea davanti.

Ond' io: "Maestro, dì, qual cosa greve   118
levata s'è da me, che nulla quasi
per me fatica, andando, si riceve?"

Rispuose: "Quando i P che son rimasi   121
ancor nel volto tuo presso che stinti,
saranno, com' è l'un, del tutto rasi,

fier li tuoi piè dal buon voler sì vinti,   124
che non pur non fatica sentiranno,
ma fia diletto loro esser sù pinti."

Allor fec' io come color che vanno   127
con cosa in capo non da lor saputa,
se non che ' cenni altrui sospecciar fanno;

per che la mano ad accertar s'aiuta,   130
e cerca e truova e quello officio adempie
che non si può fornir per la veduta;

e con le dita de la destra scempie   133
trovai pur sei le lettere che 'ncise
quel da le chiavi a me sovra le tempie:

a che guardando, il mio duca sorrise.   136

While we began to move in that direction,   109
"Beati pauperes spiritu" was sung
so sweetly—it can not be told in words.

How different were these entryways from those   112
of Hell! For here it is with song one enters;
down there, it is with savage lamentations.

Now we ascended by the sacred stairs,   115
but I seemed to be much more light than I
had been, before, along the level terrace.

At this I asked: "Master, tell me, what heavy   118
weight has been lifted from me, so that I,
in going, notice almost no fatigue?"

He answered: "When the *P*'s that still remain   121
upon your brow—now almost all are faint—
have been completely, like this *P*, erased,

your feet will be so mastered by good will   124
that they not only will not feel travail
but will delight when they are urged uphill."

Then I behaved like those who make their way   127
with something on their head of which they're not
aware, till others' signs make them suspicious,

at which, the hand helps them to ascertain;   130
it seeks and finds and touches and provides
the services that sight cannot supply;

so, with my right hand's outspread fingers, I   133
found just six of the letters once inscribed
by him who holds the keys, upon my forehead;

and as he watched me do this, my guide smiled.   136

CANTO XIII

Noi eravamo al sommo de la scala,
 dove secondamente si risega
lo monte che salendo altrui dismala.

  Ivi così una cornice lega   4
dintorno il poggio, come la primaia;
se non che l'arco suo più tosto piega.

  Ombra non li è né segno che si paia: 7
parsi la ripa e parsi la via schietta
col livido color de la petraia.

  "Se qui per dimandar gente s'aspetta,"   10
ragionava il poeta, "io temo forse
che troppo avrà d'indugio nostra eletta."

  Poi fisamente al sole li occhi porse;   13
fece del destro lato a muover centro,
e la sinistra parte di sé torse.

  "O dolce lume a cui fidanza i' entro   1
per lo novo cammin, tu ne conduci,"
dicea, "come condur si vuol quinc' entro.

  Tu scaldi il mondo, tu sovr' esso luci;   19
s'altra ragione in contrario non ponta,
esser dien sempre li tuoi raggi duci."

  Quanto di qua per un migliaio si conta,   22
tanto di là eravam noi già iti,
con poco tempo, per la voglia pronta;

  e verso noi volar furon sentiti,   25
non però visti, spiriti parlando
a la mensa d'amor cortesi inviti.

  La prima voce che passò volando   28
"Vinum non habent" altamente disse,
e dietro a noi l'andò reïterando.

We now had reached the summit of the stairs
    where once again the mountain whose ascent
delivers man from sin has been indented.

    There, just as in the case of the first terrace,   4
a second terrace runs around the slope,
except that it describes a sharper arc.

    No effigy is there and no outline: 7
the bank is visible, the naked path—
only the livid color of raw rock.

    "If we wait here in order to inquire   10
of those who pass," the poet said, "I fear
our choice of path may be delayed too long."

    And then he fixed his eyes upon the sun;   13
letting his right side serve to guide his movement,
he wheeled his left around and changed direction.

    "O gentle light, through trust in which I enter   16
on this new path, may you conduct us here,"
he said, "for men need guidance in this place.

    You warm the world and you illumine it;   19
unless a higher Power urge us elsewhere,
your rays must always be the guides that lead."

    We had already journeyed there as far   22
as we should reckon here to be a mile,
and done it in brief time—our will was eager—

    when we heard spirits as they flew toward us,   25
though they could not be seen—spirits pronouncing
courteous invitations to love's table.

    The first voice that flew by called out aloud: 28
"Vinum non habent," and behind us that
same voice reiterated its example.

    E prima che del tutto non si udisse   31
per allungarsi, un'altra "I' sono Oreste"
passò gridando, e anco non s'affisse.

    "Oh!" diss' io, "padre, che voci son queste?"   34
E com' io domandai, ecco la terza
dicendo: "Amate da cui male aveste."

    E 'l buon maestro: "Questo cinghio sferza   37
la colpa de la invidia, e però sono
tratte d'amor le corde de la ferza.

    Lo fren vuol esser del contrario suono;   40
credo che l'udirai, per mio avviso,
prima che giunghi al passo del perdono.

    Ma ficca li occhi per l'aere ben fiso,   43
e vedrai gente innanzi a noi sedersi,
e ciascun è lungo la grotta assiso."

    Allora più che prima li occhi apersi;   46
guarda'mi innanzi, e vidi ombre con manti
al color de la pietra non diversi.

    E poi che fummo un poco più avanti,   49
udia gridar: "Maria, òra per noi":
gridar "Michele" e "Pietro" e "Tutti santi."

    Non credo che per terra vada ancoi   52
omo sì duro, che non fosse punto
per compassion di quel ch'i' vidi poi;

    ché, quando fui sì presso di lor giunto,   55
che li atti loro a me venivan certi,
per li occhi fui di grave dolor munto.

    Di vil ciliccio mi parean coperti,   58
e l'un sofferia l'altro con la spalla,
e tutti da la ripa eran sofferti.

    Così li ciechi a cui la roba falla,   61
stanno a' perdoni a chieder lor bisogna,
e l'uno il capo sopra l'altro avvalla,

    perché 'n altrui pietà tosto si pogna,   64
non pur per lo sonar de le parole,
ma per la vista che non meno agogna.

    E come a li orbi non approda il sole,   67
così a l'ombre quivi, ond' io parlo ora,
luce del ciel di sé largir non vole;

And as that voice drew farther off, before   31
it faded finally, another cried:
"I am Orestes." It, too, did not stop.

"What voices are these, father?" were my words;   34
and as I asked him this, I heard a third
voice say: "Love those by whom you have been hurt."

And my good master said: "The sin of envy   37
is scourged within this circle; thus, the cords
that form the scourging lash are plied by love.

The sounds of punished envy, envy curbed,   40
are different; if I judge right, you'll hear
those sounds before we reach the pass of pardon.

But let your eyes be fixed attentively   43
and, through the air, you will see people seated
before us, all of them on the stone terrace."

I opened—wider than before—my eyes;   46
I looked ahead of me, and I saw shades
with cloaks that shared their color with the rocks.

And once we'd moved a little farther on,   49
I heard the cry of, "Mary, pray for us,"
and then heard, "Michael," "Peter," and "All saints."

I think no man now walks upon the earth   52
who is so hard that he would not have been
pierced by compassion for what I saw next;

for when I had drawn close enough to see   55
clearly the way they paid their penalty,
the force of grief pressed tears out of my eyes.

Those souls—it seemed—were cloaked in coarse haircloth;   58
another's shoulder served each shade as prop,
and all of them were bolstered by the rocks:

so do the blind who have to beg appear   61
on pardon days to plead for what they need,
each bending his head back and toward the other,

that all who watch feel—quickly—pity's touch   64
not only through the words that would entreat
but through the sight, which can—no less—beseech.

And just as, to the blind, no sun appears,   67
so to the shades—of whom I now speak—here,
the light of heaven would not give itself;

ché a tutti un fil di ferro i cigli fóra   70
e cusce sì, come a sparvier selvaggio
si fa però che queto non dimora.

A me pareva, andando, fare oltraggio,   73
veggendo altrui, non essendo veduto:
per ch'io mi volsi al mio consiglio saggio.

Ben sapev' ei che volea dir lo muto;   76
e però non attese mia dimanda,
ma disse: "Parla, e sie breve e arguto."

Virgilio mi venìa da quella banda   79
de la cornice onde cader si puote,
perché da nulla sponda s'inghirlanda;

da l'altra parte m'eran le divote   82
ombre, che per l'orribile costura
premevan sì, che bagnavan le gote.

Volsimi a loro e: "O gente sicura,"   85
incominciai, "di veder l'alto lume
che 'l disio vostro solo ha in sua cura,

se tosto grazia resolva le schiume   88
di vostra coscïenza sì che chiaro
per essa scenda de la mente il fiume,

ditemi, ché mi fia grazioso e caro,   91
s'anima è qui tra voi che sia latina;
e forse lei sarà buon s'i' l'apparo."

"O frate mio, ciascuna è cittadina   94
d'una vera città; ma tu vuo' dire
che vivesse in Italia peregrina."

Questo mi parve per risposta udire   97
più innanzi alquanto che là dov' io stava,
ond' io mi feci ancor più là sentire.

Tra l'altre vidi un'ombra ch'aspettava   100
in vista; e se volesse alcun dir "Come?"
lo mento a guisa d'orbo in sù levava.

"Spirto," diss'io, "che per salir ti dome,   103
se tu se' quelli che mi rispondesti,
fammiti conto o per luogo o per nome."

"Io fui sanese," rispuose, "e con questi   106
altri rimendo qui la vita ria,
lagrimando a colui che sé ne presti.

for iron wire pierces and sews up   70
the lids of all those shades, as untamed hawks
are handled, lest, too restless, they fly off.

It seemed to me a gross discourtesy   73
for me, going, to see and not be seen;
therefore, I turned to my wise counselor.

He knew quite well what I, though mute, had meant;   76
and thus he did not wait for my request,
but said: "Speak, and be brief and to the point."

Virgil was to my right, along the outside,   79
nearer the terrace-edge—no parapet
was there to keep a man from falling off;

and to my other side were the devout   82
shades; through their eyes, sewn so atrociously,
those spirits forced the tears that bathed their cheeks.

I turned to them; and "You who can be certain,"   85
I then began, "of seeing that high light
which is the only object of your longing,

may, in your conscience, all impurity   88
soon be dissolved by grace, so that the stream
of memory flow through it limpidly;

tell me, for I shall welcome such dear words,   91
if any soul among you is Italian;
if I know that, then I—perhaps—can help him."

"My brother, each of us is citizen   94
of one true city: what you meant to say
was 'one who lived in Italy as pilgrim.'"

My hearing placed the point from which this answer   97
had come somewhat ahead of me; therefore,
I made myself heard farther on; moving,

I saw one shade among the rest who looked   100
expectant; and if any should ask how—
its chin was lifted as a blind man's is.

"Spirit," I said, "who have subdued yourself   103
that you may climb, if it is you who answered,
then let me know you by your place or name."

"I was a Sienese," she answered, "and   106
with others here I mend my wicked life,
weeping to Him that He grant us Himself.

Savia non fui, avvegna che Sapìa   109
fossi chiamata, e fui de li altrui danni
più lieta assai che di ventura mia.

E perché tu non creda ch'io t'inganni,   112
odi s'i' fui, com' io ti dico, folle,
già discendendo l'arco d'i miei anni.

Eran li cittadin miei presso a Colle   115
in campo giunti co' loro avversari,
e io pregava Iddio di quel ch'e' volle.

Rotti fuor quivi e vòlti ne li amari   118
passi di fuga; e veggendo la caccia,
letizia presi a tutte altre dispari,

tanto ch'io volsi in sù l'ardita faccia,   121
gridando a Dio: 'Omai più non ti temo!'
come fé 'l merlo per poca bonaccia.

Pace volli con Dio in su lo stremo   124
de la mia vita; e ancor non sarebbe
lo mio dover per penitenza scemo,

se ciò non fosse, ch'a memoria m'ebbe   127
Pier Pettinaio in sue sante orazioni,
a cui di me per caritate increbbe.

Ma tu chi se', che nostre condizioni   130
vai dimandando, e porti li occhi sciolti,
sì com' io credo, e spirando ragioni?"

"Li occhi," diss' io, "mi fieno ancor qui tolti,   133
ma picciol tempo, ché poca è l'offesa
fatta per esser con invidia vòlti.

Troppa è più la paura ond' è sospesa   136
l'anima mia del tormento di sotto,
che già lo 'ncarco di là giù mi pesa."

Ed ella a me: "Chi t'ha dunque condotto   139
qua sù tra noi, se giù ritornar credi?"
E io: "Costui ch'è meco e non fa motto.

E vivo sono; e però mi richiedi,   142
spirito eletto, se tu vuo' ch'i' mova
di là per te ancor li mortai piedi."

"Oh, questa è a udir sì cosa nuova,"   145
rispuose, "che gran segno è che Dio t'ami;
però col priego tuo talor mi giova.

I was not sapient, though I was called Sapia;   109
and I rejoiced far more at others' hurts
than at my own good fortune. And lest you

   should think I have deceived you, hear and judge   112
if I was not, as I have told you, mad
when my years' arc had reached its downward part.

   My fellow citizens were close to Colle,   115
where they'd joined battle with their enemies,
and I prayed God for that which He had willed.

   There they were routed, beaten; they were reeling   118
along the bitter paths of flight; and seeing
that chase, I felt incomparable joy,

   so that I lifted up my daring face   121
and cried to God: 'Now I fear you no more!'—
as did the blackbird after brief fair weather.

   I looked for peace with God at my life's end;   124
the penalty I owe for sin would not
be lessened now by penitence had not

   one who was sorrowing for me because   127
of charity in him—Pier Pettinaio—
remembered me in his devout petitions.

   But who are you, who question our condition   130
as you move on, whose eyes—if I judge right—
have not been sewn, who uses breath to speak?"

   "My eyes," I said, "will be denied me here,   133
but only briefly; the offense of envy
was not committed often by their gaze.

   I fear much more the punishment below;   136
my soul is anxious, in suspense; already
I feel the heavy weights of the first terrace."

   And she: "Who, then, led you up here among us,   139
if you believe you will return below?"
And I: "He who is with me and is silent.

   I am alive; and therefore, chosen spirit,   142
if you would have me move my mortal steps
on your behalf, beyond, ask me for that."

   "Oh, this," she answered, "is so strange a thing   145
to hear: the sign is clear—you have God's love.
Thus, help me sometimes with your prayers. I ask

E cheggioti, per quel che tu più brami,   148
se mai calchi la terra di Toscana,
che a' miei propinqui tu ben mi rinfami.

Tu li vedrai tra quella gente vana   151
che spera in Talamone, e perderagli
più di speranza ch'a trovar la Diana;

ma più vi perderanno li ammiragli."   154

of you, by that which you desire most,   148
if you should ever tread the Tuscan earth,
to see my name restored among my kin.

  You will see them among those vain ones who   151
have put their trust in Talamone (their loss
in hope will be more than Diana cost);

  but there the admirals will lose the most."   154

XIII · 70

AGLAUROS

CANTO XIV

"Chi è costui che 'l nostro monte cerchia
prima che morte li abbia dato il volo,
e apre li occhi a sua voglia e coverchia?"

"Non so chi sia, ma so ch'e' non è solo;   4
domandal tu che più li t'avvicini,
e dolcemente, sì che parli, acco'lo."

Così due spirti, l'uno a l'altro chini,   7
ragionavan di me ivi a man dritta;
poi fer li visi, per dirmi, supini;

e disse l'uno: "O anima che fitta   10
nel corpo ancora inver' lo ciel ten vai,
per carità ne consola e ne ditta

onde vieni e chi se'; ché tu ne fai   13
tanto maravigliar de la tua grazia,
quanto vuol cosa che non fu più mai."

E io: "Per mezza Toscana si spazia   16
un fiumicel che nasce in Falterona,
e cento miglia di corso nol sazia.

Di sovr' esso rech' io questa persona: 19
dirvi ch'i' sia, saria parlare indarno,
ché 'l nome mio ancor molto non suona."

"Se ben lo 'ntendimento tuo accarno   22
con lo 'ntelletto," allora mi rispuose
quei che diceva pria, "tu parli d'Arno."

E l'altro disse lui: "Perché nascose   25
questi il vocabol di quella riviera,
pur com' om fa de l'orribili cose?"

E l'ombra che di ciò domandata era,   28
si sdebitò così: "Non so; ma degno
ben è che 'l nome di tal valle pèra;

W ho is this man who, although death has yet
    to grant him flight, can circle round our mountain,
and can, at will, open and shut his eyes?"

  "I don't know who he is, but I do know   4
he's not alone; you're closer; question him
and greet him gently, so that he replies."

  So were two spirits, leaning toward each other,   7
discussing me, along my right-hand side;
then they bent back their heads to speak to me,

  and one began: "O soul who—still enclosed   10
within the body—make your way toward Heaven,
may you, through love, console us; tell us who

  you are, from where you come; the grace that you've   13
received—a thing that's never come to pass
before—has caused us much astonishment."

  And I: "Through central Tuscany there spreads   16
a little stream first born in Falterona;
one hundred miles can't fill the course it needs.

  I bring this body from that river's banks;   19
to tell you who I am would be to speak
in vain—my name has not yet gained much fame."

  "If, with my understanding, I have seized   22
your meaning properly," replied to me
the one who'd spoken first, "you mean the Arno."

  The other said to him: "Why did he hide   25
that river's name, even as one would do
in hiding something horrible from view?"

  The shade to whom this question was addressed   28
repaid with this: "I do not know; but it
is right for such a valley's name to perish,

ché dal principio suo, ov' è sì pregno   31
l'alpestro monte ond' è tronco Peloro,
che 'n pochi luoghi passa oltra quel segno,

infin là 've si rende per ristoro   34
di quel che 'l ciel de la marina asciuga,
ond' hanno i fiumi ciò che va con loro,

vertù così per nimica si fuga   37
da tutti come biscia, o per sventura
del luogo, o per mal uso che li fruga:

ond' hanno sì mutata lor natura   40
li abitator de la misera valle,
che par che Circe li avesse in pastura.

Tra brutti porci, più degni di galle   43
che d'altro cibo fatto in uman uso,
dirizza prima il suo povero calle.

Botoli trova poi, venendo giuso,   46
ringhiosi più che non chiede lor possa,
e da lor disdegnosa torce il muso.

Vassi caggendo; e quant' ella più 'ngrossa,   49
tanto più trova di can farsi lupi
la maladetta e sventurata fossa

Discesa poi per più pelaghi cupi,   52
trova le volpi sì piene di froda,
che non temono ingegno che le occùpi.

Né lascerò di dir perch' altri m'oda;   55
e buon sarà costui, s'ancor s'ammenta
di ciò che vero spirto mi disnoda

Io veggio tuo nepote che diventa   58
cacciator di quei lupi in su la riva
del fiero fiume, e tutti li sgomenta.

Vende la carne loro essendo viva;   61
poscia li ancide come antica belva;
molti di vita e sé di pregio priva.

Sanguinoso esce de la trista selva;   64
lasciala tal, che di qui a mille anni
ne lo stato primaio non si rinselva."

Com' a l'annunzio di dogliosi danni   67
si turba il vìso di colui ch'ascolta,
da qual che parte il periglio l'assanni,

for from its source (at which the rugged chain—   31
from which Pelorus was cut off—surpasses
most other places with its mass of mountains)

until its end point (where it offers back   34
those waters that evaporating skies
drew from the sea, that streams may be supplied),

virtue is seen as serpent, and all flee   37
from it as if it were an enemy,
either because the site is ill-starred or

their evil custom goads them so; therefore,   40
the nature of that squalid valley's people
has changed, as if they were in Circe's pasture.

That river starts its miserable course   43
among foul hogs, more fit for acorns than
for food devised to serve the needs of man.

Then, as that stream descends, it comes on curs   46
that, though their force is feeble, snap and snarl;
scornful of them, it swerves its snout away.

And, downward, it flows on; and when that ditch,   49
ill-fated and accursed, grows wider, it
finds, more and more, the dogs becoming wolves.

Descending then through many dark ravines,   52
it comes on foxes so full of deceit—
there is no trap that they cannot defeat.

Nor will I keep from speech because my comrade   55
hears me (and it will serve you, too, to keep
in mind what prophecy reveals to me).

I see your grandson: he's become a hunter   58
of wolves along the banks of the fierce river,
and he strikes every one of them with terror.

He sells their flesh while they are still alive;   61
then, like an ancient beast, he turns to slaughter,
depriving many of life, himself of honor.

Bloody, he comes out from the wood he's plundered,   64
leaving it such that in a thousand years
it will not be the forest that it was."

Just as the face of one who has heard word   67
of pain and injury becomes perturbed,
no matter from what side that menace stirs,

così vid' io l'altra' anima, che volta   70
stava a udir, turbarsi e farsi trista,
poi ch'ebbe la parola a sé raccolta.

Lo dir de l'una e de l'altra la vista   73
mi fer voglioso di saper lor nomi,
e dimanda ne fei con prieghi mista;

per che lo spirto che di pria parlòmi   76
ricominciò: "Tu vuo' ch'io mi deduca
nel fare a te ciò che tu far non vuo'mi.

Ma da che Dio in te vuol che traluca   79
tanto sua grazia, non ti sarò scarso;
però sappi ch'io fui Guido del Duca.

Fu il sangue mio d'invidia sì rïarso,   82
che se veduto avesse uom farsi lieto,
visto m'avresti di livore sparso.

Di mia semente cotal paglia mieto;   85
o gente umana, perché poni 'l core
là 'v' è mestier di consorte divieto?

Questi è Rinier; questi è 'l pregio e l'onore   88
de la casa da Calboli, ove nullo
fatto s'è reda poi del suo valore.

E non pur lo suo sangue è fatto brullo,   91
tra 'l Po e 'l monte e la marina e 'l Reno,
del ben richesto al vero e al trastullo;

ché dentro a questi termini è ripieno   94
di venenosi sterpi, sì che tardi
per coltivare omai verrebber meno.

Ov' è 'l buon Lizio e Arrigo Mainardi?   97
Pier Traversaro e Guido di Carpigna?
Oh Romagnuoli tornati in bastardi!

Quando in Bologna un Fabbro si ralligna?   100
quando in Faenza un Bernardin di Fosco,
verga gentil di picciola gramigna?

Non ti maravigliar s'io piango, Tosco,   103
quando rimembro, con Guido da Prata,
Ugolin d'Azzo che vivette nosco,

Federigo Tignoso e sua brigata,   106
la casa Traversara e li Anastagi
(e l'una gente e l'altra è diretata),

so did I see that other soul, who'd turned   70
to listen, growing anxious and dejected
when he had taken in his comrade's words.

The speech of one, the aspect of the other   73
had made me need to know their names, and I
both queried and beseeched at the same time,

at which the spirit who had spoken first   76
to me began again: "You'd have me do
for you that which, to me, you have refused.

But since God would, in you, have His grace glow   79
so brightly, I shall not be miserly;
know, therefore, that I was Guido del Duca.

My blood was so afire with envy that,   82
when I had seen a man becoming happy,
the lividness in me was plain to see.

From what I've sown, this is the straw I reap: 85
o humankind, why do you set your hearts
there where our sharing cannot have a part?

This is Rinieri, this is he—the glory,   88
the honor of the house of Calboli;
but no one has inherited his worth.

It's not his kin alone, between the Po   91
and mountains, and the Reno and the coast,
who've lost the truth's grave good and lost the good

of gentle living, too; those lands are full   94
of poisoned stumps; by now, however much
one were to cultivate, it is too late.

Where is good Lizio? Arrigo Mainardi?   97
Pier Traversaro? Guido di Carpigna?
O Romagnoles returned to bastardy!

When will a Fabbro flourish in Bologna?   100
When, in Faenza, a Bernadin di Fosco,
the noble offshoot of a humble plant?

Don't wonder, Tuscan, if I weep when I   103
remember Ugolino d'Azzo, one
who lived among us, and Guido da Prata,

the house of Traversara, of Anastagi   106
(both houses without heirs), and Federigo
Tignoso and his gracious company,

le donne e ' cavalier, li affanni e li agi   109
che ne 'nvogliava amore e cortesia
là dove i cuor son fatti sì malvagi.

O Bretinoro, ché non fuggi via,   112
poi che gita se n'è la tua famiglia
e molta gente per non esser ria?

Ben fa Bagnacaval, che non rifiglia;   115
e mal fa Castrocaro, e peggio Conio,
che di figliar tai conti più s'impiglia.

Ben faranno i Pagan, da che 'l demonio   118
lor sen girà; ma non però che puro
già mai rimagna d'essi testimonio.

O Ugolin de' Fantolin, sicuro   121
è 'l nome tuo, da che più non s'aspetta
chi far lo possa, tralignando, scuro.

Ma va via, Tosco omai; ch'or mi diletta   124
troppo di pianger più che di parlare,
sì m'ha nostra ragion la mente stretta."

Noi sapavam che quell' anime care   127
ci sentivano andar; però, tacendo,
facëan noi del cammin confidare.

Poi fummo fatti soli procedendo,   130
folgore parve quando l'aere fende,
voce che giunse di contra dicendo:

"Anciderammi qualunque m'apprende";   133
e fuggì come tuon che si dilegua,
se sùbito la nuvola scoscende.

Come da lei l'udir nostro ebbe triegua,   136
ed ecco l'altra con sì gran fracasso,
che somigliò tonar che tosto segua:

"Io sono Aglauro che divenni sasso";   139
e allor, per ristrignermi al poeta,
in destro feci, e non innanzi, il passo.

Già era l'aura d'ogne parte queta;   142
ed el mi disse: "Quel fu 'l duro camo
che dovria l'uom tener dentro a sua meta.

Ma voi prendete l'esca, sì che l'amo   145
de l'antico avversaro a sé vi tira;
e però poco val freno o richiamo.

the ladies and the knights, labors and leisure 109
to which we once were urged by courtesy
and love, where hearts now host perversity.

O Bretinoro, why do you not flee— 112
when you've already lost your family
and many men who've fled iniquity?

Bagnacaval does well: it breeds no more— 115
and Castrocuro ill, and Conio worse,
for it insists on breeding counts so cursed.

Once freed of their own demon, the Pagani 118
will do quite well, but not so well that any
will testify that they are pure and worthy.

Your name, o Ugolin de' Fantolini, 121
is safe, since one no longer waits for heirs
to blacken it with their degeneracy.

But, Tuscan, go your way; I am more pleased 124
to weep now than to speak: for that which we
have spoken presses heavily on me!"

We knew those gentle souls had heard us move 127
away; therefore, their silence made us feel
more confident about the path we took.

When we, who'd gone ahead, were left alone, 130
a voice that seemed like lightning as it splits
the air encountered us, a voice that said:

"Whoever captures me will slaughter me"; 133
and then it fled like thunder when it fades
after the cloud is suddenly ripped through.

As soon as that first voice had granted us 136
a truce, another voice cried out with such
uproar—like thunder quick to follow thunder:

"I am Aglauros, who was turned to stone"; 139
and then, to draw more near the poet, I
moved to my right instead of moving forward.

By now the air on every side was quiet; 142
and he told me: "That is the sturdy bit
that should hold every man within his limits.

But you would take the bait, so that the hook 145
of the old adversary draws you to him;
thus, neither spur nor curb can serve to save you.

Chiamavi 'l cielo e 'ntorno vi si gira,   148
mostrandovi le sue bellezze etterne,
e l'occhio vostro pur a terra mira;
   onde vi batte chi tutto discerne."   151

Heaven would call—and it encircles—you;
it lets you see its never-ending beauties;
and yet your eyes would only see the ground;
    thus, He who sees all things would strike you down."

CANTO XV

Quanto tra l'ultimar de l'ora terza
   e 'l principio del dì par de la spera
che sempre a guisa di fanciullo scherza,

   tanto pareva già inver' la sera   4
essere al sol del suo corso rimaso;
vespero là, e qui mezza notte era.

   E i raggi ne ferien per mezzo 'l naso,   7
perché per noi girato era sì 'l monte,
che già dritti andavamo inver' l'occaso,

   quand' io senti' a me gravar la fronte   10
a lo splendore assai più che di prima,
e stupor m'eran le cose non conte;

   ond' io levai le mani inver' la cima   13
de le mie ciglia, e fecimi 'l solecchio,
che del soverchio visibile lima.

   Come quando da l'acqua o da lo specchio   16
salta lo raggio a l'opposita parte,
salendo su per lo modo parecchio

   a quel che scende, e tanto si diparte   19
dal cader de la pietra in igual tratta,
sì come mostra esperïenza e arte;

   così mi parve da luce rifratta   22
quivi dinanzi a me esser percosso;
per che a fuggir la mia vista fu ratta.

   "Che è quel, dolce padre, a che non posso 25
schermar lo viso tanto che mi vaglia,"
diss' io, "e pare inver' noi esser mosso?"

   "Non ti maravigliar s'ancor t'abbaglia   28
la famiglia del cielo," a me rispuose:
"messo è che viene ad invitar ch'om saglia.

From the Second to the Third Terrace: the Wrathful. Mid-afternoon. The Fifth Beatitude. Virgil on the sharing of heavenly goods. The Third Terrace, where Dante sees, in ecstatic vision, examples of gentleness: the Virgin Mary, Pisistratus, St. Stephen. Virgil on Dante's vision. Black smoke.

As many as the hours in which the sphere
that's always playing like a child appears
from daybreak to the end of the third hour,

so many were the hours of light still left   4
before the course of day had reached sunset;
vespers was there; and where we are, midnight.

When sunlight struck directly at our faces,   7
for we had circled so much of the mountain
that now we headed straight into the west,

then I could feel my vision overcome   10
by radiance greater than I'd sensed before,
and unaccounted things left me amazed;

at which, that they might serve me as a shade,   13
I lifted up my hands above my brow,
to limit some of that excessive splendor.

As when a ray of light, from water or   16
a mirror, leaps in the opposed direction
and rises at an angle equal to

its angle of descent, and to each side   19
the distance from the vertical is equal,
as science and experiment have shown;

so did it seem to me that I had been   22
struck there by light reflected, facing me,
at which my eyes turned elsewhere rapidly.

"Kind father, what is that against which I   25
have tried in vain," I said, "to screen my eyes?
It seems to move toward us." And he replied:

"Don't wonder if you are still dazzled by   28
the family of Heaven: a messenger
has come, and he invites us to ascend.

Tosto sarà ch'a veder queste cose   31
non ti fia grave, ma fieti diletto
quanto natura a sentir ti dispuose."

Poi giunti fummo a l'angel benedetto,   34
con lieta voce disse: "Intrate quinci
ad un scaleo vie men che li altri eretto."

Noi montavam, già partiti di linci,   37
e *"Beati misericordes!"* fue
cantato retro, e "Godi tu che vinci!"

Lo mio maestro e io soli amendue   40
suso andavamo; e io pensai, andando,
prode acquistar ne le parole sue;

e dirizza'mi a lui sì dimandando: 43
"Che volse dir lo spirto di Romagna,
e 'divieto' e 'consorte' menzionando?"

Per ch'elli a me: "Di sua maggior magagna   46
conosce il danno; e però non s'ammiri
se ne riprende perché men si piagna.

Perché s'appuntano i vostri disiri   49
dove per compagnia parte si scema,
invidia move il mantaco a' sospiri.

Ma se l'amor de la spera supprema   52
torcesse in suso il disiderio vostro,
non vi sarebbe al petto quella tema;

ché, per quanti si dice più lì 'nostro,'   55
tanto possiede più di ben ciascuno,
e più di caritate arde in quel chiostro."

"Io son d'esser contento più digiuno,"   58
diss' io, "che se mi fosse pria taciuto,
e più di dubbio ne la mente aduno.

Com' esser puote ch'un ben, distributo   61
in più posseditor, faccia più ricchi
di sé che se da pochi è posseduto?"

Ed elli a me: "Però che tu rificchi   64
la mente pur a le cose terrene,
di vera luce tenebre dispicchi.

Quello infinito e ineffabil bene   67
che là sù è, così corre ad amore
com' a lucido corpo raggio vene.

Soon, in the sight of such things, there will be   31
no difficulty for you, but delight—
as much as nature fashioned you to feel."

No sooner had we reached the blessed angel   34
than with glad voice he told us: "Enter here;
these are less steep than were the other stairs."

We climbed, already past that point; behind us,   37
we heard *"Beati misericordes"* sung
and then "Rejoice, you who have overcome."

I and my master journeyed on alone,   40
we two together, upward; as we walked,
I thought I'd gather profit from his words;

and even as I turned toward him, I asked: 43
"What did the spirit of Romagna mean
when he said, 'Sharing cannot have a part'?"

And his reply: "He knows the harm that lies   46
in his worst vice; if he chastises it,
to ease its expiation—do not wonder.

For when your longings center on things such   49
that sharing them apportions less to each,
then envy stirs the bellows of your sighs.

But if the love within the Highest Sphere   52
should turn your longings heavenward, the fear
inhabiting your breast would disappear;

for there, the more there are who would say 'ours,'   55
so much the greater is the good possessed
by each—so much more love burns in that cloister."

"I am more hungry now for satisfaction,"   58
I said, "than if I'd held my tongue before;
I host a deeper doubt within my mind.

How can a good that's shared by more possessors   61
enable each to be more rich in it
than if that good had been possessed by few?"

And he to me: "But if you still persist   64
in letting your mind fix on earthly things,
then even from true light you gather darkness.

That Good, ineffable and infinite,   67
which is above, directs Itself toward love
as light directs itself to polished bodies.

Tanto si dà quanto trova d'ardore;   70
sì che, quantunque carità si stende,
cresce sovr' essa l'etterno valore.

E quanta gente più là sù s'intende,   73
più v'è da bene amare, e più vi s'ama,
e come specchio l'uno a l'altro rende.

E se la mia ragion non ti disfama,   76
vedrai Beatrice, ed ella pienamente
ti torrà questa e ciascun' altra brama.

Procaccia pur che tosto sieno spente,   79
come son già le due, le cinque piaghe,
che si richiudon per esser dolente."

Com' io voleva dicer "Tu m'appaghe,"   82
vidimi giunto in su l'altro girone,
sì che tacer mi fer le luci vaghe.

Ivi mi parve in una visïone   85
estatica di sùbito esser tratto,
e vedere in un tempio più persone;

e una donna, in su l'entrar, con atto   88
dolce di madre dicer: "Figliuol mio,
perché hai tu così verso noi fatto?

Ecco, dolenti, lo tuo padre e io   91
ti cercavamo." E come qui si tacque,
ciò che pareva prima, disparìo.

Indi m'apparve un'altra con quell' acque   94
giù per le gote che 'l dolor distilla
quando di gran dispetto in altrui nacque,

e dir: "Se tu se' sire de la villa   97
del cui nome ne' dèi fu tanta lite,
e onde ogne scïenza disfavilla,

vendica te di quelle braccia ardite   100
ch'abbracciar nostra figlia, o Pisistràto."
E 'l segnor mi parea, benigno e mite,

risponder lei con viso temperato: 103
"Che farem noi a chi mal ne disira,
se quei che ci ama è per noi condannato?"

Poi vidi genti accese in foco d'ira   106
con pietre un giovinetto ancider, forte
gridando a sé pur: "Martira, martira!"

Where ardor is, that Good gives of Itself;   70
and where more love is, there that Good confers
a greater measure of eternal worth.

And when there are more souls above who love,   73
there's more to love well there, and they love more,
and, mirror-like, each soul reflects the other.

And if my speech has not appeased your hunger,   76
you will see Beatrice—she will fulfill
this and all other longings that you feel.

Now only strive, so that the other five   79
wounds may be canceled quickly, as the two
already are—the wounds contrition heals."

But wanting then to say, "You have appeased me,"   82
I saw that I had reached another circle,
and my desiring eyes made me keep still.

There I seemed, suddenly, to be caught up   85
in an ecstatic vision and to see
some people in a temple; and a woman

just at the threshold, in the gentle manner   88
that mothers use, was saying: "O my son,
why have you done this to us? You can see

how we have sought you—sorrowing, your father   91
and I." And at this point, as she fell still,
what had appeared at first now disappeared.

Then there appeared to me another woman: 94
upon her cheeks—the tears that grief distills
when it is born of much scorn for another.

She said: "If you are ruler of that city   97
to name which even goddesses once vied—
where every science had its source of light—

revenge yourself on the presumptuous   100
arms that embraced our daughter, o Pisistratus."
And her lord seemed to me benign and mild,

his aspect temperate, as he replied: 103
"What shall we do to one who'd injure us
if one who loves us earns our condemnation?"

Next I saw people whom the fire of wrath   106
had kindled, as they stoned a youth and kept
on shouting loudly to each other: "Kill!"

E lui vedea chinarsi, per la morte   109
che l'aggravava già, inver' la terra,
ma de li occhi facea sempre al ciel porte,

orando a l'alto Sire, in tanta guerra,   112
che perdonasse a' suoi persecutori,
con quello aspetto che pietà diserra.

Quando l'anima mia tornò di fori   115
a le cose che son fuor di lei vere,
io riconobbi i miei non falsi errori.

Lo duca mio, che mi potea vedere   118
far sì com' om che dal sonno si slega,
disse: "Che hai che non ti puoi tenere,

ma se' venuto più che mezza lega   121
velando li occhi e con le gambe avvolte,
a guisa di cui vino o sonno piega?"

"O dolce padre mio, se tu m'ascolte,   124
io ti dirò," diss' io, "ciò che m'apparve
quando le gambe mi furon sì tolte."

Ed ei: "Se tu avessi cento larve   127
sovra la faccia, non mi sarian chiuse
le tue cogitazion, quantunque parve.

Ciò che vedesti fu perché non scuse   130
d'aprir lo core a l'acque de la pace
che da l'etterno fonte son diffuse.

Non dimandai 'Che hai?' per quel che face   133
chi guarda pur con l'occhio che non vede,
quando disanimato il corpo giace;

ma dimandai per darti forza al piede: 136
così frugar conviensi i pigri, lenti
ad usar lor vigilia quando riede."

Noi andavam per lo vespero, attenti   139
oltre quanto potean li occhi allungarsi
contra i raggi serotini e lucenti.

Ed ecco a poco a poco un fummo farsi   142
verso di noi come la notte oscuro;
né da quello era loco da cansarsi.

Questo ne tolse li occhi e l'aere puro.   145

"Kill!" "Kill!" I saw him now, weighed down by death,   109
sink to the ground, although his eyes were bent
always on Heaven—they were Heaven's gates—

praying to his high Lord, despite the torture,   112
to pardon those who were his persecutors;
his look was such that it unlocked compassion.

And when my soul returned outside itself   115
and met the things outside it that are real,
I then could recognize my not false errors.

My guide, on seeing me behave as if   118
I were a man who's freed himself from sleep,
said: "What is wrong with you? You can't walk straight;

for more than half a league now you have moved   121
with clouded eyes and lurching legs, as if
you were a man whom wine or sleep has gripped!"

"Oh, my kind father, if you hear me out,   124
I'll tell you what appeared to me," I said,
"when I had lost the right use of my legs."

And he: "Although you had a hundred masks   127
upon your face, that still would not conceal
from me the thoughts you thought, however slight.

What you have seen was shown lest you refuse   130
to open up your heart unto the waters
of peace that pour from the eternal fountain.

I did not ask 'What's wrong with you?' as one   133
who only sees with earthly eyes, which—once
the body, stripped of soul, lies dead—can't see;

I asked so that your feet might find more force: 136
so must one urge the indolent, too slow
to use their waking time when it returns."

We made our way until the end of vespers,   139
peering, as far ahead as sight could stretch,
at rays of light that, although late, were bright.

But, gradually, smoke as black as night   142
began to overtake us; and there was
no place where we could have avoided it.

This smoke deprived us of pure air and sight.   145

XV·107

XVI · 6

CANTO XVI

Buio d'inferno e di notte privata
d'ogne pianeto, sotto pover cielo,
quant' esser può di nuvol tenebrata,

non fece al viso mio sì grosso velo   4
come quel fummo ch'ivi ci coperse,
né a sentir di così aspro pelo,

che l'occhio stare aperto non sofferse;   7
onde la scorta mia saputa e fida
mi s'accostò e l'omero m'offerse.

Sì come cieco va dietro a sua guida   10
per non smarrirsi e per non dar di cozzo
in cosa che 'l molesti, o forse ancida,

m'andava io per l'aere amaro e sozzo,   13
ascoltando il mio duca che diceva
pur: "Guarda che da me tu non sia mozzo."

Io sentia voci, e ciascuna pareva   16
pregar per pace e per misericordia
l'Agnel di Dio che le peccata leva.

Pur *"Agnus Dei"* eran le loro essordia;   19
una parola in tutte era e un modo,
sì che parea tra esse ogne concordia.

"Quei sono spirti, maestro, ch'i' odo?"   22
diss' io. Ed elli a me: "Tu vero apprendi,
e d'iracundia van solvendo il nodo."

"Or tu chi se' che 'l nostro fummo fendi,   25
e di noi parli pur come se tue
partissi ancor lo tempo per calendi?"

Così per una voce detto fue;   28
onde 'l maestro mio disse: "Rispondi,
e domanda se quinci si va sùe."

Still the Third Terrace: the Wrathful. Their sin punished by dark smoke.
Marco Lombardo's discourse on free will, on the causes of corruption,
and on three worthy old men, living examples of ancient virtue.

D arkness of Hell and of a night deprived
　　of every planet, under meager skies,
as overcast by clouds as sky can be,

　　had never served to veil my eyes so thickly 　　　　4
nor covered them with such rough-textured stuff
as smoke that wrapped us there in Purgatory;

　　my eyes could not endure remaining open; 　　　　7
so that my faithful, knowledgeable escort
drew closer as he offered me his shoulder.

　　Just as a blind man moves behind his guide, 　　　10
that he not stray or strike against some thing
that may do damage to—or even kill—him,

　　so I moved through the bitter, filthy air, 　　　　13
while listening to my guide, who kept repeating:
"Take care that you are not cut off from me."

　　But I heard voices, and each seemed to pray 　　　16
unto the Lamb of God, who takes away
our sins, for peace and mercy. *"Agnus Dei"*

　　was sung repeatedly as their exordium, 　　　　19
words sung in such a way—in unison—
that fullest concord seemed to be among them.

　　"Master, are those whom I hear, spirits?" I 　　　22
asked him. "You have grasped rightly," he replied,
"and as they go they loose the knot of anger."

　　"Then who are you whose body pierces through 　　25
our smoke, who speak of us exactly like
a man who uses months to measure time?"

　　A voice said this. On hearing it, my master 　　　28
turned round to me: "Reply to him, then ask
if this way leads us to the upward path."

E io: "O creatura che ti mondi   31
per tornar bella a colui che ti fece,
maraviglia udirai, se mi secondi."

"Io ti seguiterò quanto mi lece,"   34
rispuose; "e se veder fummo non lascia,
l'udir ci terrà giunti in quella vece."

Allora incominciai: "Con quella fascia   37
che la morte dissolve men vo suso,
e venni qui per l'infernale ambascia.

E se Dio m'ha in sua grazia rinchiuso,   40
tanto che vuol ch'i' veggia la sua corte
per modo tutto fuor del moderno uso,

non mi celar chi fosti anzi la morte,   43
ma dilmi, e dimmi s'i' vo bene al varco;
e tue parole fier le nostre scorte."

"Lombardo fui, e fu' chiamato Marco;   46
del mondo seppi, e quel valore amai
al quale ha or ciascun disteso l'arco.

Per montar sù dirittamente vai."   49
Così rispuose, e soggiunse: "I' ti prego
che per me prieghi quando sù sarai."

E io a lui: "Per fede mi ti lego   52
di far ciò che mi chiedi; ma io scoppio
dentro ad un dubbio, s'io non me ne spiego.

Prima era scempio, e ora è fatto doppio   55
ne la sentenza tua, che mi fa certo
qui, e altrove, quello ov' io l'accoppio.

Lo mondo è ben così tutto diserto   58
d'ogne virtute, come tu mi sone,
e di malizia gravido e coverto;

ma priego che m'addite la cagione,   61
sì ch'i' la veggia e ch'i' la mostri altrui;
ché nel cielo uno, e un qua giù la pone."

Alto sospir, che duolo strinse in "uhi!"   64
mise fuor prima; e poi cominciò: "Frate,
lo mondo è cieco, e tu vien ben da lui.

Voi che vivete ogne cagion recate   67
pur suso al cielo, pur come se tutto
movesse seco di necessitate.

And I: "O creature who—that you return 31
fair unto Him who made you—cleanse yourself,
you shall hear wonders if you follow me."

"I'll follow you as far as I'm allowed," 34
he answered, "and if smoke won't let us see,
hearing will serve instead to keep us linked."

Then I began: "With those same swaddling-bands 37
that death unwinds I take my upward path:
I have come here by way of Hell's exactions;

since God's so gathered me into His grace 40
that He would have me, in a manner most
unusual for moderns, see His court,

do not conceal from me who you once were, 43
before your death, and tell me if I go
straight to the pass; your words will be our escort."

"I was a Lombard and I was called Marco; 46
I knew the world's ways, and I loved those goods
for which the bows of all men now grow slack.

The way you've taken leads directly upward." 49
So he replied, and then he added: "I
pray you to pray for me when you're above."

And I to him: "I pledge my faith to you 52
to do what you have asked; and yet a doubt
will burst in me if it finds no way out.

Before, my doubt was simple; but your statement 55
has doubled it and made me sure that I
am right to couple your words with another's.

The world indeed has been stripped utterly 58
of every virtue; as you said to me,
it cloaks—and is cloaked by—perversity.

Some place the cause in heaven, some, below; 61
but I beseech you to define the cause,
that, seeing it, I may show it to others."

A sigh, from which his sorrow formed an "Oh," 64
was his beginning; then he answered: "Brother,
the world is blind, and you come from the world.

You living ones continue to assign 67
to heaven every cause, as if it were
the necessary source of every motion.

    Se così fosse, in voi fora distrutto   70
libero arbitrio, e non fora giustizia
per ben letizia, e per male aver lutto.

    Lo cielo i vostri movimenti inizia;   73
non dico tutti, ma, posto ch'i' 'l dica,
lume v'è dato a bene e a malizia,

    e libero voler; che, se fatica   76
ne le prime battaglie col ciel dura,
poi vince tutto, se ben si notrica.

    A maggior forza e a miglior natura   79
liberi soggiacete; e quella cria
la mente in voi, che 'l ciel non ha in sua cura.

    Però, se 'l mondo presente disvia,   82
in voi è la cagione, in voi si cheggia;
e io te ne sarò or vera spia.

    Esce di mano a lui che la vagheggia   85
prima che sia, a guisa di fanciulla
che piangendo e ridendo pargoleggia,

    l'anima semplicetta che sa nulla,   88
salvo che, mossa da lieto fattore,
volontier torna a ciò che la trastulla.

    Di picciol bene in pria sente sapore;   91
quivi s'inganna, e dietro ad esso corre,
se guida o fren non torce suo amore.

    Onde convenne legge per fren porre;   94
convenne rege aver, che discernesse
de la vera cittade almen la torre.

    Le leggi son, ma chi pon mano ad esse?   97
Nullo, però che 'l pastor che procede,
rugumar può, ma non ha l'unghie fesse;

    per che la gente, che sua guida vede   100
pur a quel ben fedire ond' ella è ghiotta,
di quel si pasce, e più oltre non chiede.

    Ben puoi veder che la mala condotta   103
è la cagion che 'l mondo ha fatto reo,
e non natura che 'n voi sia corrotta.

    Soleva Roma, che 'l buon mondo feo,   106
due soli aver, che l'una e l'altra strada
facean vedere, e del mondo e di Deo.

If this were so, then your free will would be   70
destroyed, and there would be no equity
in joy for doing good, in grief for evil.

The heavens set your appetites in motion—   73
not all your appetites, but even if
that were the case, you have received both light

on good and evil, and free will, which though   76
it struggle in its first wars with the heavens,
then conquers all, if it has been well nurtured.

On greater power and a better nature   79
you, who are free, depend; that Force engenders
the mind in you, outside the heavens' sway.

Thus, if the present world has gone astray,   82
in you is the cause, in you it's to be sought;
and now I'll serve as your true exegete.

Issuing from His hands, the soul—on which   85
He thought with love before creating it—
is like a child who weeps and laughs in sport;

that soul is simple, unaware; but since   88
a joyful Maker gave it motion, it
turns willingly to things that bring delight.

At first it savors trivial goods; these would   91
beguile the soul, and it runs after them,
unless there's guide or rein to rule its love.

Therefore, one needed law to serve as curb;   94
a ruler, too, was needed, one who could
discern at least the tower of the true city.

The laws exist, but who applies them now?   97
No one—the shepherd who precedes his flock
can chew the cud but does not have cleft hooves;

and thus the people, who can see their guide   100
snatch only at that good for which they feel
some greed, would feed on that and seek no further.

Misrule, you see, has caused the world to be   103
malevolent; the cause is clearly not
celestial forces—they do not corrupt.

For Rome, which made the world good, used to have   106
two suns; and they made visible two paths—
the world's path and the pathway that is God's.

L'un l'altro ha spento; ed è giunta la spada   109
col pasturale, e l'un con l'altro insieme
per viva forza mal convien che vada;

   però che, giunti, l'un l'altro non teme: 112
se non mi credi, pon mente a la spiga,
ch'ogn' erba si conosce per lo seme.

   In sul paese ch'Adice e Po riga,   115
solea valore e cortesia trovarsi,
prima che Federigo avesse briga;

   or può sicuramente indi passarsi   118
per qualunque lasciasse, per vergogna,
di ragionar coi buoni o d'appressarsi.

   Ben v'èn tre vecchi ancora in cui rampogna   121
l'antica età la nova, e par lor tardo
che Dio a miglior vita li ripogna:

   Currado da Palazzo e 'l buon Gherardo   124
e Guido da Castel, che mei si noma,
francescamente, il semplice Lombardo.

   Dì oggimai che la Chiesa di Roma,   127
per confondere in sé due reggimenti,
cade nel fango, e sé brutta e la soma."

   "O Marco mio," diss' io, "bene argomenti;   130
e or discerno perché dal retaggio
li figli di Levì furono essenti.

   Ma qual Gherardo è quel che tu per saggio   133
di' ch'è rimaso de la gente spenta,
in rimprovèro del secol selvaggio?"

   "O tuo parlar m'inganna, o el mi tenta,"   136
rispuose a me; "ché, parlandomi tosco,
par che del buon Gherardo nulla senta.

   Per altro sopranome io nol conosco,   139
s'io nol togliessi da sua figlia Gaia.
Dio sia con voi, ché più non vegno vosco.

   Vedi l'albor che per lo fummo raia   142
già biancheggiare, e me convien partirmi
(l'angelo è ivi) prima ch'io li paia."

   Così tornò, e più non volle udirmi.   145

Each has eclipsed the other; now the sword 109
has joined the shepherd's crook; the two together
must of necessity result in evil,

because, so joined, one need not fear the other: 112
and if you doubt me, watch the fruit and flower,
for every plant is known by what it seeds.

Within the territory watered by 115
the Adige and Po, one used to find
valor and courtesy—that is, before

Frederick was met by strife; now anyone 118
ashamed of talking with the righteous or
of meeting them can journey there, secure.

True, three old men are there, in whom old times 121
reprove the new; and they find God is slow
in summoning them to a better life:

Currado da Palazzo, good Gherardo, 124
and Guido da Castel, whom it is better
to call, as do the French, the candid Lombard.

You can conclude: the Church of Rome confounds 127
two powers in itself; into the filth,
it falls and fouls itself and its new burden."

"Good Marco," I replied, "you reason well; 130
and now I understand why Levi's sons
were not allowed to share in legacies.

But what Gherardo is this whom you mention 133
as an example of the vanished people
whose presence would reproach this savage age?"

"Either your speech deceives me or would tempt me," 136
he answered then, "for you, whose speech is Tuscan,
seem to know nothing of the good Gherardo.

There is no other name by which I know him, 139
unless I speak of him as Gaia's father.
God be with you; I come with you no farther.

You see the rays that penetrate the smoke 142
already whitening; I must take leave—
the angel has arrived—before he sees me."

So he turned back and would not hear me more. 145

CANTO XVII

Ricorditi, lettor, se mai ne l'alpe
  ti colse nebbia per la qual vedessi
non altrimenti che per pelle talpe,

  come, quando i vapori umidi e spessi   4
a diradar cominciansi, la spera
del sol debilemente entra per essi;

  e fia la tua imagine leggera   7
in giugnere a veder com' io rividi
lo sole in pria, che già nel corcar era.

  Sì, pareggiando i miei co' passi fidi   10
del mio maestro, usci' fuor di tal nube
ai raggi morti già ne' bassi lidi.

  O imaginativa che ne rube   13
talvolta sì di fuor, ch'om non s'accorge
perché dintorno suonin mille tube,

  chi move te, se 'l senso non ti porge?   16
Moveti lume che nel ciel s'informa,
per sé o per voler che giù lo scorge.

  De l'empiezza di lei che mutò forma   19
ne l'uccel ch'a cantar più si diletta,
ne l'imagine mia apparve l'orma:

  e qui fu la mia mente sì ristretta   22
dentro da sé, che di fuor non venìa
cosa che fosse allor da lei ricetta.

  Poi piovve dentro a l'alta fantasia   25
un crucifisso, dispettoso e fero
ne la sua vista, e cotal si moria;

  intorno ad esso era il grande Assüero,   28
Estèr sua sposa e 'l giusto Mardoceo,
che fu al dire e al far così intero.

From the Third to the Fourth Terrace. Examples of wrath: Procne, Haman, Amata. The angel of gentleness. The Seventh Beatitude. Ascent to the Fourth Terrace. Virgil on love and on Purgatory's seven terraces punishing the seven sins: pride, envy, and wrath—resulting from perverted love; sloth—from defective love; avarice, gluttony, and lust—from excessive love of earthly goods.

Remember, reader, if you've ever been
    caught in the mountains by a mist through which
you only saw as moles see through their skin,

    how, when the thick, damp vapors once begin   4
to thin, the sun's sphere passes feebly through them,
then your imagination will be quick

    to reach the point where it can see how I   7
first came to see the sun again—when it
was almost at the point at which it sets.

    So, my steps matched my master's trusty steps;   10
out of that cloud I came, reaching the rays
that, on the shores below, by now were spent.

    O fantasy, you that at times would snatch   13
us so from outward things—we notice nothing
although a thousand trumpets sound around us—

    who moves you when the senses do not spur you?   16
A light that finds its form in Heaven moves you—
directly or led downward by God's will.

    Within my fantasy I saw impressed   19
the savagery of one who then, transformed,
became the bird that most delights in song;

    at this, my mind withdrew to the within,   22
to what imagining might bring; no thing
that came from the without could enter in.

    Then into my deep fantasy there rained   25
one who was crucified; and as he died,
he showed his savagery and his disdain.

    Around him were great Ahasuerus and   28
Esther his wife, and the just Mordecai,
whose saying and whose doing were so upright.

E come questa imagine rompeo   31
sé per sé stessa, a guisa d'una bulla
cui manca l'acqua sotto qual si feo,

surse in mia visïone una fanciulla   34
piangendo forte, e dicea: "O regina,
perché per ira hai voluto esser nulla?

Ancisa t'hai per non perder Lavina;   37
or m'hai perduta! Io son essa che lutto,
madre, a la tua pria ch'a l'altrui ruina."

Come si frange il sonno ove di butto   40
nova luce percuote il viso chiuso,
che fratto guizza pria che muoia tutto;

così l'imaginar mio cadde giuso   43
tosto che lume il volto mi percosse,
maggior assai che quel ch'è in nostro uso.

I' mi volgea per veder ov' io fosse,   46
quando una voce disse "Qui si monta,"
che da ogne altro intento mi rimosse;

e fece la mia voglia tanto pronta   49
di riguardar chi era che parlava,
che mai non posa, se non si raffronta.

Ma come al sol che nostra vista grava   52
e per soverchio sua figura vela,
così la mia virtù quivi mancava.

"Questo è divino spirito, che ne la   55
via da ir sù ne drizza sanza prego,
e col suo lume sé medesmo cela.

Sì fa con noi, come l'uom si fa sego;   58
ché quale aspetta prego e l'uopo vede,
malignamente già si mette al nego.

Or accordiamo a tanto invito il piede;   61
procacciam di salir pria che s'abbui,
ché poi non si poria, se 'l dì non riede."

Così disse il mio duca, e io con lui   64
volgemmo i nostri passi ad una scala;
e tosto ch'io al primo grado fui,

senti'mi presso quasi un muover d'ala   67
e ventarmi nel viso e dir: *Beati
pacifici,* che son sanz' ira mala!"

And when this image shattered of itself,   31
just like a bubble that has lost the water
beneath which it was formed, there then rose up

    in my envisioning a girl who wept   34
most bitterly and said: "O queen, why did
you, in your wrath, desire to be no more?

    So as to keep Lavinia, you killed   37
yourself; now you have lost me! I am she,
mother, who mourns your fall before another's."

    Even as sleep is shattered when new light   40
strikes suddenly against closed eyes and, once
it's shattered, gleams before it dies completely,

    so my imagination fell away   43
as soon as light—more powerful than light
we are accustomed to—beat on my eyes.

    I looked about to see where I might be;   46
but when a voice said: "Here one can ascend,"
then I abandoned every other intent.

    That voice made my will keen to see the one   49
who'd spoken—with the eagerness that cannot
be still until it faces what it wants.

    But even as the sun, become too strong,   52
defeats our vision, veiling its own form,
so there my power of sight was overcome.

    "This spirit is divine; and though unasked,   55
he would conduct us to the upward path;
he hides himself with that same light he sheds.

    He does with us as men do with themselves;   58
for he who sees a need but waits to be
asked is already set on cruel refusal.

    Now let our steps accept his invitation,   61
and let us try to climb before dark falls—
then, until day returns, we'll have to halt."

    So said my guide; and toward a stairway, he   64
and I, together, turned; and just as soon
as I was at the first step, I sensed something

    much like the motion of a wing, and wind   67
that beat against my face, and words: *"Beati
pacifici,* those free of evil anger!"

Già eran sovra noi tanto levati   70
li ultimi raggi che la notte segue,
che le stelle apparivan da più lati.

"O virtù mia, perché sì ti dilegue?"   73
fra me stesso dicea, ché mi sentiva
la possa de le gambe posta in triegue.

Noi eravam dove più non saliva   76
la scala sù, ed eravamo affissi,
pur come nave ch'a la piaggia arriva.

E io attesi un poco, s'io udissi   79
alcuna cosa nel novo girone;
poi mi volsi al maestro mio, e dissi:

"Dolce mio padre, dì, quale offensione   82
si purga qui nel giro dove semo?
Se i piè si stanno, non stea tuo sermone."

Ed elli a me: "L'amor del bene, scemo   85
del suo dover, quiritta si ristora;
qui si ribatte il mal tardato remo.

Ma perché più aperto intendi ancora,   88
volgi la mente a me, e prenderai
alcun buon frutto di nostra dimora."

"Né creator né creatura mai,"   91
cominciò el, "figliuol, fu sanza amore,
o naturale o d'animo; e tu 'l sai.

Lo naturale è sempre sanza errore,   94
ma l'altro puote errar per malo obietto
o per troppo o per poco di vigore.

Mentre ch'elli è nel primo ben diretto,   97
e ne' secondi sé stesso misura,
esser non può cagion di mal diletto;

ma quando al mal si torce, o con più cura   100
o con men che non dee corre nel bene,
contra 'l fattore adovra sua fattura.

Quinci comprender puoi ch'esser convene   103
amor sementa in voi d'ogne virtute
e d'ogne operazion che merta pene.

Or, perché mai non può da la salute   106
amor del suo subietto volger viso,
da l'odio proprio son le cose tute;

Above us now the final rays before   70
the fall of night were raised to such a height
that we could see the stars on every side.

"O why, my strength, do you so melt away?"   73
I said within myself, because I felt
the force within my legs compelled to halt.

We'd reached a point at which the upward stairs   76
no longer climbed, and we were halted there
just like a ship when it has touched the shore.

I listened for a while, hoping to hear   79
whatever there might be in this new circle;
then I turned toward my master, asking him:

"Tell me, my gentle father: what offense   82
is purged within the circle we have reached?
Although our feet must stop, your words need not."

And he to me: "Precisely here, the love   85
of good that is too tepidly pursued
is mended; here the lazy oar plies harder.

But so that you may understand more clearly,   88
now turn your mind to me, and you will gather
some useful fruit from our delaying here.

My son, there's no Creator and no creature   91
who ever was without love—natural
or mental; and you know that," he began.

"The natural is always without error,   94
but mental love may choose an evil object
or err through too much or too little vigor.

As long as it's directed toward the First Good   97
and tends toward secondary goods with measure,
it cannot be the cause of evil pleasure;

but when it twists toward evil, or attends   100
to good with more or less care than it should,
those whom He made have worked against their Maker.

From this you see that—of necessity—   103
love is the seed in you of every virtue
and of all acts deserving punishment.

Now, since love never turns aside its eyes   106
from the well-being of its subject, things
are surely free from hatred of themselves;

    e perché intender non si può diviso,   109
e per sé stante, alcuno esser dal primo,
da quello odiare ogne effetto è deciso.

    Resta, se dividendo bene stimo,   112
che 'l mal che s'ama è del prossimo; ed esso
amor nasce in tre modi in vostro limo.

    E chi, per esser suo vicin soppresso,   115
spera eccellenza, e sol per questo brama
ch'el sia di sua grandezza in basso messo;

    è chi podere, grazia, onore e fama   118
teme di perder perch' altri sormonti,
onde s'attrista sì che 'l contrario ama;

    ed è chi per ingiuria par ch'aonti,   121
sì che si fa de la vendetta ghiotto,
e tal convien che 'l male altrui impronti.

    Questo triforme amor qua giù di sotto   124
si piange: or vo' che tu de l'altro intende,
che corre al ben con ordine corrotto.

    Ciascun confusamente un bene apprende   127
nel qual si queti l'animo, e disira;
per che di giugner lui ciascun contende.

    Se lento amore a lui veder vi tira   130
o a lui quistar, acquesta cornice,
dopo giusto penter, ve ne martira.

    Altro ben è che non fa l'uom felice;   133
non è felicità, non è la buona
essenza, d'ogne ben frutto e radice.

    L'amor ch'ad esso troppo s'abbandona,   136
di sovr' a noi si piange per tre cerchi;
ma come tripartito si ragiona,

    tacciolo, acciò che tu per te ne cerchi."   139

and since no being can be seen as self-   109
existing and divorced from the First Being,
each creature is cut off from hating Him.

Thus, if I have distinguished properly,   ·   112
ill love must mean to wish one's neighbor ill;
and this love's born in three ways in your clay.

There's he who, through abasement of another,   115
hopes for supremacy; he only longs
to see his neighbor's excellence cast down.

Then there is one who, when he is outdone,   118
fears his own loss of fame, power, honor, favor;
his sadness loves misfortune for his neighbor.

And there is he who, over injury   121
received, resentful, for revenge grows greedy
and, angrily, seeks out another's harm.

This threefold love is expiated here   124
below; now I would have you understand
the love that seeks the good distortedly.

Each apprehends confusedly a Good   127
in which the mind may rest, and longs for It;
and, thus, all strive to reach that Good; but if

the love that urges you to know It or   130
to reach that Good is lax, this terrace, after
a just repentance, punishes for that.

There is a different good, which does not make   133
men glad; it is not happiness, is not
true essence, fruit and root of every good.

The love that—profligately—yields to that   136
is wept on in three terraces above us;
but I'll not say what three shapes that loves takes—

may you seek those distinctions for yourself."   139

HAMAN

XVIII · 76

CANTO XVIII

Posto avea fine al suo ragionamento
 l'alto dottore, e attento guardava
ne la mia vista s'io parea contento;

 e io, cui nova sete ancor frugava,   4
di fuor tacea, e dentro dicea: "Forse
lo troppo dimandar ch'io fo li grava."

 Ma quel padre verace, che s'accorse   7
del timido voler che non s'apriva,
parlando, di parlare ardir mi porse.

 Ond' io: "Maestro, il mio veder s'avviva   10
sì nel tuo lume, ch'io discerno chiaro
quanto la tua ragion parta o descriva.

 Però ti prego, dolce padre caro,   13
che mi dimostri amore, a cui reduci
ogne buono operare e 'l suo contraro."

 "Drizza," disse, "ver' me l'agute luci   16
de lo 'ntelletto, e fieti manifesto
l'error de' ciechi che si fanno duci.

 L'animo, ch'è creato ad amar presto,   19
ad ogne cosa è mobile che piace,
tosto che dal piacere in atto è desto.

 Vostra apprensiva da esser verace   22
tragge intenzione, e dentro a voi la spiega,
sì che l'animo ad essa volger face;

 e se, rivolto, inver' di lei si piega,   25
quel piegare è amor, quell'è natura
che per piacer di novo in voi si lega.

 Poi, come 'l foco movesi in altura   28
per la sua forma ch'è nata a salire
là dove più in sua matera dura,

T he subtle teacher had completed his
    discourse to me; attentively he watched
my eyes to see if I seemed satisfied.

And I, still goaded by new thirst, was silent   4
without, although within I said: "Perhaps
I have displeased him with too many questions."

But that true father, who had recognized   7
the timid want I would not tell aloud,
by speaking, gave me courage to speak out.

At which I said: "Master, my sight is so   10
illumined by your light—I recognize
all that your words declare or analyze.

Therefore, I pray you, gentle father dear,   13
to teach me what love is: you have reduced
to love both each good and its opposite."

He said: "Direct your intellect's sharp eyes   16
toward me, and let the error of the blind
who'd serve as guides be evident to you.

The soul, which is created quick to love,   19
responds to everything that pleases, just
as soon as beauty wakens it to act.

Your apprehension draws an image from   22
a real object and expands upon
that object until soul has turned toward it;

and if, so turned, the soul tends steadfastly,   25
then that propensity is love—it's nature
that joins the soul in you, anew, through beauty.

Then, just as flames ascend because the form   28
of fire was fashioned to fly upward, toward
the stuff of its own sphere, where it lasts longest,

così l'animo preso entra in disire,   31
ch'è moto spiritale, e mai non posa
fin che la cosa amata il fa gioire.

Or ti puote apparer quant' è nascosa   34
la veritate a la gente ch'avvera
ciascun amore in sé laudabil cosa;

però che forse appar la sua matera   37
sempre esser buona, ma non ciascun segno
è buono, ancor che buona sia la cera."

"Le tue parole e 'l mio seguace ingegno,"   40
rispuos' io lui, "m'hanno amor discoverto,
ma ciò m'ha fatto di dubbiar più pregno;

ché, s'amore è di fuori a noi offerto   43
e l'anima non va con altro piede,
se dritta o torta va, non è suo merto."

Ed elli a me: "Quanto ragion qui vede,   46
dir ti poss' io; da indi in là t'aspetta
pur a Beatrice, ch'è opra di fede.

Ogne forma sustanzïal, che setta   49
è da matera ed è con lei unita,
specifica vertute ha in sé colletta,

la qual sanza operar non è sentita,   52
né si dimostra mai che per effetto,
come per verdi fronde in pianta vita.

Però, là onde vegna lo 'ntelletto   55
de le prime notizie, omo non sape,
e de' primi appetibili l'affetto,

che sono in voi sì come studio in ape   58
di far lo mele; e questa prima voglia
merto di lode o di biasmo non cape.

Or perché a questa ogn' altra si raccoglia,   61
innata v'è la virtù che consiglia,
e de l'assenso de' tener la soglia.

Quest' è 'l principio là onde si piglia   64
ragion di meritare in voi, secondo
che buoni e rei amori accoglie e viglia.

Color che ragionando andaro al fondo,   67
s'accorser d'esta innata libertate;
però moralità lasciaro al mondo.

so does the soul, when seized, move into longing,   31
a motion of the spirit, never resting
till the beloved thing has made it joyous.

Now you can plainly see how deeply hidden   34
truth is from scrutinists who would insist
that every love is, in itself, praiseworthy;

and they are led to error by the matter   37
of love, because it may seem—always—good;
but not each seal is fine, although the wax is."

"Your speech and my own wit that followed it,"   40
I answered him, "have shown me what love is;
but that has filled me with still greater doubt;

for if love's offered to us from without   43
and is the only foot with which soul walks,
soul—going straight or crooked—has no merit."

And he to me: "What reason can see here,   46
I can impart; past that, for truth of faith,
it's Beatrice alone you must await.

Every substantial form, at once distinct   49
from matter and conjoined to it, ingathers
the force that is distinctively its own,

a force unknown to us until it acts—   52
it's never shown except in its effects,
just as green boughs display the life in plants.

And thus man does not know the source of his   55
intelligence of primal notions and
his tending toward desire's primal objects:

both are in you just as in bees there is   58
the honey-making urge; such primal will
deserves no praise, and it deserves no blame.

Now, that all other longings may conform   61
to this first will, there is in you, inborn,
the power that counsels, keeper of the threshold

of your assent: this is the principle   64
on which your merit may be judged, for it
garners and winnows good and evil longings.

Those reasoners who reached the roots of things   67
learned of this inborn freedom; the bequest
that, thus, they left unto the world is ethics.

Onde, poniam che di necessitate   70
surga ogne amor che dentro a voi s'accende,
di ritenerlo è in voi la podestate.

La nobile virtù Beatrice intende   73
per lo libero arbitrio, e però guarda
che l'abbi a mente, s'a parlar ten prende."

La luna, quasi a mezza notte tarda,   76
facea le stelle a noi parer più rade,
fatta com' un secchion che tuttor arda;

e correa contra 'l ciel per quelle strade   79
che 'l sole infiamma allor che quel da Roma
tra ' Sardi e ' Corsi il vede quando cade.

E quell' ombra gentil per cui si noma   82
Pietola più che villa mantoana,
del mio carcar diposta avea la soma;

per ch'io, che la ragione aperta e piana   85
sovra le mie quistioni avea ricolta,
stava com' om che sonnolento vana.

Ma questa sonnolenza mi fu tolta   88
subitamente da gente che dopo
le nostre spalle a noi era già volta.

E quale Ismeno già vide e Asopo   91
lungo di sé di notte furia e calca,
pur che i Teban di Bacco avesser uopo,

cotal per quel giron suo passo falca,   94
per quel ch'io vidi di color, venendo,
cui buon volere e giusto amor cavalca.

Tosto fur sovr' a noi, perché correndo   97
si movea tutta quella turba magna;
e due dinanzi gridavan piangendo:

"Maria corse con fretta a la montagna;   100
e Cesare, per soggiogare Ilerda,
punse Marsilia e poi corse in Ispagna."

"Ratto, ratto, che 'l tempo non si perda   103
per poco amor," gridavan li altri appresso,
"che studio di ben far grazia rinverda."

"O gente in cui fervore aguto adesso   106
ricompie forse negligenza e indugio
da voi per tepidezza in ben far messo,

Even if we allow necessity   70
as source for every love that flames in you,
the power to curb that love is still your own.

This noble power is what Beatrice   73
means by free will; therefore, remember it,
if she should ever speak of it to you."

The moon, with midnight now behind us, made   76
the stars seem scarcer to us; it was shaped
just like a copper basin, gleaming, new;

and countercourse, it crossed those paths the sun   79
ignites when those in Rome can see it set
between the Corsicans and the Sardinians.

That gracious shade for whom Pietola   82
won more renown than any Mantuan town,
had freed me from the weight of doubt I bore;

so that I, having harvested his clear   85
and open answers to my questions, stood
like one who, nearing sleep, has random visions.

But readiness for sleep was suddenly   88
taken from me by people who, behind
our backs, already turned in our direction.

Just as—of old—Ismenus and Asopus,   91
at night, along their banks, saw crowds and clamor
whenever Thebans had to summon Bacchus,

such was the arching crowd that curved around   94
that circle, driven on, as I made out,
by righteous will as well as by just love.

Soon all that mighty throng drew near us, for   97
they ran and ran; and two, in front of them,
who wept, were crying: "In her journey, Mary

made haste to reach the mountain, and, in order   100
to conquer Lérida, first Caesar thrust
against Marseilles, and then to Spain he rushed."

Following them, the others cried: "Quick, quick,   103
lest time be lost through insufficient love;
where urge for good is keen, grace finds new green."

"O people in whom eager fervor now   106
may compensate for sloth and negligence
you showed in doing good half-heartedly,

questi che vive, e certo i' non vi bugio,   109
vuole andar sù, pur che 'l sol ne riluca;
però ne dite ond' è presso il pertugio."

Parole furon queste del mio duca;   112
e un di quelli spirti disse: "Vieni
di retro a noi, e troverai la buca.

Noi siam di voglia a muoverci sì pieni,   115
che restar non potem; però perdona,
se villania nostra giustizia tieni.

Io fui abate in San Zeno a Verona   118
sotto lo 'mperio del buon Barbarossa,
di cui dolente ancor Milan ragiona.

E tale ha già l'un piè dentro la fossa,   121
che tosto piangerà quel monastero,
e tristo fia d'avere avuta possa;

perché suo figlio, mal del corpo intero,   124
e de la mente peggio, e che mal nacque,
ha posto in loco di suo pastor vero."

Io non so se piu disse o s'ei si tacque,   127
tant' era già di là da noi trascorso;
ma questo intesi, e ritener mi piacque.

E quei che m'era ad ogne uopo soccorso   130
disse: "Volgiti qua: vedine due
venir dando a l'accidia di morso."

Di retro a tutti dicean: "Prima fue   133
morta la gente a cui il mar s'aperse,
che vedesse Iordan le rede sue.

E quella che l'affanno non sofferse   136
fino a la fine col figlio d'Anchise,
sé stessa a vita sanza gloria offerse."

Poi quando fuor da noi tanto divise   139
quell' ombre, che veder più non potiersi,
novo pensiero dentro a me si mise,

del qual più altri nacquero e diversi;   142
e tanto d'uno in altro vaneggiai,
che li occhi per vaghezza ricopersi,

e 'l pensamento in sogno trasmutai.   145

he—who's alive, and surely I don't lie   109
to you—would climb above as soon as he
has seen the sun shed light on us again;

  then, tell us where the passage lies at hand."   112
My guide said this. One of the souls replied:
"Come, follow us, and you will find the gap.

  We are so fully anxious to advance—   115
we cannot halt; and do forgive us, should
you take our penance for discourtesy.

  I was St. Zeno's abbot in Verona   118
under the rule of valiant Barbarossa,
of whom Milan still speaks with so much sorrow.

  And there is one with one foot in the grave,   121
who soon will weep over that monastery,
lamenting that he once had power there,

  because, in place of its true shepherd, he   124
put one who was unsound of body and,
still more, of mind, and born in sin—his son."

  I don't know if he said more or was silent—   127
he had already raced so far beyond us;
but I heard this much and was pleased to hear it.

  And he who was my help in every need   130
said: "Turn around: see those two coming—they
whose words mock sloth." And I heard those two say

  behind all of the rest: "The ones for whom   133
the sea parted were dead before the Jordan
saw those who had inherited its lands;

  and those who did not suffer trials until   136
the end together with Anchises' son
gave themselves up to life without renown."

  Then, when those shades were so far off from us   139
that seeing them became impossible,
a new thought rose inside of me and, from

  that thought, still others—many and diverse—   142
were born: I was so drawn from random thought
to thought that, wandering in mind, I shut

  my eyes, transforming thought on thought to dream.   145

CANTO XIX

Ne l'ora che non può 'l calor dïurno
intepidar più 'l freddo de la luna,
vinto da terra, e talor da Saturno

   —quando i geomanti lor Maggior Fortuna   4
veggiono in orïente, innanzi a l'alba,
surger per via che poco le sta bruna—

   mi venne in sogno una femmina balba,   7
ne li occhi guercia, e sovra i piè distorta,
con le man monche, e di colore scialba.

   Io la mirava; e come 'l sol conforta   10
le fredde membra che la notte aggrava,
così lo sguardo mio le facea scorta

   la lingua, e poscia tutta la drizzava   13
in poco d'ora, e lo smarrito volto,
com' amor vuol, così le colorava.

   Poi ch'ell' avea 'l parlar così disciolto,   16
cominciava a cantar sì, che con pena
da lei avrei mio intento rivolto.

   "Io son," cantava, "io son dolce serena,   19
che ' marinari in mezzo mar dismago;
tanto son di piacere a sentir piena!

   Io volsi Ulisse del suo cammin vago   22
al canto mio; e qual meco s'ausa,
rado sen parte; sì tutto l'appago!"

   Ancor non era sua bocca richiusa,   25
quand' una donna apparve santa e presta
lunghesso me per far colei confusa.

   "O Virgilio, Virgilio, chi è questa?"   28
fieramente dicea; ed el venìa
con li occhi fitti pur in quella onesta.

From the Fourth to the Fifth Terrace: the Avaricious and the Prodigal.
Dante's dream of the Siren. Waking to the third morning. The angel of
zeal. The Third Beatitude. Ascent to the Fifth Terrace. Colloquy with
Pope Adrian V. The punishment of the Avaricious: given to earthly goods,
they now, bound hand and foot, lie stretched on the ground, face down.

I n that hour when the heat of day, defeated
  by Earth and, sometimes, Saturn, can no longer
warm up the moon-sent cold, when geomancers

    can, in the east, see their *Fortuna major*   4
rising before the dawn along a path
that will be darkened for it only briefly—

    a stammering woman came to me in dream: 7
her eyes askew, and crooked on her feet,
her hands were crippled, her complexion sallow.

    I looked at her; and just as sun revives   10
cold limbs that night made numb, so did my gaze
loosen her tongue and then, in little time,

    set her contorted limbs in perfect order;   13
and, with the coloring that love prefers,
my eyes transformed the wanness of her features.

    And when her speech had been set free, then she   16
began to sing so, that it would have been
most difficult for me to turn aside.

    "I am," she sang, "I am the pleasing siren,   19
who in midsea leads mariners astray—
there is so much delight in hearing me.

    I turned aside Ulysses, although he   22
had longed to journey; who grows used to me
seldom departs—I satisfy him so."

    Her lips were not yet done when, there beside me,   25
a woman showed herself, alert and saintly,
to cast the siren into much confusion.

    "O Virgil, Virgil, tell me: who is this?"   28
she asked most scornfully; and he came forward,
his eyes intent upon that honest one.

L'altra prendea, e dinanzi l'apria   31
fendendo i drappi, e mostravami 'l ventre;
quel mi svegliò col puzzo che n'uscia.

Io mossi li occhi, e 'l buon maestro: "Almen tre   34
voci t'ho messe!" dicea. "Surgi e vieni;
troviam l'aperta per la qual tu entre."

Sù mi levai, e tutti eràn già pieni   37
de l'alto di i giron del sacro monte,
e andavam col sol novo a le reni.

Seguendo lui, portava la mia fronte   40
come colui che l'ha di pensier carca,
che fa di sé un mezzo arco di ponte;

quand' io udi' "Venite; qui si varca,"   43
parlare in modo soave e benigno,
qual non si sente in questa mortal marca.

Con l'ali aperte, che parean di cigno,   46
volseci in sù colui che sì parlonne
tra due pareti del duro macigno.

Mosse le penne poi e ventilonne,   49
"Qui lugent" affermando esser beati,
ch'avran di consolar l'anime donne.

"Che hai che pur inver' la terra guati?"   52
la guida mia incominciò a dirmi,
poco amendue da l'angel sormontati.

E io: "Con tanta sospeccion fa irmi   55
novella visïon ch'a sé mi piega,
sì ch'io non posso dal pensar partirmi."

"Vedesti," disse, "quell'antica strega   58
che sola sovr' a noi omai si piagne;
vedesti come l'uom da lei si slega.

Bastiti, e batti a terra le calcagne;   61
li occhi rivolgi al logoro che gira
lo rege etterno con le rote magne."

Quale 'l falcon, che prima a' piè si mira,   64
indi si volge al grido e si protende
per lo disio del pasto che là il tira,

tal mi fec' io; e tal, quanto si fende   67
la roccia per dar via a chi va suso,
n'andai infin dove 'l cerchiar si prende.

He seized the other, baring her in front,   31
tearing her clothes, and showing me her belly;
the stench that came from there awakened me.

I moved my eyes, and my good master cried: 34
"At least three times I've called you. Rise and come:
let's find the opening where you may enter."

I rose; the daylight had already filled   37
the circles of the sacred mountain—we
were journeying with new sun at our back.

I followed him, bearing my brow like one   40
whose thoughts have weighed him down, who bends as if
he were the semiarch that forms a bridge,

and then I heard: "Draw near; the pass is here,"   43
said in a manner so benign and gentle
as, in our mortal land, one cannot hear.

He who addressed us so had open wings,   46
white as a swan's; and he directed us
upward, between two walls of the hard rock.

And then he moved his plumes and, fanning us,   49
affirmed that those "Qui lugent" would be blessed—
their souls would be possessed of consolation.

"What makes you keep your eyes upon the ground?"   52
my guide began to say to me when both
of us had climbed a little, past the angel.

And I: "What makes me move with such misgiving   55
is a new vision: it has so beguiled me
that I cannot relinquish thoughts of it."

"The one you saw," he said, "that ancient witch—   58
for her alone one must atone above;
you saw how man can free himself from her.

Let that suffice, and hurry on your way;   61
fasten your eyes upon the lure that's spun
by the eternal King with His great spheres."

Just like a falcon, who at first looks down,   64
then, when the falconer has called, bends forward,
craving the food that's ready for him there,

so I became—and so remained until,   67
through the cleft rock that lets one climb above,
I reached the point at which the circle starts.

Com' io nel quinto giro fui dischiuso,   70
vidi gente per esso che piangea,
giacendo a terra tutta volta in giuso.

  "Adhaesit pavimento anima mea,"   73
sentia dir lor con sì alti sospiri,
che la parola a pena s'intendea.

  "O eletti di Dio, li cui soffriri   76
e giustizia e speranza fa men duri,
drizzate noi verso li alti saliri."

  "Se voi venite dal giacer sicuri,   79
e volete trovar la via più tosto,
le vostre destre sien sempre di fori."

  Così pregò 'l poeta, e sì risposto   82
poco dinanzi a noi ne fu; per ch'io
nel parlare avvisai l'altro nascosto,

  e volsi li occhi a li occhi al segnor mio: 85
ond' elli m'assentì con lieto cenno
ciò che chiedea la vista del disio.

  Poi ch'io potei di me fare a mio senno,   88
trassimi sovra quella creatura
le cui parole pria notar mi fenno,

  dicendo: "Spirto in cui pianger matura   91
quel sanza 'l quale a Dio tornar non pòssi.
sosta un poco per me tua maggior cura.

  Chi fosti e perché vòlti avete i dossi   94
al sù, mi dì, e se vuo' ch'io t'impetri
cosa di là ond' io vivendo mossi."

  Ed elli a me: "Perché i nostri diretri   97
rivolga il cielo a sé, saprai; ma prima
scias quod ego fui successor Petri.

  Intra Sïestri e Chiaveri s'adima   100
una fiumana bella, e del suo nome
lo titol del mio sangue fa sua cima.

  Un mese e poco più prova' io come   103
pesa il gran manto a chi dal fango il guarda,
che piuma sembran tutte l'altre some.

  La mia conversïone, omè!, fu tarda;   106
ma, come fatto fui roman pastore,
così scopersi la vita bugiarda.

When I was in the clearing, the fifth level,   70
my eyes discovered people there who wept,
lying upon the ground, all turned face down.

"Adhaesit pavimento anima mea,"   73
I heard them say with sighs so deep that it
was hard to comprehend the words they spoke.

"O God's elect, whose sufferings both hope   76
and justice make less difficult, direct
us to the stairway meant for our ascent."

"If you come here but do not need to be   79
prostrate, and you would find the path most quickly,
then keep your right hand always to the outside."

So did the poet ask, so did reply   82
come from a little way ahead; and I,
hearing that voice reply, learned what was hidden.

I turned my eyes to find my master's eyes;   85
at this, with a glad sign, he ratified
what I had asked for with my eager eyes.

When, free to do as I had wanted to,   88
I moved ahead and bent over that soul
whose words—before—had made me notice him,

saying: "Spirit, within whom weeping ripens   91
that without which there's no return to God,
suspend awhile—for me—your greater care.

Tell me: Who were you? And why are your backs   94
turned up? And there—where I, alive, set out—
would you have me beseech some good for you?"

And he to me: "Why Heaven turns our backs   97
against itself, you are to know; but first
scias quod ego fui successor Petri.

Between Sestri and Chiavari descends   100
a handsome river; and its name is set
upon the upper portion of my crest.

For one month and a little more I learned   103
how the great mantle weighs on him who'd keep it
out of the mire—all other weights seem feathers.

Alas, how tardy my conversion was!   106
But when I had been named the Roman shepherd,
then I discovered the deceit of life.

Vidi che lì non s'acquetava il core,   109
né più salir potiesi in quella vita;
per che di questa in me s'accese amore.

Fino a quel punto misera e partita   112
da Dio anima fui, del tutto avara;
or, come vedi, qui ne son punita.

Quel ch'avarizia fa, qui si dichiara   115
in purgazion de l'anime converse;
e nulla pena il monte ha più amara.

Sì come l'occhio nostro non s'aderse   118
in alto, fisso a le cose terrene,
così giustizia qui a terra il merse.

Come avarizia spense a ciascun bene   121
lo nostro amore, onde operar perdési,
così giustizia qui stretti ne tene,

ne' piedi e ne le man legati e presi;   124
e quanto fia piacer del giusto Sire,
tanto staremo immobili e distesi."

Io m'era iginocchiato e volea dire;   127
ma com' io cominciai ed el s'accorse,
solo ascoltando, del mio reverire,

"Qual cagion," disse, "in giù così ti torse?"   130
E io a lui: "Pur vostra dignitate
mia coscïenza dritto mi rimorse."

"Drizza le gambe, lèvati sù, frate!"   133
rispuose; "non errar: conservo sono
teco e con li altri ad una podestate.

Se mai quel santo evangelico suono   136
che dice *'Neque nubent,'* intendesti,
ben puoi veder perch' io così ragiono.

Vattene omai: non vo' che più t'arresti;   139
ché la tua stanza mio pianger disagia,
col qual maturo ciò che tu dicesti.

Nepote ho io di là c'ha nome Alagia,   142
buona da sé, pur che la nostra casa
non faccia lei per essempro malvagia;

e questa sola di là m'è rimasa."   145

I saw that there the heart was not at rest,   109
nor could I, in that life, ascend more high;
so that, in me, love for this life was kindled.

Until that point I was a squalid soul,   112
from God divided, wholly avaricious;
now, as you see, I'm punished here for that.

What avarice enacts is here declared   115
in the purgation of converted souls;
the mountain has no punishment more bitter.

Just as we did not lift our eyes on high   118
but set our sight on earthly things instead,
so justice here impels our eyes toward earth.

As avarice annulled in us the love   121
of any other good, and thus we lost
our chance for righteous works, so justice here

fetters our hands and feet and holds us captive;   124
and for as long as it may please our just
Lord, here we'll be outstretched and motionless."

I'd kneeled, wishing to speak: but just as I   127
began—and through my voice alone—he sensed
that I had meant to do him reverence.

"What reason makes you bend your body so?"   130
he said. And I to him: "Your dignity
made conscience sting me as I stood erect."

"Brother, straighten your legs; rise up!" he answered.   133
"Don't be mistaken; I, with you and others,
am but a fellow-servant of one Power.

If you have ever understood the holy   136
sound of the Gospel that says *'Neque nubent,'*
then you will see why I have spoken so.

Now go your way: I'd not have you stop longer;   139
your staying here disturbs my lamentations,
the tears that help me ripen what you mentioned.

Beyond, I have a niece whose name's Alagia;   142
she in herself is good, as long as our
house, by example, brings her not to evil;

and she alone is left to me beyond."   145

XIX · 124

CANTO XX

Contra miglior voler voler mal pugna;
onde contra 'l piacer mio, per piacerli,
trassi de l'acqua non sazia la spugna.

Mossimi; e 'l duca mio si mosse per li   4
luoghi spediti pur lungo la roccia,
come si va per muro stretto a' merli;

ché la gente che fonde a goccia a goccia   7
per li occhi il mal che tutto 'l mondo occupa,
da l'altra parte in fuor troppo s'approccia.

Maladetta sie tu, antica lupa,   10
che più che tutte l'altre bestie hai preda
per la tua fame sanza fine cupa!

O ciel, nel cui girar par che si creda   13
le condizion di qua giù trasmutarsi,
quando verrà per cui questa disceda?

Noi andavam con passi lenti e scarsi,   16
e io attento a l'ombre, ch'i' sentia
pietosamente piangere e lagnarsi;

e per ventura udi' "Dolce Maria!"   19
dinanzi a noi chiamar così nel pianto
come fa donna che in parturir sia;

e seguitar: "Povera fosti tanto,   22
quanto veder si può per quello ospizio
dove sponesti il tuo portato santo."

Seguentemente intesi: "O buon Fabrizio,   25
con povertà volesti anzi virtute
che gran ricchezza posseder con vizio."

Queste parole m'eran sì piaciute,   28
ch'io mi trassi oltre per aver contezza
di quello spirto onde parean venute.

Still the Fifth Terrace, the Avaricious and the Prodigal. Excoriation of avarice. Examples of poverty and generosity: the Virgin Mary, Fabricius, St. Nicholas. Hugh Capet's condemnation of his descendants. Examples of avarice: Pygmalion, Midas, Acan, Sapphira and her husband Ananias, Heliodorus, Polymnestor, Crassus. The mountain's trembling. The shout of the souls on Purgatory.

Against a better will, the will fights weakly;
    therefore, to please him, though against my pleasure,
I drew my unquenched sponge out of the water.

I moved on, and my guide moved through the un-   4
encumbered space, hugging the rock, as one
walks on a wall, close to the battlements;

for those whose eyes would melt down, drop by drop,   7
the evil that possesses all the world,
were too close to the edge, on the far side.

May you be damned, o ancient wolf, whose power   10
can claim more prey than all the other beasts—
your hungering is deep and never-ending!

O heavens, through whose revolutions many   13
think things on earth are changed, when will he come—
the one whose works will drive that wolf away?

Our steps were short and slow as we moved on;   16
I was attentive to the shades; I heard
the sorrow in their tears and lamentations.

Then I, by chance, heard one ahead of us   19
crying in his lament, "Sweet Mary," as
a woman would outcry in labor pains.

And he continued: "In that hostel where   22
you had set down your holy burden, there
one can discover just how poor you were."

Following this I heard: "O good Fabricius,   25
you chose, as your possessions, indigence
with virtue rather than much wealth with vice."

These words had been so pleasing to me—I   28
moved forward, so that I might come to know
the spirit from whom they had seemed to come.

Esso parlava ancor de la larghezza   31
che fece Niccolò a le pulcelle,
per condurre ad onor lor giovinezza.

"O anima che tanto ben favelle,   34
dimmi chi fosti," dissi, "e perché sola
tu queste degne lode rinovelle.

Non fia sanza mercé la tua parola,   37
s'io ritorno a compiér lo cammin corto
di quella vita ch'al termine vola."

Ed elli: "Io ti dirò, non per conforto   40
ch'io attenda di là, ma perché tanta
grazia in te luce prima che sie morto.

Io fui radice de la mala pianta   43
che la terra cristiana tutta aduggia,
sì che buon frutto rado se ne schianta.

Ma se Doagio, Lilla, Guanto e Bruggia   46
potesser, tosto ne saria vendetta;
e io la cheggio a lui che tutto giuggia.

Chiamato fui di là Ugo Ciappetta;   49
di me son nati i Filippi e i Luigi
per cui novellamente è Francia retta.

Figliuol fu' io d'un beccaio di Parigi: 52
quando li regi antichi venner meno
tutti, fuor ch'un renduto in panni bigi,

trova'mi stretto ne le mani il freno   55
del governo del regno, e tanta possa
di nuovo acquisto, e sì d'amici pieno,

ch'a la corona vedova promossa   58
la testa di mio figlio fu, dal quale
cominciar di costor le sacrate ossa.

Mentre che la gran dota provenzale   61
al sangue mio non tolse la vergogna,
poco valea, ma pur non facea male.

Lì cominciò con forza e con menzogna   64
la sua rapina; e poscia, per ammenda,
Pontì e Normandia prese e Guascogna.

Carlo venne in Italia e, per ammenda,   67
vittima fé di Curradino; e poi
ripinse al ciel Tommaso, per ammenda.

He kept on speaking, telling the largesse   31
of Nicholas—the gifts he gave the maidens
so that they might be honorably wed.

"O soul who speaks of so much righteousness,   34
do tell me who you were," I said, "and why
just you alone renew these seemly praises.

Your speaking to me will not go unthanked   37
when I return to finish the short span
of that life which now hurries toward its end."

And he: "I'll tell you—not because I hope   40
for solace from your world, but for such grace
as shines in you before your death's arrived.

I was the root of the obnoxious plant   43
that overshadows all the Christian lands,
so that fine fruit can rarely rise from them.

But if Douai and Lille and Bruges and Ghent   46
had power, they would soon take vengeance on it;
and this I beg of Him who judges all.

The name I bore beyond was Hugh Capet: 49
of me were born the Louises and Philips
by whom France has been ruled most recently.

I was the son of a Parisian butcher.   52
When all the line of ancient kings was done
and only one—a monk in gray—survived,

I found the reins that ruled the kingdom tight   55
within my hands, and I held so much new-
gained power and possessed so many friends

that, to the widowed crown, my own son's head   58
was elevated, and from him began
the consecrated bones of all those kings.

Until the giant dowry of Provence   61
removed all sense of shame within my house,
my line was not worth much, but did no wrong.

There its rapine began with lies and force;   64
and then it seized—that it might make amends—
Ponthieu and Normandy and Gascony.

Charles came to Italy and, for amends,   67
made Conradin a victim, and then thrust
back Thomas into Heaven, for amends.

Tempo vegg' io, non molto dopo ancoi,   70
che tragge un altro Carlo fuor di Francia,
per far conoscer meglio e sé e ' suoi.

Sanz' arme n'esce e solo con la lancia   73
con la qual giostrò Giuda, e quella ponta
sì, ch'a Fiorenza fa scoppiar la pancia.

Quindi non terra, ma peccato e onta   76
guadagnerà, per sé tanto più grave
quanto più lieve simil danno conta.

L'altro, che già uscì preso di nave,   79
veggio vender sua figlia e patteggiarne
come fanno i corsar de l'altre schiave.

O avarizia, che puoi tu più farne,   82
poscia c'ha' il mio sangue a te sì tratto,
che non si cura de la propria carne?

Perché men paia il mal futuro e 'l fatto,   85
veggio in Alagna intrar lo fiordaliso,
e nel vicario suo Cristo esser catto.

Veggiolo un'altra volta esser deriso;   88
veggio rinovellar l'aceto e 'l fiele,
e tra vivi ladroni esser anciso.

Veggio il novo Pilato sì crudele,   91
che ciò nol sazia, ma sanza decreto
portar nel Tempio le cupide vele.

O Segnor mio, quando sarò io lieto   94
a veder la vendetta che, nascosa,
fa dolce l'ira tua nel tuo secreto?

Ciò ch'io dicea di quell' unica sposa   97
de lo Spirito Santo e che ti fece
verso me volger per alcuna chiosa,

tanto è risposto a tutte nostre prece   100
quanto 'l dì dura; ma com' el s'annotta,
contrario suon prendemo in quella vece.

Noi repetiam Pigmalïon allotta,   103
cui traditore e ladro e paricida
fece la voglia sua de l'oro ghiotta;

e la miseria de l'avaro Mida,   106
che seguì a la sua dimanda gorda,
per la qual semper convien che si rida.

I see a time—not too far off—in which 70
another Charles advances out of France
to make himself and his descendants famous.

He does not carry weapons when he comes, 73
only the lance that Judas tilted; this
he couches so—he twists the paunch of Florence.

From this he'll gain not land, just shame and sin, 76
which will be all the heavier for him
as he would reckon lightly such disgrace.

The other, who once left his ship as prisoner— 79
I see him sell his daughter, bargaining
as pirates haggle over female slaves.

O avarice, my house is now your captive: 82
it traffics in the flesh of its own children—
what more is left for you to do to us?

That past and future evil may seem less, 85
I see the fleur-de-lis enter Anagni
and, in His vicar, Christ made prisoner.

I see Him mocked a second time; I see 88
the vinegar and gall renewed—and He
is slain between two thieves who're still alive.

And I see the new Pilate, one so cruel 91
that, still not sated, he, without decree,
carries his greedy sails into the Temple.

O You, my Lord, when will You let me be 94
happy on seeing vengeance that, concealed,
makes sweet Your anger in Your secrecy?

What I have said about the only bride 97
the Holy Ghost has known, the words that made
you turn to me for commentary—these

words serve as answer to our prayers as long 100
as it is day; but when night falls, then we
recite examples that are contrary.

Then we tell over how Pygmalion, 103
out of his greedy lust for gold, became
a thief and traitor and a parricide;

the wretchedness of avaricious Midas, 106
resulting from his ravenous request,
the consequence that always makes men laugh;

Del folle Acàn ciascun poi si ricorda,   109
come furò le spoglie, sì che l'ira
di Iosüè qui par ch'ancor lo morda.

Indi accusiam col marito Saffira;   112
lodiamo i calci ch'ebbe Elïodoro;
e in infamia tutto 'l monte gira

Polinestòr ch'ancise Polidoro;   115
ultimamente ci si grida: 'Crasso,
dilci, che 'l sai: di che sapore è l'oro?'

Talor parla l'uno alto e l'altro basso,   118
secondo l'affezion ch'ad ir ci sprona
ora a maggiore e ora a minor passo:

però al ben che 'l dì ci si ragiona,   121
dianzi non era io sol; ma qui da presso
non alzava la voce altra persona."

Noi eravam partiti già da esso,   124
e brigavam di soverchiar la strada
tanto quanto al poder n'era permesso,

quand' io senti', come cosa che cada,   127
tremar lo monte; onde mi prese un gelo
qual prender suol colui ch'a morte vada.

Certo non si scoteo sì forte Delo,   130
pria che Latona in lei facesse 'l nido
a parturir li due occhi del cielo.

Poi cominciò da tutte parti un grido   133
tal, che 'l maestro inverso me si feo,
dicendo: "Non dubbiar, mentr' io ti guido."

"Glorïa in excelsis" tutti *"Deo"*   136
dicean, per quel ch'io da' vicin compresi,
onde intender lo grido si poteo.

No' istavamo immobili e sospesi   139
come i pastor che prima udir quel canto,
fin che 'l tremar cessò ed el compiési.

Poi ripigliammo nostro cammin santo,   142
guardando l'ombre che giacean per terra,
tornate già in su l'usato pianto.

Nulla ignoranza mai con tanta guerra   145
mi fé desideroso di sapere,
se la memoria mia in ciò non erra,

and each of us recalls the foolish Achan—   109
how he had robbed the spoils, so that the anger
of Joshua still seems to sting him here.

Then we accuse Sapphira and her husband;   112
we praise the kicks Heliodorus suffered;
and Polymnestor, who killed Polydorus,

resounds, in infamy, round all this mountain;   115
and finally, what we cry here is: 'Crassus,
tell us, because you know: "How does gold taste?"'

At times one speaks aloud, another low,   118
according to the sentiment that goads
us now to be more swift and now more slow:

thus, I was not alone in speaking of   121
the good we cite by day, but here nearby
no other spirit raised his voice as high."

We had already taken leave of him   124
and were already struggling to advance
along that road as far as we were able,

when I could feel the mountain tremble like   127
a falling thing; at which a chill seized me
as cold grips one who goes to meet his death.

Delos had surely not been buffeted   130
so hard before Latona planted there
the nest in which to bear the sky's two eyes.

Then such a shout rose up on every side   133
that, drawing near to me, my master said:
"Don't be afraid, as long as I'm your guide."

"Gloria in excelsis Deo," they all cried—   136
so did I understand from those nearby,
whose shouted words were able to be heard.

Just like the shepherds who first heard that song,   139
we stood, but did not move, in expectation,
until the trembling stopped, the song was done.

Then we took up again our holy path,   142
watching the shades who lay along the ground,
who had resumed their customary tears.

My ignorance has never struggled so,   145
has never made me long so much to know—
if memory does not mislead me now—

quanta pareami allor, pensando, avere;   148
né per la fretta dimandare er' oso,
né per me lì potea cosa vedere:
  così m'andava timido e pensoso.   151

as it seemed then to long within my thoughts;   148
nor did I dare to ask—we were so rushed;
nor, by myself, could I discern the cause.

So, timid, pensive, I pursued my way.   151

CANTO XXI

La sete natural che mai non sazia
se non con l'acqua onde la femminetta
samaritana domandò la grazia,

mi travagliava, e pungeami la fretta   4
per la 'mpacciata via dietro al mio duca,
e condoleami a la giusta vendetta.

Ed ecco, sì come ne scrive Luca   7
che Cristo apparve a' due ch'erano in via,
giù surto fuor de la sepulcral buca,

ci apparve un'ombra, e dietro a noi venìa,   10
dal piè guardando la turba che giace;
né ci addemmo di lei, sì parlò pria,

dicendo: "O frati miei, Dio vi dea pace."   13
Noi ci volgemmo sùbiti, e Virgilio
rendéli 'l cenno ch'a ciò si conface.

Poi cominciò: "Nel beato concilio   16
ti ponga in pace la verace corte
che me rilega ne l'etterno essilio."

"Come!" diss' elli, e parte andavam forte: 19
"se voi siete ombre che Dio sù non degni,
chi v'ha per la sua scala tanto scorte?"

E 'l dottor mio: "Se tu riguardi a' segni   22
che questi porta e che l'angel profila,
ben vedrai che coi buon convien ch'e' regni.

Ma perché lei che dì e notte fila   25
non li avea tratta ancora la conocchia
che Cloto impone a ciascuno e compila,

l'anima sua, ch'è tua e mia serocchia,   28
venendo sù, non potea venir sola,
però ch'al nostro modo non adocchia.

T he natural thirst that never can be quenched
   except by water that gives grace—the draught
the simple woman of Samaria sought—

   tormented me; haste spurred me on the path   4
crowded with souls, behind my guide; and I
felt pity, though their pain was justified.

   And here—even as Luke records for us   7
that Christ, new-risen from his burial cave,
appeared to two along his way—a shade

   appeared; and he advanced behind our backs   10
while we were careful not to trample on
the outstretched crowd. We did not notice him

   until he had addressed us with: "God give   13
you, o my brothers, peace!" We turned at once;
then, after offering suitable response,

   Virgil began: "And may that just tribunal   16
which has consigned me to eternal exile
place you in peace within the blessed assembly!"

   "What!" he exclaimed, as we moved forward quickly.   19
"If God's not deemed you worthy of ascent,
who's guided you so far along His stairs?"

   "If you observe the signs the angel traced   22
upon this man," my teacher said, "you'll see
plainly—he's meant to reign with all the righteous;

   but since she who spins night and day had not   25
yet spun the spool that Clotho sets upon
the distaff and adjusts for everyone,

   his soul, the sister of your soul and mine,   28
in its ascent, could not—alone—have climbed
here, for it does not see the way we see.

Ond' io fui tratto fuor de l'ampia gola   31
d'inferno per mostrarli, e mosterrolli
oltre, quanto 'l potrà menar mia scola.

Ma dimmi, se tu sai, perché tai crolli   34
diè dianzi 'l monte, e perché tutto ad una
parve gridare infino a' suoi piè molli."

Sì mi diè, dimandando, per la cruna   37
del mio disio, che pur con la speranza
si fece la mia sete men digiuna.

Quei cominciò: "Cosa non è che sanza   40
ordine senta la religïone
de la montagna, o che sia fuor d'usanza.

Libero è qui da ogne alterazione: 43
di quel che 'l ciel da sé in sé riceve
esser ci puote, e non d'altro, cagione.

Per che non pioggia, non grando, non neve,   46
non rugiada, non brina più sù cade
che la scaletta di tre gradi breve;

nuvole spesse non paion né rade,   49
né coruscar, né figlia di Taumante,
che di là cangia sovente contrade;

secco vapor non surge più avante   52
ch'al sommo d'i tre gradi ch'io parlai,
dov' ha 'l vicario di Pietro le piante.

Trema forse più giù poco o assai;   55
ma per vento che 'n terra si nasconda,
non so come, qua sù non tremò mai.

Tremaci quando alcuna anima monda   58
sentesi, sì che surga o che si mova
per salir sù; e tal grido seconda.

De la mondizia sol voler fa prova,   61
che, tutto libero a mutar convento,
l'alma sorprende, e di voler le giova.

Prima vuol ben, ma non lascia il talento   64
che divina giustizia, contra voglia,
come fu al peccar, pone al tormento.

E io, che son giaciuto a questa doglia   67
cinquecent' anni e più, pur mo sentii
libera volontà di miglior soglia:

Therefore, I was brought forth from Hell's broad jaws   31
to guide him in his going; I shall lead
him just as far as where I teach can reach.

But tell me, if you can, why, just before,   34
the mountain shook and shouted, all of it—
for so it seemed—down to its sea-bathed shore."

His question threaded so the needle's eye   37
of my desire that just the hope alone
of knowing left my thirst more satisfied.

That other shade began: "The sanctity   40
of these slopes does not suffer anything
that's without order or uncustomary.

This place is free from every perturbation: 43
what heaven from itself and in itself
receives may serve as cause here—no thing else.

Therefore, no rain, no hail, no snow, no dew,   46
no hoarfrost falls here any higher than
the stairs of entry with their three brief steps;

neither thick clouds nor thin appear, nor flash   49
of lightning; Thaumas' daughter, who so often
shifts places in your world, is absent here.

Dry vapor cannot climb up any higher   52
than to the top of the three steps of which
I spoke—where Peter's vicar plants his feet.

Below that point, there may be small or ample   55
tremors; but here above, I know not why,
no wind concealed in earth has ever caused

a tremor; for it only trembles here   58
when some soul feels it's cleansed, so that it rises
or stirs to climb on high; and that shout follows.

The will alone is proof of purity   61
and, fully free, surprises soul into
a change of dwelling place—effectively.

Soul had the will to climb before, but that   64
will was opposed by longing to do penance
(as once, to sin), instilled by divine justice.

And I, who have lain in this suffering   67
five hundred years and more, just now have felt
my free will for a better threshold: thus,

però sentisti il tremoto e li pii   70
spiriti per lo monte render lode
a quel Segnor, che tosto sù li 'nvii."

Così ne disse; e però ch'el si gode   73
tanto del ber quant' è grande la sete,
non saprei dir quant' el mi fece prode.

E 'l savio duca: "Omai veggio la rete   76
che qui vi 'mpiglia e come si scalappia,
perché ci trema e di che congaudete.

Ora chi fosti, piacciati ch'io sappia,   79
e perché tanti secoli giaciuto
qui se', ne le parole tue mi cappia."

"Nel tempo che 'l buon Tito, con l'aiuto   82
del sommo rege, vendicò le fóra
ond' uscì 'l sangue per Giuda venduto,

col nome che più dura e più onora   85
era io di là," rispuose quello spirto,
"famoso assai, ma non con fede ancora.

Tanto fu dolce mio vocale spirto,   88
che, tolosano, a sé mi trasse Roma,
dove mertai le tempie ornar di mirto.

Stazio la gente ancor di là mi noma: 91
cantai di Tebe, e poi del grande Achille;
ma caddi in via con la seconda soma.

Al mio ardor fuor seme le faville,   94
che mi scaldar, de la divina fiamma
onde sono allumati più di mille;

de l'Eneïda dico, la qual mamma   97
fummi, e fummi nutrice, poetando:
sanz' essa non fermai peso di dramma.

E per esser vivuto di là quando   100
visse Virgilio, assentirei un sole
più che non deggio al mio uscir di bando."

Volser Virgilio a me queste parole   103
con viso che, tacendo, disse "Taci";
ma non può tutto la virtù che vuole;

ché riso e pianto son tanto seguaci   106
a la passion di che ciascun si spicca,
che men seguon voler ne' più veraci.

you heard the earthquake and the pious spirits   70
throughout the mountain as they praised the Lord—
and may He send them speedily upward."

So did he speak to us; and just as joy   73
is greater when we quench a greater thirst,
the joy he brought cannot be told in words.

And my wise guide: "I now can see the net   76
impeding you, how one slips through, and why
it quakes here, and what makes you all rejoice.

And now may it please you to tell me who   79
you were, and in your words may I find why
you've lain here for so many centuries."

"In that age when the worthy Titus, with   82
help from the Highest King, avenged the wounds
from which the blood that Judas sold had flowed,

I had sufficient fame beyond," that spirit   85
replied; "I bore the name that lasts the longest
and honors most—but faith was not yet mine.

So gentle was the spirit of my verse   88
that Rome drew me, son of Toulouse, to her,
and there my brow deserved a crown of myrtle.

On earth my name is still remembered—Statius: 91
I sang of Thebes and then of great Achilles;
I fell along the way of that last labor.

The sparks that warmed me, the seeds of my ardor,   94
were from the holy fire—the same that gave
more than a thousand poets light and flame.

I speak of the *Aeneid;* when I wrote   97
verse, it was mother to me, it was nurse;
my work, without it, would not weigh an ounce.

And to have lived on earth when Virgil lived—   100
for that I would extend by one more year
the time I owe before my exile's end."

These words made Virgil turn to me, and as   103
he turned, his face, through silence, said: "Be still"
(and yet the power of will cannot do all,

for tears and smiles are both so faithful to   106
the feelings that have prompted them that true
feeling escapes the will that would subdue).

Io pur sorrisi come l'uom ch'ammicca;   109
per che l'ombra si tacque, e riguardommi
ne li occhi ove 'l sembiante più si ficca;

e "Se tanto labore in bene assommi,"   112
disse, "perché la tua faccia testeso
un lampeggiar di riso dimostrommi?"

Or son io d'una parte e d'altra preso: 115
l'una mi fa tacer, l'altra scongiura
ch'io dica; ond' io sospiro, e sono inteso

dal mio maestro, e "Non aver paura,"   118
mi dice, "di parlar; ma parla e digli
quel ch'e' dimanda con cotanta cura."

Ond' io: "Forse che tu ti maravigli,   121
antico spirto, del rider ch'io fei;
ma più d'ammirazion vo' che ti pigli.

Questi che guida in alto li occhi miei,   124
è quel Virgilio dal qual tu togliesti
forte a cantar de li uomini e d'i dèi.

Se cagion altra al mio rider credesti,   127
lasciala per non vera, ed esser credi
quelle parole che di lui dicesti."

Già s'inchinava ad abbracciar li piedi   130
al mio dottor, ma el li disse: "Frate,
non far, ché tu se' ombra e ombra vedi."

Ed ei surgendo: "Or puoi la quantitate   133
comprender de l'amor ch'a te mi scalda,
quand' io dismento nostra vanitate,

trattando l'ombre come cosa salda."   136

But I smiled like a man whose eyes would signal;   109
at this, the shade was silent, and he stared
where sentiment is clearest—at my eyes—

and said: "So may your trying labor end   112
successfully, do tell me why—just now—
your face showed me the flashing of a smile."

Now I am held by one side and the other: 115
one keeps me still, the other conjures me
to speak; but when, therefore, I sigh, my master

knows why and tells me: "Do not be afraid   118
to speak, but speak and answer what he has
asked you to tell him with such earnestness."

At this, I answered: "Ancient spirit, you   121
perhaps are wondering at the smile I smiled:
but I would have you feel still more surprise.

He who is guide, who leads my eyes on high,   124
is that same Virgil from whom you derived
the power to sing of men and of the gods.

Do not suppose my smile had any source   127
beyond the speech you spoke; be sure—it was
those words you said of him that were the cause."

Now he had bent to kiss my teacher's feet,   130
but Virgil told him: "Brother, there's no need—
you are a shade, a shade is what you see."

And, rising, he: "Now you can understand   133
how much love burns in me for you, when I
forget our insubstantiality,

treating the shades as one treats solid things."   136

VIRGIL & STATIUS

XXII ·131

CANTO XXII

Già era l'angel dietro a noi rimaso,
l'angel che n'avea vòlti al sesto giro,
avendomi dal viso un colpo raso;

e quei c'hanno a giustizia lor disiro   4
detto n'avea beati, e le sue voci
con *"sitiunt,"* sanz' altro, ciò forniro.

E io più lieve che per l'altre foci   7
m'andava, sì che sanz' alcun labore
seguiva in sù li spiriti veloci;

quando Virgilio incominciò: "Amore,   10
acceso di virtù, sempre altro accese,
pur che la fiamma sua paresse fore;

onde da l'ora che tra noi discese   13
nel limbo de lo 'nferno Giovenale,
che la tua affezion mi fé palese,

mia benvoglienza inverso te fu quale   16
più strinse mai di non vista persona,
sì ch'or mi parran corte queste scale.

Ma dimmi, e come amico mi perdona   19
se troppa sicurtà m'allarga il freno,
e come amico omai meco ragiona:

come poté trovar dentro al tuo seno   22
loco avarizia, tra cotanto senno
di quanto per tua cura fosti pieno?"

Queste parole Stazio mover fenno   25
un poco a riso pria; poscia rispuose:
"Ogne tuo dir d'amor m'è caro cenno.

Veramente più volte appaion cose   28
che danno a dubitar falsa matera
per le vere ragion che son nascose.

From the Fifth to the Sixth Terrace: the Gluttonous. The angel of justice.
First part of the Fourth Beatitude. Ascent to the Sixth Terrace. Statius:
his true sin, prodigality; his conversion. Virgil on the other souls in
Limbo. The Sixth Terrace. The strange tree. Voices citing examples of
temperance: the Virgin Mary, the women of ancient Rome, the Golden
Age, John the Baptist.

T he angel now was left behind us, he
    who had directed us to the sixth terrace,
having erased one *P* that scarred my face;

    he had declared that those who longed for justice   4
are blessed, and his voice concluded that
message with *"sitiunt,"* without the rest.

    And while I climbed behind the two swift spirits,   7
not laboring at all, for I was lighter
than I had been along the other stairs,

    Virgil began: "Love that is kindled by   10
virtue, will, in another, find reply,
as long as that love's flame appears without;

    so, from the time when Juvenal, descending   13
among us, in Hell's Limbo, had made plain
the fondness that you felt for me, my own

    benevolence toward you has been much richer   16
than any ever given to a person
one has not seen; thus, now these stairs seem short.

    But tell me (and, as friend, forgive me if   19
excessive candor lets my reins relax,
and, as a friend, exchange your words with me):

    how was it that you found within your breast   22
a place for avarice, when you possessed
the wisdom you had nurtured with such care?"

    These words at first brought something of a smile   25
to Statius; then he answered: "Every word
you speak, to me is a dear sign of love.

    Indeed, because true causes are concealed,   28
we often face deceptive reasoning
and things provoke perplexity in us.

La tua diamanda tuo creder m'avvera   31
esser ch'i' fossi avaro in l'altra vita,
forse per quella cerchia dov' io era.

Or sappi ch'avarizia fu partita   34
troppo da me, e questa dismisura
migliaia di lunari hanno punita.

E se non fosse ch'io drizzai mia cura,   37
quand' io intesi là dove tu chiame,
crucciato quasi a l'umana natura:

'Perché non reggi tu, o sacra fame   40
de l'oro, l'appetito de' mortali?'
voltando sentirei le giostre grame.

Allor m'accorsi che troppo aprir l'ali   43
potean le mani a spendere, e pente'mi
così di quel come de li altri mali.

Quanti risurgeran coi crini scemi   46
per ignoranza, che di questa pecca
toglie 'l penter vivendo e ne li stremi!

E sappie che la colpa che rimbecca   49
per dritta opposizione alcun peccato,
con esso insieme qui suo verde secca;

però, s'io son tra quella gente stato   52
che piange l'avarizia, per purgarmi,
per lo contrario suo m'è incontrato."

"Or quando tu cantasti le crude armi   55
de la doppia trestizia di Giocasta,"
disse 'l cantor de' buccolici carmi,

"per quello che Clïò teco lì tasta,   58
non par che ti facesse ancor fedele
la fede, sanza qual ben far non basta.

Se così è, qual sole quai candele   61
ti stenebraron sì, che tu drizzasti
poscia di retro al pescator le vele?"

Ed elli a lui: "Tu prima m'invïasti   64
verso Parnaso a ber ne le sue grotte,
e prima appresso Dio m'alluminasti.

Facesti come quei che va di notte,   67
che porta il lume dietro e sé non giova,
ma dopo sé fa le persone dotte,

Your question makes me sure that you're convinced— 31
perhaps because my circle was the fifth—
that, in the life I once lived, avarice

had been my sin. Know then that I was far 34
from avarice—it was my lack of measure
thousands of months have punished. And if I

had not corrected my assessment by 37
my understanding what your verses meant
when you, as if enraged by human nature,

exclaimed: 'Why cannot you, o holy hunger 40
for gold, restrain the appetite of mortals?'—
I'd now, while rolling weights, know sorry jousts.

Then I became aware that hands might open 43
too wide, like wings, in spending; and of this,
as of my other sins, I did repent.

How many are to rise again with heads 46
cropped close, whom ignorance prevents from reaching
repentance in—and at the end of—life!

And know that when a sin is countered by 49
another fault—directly opposite
to it—then, here, both sins see their green wither.

Thus, I join those who pay for avarice 52
in my purgation, though what brought me here
was prodigality—its opposite."

"Now, when you sang the savage wars of those 55
twin sorrows of Jocasta," said the singer
of the bucolic poems, "it does not seem—

from those notes struck by you and Clio there— 58
that you had yet turned faithful to the faith
without which righteous works do not suffice.

If that is so, then what sun or what candles 61
drew you from darkness so that, in their wake,
you set your sails behind the fisherman?"

And he to him: "You were the first to send me 64
to drink within Parnassus' caves and you,
the first who, after God, enlightened me.

You did as he who goes by night and carries 67
the lamp behind him—he is of no help
to his own self but teaches those who follow—

    quando dicesti: 'Secol si rinova;   70
torna giustizia e primo tempo umano,
e progenïe scende da ciel nova.'

    Per te poeta fui, per te cristiano: 73
ma perché veggi mei ciò ch'io disegno,
a colorare stenderò la mano.

    Già era 'l mondo tutto quanto pregno   76
de la vera credenza, seminata
per li messaggi de l'etterno regno;

    e la parola tua sopra toccata   79
si consonava a' nuovi predicanti;
ond' io a visitarli presi usata.

    Vennermi poi parendo tanto santi,   82
che, quando Domizian li perseguette,
sanza mio lagrimar non fur lor pianti;

    e mentre che di là per me si stette,   85
io li sovvenni, e i lor dritti costumi
fer dispregiare a me tutte altre sette.

    E pria ch'io conducessi i Greci a' fiumi   88
di Tebe poetando, ebb' io battesmo;
ma per paura chiuso cristian fu'mi,

    lungamente mostrando paganesmo;   91
e questa tepidezza il quarto cerchio
cerchiar mi fé più che 'l quarto centesmo.

    Tu dunque, che levato hai il coperchio   94
che m'ascondeva quanto bene io dico,
mentre che del salire avem soverchio,

    dimmi dov' è Terrenzio nostro antico,   97
Cecilio e Plauto e Varro, se lo sai:
dimmi se son dannati, e in qual vico."

    "Costoro e Persio e io e altri assai,"   100
rispuose il duca mio, "siam con quel Greco
che le Muse lattar più ch'altri mai,

    nel primo cinghio del carcere cieco;   103
spesse fïate ragioniam del monte
che sempre ha le nutrice nostre seco.

    Euripide v'è nosco e Antifonte,   106
Simonide, Agatone e altri piùe
Greci che già di lauro ornar la fronte.

when you declared: 'The ages are renewed;   70
justice and man's first time on earth return;
from Heaven a new progeny descends.'

Through you I was a poet and, through you,   73
a Christian; but that you may see more plainly,
I'll set my hand to color what I sketch.

Disseminated by the messengers   76
of the eternal kingdom, the true faith
by then had penetrated all the world,

and the new preachers preached in such accord   79
with what you'd said (and I have just repeated),
that I was drawn into frequenting them.

Then they appeared to me to be so saintly   82
that, when Domitian persecuted them,
my own laments accompanied their grief;

and while I could—as long as I had life—   85
I helped them, and their honest practices
made me disdainful of all other sects.

Before—within my poem—I'd led the Greeks   88
unto the streams of Thebes, I was baptized;
but out of fear, I was a secret Christian

and, for a long time, showed myself as pagan;   91
for this halfheartedness, for more than four
centuries, I circled the fourth circle.

And now may you, who lifted up the lid   94
that hid from me the good of which I speak,
while time is left us as we climb, tell me

where is our ancient Terence, and Caecilius   97
and Plautus, where is Varius, if you know;
tell me if they are damned, and in what quarter."

"All these and Persius, I, and many others,"   100
my guide replied, "are with that Greek to whom
the Muses gave their gifts in greatest measure.

Our place is the blind prison, its first circle;   103
and there we often talk about the mountain
where those who were our nurses always dwell.

Euripides is with us, Antiphon,   106
Simonides, and Agathon, as well
as many other Greeks who once wore laurel

Quivi si veggion de le genti tue   109
Antigone, Deïfile e Argia,
e Ismene sì trista come fue.

Védeisi quella che mostrò Langia;   112
èvvi la figlia di Tiresia, e Teti,
e con le suore sue Deïdamia."

Tacevansi ambedue già li poeti,   115
di novo attenti a riguardar dintorno,
liberi da saliri e da pareti;

e già le quattro ancelle eran del giorno   118
rimase a dietro, e la quinta era al temo,
drizzando pur in sù l'ardente corno,

quando il mio duca: "Io credo ch'a lo stremo   121
le destre spalle volger ne convegna,
girando il monte come far solemo."

Così l'usanza fu lì nostra insegna,   124
e prendemmo la via con men sospetto
per l'assentir di quell' anima degna.

Elli givan dinanzi, e io soletto   127
di retro, e ascoltava i lor sermoni,
ch'a poetar mi davano intelletto.

Ma tosto ruppe le dolci ragioni   130
un alber che trovammo in mezza strada,
con pomi a odorar soavi e buoni;

e come abete in alto si digrada   133
di ramo in ramo, così quello in giuso,
cred' io, perché persona sù non vada.

Dal lato onde 'l cammin nostro era chiuso,   136
cadea de l'alta roccia un liquor chiaro
e si spandeva per le foglie suso.

Li due poeti a l'alber s'appressaro;   139
e una voce per entro le fronde
gridò: "Di questo cibo avrete caro."

Poi disse: "Più pensava Maria onde   142
fosser le nozze orrevoli e intere,
ch'a la sua bocca, ch'or per voi risponde.

E le Romane antiche, per lor bere,   145
contente furon d'acqua; e Daniello
dispregiò cibo e acquistò savere.

upon their brow; and there—of your own people—   109
one sees Antigone, Deiphyle,
Ismene, sad still, Argia as she was.

There one can see the woman who showed Langia,   112
and there, Tiresias' daughter; there is Thetis;
and, with her sisters, there, Deidamia."

Both poets now were silent, once again   115
intent on their surroundings—they were free
of stairs and walls; with day's first four handmaidens

already left behind, and with the fifth   118
guiding the chariot-pole and lifting it,
so that its horn of flame rose always higher,

my master said: "I think it's time that we   121
turn our right shoulders toward the terrace edge,
circling the mountain in the way we're used to."

In this way habit served us as a banner;   124
and when we chose that path, our fear was less
because that worthy soul gave his assent.

Those two were in the lead; I walked alone,   127
behind them, listening to their colloquy,
which taught me much concerning poetry.

But their delightful conversation soon   130
was interrupted by a tree that blocked
our path; its fruits were fine, their scent was sweet,

and even as a fir-tree tapers upward   133
from branch to branch, that tree there tapered downward,
so as—I think—to ward off any climber.

Upon our left, where wall enclosed our path,   136
bright running water fell from the high rock
and spread itself upon the leaves above.

When the two poets had approached the tree,   139
a voice emerging from within the leaves
cried out: "This food shall be denied to you."

Then it cried: "Mary's care was for the marriage—   142
feast's being seemly and complete, not for
her mouth (which now would intercede for you).

And when they drank, of old, the Roman women   145
were satisfied with water; and young Daniel,
through his disdain of food, acquired wisdom.

    Lo secol primo quant' oro fu bello,   148
fé savorose con fame le ghiande,
e nettare con sete ogne ruscello.

    Mele e locuste furon le vivande   151
che nodriro il Batista nel diserto;
per ch'elli è glorïoso e tanto grande
    quanto per lo Vangelio v'è aperto."   154

The first age was as fair as gold: when hungry, 148
men found the taste of acorns good; when thirsty,
they found that every little stream was nectar.

When he was in the wilderness, the Baptist 151
had fed on nothing more than honey, locusts:
for this he was made great, as glorious

as, in the Gospel, is made plain to you." 154

CANTO XXIII

Mentre che li occhi per la fronda verde
ficcava ïo sì come far suole
chi dietro a li uccellin sua vita perde,

lo più che padre mi dicea: "Figliuole,   4
vienne oramai, ché 'l tempo che n'è imposto
più utilmente compartir si vuole."

Io volsi 'l viso, e 'l passo non men tosto,   7
appresso i savi, che parlavan sìe,
che l'andar mi facean di nullo costo.

Ed ecco piangere e cantar s'udìe   10
"Labïa mëa, Domine" per modo
tal, che diletto e doglia parturìe.

"O dolce padre, che è quel ch'i' odo?"   13
comincia' io; ed elli: "Ombre che vanno
forse di lor dover solvendo il nodo."

Sì come i peregrin pensosi fanno,   16
giugnendo per cammin gente non nota,
che si volgono ad essa e non restanno,

così di retro a noi, più tosto mota,   19
venendo e trapassando ci ammirava
d'anime turba tacita e devota.

Ne li occhi era ciascuna oscura e cava,   22
palida ne la faccia, e tanto scema
che da l'ossa la pelle s'informava.

Non credo che così a buccia strema   25
Erisittone fosse fatto secco,
per digiunar, quando più n'ebbe tema.

Io dicea fra stesso pensando: "Ecco   28
la gente che perdé Ierusalemme,
quando Maria nel figlio diè di becco!"

*Still the Sixth Terrace: the Gluttonous. Encounter with Forese Donati,
Dante's friend, who explains the punishment of the Gluttonous, condemned to emaciating hunger and thirst; praises his widow, Nella; and
rebukes the shameless women of Florence. Dante's presentation of Virgil
and Statius.*

While I was peering so intently through
   the green boughs, like a hunter who, so used,
would waste his life in chasing after birds,

   my more than father said to me: "Now come,   4
son, for the time our journey can permit
is to be used more fruitfully than this."

   I turned my eyes, and I was no less quick   7
to turn my steps; I followed those two sages,
whose talk was such, my going brought no loss.

   And—there!—*"Labï mëa, Domine"*   10
was wept and sung and heard in such a manner
that it gave birth to both delight and sorrow.

   "O gentle father, what is this I hear?"   13
I asked. And he: "Perhaps they're shades who go
loosening the knot of what they owe."

   Even as pensive pilgrims do, who when   16
they've overtaken folk unknown to them
along the way, will turn but will not stop,

   so, overtaking us—they had come from   19
behind but were more swift—a crowd of souls,
devout and silent, looked at us in wonder.

   Each shade had dark and hollow eyes; their faces   22
were pale and so emaciated that
their taut skin took its shape from bones beneath.

   I don't believe that even Erysichthon   25
had been so dried, down to his very hide,
by hunger, when his fast made him fear most.

   Thinking, I told myself: "I see the people   28
who lost Jerusalem, when Mary plunged
her beak into her son." The orbits of

Parean l'occhiaie anella sanza gemme: 31
chi nel viso de li uomini legge "omo"
ben avria quivi conosciuta l'emme.

Chi crederebbe che l'odor d'un pomo   34
sì governasse, generando brama,
e quel d'un'acqua, non sappiendo como?

Già era in ammirar che sì li affama,   37
per la cagione ancor non manifesta
di lor magrezza e di lor trista squama,

ed ecco del profondo de la testa   40
volse a me li occhi un'ombra e guardò fiso;
poi gridò forte: "Qual grazia m'è questa?"

Mai non l'avrei riconosciuto al viso;   43
ma ne la voce sua mi fu palese
ciò che l'aspetto in sé avea conquiso.

Questa favilla tutta mi raccese   46
mia conoscenza a la cangiata labbia,
e ravvisai la faccia di Forese.

"Deh, non contendere a l'asciutta scabbia   49
che mi scolora," pregava, "la pelle,
né a difetto di carne ch'io abbia;

ma dimmi il ver di te, dì chi son quelle   52
due anime che là ti fanno scorta;
non rimaner che tu non mi favelle!"

"La faccia tua, ch'io lagrimai già morta,   55
mi dà di pianger mo non minor doglia,"
rispuos' io lui, "veggendola sì torta.

Però mi dì, per Dio, che sì vi sfoglia;   58
non mi far dir mentr' io mi maraviglio,
ché mal può dir chi è pien d'altra voglia."

Ed elli a me: "De l'etterno consiglio   61
cade vertù ne l'acqua e ne la pianta
rimasa dietro, ond' io sì m'assottiglio.

Tutta esta gente che piangendo canta   64
per seguitar la gola oltra misura,
in fame e 'n sete qui si rifà santa.

Di bere e di mangiar n'accende cura   67
l'odor ch'esce del pomo e de lo sprazzo
che si distende su per sua verdura.

their eyes seemed like a ring that's lost its gems;   31
and he who, in the face of man, would read
OMO would here have recognized the *M*.

Who—if he knew not how—would have believed   34
that longing born from odor of a tree,
odor of water, could reduce souls so?

I was already wondering what had   37
so famished them (for I had not yet learned
the reason for their leanness and sad scurf),

when—there!—a shade, his eyes deep in his head,   40
turned toward me, staring steadily; and then
he cried aloud: "What grace is granted me!"

I never would have recognized him by   43
his face; and yet his voice made plain to me
what his appearance had obliterated.

This spark rekindled in me everything   46
I knew about those altered features; thus,
I realized it was Forese's face.

"Ah, don't reproach me for the dried-out scabs   49
that stain my skin," he begged, "nor for the lack
of flesh on me; but do tell me the truth

about yourself, do tell me who those two   52
souls there are, those who are escorting you;
may you not keep yourself from speaking to me!"

"Your face, which I once wept on when you died,"   55
I answered him, "now gives me no less cause
for sad lament, seeing you so deformed.

But tell me, for God's sake, what has unleaved   58
you so; don't make me speak while I'm amazed—
he who's distracted answers clumsily."

And he to me: "From the eternal counsel,   61
the water and the tree you left behind
receive the power that makes me waste away.

All of these souls who, grieving, sing because   64
their appetite was gluttonous, in thirst
and hunger here resanctify themselves.

The fragrance of the fruit and of the water   67
that's sprayed through that green tree kindles in us
craving for food and drink; and not once only,

E non pur una volta, questo spazzo   70
girando, si rinfresca nostra pena:
io dico pena, e dovria dir sollazzo,

    ché quella voglia a li alberi ci mena   73
che menò Cristo lieto a dire *'Eli,'*
quando ne liberò con la sua vena."

    E io a lui: "Forese, da quel dì   76
nel qual mutasti mondo a miglior vita,
cinqu' anni non son vòlti infino a qui.

    Se prima fu la possa in te finita   79
di peccar più, che sovvenisse l'ora
del buon dolor ch'a Dio ne rimarita,

    come se' tu qua sù venuto ancora?   82
Io ti credea trovar là giù di sotto,
dove tempo per tempo si ristora."

    Ond' elli a me: "Sì tosto m'ha condotto   85
a ber lo dolce assenzo d'i martìri
la Nella mia con suo pianger dirotto.

    Con suoi prieghi devoti e con sospiri   88
tratto m'ha de la costa ove s'aspetta,
e liberato m'ha de li altri giri.

    Tanto è a Dio più cara e più diletta   91
la vedovella mia, che molto amai,
quanto in bene operare è più soletta;

    ché la Barbagia di Sardigna assai   94
ne le femmine sue più è pudica
che la Barbagia dov' io la lasciai.

    O dolce frate, che vuo' tu ch'io dica?   97
Tempo futuro m'è già nel cospetto,
cui non sarà quest' ora molto antica,

    nel qual sarà in pergamo interdetto   100
a le sfacciate donne fiorentine
l'andar mostrando con le poppe il petto.

    Quai barbare fuor mai, quai saracine,   103
cui bisognasse, par farle ir coperte,
o spiritali o altre discipline?

    Ma se le svergognate fosser certe   106
di quel che 'l ciel veloce loro ammanna,
già per urlare avrian le bocche aperte;

    as we go round this space, our pain's renewed—   70
I speak of pain but I should speak of solace,
for we are guided to those trees by that

    same longing that had guided Christ when He   73
had come to free us through the blood He shed
and, in His joyousness, called out: *'Eli.'* "

    And I to him: "Forese, from that day   76
when you exchanged the world for better life
until now, less than five years have revolved;

    and if you waited for the moment when   79
the power to sin was gone before you found
the hour of the good grief that succors us

    and weds us once again to God, how have   82
you come so quickly here? I thought to find
you down below, where time must pay for time."

    And he to me: "It is my Nella who,   85
with her abundant tears, has guided me
to drink the sweet wormwood of torments: she,

    with sighs and prayers devout has set me free   88
of that slope where one waits and has freed me
from circles underneath this circle. She—

    my gentle widow, whom I loved most dearly—   91
was all the more beloved and prized by God
as she is more alone in her good works.

    For even the Barbagia of Sardinia   94
is far more modest in its women than
is that Barbagia where I left her. O

    sweet brother, what would you have had me say?   97
A future time's already visible
to me—a time not too far-off from now—

    when, from the pulpit, it shall be forbidden   100
to those immodest ones—Florentine women—
to go displaying bosoms with bare paps.

    What ordinances—spiritual, civil—   103
were ever needed by barbarian or
Saracen women to make them go covered?

    But if those shameless ones had certain knowledge   106
of what swift Heaven's readying for them,
then they would have mouths open now to howl;

ché, se l'antiveder qui non m'inganna,   109
prima fien triste che le guance impeli
colui che mo si consola con nanna.

Deh, frate, or fa che più non mi ti celi!   112
vedi che non pur io, ma questa gente
tutta rimira là dove 'l sol veli."

Per ch'io a lui: "Se tu riduci a mente   115
qual fosti meco, e qual io teco fui,
ancor fia grave il memorar presente.

Di quella vita mi volse costui   118
che mi va innanzi, l'altr' ier, quando tonda
vi si mostrò la suora di colui,"

e 'l sol mostrai; "costui per la profonda   121
notte menato m'ha d'i veri morti
con questa vera carne che 'l seconda.

Indi m'han tratto sù li suoi conforti,   124
salendo e rigirando la montagna
che drizza voi che 'l mondo fece torti.

Tanto dice di farmi sua compagna   127
che io sarò là dove fia Beatrice;
quivi convien che sanza lui rimagna.

Virgilio è questi che così mi dice,"   130
e addita'lo; "e quest' altro è quell' ombra
per cuï scosse dianzi ogne pendice

lo vostro regno, che da sé lo sgombra."   133

for if our foresight here does not deceive me,   109
they will be sad before the cheeks of those
whom lullabies can now appease grow beards.

Ah, brother, do not hide things any longer!   112
You see that I am not alone, for all
these people stare at where you veil the sun."

At this I said to him: "If you should call   115
to mind what you have been with me and I
with you, remembering now will still be heavy.

He who precedes me turned me from that life   118
some days ago, when she who is the sister
of him"—I pointed to the sun—"was showing

her roundness to you. It is he who's led   121
me through the deep night of the truly dead
with this true flesh that follows after him.

His help has drawn me up from there, climbing   124
and circling round this mountain, which makes straight
you whom the world made crooked. And he says

that he will bear me company until   127
I reach the place where Beatrice is; there
I must remain without him. It is Virgil

who speaks to me in this way," and I pointed   130
to him; "this other is the shade for whom,
just now, your kingdom caused its every slope

to tremble as it freed him from itself."   133

XXIII

22

XXIV·123

CANTO XXIV

Né 'l dir l'andar, né l'andar lui più lento
  facea, ma ragionando andavam forte,
sì come nave pinta da buon vento;

  e l'ombre, che parean cose rimorte,   4
per le fosse de li occhi ammirazione
traean di me, di mio vivere accorte.

  E io, continüando al mio sermone,   7
disse: "Ella sen va sù forse più tarda
che non farebbe, per altrui cagione.

  Ma dimmi, se tu sai, dov' è Piccarda;   10
dimmi s'io veggio da notar persona
tra questa gente che sì mi riguarda."

  "La mia sorella, che tra bella e buona   13
non so qual fosse più, trïunfa lieta
ne l'alto Olimpo già di sua corona."

  Sì disse prima; e poi: "Qui non si vieta   16
di nominar ciascun, da ch'è sì munta
nostra sembianza via per la dïeta.

  "Questi," e mostrò col dito, "è Bonagiunta,   19
Bonagiunta da Lucca; e quella faccia
di là da lui più che l'altre trapunta

  ebbe la Santa Chiesa in le sue braccia: 22
dal Torso fu, e purga per digiuno
l'anguille di Bolsena e la vernaccia."

  Molti altri mi nomò ad uno ad uno;   25
e del nomar parean tutti contenti,
sì ch'io però non vidi un atto bruno.

  Vidi per fame a vòto usar li denti   28
Ubaldin da la Pila e Bonifazio
che pasturò col rocco molte genti.

Our talking did not slow our pace, our pace
    not slow our talking; but conversing, we
moved quickly, like a boat a fair wind drives.

    And recognizing that I was alive,   4
the shades—they seemed to be things twice dead—drew
amazement from the hollows of their eyes.

    And I, continuing my telling, added: 7
"Perhaps he is more slow in his ascent
than he would be had he not met the other.

    But tell me, if you can: where is Piccarda?   10
And tell me if, among those staring at me,
I can see any person I should note."

    "My sister—and I know not whether she   13
was greater in her goodness or her beauty—
on high Olympus is in triumph; she

    rejoices in her crown already," he   16
began, then added: "It is not forbidden
to name each shade here—abstinence has eaten

    away our faces." And he pointed: "This   19
is Bonagiunta, Bonagiunta da
Lucca; the one beyond him, even more

    emaciated than the rest, had clasped   22
the Holy Church; he was from Tours; his fast
purges Bolsena's eels, Vernaccia's wine."

    And he named many others, one by one,   25
and, at their naming, they all seemed content;
so that—for this—no face was overcast.

    I saw—their teeth were biting emptiness—   28
both Ubaldin da la Pila and Boniface,
who shepherded so many with his staff.

Vidi messer Marchese, ch'ebbe spazio   31
già di bere a Forlì con men secchezza,
e sì fu tal, che non si sentì sazio.

Ma come fa chi guarda e poi s'apprezza   34
più d'un che d'altro, fei a quel da Lucca,
che più parea di me aver contezza.

El mormorava; e non so che "Gentucca"   37
sentiv' io là, ov' el sentia la piaga
de la giustizia che sì li pilucca.

"O anima," diss' io, "che par sì vaga   40
di parlar meco, fa sì ch'io t'intenda,
e te e me col tuo parlare appaga."

"Femmina è nata, e non porta ancor benda,"   43
cominciò el, "che ti farà piacere
la mia città, come ch'om la riprenda.

Tu te n'andrai con questo antivedere: 46
se nel mio mormorar prendesti errore,
dichiareranti ancor le cose vere.

Ma dì s'i' veggio qui colui che fore   49
trasse le nove rime, cominciando
'Donne ch'avete intelletto d'amore.' "

E io a lui: "I' mi son un che, quando   52
Amor mi spira, noto, e a quel modo
ch'e' ditta dentro vo significando."

"O frate, issa vegg' io," diss' elli, "il nodo   55
che 'l Notaro e Guittone e me ritenne
di qua dal dolce stil novo ch'i' odo.

Io veggio ben come le vostre penne   58
di retro al dittator sen vanno strette,
che de le nostre certo non avvenne;

e qual più a gradire oltre si mette,   61
non vede più da l'uno a l'altro stilo";
e, quasi contentato, si tacette.

Come li augei che vernan lungo 'l Nilo,   64
alcuna volta in aere fanno schiera,
poi volan più a fretta e vanno in filo,

così tutta la gente che lì era,   67
volgendo 'l viso, raffrettò suo passo,
e per magrezza e per voler leggera.

    I saw Messer Marchese, who once had   31
more ease, less dryness, drinking at Forlì
and yet could never satisfy his thirst.

    But just as he who looks and then esteems   34
one more than others, so did I prize him
of Lucca, for he seemed to know me better.

    He murmured; something like "Gentucca" was   37
what I heard from the place where he could feel
the wound of justice that denudes them so.

    "O soul," I said, "who seems so eager to   40
converse with me, do speak so that I hear you,
for speech may satisfy both you and me."

    He answered: "Although men condemn my city,   43
there is a woman born—she wears no veil
as yet—because of whom you'll find it pleasing.

    You are to journey with this prophecy;   46
and if there's something in my murmuring
you doubt, events themselves will bear me out.

    But tell me if the man whom I see here   49
is he who brought the new rhymes forth, beginning:
'Ladies who have intelligence of love.' "

    I answered: "I am one who, when Love breathes   52
in me, takes note; what he, within, dictates,
I, in that way, without, would speak and shape."

    "O brother, now I see," he said, "the knot   55
that kept the Notary, Guittone, and me
short of the sweet new manner that I hear.

    I clearly see how your pens follow closely   58
behind him who dictates, and certainly
that did not happen with our pens; and he

    who sets himself to ferreting profoundly   61
can find no other difference between
the two styles." He fell still, contentedly.

    Even as birds that winter on the Nile   64
at times will slow and form a flock in air,
then speed their flight and form a file, so all

    the people who were there moved much more swiftly,   67
turning away their faces, hurrying
their pace because of leanness and desire.

E come l'uom che di trottare è lasso,   70
lascia andar li compagni, e sì passeggia
fin che si sfoghi l'affollar del casso,

sì lasciò trapassar la santa greggia   73
Forese, e dietro meco sen veniva,
dicendo: "Quando fïa ch'io ti riveggia?"

"Non so," rispuos' io lui, "quant' io mi viva;   76
ma già non fïa il tornar mio tantosto,
ch'io non sia col voler prima a la riva;

però che 'l loco u' fui a viver posto,   79
di giorno in giorno più di ben si spolpa,
e a trista ruina par disposto."

"Or va," diss' el; "che quei che più n'ha colpa,   82
vegg' ïo a coda d'una bestia tratto
inver' la valle ove mai non si scolpa.

La bestia ad ogne passo va più ratto,   85
crescendo sempre, fin ch'ella il percuote,
e lascia il corpo vilmente disfatto.

Non hanno molto a volger quelle ruote,"   88
e drizzò li occhi al ciel, "che ti fia chiaro
ciò che 'l mio dir più dichiarar non puote.

Tu ti rimani omai; ché 'l tempo è caro   91
in questo regno, sì ch'io perdo troppo
venendo teco sì a paro a paro."

Qual esce alcuna volta di gualoppo   94
lo cavalier di schiera che cavalchi,
e va per farsi onor del primo intoppo,

tal si partì da noi con maggior valchi;   97
e io rimasi in via con esso i due
che fuor del mondo sì gran marescalchi.

E quando innanzi a noi intrato fue,   100
che li occhi miei si fero a lui seguaci,
come la mente a le parole sue,

parvermi i rami gravidi e vivaci   103
d'un altro pomo, e non molto lontani
per esser pur allora vòlto in laci.

Vidi gente sott' esso alzar le mani   106
e gridar non so che verso le fronde,
quasi bramosi fantolini e vani

And just as he who's tired of running lets   70
his comrades go ahead and slows his steps
until he's eased the panting of his chest,

so did Forese let the holy flock   73
pass by and move, behind, with me, saying:
"How long before I shall see you again?"

"I do not know," I said, "how long I'll live;   76
and yet, however quick is my return,
my longing for these shores would have me here

sooner—because the place where I was set   79
to live is day by day deprived of good
and seems along the way to wretched ruin."

"Do not be vexed," he said, "for I can see   82
the guiltiest of all dragged by a beast's
tail to the valley where no sin is purged.

At every step the beast moves faster, always   85
gaining momentum, till it smashes him
and leaves his body squalidly undone.

Those wheels," and here he looked up at the sky,   88
"do not have long to turn before you see
plainly what I can't tell more openly.

Now you remain behind, for time is costly   91
here in this kingdom; I should lose too much
by moving with you thus, at equal pace."

Just as a horseman sometimes gallops out,   94
leaving behind his troop of riders, so
that he may gain the honor of the first

clash—so, with longer strides, did he leave us;   97
and I remained along my path with those
two who were such great marshals of the world.

And when he'd gone so far ahead of us   100
that my eyes strained to follow him, just as
my mind was straining after what he'd said,

the branches of another tree, heavy   103
with fruit, alive with green, appeared to me
nearby, just past a curve where I had turned.

Beneath the tree I saw shades lifting hands,   106
crying I know not what up toward the branches,
like little eager, empty-headed children,

che pregano, e 'l pregato non risponde,   109
ma, per fare esser ben la voglia acuta,
tien alto lor disio e nol nasconde.

Poi si partì sì come ricreduta;   112
e noi venimmo al grande arbore adesso,
che tanti prieghi e lagrime rifiuta.

"Trapassate oltre sanza farvi presso: 115
legno è più sù che fu morso da Eva,
e questa pianta si levò da esso."

Sì tra le frasche non so chi diceva;   118
per che Virgilio e Stazio e io, ristretti,
oltre andavam dal lato che si leva.

"Ricordivi," dicea, "d'i maladetti   121
nei nuvoli formati, che, satolli,
Tesëo combatter co' doppi petti;

e de li Ebrei ch'al ber si mostrar molli,   124
per che no i volle Gedeon compagni,
quando inver' Madïan discese i colli."

Sì accostati a l'un d'i due vivagni   127
passammo, udendo colpe de la gola
seguite già da miseri guadagni.

Poi, rallargati per la strada sola,   130
ben mille passi e più ci portar oltre,
contemplando ciascun sanza parola.

"Che andate pensando sì voi sol tre?"   133
sùbita voce disse; ond' io mi scossi
come fan bestie spaventate e poltre.

Drizzai la testa per veder chi fossi;   136
e già mai non si videro in fornace
vetri o metalli sì lucenti e rossi,

com' io vidi un che dicea: "S'a voi piace   139
montare in sù, qui si convien dar volta;
quinci si va chi vuole andar per pace."

L'aspetto suo m'avea la vista tolta;   142
per ch'io mi volsi dietro a' miei dottori,
com' om che va secondo ch'elli ascolta.

E quale, annunziatrice de li albori,   145
l'aura di maggio movesi e olezza,
tutta impregnata da l'erba e da' fiori;

who beg—but he of whom they beg does not   109
reply, but to provoke their longing, he
holds high, and does not hide, the thing they want.

Then they departed as if disabused;   112
and we—immediately—reached that great tree,
which turns aside so many prayers and tears.

"Continue on, but don't draw close to it;   115
there is a tree above from which Eve ate,
and from that tree above, this plant was raised."

Among the boughs, a voice—I know not whose—   118
spoke so; thus, drawing closer, Virgil, Statius,
and I edged on, along the side that rises.

It said: "Remember those with double chests,   121
the miserable ones, born of the clouds,
whom Theseus battled when they'd gorged themselves;

and those whom Gideon refused as comrades—   124
those Hebrews who had drunk too avidly—
when he came down the hills to Midian."

So, keeping close to one of that road's margins,   127
we moved ahead, hearing of gluttony—
its sins repaid by sorry penalties.

Then, with more space along the lonely path,   130
a thousand steps and more had brought us forward,
each of us meditating wordlessly.

"What are you thinking of, you three who walk   133
alone?" a sudden voice called out; at which
I started—like a scared young animal.

I raised my head to see who it might be;   136
no glass or metal ever seen within
a furnace was so glowing or so red

as one I saw, who said: "If you'd ascend,   139
then you must turn at this point; for whoever
would journey unto peace must pass this way."

But his appearance had deprived me of   142
my sight, so that—as one who uses hearing
as guide—I turned and followed my two teachers.

And like the breeze of May that—heralding   145
the dawning of the day—when it is steeped
in flowers and in grass, stirs fragrantly,

   tal mi senti' un vento dar per mezza   148
la fronte, e ben senti' mover la piuma,
che fé sentir d'ambrosïa l'orezza.

   E senti' dir: "Beati cui alluma   151
tanto di grazia, che l'amor del gusto
nel petto lor troppo disir non fuma,

      esurïendo sempre quanto è giusto!"   154

so did I feel the wind that blew against 148
the center of my brow, and clearly sensed
the movement of his wings, the air's ambrosia.

And then I heard: "Blessed are those whom grace 151
illumines so, that, in their breasts, the love
of taste does not awake too much desire—

whose hungering is always in just measure." 154

CANTO XXV

Ora era onde 'l salir non volea storpio;
   ché 'l sole avëa il cerchio di merigge
lasciato al Tauro e la notte a lo Scorpio:

   per che, come fa l'uom che non s'affigge   4
ma vassi a la via sua, che che li appaia,
se di bisogno stimolo il trafigge,

   così intrammo noi per la callaia,   7
uno innanzi altro prendendo la scala
che per artezza i salitor dispaia.

   E quale il cicognin che leva l'ala   10
per voglia di volare, e non s'attenta
d'abbandonar lo nido, e giù la cala;

   tal era io con voglia accesa e spenta   13
di dimandar, venendo infino a l'atto
che fa colui ch'a dicer s'argomenta.

   Non lasciò, per l'andar che fosse ratto,   16
lo dolce padre mio, ma disse: "Scocca
l'arco del dir, che 'nfino al ferro hai tratto."

   Allor sicuramente apri' la bocca   19
e cominciai: "Come si può far magro
là dove l'uopo di nodrir non tocca?"

   "Se t'ammentassi come Meleagro   22
si consumò al consumar d'un stizzo,
non fora," disse, "a te questo sì agro;

   e se pensassi come, al vostro guizzo,   25
guizza dentro a lo specchio vostra image,
ciò che par duro ti parrebbe vizzo.

   Ma perché dentro a tuo voler t'adage,   28
ecco qui Stazio; e io lui chiamo e prego
che sia or sanator de le tue piage."

From the Sixth to the Seventh Terrace: the Lustful. Hour and mode of as-cent to the Seventh Terrace. Dante's queries about the leanness of bodi-less shades. Statius' explanation of generation, souls after death, and aerial bodies. The punishment of the Lustful, purification through fire. The Lustful shouting examples of chastity: the Virgin Mary and Diana.

The hour when climbers cannot pause had come:
　　the sun had left to Taurus the meridian,
and night had left it to the Scorpion.

　　Therefore, like one who will not stop but moves   4
along his path, no matter what he sees,
if he is goaded by necessity,

　　we made our way into the narrow gap   7
and, one behind the other, took the stairs
so strait that climbers there must separate.

　　And as the fledgling stork will lift its wing   10
because it wants to fly, but dares not try
to leave the nest, and lets its wing drop back,

　　so I, with my desire to question kindled   13
then spent, arrived as far as making ready
to speak. But my dear father, though our steps

　　were hurrying, did not stop talking, for   16
he said: "The iron of the arrow's touched
the longbow; let the shaft of speech fly off."

　　Then I had confidence enough to open   19
my mouth and ask him: "How can one grow lean
where there is never need for nourishment?"

　　"If you recall how Meleager was   22
consumed," he said, "just when the firebrand
was spent, this won't be hard to understand;

　　and if you think how, though your body's swift,   25
your image in the mirror captures it,
then what perplexed will seem to you transparent.

　　But that your will to know may be appeased,   28
here's Statius, and I call on him and ask
that he now be the healer of your doubts."

"Se la veduta etterna li dislego,"   31
rispuose Stazio, "là dove tu sie,
discolpi me non potert' io far nego."

Poi cominciò: "Se le parole mie,   34
figlio, la mente tua guarda e riceve,
lume ti fiero al come che tu die.

Sangue perfetto, che poi non si beve   37
da l'assetate vene, e si rimane
quasi alimento che di mensa leve,

prende nel core a tutte membra umane   40
virtute informativa, come quello
ch'a farsi quelle per le vene vane.

Ancor digesto, scende ov' è più bello   43
tacer che dire; e quindi poscia geme
sovr' altrui sangue in natural vasello.

Ivi s'accoglie l'uno e l'altro insieme,   46
l'un disposto a patire, e l'altro a fare
per lo perfetto loco onde si preme;

e, giunto lui, comincia ad operare   49
coagulando prima, e poi avviva
ciò che per sua matera fé constare.

Anima fatta la virtute attiva   52
qual d'una pianta, in tanto differente,
che questa è in via e quella è già a riva,

tanto ovra poi, che già si move e sente,   55
come spungo marino; e indi imprende
ad organar le posse ond' è semente.

Or si spiega, figliuolo, or si distende   58
la virtù ch'è dal cor del generante,
dove natura a tutte membra intende.

Ma come d'animal divegna fante,   61
non vedi tu ancor: quest' è tal punto,
che più savio di te fé già errante,

sì che per sua dottrina fé disgiunto   64
da l'anima il possibile intelletto,
perché da lui non vide organo assunto.

Apri a la verità che viene il petto;   67
e sappi che, sì tosto come al feto
l'articular del cerebro è perfetto,

"If I explain eternal ways to him,"   31
Statius replied, "while you are present here,
let my excuse be: I cannot refuse you."

Then he began: "If, son, your mind receives   34
and keeps my words, then what I say will serve
as light upon the *how* that you have asked.

The thirsty veins drink up the perfect blood—   37
but not all of that blood: a portion's left,
like leavings that are taken from the table.

Within the heart, that part acquires power   40
to form all of another's human limbs,
as blood that flows through veins feeds one's own limbs.

Digested yet again, that part descends   43
to what is best not named; from there it drips
into the natural receptacle,

upon another's blood; the two bloods mix,   46
one ready to be passive and one active
because a perfect place, the heart, prepared them.

The active, having reached the passive, starts   49
to work: first it coagulates—and then
quickens—the matter it has made more dense.

Having become a soul (much like a plant,   52
though with this difference—a plant's complete,
whereas a fetus still is journeying),

the active virtue labors, so the fetus   55
may move and feel, like a sea-sponge; and then
it starts to organize the powers it's seeded.

At this point, son, the power that had come   58
from the begetter's heart unfolds and spreads,
that nature may see every limb perfected.

But how the animal becomes a speaking   61
being, you've not yet seen; this point's so hard,
it led one wiser than you are to err

in separating from the possible   64
intellect the soul, since he could see
no organ for the mind—so did he teach.

Open your heart to truth we now have reached   67
and know that, once the brain's articulation
within the fetus has attained perfection,

   lo motor primo a lui si volge lieto   70
sovra tant' arte di natura, e spira
spirito novo, di vertù repleto,

   che ciò che trova attivo quivi, tira   73
in sua sustanzia, e fassi un'alma sola,
che vive e sente e sé in sé rigira.

   E perché meno ammiri la parola,   76
guarda il calor del sol che si fa vino,
giunto a l'omor che de la vite cola.

   Quando Làchesis non ha più del lino,   79
solvesi da la carne, e in virtute
ne porta seco e l'umano e 'l divino:

   l'altre potenze tutte quante mute;   82
memoria, intelligenza e volontade
in atto molto più che prima agute.

   Sanza restarsi, per sé stessa cade   85
mirabilmente a l'una de le rive;
quivi conosce prima le sue strade.

   Tosto che loco lì la circunscrive,   88
la virtù formativa raggia intorno
così e quanto ne le membra vive.

   E come l'aere, quand' è ben pïorno,   91
per l'altrui raggio che 'n sé si reflette,
di diversi color diventa addorno;

   così l'aere vicin quivi si mette   94
e in quella forma ch'è in lui suggella
virtüalmente l'alma che ristette;

   e simigliante poi a la fiammella   97
che segue il foco là 'vunque si muta,
segue lo spirto sua forma novella.

   Però che quindi ha poscia sua paruta,   100
è chiamata ombra; e quindi organa poi
ciascun sentire infino a la veduta.

   Quindi parliamo e quindi ridiam noi;   103
quindi facciam le lagrime e ' sospiri
che per lo monte aver sentiti puoi.

   Secondo che ci affliggono i disiri   106
e li altri affetti, l'ombra si figura;
e quest' è la cagion di che tu miri."

then the First Mover turns toward it with joy   70
on seeing so much art in nature and
breathes into it new spirit—vigorous—

which draws all that is active in the fetus   73
into its substance and becomes one soul
that lives and feels and has self-consciousness.

That what I say may leave you less perplexed,   76
consider the sun's heat that, when combined
with sap that flows from vines, is then made wine.

And when Lachesis lacks more thread, then soul's   79
divided from the flesh; potentially,
it bears with it the human and divine;

but with the human powers mute, the rest—   82
intelligence and memory and will—
are more acute in action than they were.

With no delay, the soul falls of itself—   85
astonishingly—on one of two shores;
there it learns—early—what way it will journey.

There, once the soul is circumscribed by space,   88
the power that gives form irradiates
as—and as much as—once it formed live limbs.

And even as the saturated air,   91
since it reflects the rays the sun has sent,
takes rainbow colors as its ornament,

so there, where the soul stopped, the nearby air   94
takes on the form that soul impressed on it,
a shape that is, potentially, real body;

and then, just as a flame will follow after   97
the fire whenever fire moves, so that
new form becomes the spirit's follower.

Since from that airy body it takes on   100
its semblance, that soul is called 'shade': that shape
forms organs for each sense, even for sight.

This airy body lets us speak and laugh;   103
with it we form the tears and sigh the sighs
that you, perhaps, have heard around this mountain.

Just as we are held fast by longings and   106
by other sentiments, our shade takes form:
this is the cause of your astonishment."

E già venuto a l'ultima tortura   109
s'era per noi, e vòlto a la man destra,
ed eravamo attenti ad altra cura.

Quivi la ripa fiamma in fuor balestra,   112
e la cornice spira fiato in suso
che la reflette e via da lei sequestra;

ond' ir ne convenia dal lato schiuso   115
ad uno ad uno; e io temëa 'l foco
quinci, e quindi temeva cader giuso.

Lo duca mio dicea: "Per questo loco   118
si vuol tenere a li occhi stretto il freno,
però ch'errar potrebbesi per poco."

"Summae Deus clementïae" nel seno   121
al grande ardore allora udi' cantando,
che di volger mi fé caler non meno;

e vidi spirti per la fiamma andando;   124
per ch'io guardava a loro e a' miei passi,
compartendo la vista a quando a quando.

Appresso il fine ch'a quell' inno fassi,   127
gridavano alto: "Virum non cognosco";
indi ricominciavan l'inno bassi.

Finitolo anco, gridavano: "Al bosco   130
si tenne Diana, ed Elice caccionne
che di Venere avea sentito il tòsco."

Indi al cantar tornavano; indi donne   133
gridavano e mariti che fuor casti
come virtute e matrimonio imponne.

E questo modo credo che lor basti   136
per tutto il tempo che 'l foco li abbruscia:
con tal cura conviene e con tai pasti

che la piaga da sezzo si ricuscia.   139

By now we'd reached the final turning we   109
would meet and took the pathway right, at which
we were preoccupied with other cares.

There, from the wall, the mountain hurls its flames;   112
but, from the terrace side, there whirls a wind
that pushes back the fire and limits it;

thus, on the open side, proceeding one   115
by one, we went; I feared the fire on
the left and, on the right, the precipice.

My guide said: "On this terrace, it is best   118
to curb your eyes: the least distraction—left
or right—can mean a step you will regret."

Then, from the heart of that great conflagration,   121
I heard *"Summae Deus clementiae"*
sung—and was not less keen to turn my eyes;

and I saw spirits walking in the flames,   124
so that I looked at them and at my steps,
sharing the time I had to look at each.

After they'd reached that hymn's end, *"Virum non*   127
cognosco" were the words they cried aloud;
then they began the hymn in a low voice

again, and, done again, they cried: "Diana   130
kept to the woods and banished Helice
after she'd felt the force of Venus' poison."

Then they returned to singing; and they praised   133
aloud those wives and husbands who were chaste,
as virtue and as matrimony mandate.

This is—I think—the way these spirits act   136
as long as they are burned by fire: this is
the care and this the nourishment with which

one has to heal the final wound of all.   139

XXV · 127-133

XXVI · 42

CANTO XXVI

Mentre che sì per l'orlo, uno innanzi altro,
ce n'andavamo, e spesso il buon maestro
diceami: "Guarda: giovi ch'io ti scaltro";

   feriami il sole in su l'omero destro,   4
che già, raggiando, tutto l'occidente
mutava in bianco aspetto di cilestro;

   e io facea con l'ombra più rovente   7
parer la fiamma; e pur a tanto indizio
vidi molt' ombre, andando, poner mente.

   Questa fu la cagion che diede inizio   10
loro a parlar di me; e cominciarsi
a dir: "Colui non par corpo fittizio";

   poi verso me, quanto potëan farsi,   13
certi si fero, sempre con riguardo
di non uscir dove non fosser arsi.

   "O tu che vai, non per esser più tardo,   16
ma forse reverente, a li altri dopo,
rispondi a me che 'n sete e 'n foco ardo.

   Né solo a me la tua risposta è uopo;   19
ché tutti questi n'hanno maggior sete
che d'acqua fredda Indo o Etïopo.

   Dinne com' è che fai di te parete   22
al sol, pur come tu non fossi ancora
di morte intrato dentro da la rete."

   Sì mi parlava un d'essi; e io mi fora   25
già manifesto, s'io non fossi atteso
ad altra novità ch'apparve allora;

   ché per lo mezzo del cammino acceso   28
venne gente col viso incontro a questa,
la qual mi fece a rimirar sospeso.

Still the Seventh Terrace: the Lustful. The souls' amazement at Dante's having a body. His explanation to them. Souls coming from the opposite direction: the Lustful who sinned through unnatural acts. Colloquy with the poet Guido Guinizzelli. The poet Arnaut Daniel, who addresses Dante in Provençal.

While we moved at the edge, one first, one after,
　　and I could often hear my gentle master
saying: "Take care—and do not waste my warning,"

　　the sun, its rays already altering   4
the coloring of all the west from azure
to white, was striking me on my right shoulder.

　　And where my shadow fell, it made the flames   7
seem more inflamed; and I saw many shades
walking, intent upon a sight so strange.

　　This was the reason that first prompted them   10
to speak to me. Among themselves they said:
"He does not seem to have a fictive body."

　　Then certain of them came as close to me   13
as they were able to while, cautiously,
they never left the boundaries of their burning.

　　"O you who move behind the others not   16
because of sloth but reverence perhaps,
give me who burn in thirst and fire your answer.

　　I'm not alone in needing your response: 19
for all these shades thirst so for it—more than
an Indian or Ethiopian

　　thirsts for cool water. Tell us how you can—   22
as if you're not yet caught within death's net—
make of yourself a wall against the sun."

　　Thus one of them had spoken to me; I   25
should now have answered clearly, had I not
been fixed on something strangely evident;

　　for in the middle of the burning path,   28
came people moving opposite to these—
and I, since they moved left, stared in suspense.

Lì veggio d'ogne parte farsi presta   31
ciascun' ombra e basciarsi una con una
sanza restar, contente a brieve festa;

    così per entro loro schiera bruna   34
s'ammusa l'una con l'altra formica,
forse a spïar lor via e lor fortuna.

Tosto che parton l'accoglienza amica,   37
prima che 'l primo passo lì trascorra,
sopragridar ciascuna s'affatica:

    la nova gente: "Soddoma e Gomorra";   40
e l'altra: "Ne la vacca entra Pasife,
perché 'l torello a sua lussuria corra."

Poi, come grue ch'a le montagne Rife   43
volasser parte, e parte inver' l'arene,
queste del gel, quelle del sole schife,

    l'una gente sen va, l'altra sen vene;   46
e tornan, lagrimando, a' primi canti
e al gridar che più lor si convene;

    e raccostansi a me, come davanti,   49
essi medesmi che m'avean pregato,
attenti ad ascoltar ne' lor sembianti.

Io, che due volte avea visto lor grato,   52
incominciai: "O anime sicure
d'aver, quando che sia, di pace stato,

    non son rimase acerbe né mature   55
le membra mie di là, ma son qui meco
col sangue suo e con le sue giunture.

Quinci sù vo per non esser più cieco;   58
donna è di sopra che m'acquista grazia,
per che 'l mortal per vostro mondo reco.

Ma se la vostra maggior voglia sazia   61
tosto divegna, sì che 'l ciel v'alberghi
ch'è pien d'amore e più ampio si spazia,

    ditemi, acciò ch'ancor carte ne verghi,   64
chi siete voi, e chi è quella turba
che se ne va di retro a' vostri terghi."

Non altrimenti stupido si turba   67
lo montanaro, e rimirando ammuta,
quando rozzo e salvatico s'inurba,

There, on all sides, I can see every shade 31
move quickly to embrace another shade,
content—they did not pause—with their brief greeting,

as ants, in their dark company, will touch 34
their muzzles, each to each, perhaps to seek
news of their fortunes and their journeyings.

No sooner is their friendly greeting done 37
than each shade tries to outcry all the rest
even before he starts to move ahead,

the new group shouting: "Sodom and Gomorrah"; 40
the other: "That the bull may hurry toward
her lust, Pasiphaë hides in the cow."

Then, just like cranes, of whom a part, to flee 43
the sun, fly north to Riphean mountains, while
the rest, to flee the frost, fly toward the sands,

one group moves with—the other opposite—us; 46
and they return with tears to their first chants
and to the shout appropriate to each.

And those who had entreated me came close 49
again, in the same way they'd done before;
their faces showed how keen they were to listen.

I, seeing their desire once again, 52
began: "O souls who can be sure of gaining
the state of peace, whenever that may be,

my limbs—mature or green—have not been left 55
within the world beyond; they're here with me,
together with their blood and with their bones.

That I be blind no longer, through this place 58
I pass; above, a lady has gained grace
for me; therefore, I bear my mortal body

across your world. So may your deepest longing 61
soon be appeased and you be lodged within
the heaven that's most full of love, most spacious,

please tell me, so that I may yet transcribe it 64
upon my pages, who you are, and what
crowd moves in the direction opposite."

Each shade displayed no less astonishment 67
or less confusion than a mountaineer,
who, even as he stares about, falls silent

che ciascun' ombra fece in sua paruta;   70
ma poi che furon di stupore scarche,
lo qual ne li alti cuor tosto s'attuta,

"Beato te, che de le nostre marche,"   73
ricominciò colei che pria m'inchiese,
"per morir meglio, esperïenza imbarche!

La gente che non vien con noi, offese   76
di ciò per che già Cesar, trïunfando,
'Regina' contra sé chiamar s'intese:

però si parton 'Soddoma' gridando,   79
rimproverando a sé com' hai udito,
e aiutan l'arsura vergognando.

Nostro peccato fu ermafrodito;   82
ma perché non servammo umana legge,
seguendo come bestie l'appetito,

in obbrobrio di noi, per noi si legge,   85
quando partinci, il nome di colei
che s'imbestiò ne le 'mbestiate schegge.

Or sai nostri atti e di che fummo rei: 88
se forse a nome vuo' saper chi semo,
tempo non è di dire, e non saprei.

Farotti ben di me volere scemo: 91
son Guido Guinizzelli, e già mi purgo
per ben dolermi prima ch'a lo stremo."

Quali ne la tristizia di Ligurgo   94
si fer due figli a riveder la madre,
tal mi fec' io, ma non a tanto insurgo,

quand' io odo nomar sé stesso il padre   97
mio e de li altri miei miglior che mai
rime d'amor usar dolci e leggiadre;

e sanza udire e dir pensoso andai   100
lunga fïata rimirando lui,
né, per lo foco, in là più m'appressai.

Poi che di riguardar pasciuto fui,   103
tutto m'offersi pronto al suo servigio
con l'affermar che fa credere altrui.

Ed elli a me: "Tu lasci tal vestigio,   106
per quel ch'i' odo, in me, e tanto chiaro,
che Letè nol può tòrre né far bigio.

when, rough and rustic, he comes to the city;   70
but when they'd set aside astonishment—
that's soon subdued in noble hearts—he who

had questioned me before, began again: 73
"Blessed are you who would, in order to
die better, store experience of our lands!

The people moving opposite us shared   76
the sin for which once, while in triumph, Caesar
heard 'Queen' called out against him; that is why,

as they move off from us, they cry out 'Sodom,'   79
reproaching their own selves, as you have heard,
and through their shame abet the fire's work.

Our sin was with the other sex; but since   82
we did not keep the bounds of human law,
but served our appetites like beasts, when we

part from the other ranks, we then repeat,   85
to our disgrace, the name of one who, in
the bestial planks, became herself a beast.

You now know why we act so, and you know   88
what our sins were; if you would know our names,
time is too short, and I don't know them all.

But with regard to me, I'll satisfy   91
your wish to know: I'm Guido Guinizzelli,
purged here because I grieved before my end."

As, after the sad raging of Lycurgus,   94
two sons, finding their mother, had embraced her,
so I desired to do—but dared not to—

when I heard him declare his name: the father   97
of me and of the others—those, my betters—
who ever used sweet, gracious rhymes of love.

And without hearing, speaking, pensive, I   100
walked on, still gazing at him, a long time,
prevented by the fire from drawing closer.

When I had fed my sight on him, I offered   103
myself—with such a pledge that others must
believe—completely ready for his service.

And he to me: "Because of what I hear,   106
you leave a trace within me—one so clear,
Lethe itself can't blur or cancel it.

Ma se le tue parole or ver giuraro,   109
dimmi che è cagion per che dimostri
nel dire e nel guardar d'avermi caro."

E io a lui: "Li dolci detti vostri,   112
che, quanto durerà l'uso moderno,
faranno cari ancora i loro incostri."

"O frate," disse, "questi ch'io ti cerno   115
col dito," e additò un spirto innanzi,
"fu miglior fabbro del parlar materno.

Versi d'amore e prose di romanzi   118
soverchiò tutti; e lascia dir li stolti
che quel di Lemosì credon ch'avanzi.

A voce più ch'al ver drizzan li volti,   121
e così ferman sua oppinïone
prima ch'arte o ragion per lor s'ascolti.

Così fer molti antichi di Guittone,   124
di grido in grido pur lui dando pregio,
fin che l'ha vinto il ver con più persone.

Or se tu hai sì ampio privilegio,   127
che licito ti sia l'andare al chiostro
nel quale è Cristo abate del collegio,

falli per me un dir d'un paternostro,   130
quanto bisogna a noi di questo mondo,
dove poter peccar non è più nostro."

Poi, forse per dar luogo altrui secondo   133
che presso avea, disparve per lo foco,
come per l'acqua il pesce andando al fondo.

Io mi fei al mostrato innanzi un poco,   136
e dissi ch'al suo nome il mio disire
apparecchiava grazïoso loco.

El cominciò liberamente a dire: 139
"Tan m'abellis vostre cortes deman,
qu'ieu no me puesc ni voill a vos cobrire.

Ieu sui Arnaut, que plor e vau cantan;   142
consiros vei la passada folor,
e vei jausen lo joi qu'esper, denan.

Ara vos prec, per aquella valor   145
que vos guida al som de l'escalina,
sovenha vos a temps de ma dolor!"

Poi s'ascose nel foco che li affina.   148

    But if your words have now sworn truthfully,   109
do tell me why it is that you have shown
in speech and gaze that I am dear to you."
    And I to him: "It's your sweet lines that, for   112
as long as modern usage lasts, will still
make dear their very inks." "Brother," he said,
    "he there, whom I point out to you"—he showed   115
us one who walked ahead—"he was a better
artisan of the mother tongue, surpassing
    all those who wrote their poems of love or prose   118
romances—let the stupid ones contend,
who think that from Limoges there came the best.
    They credit rumor rather than the truth,   121
allowing their opinion to be set
before they hear what art or reason says.
    So, many of our fathers once persisted,   124
voice after voice, in giving to Guittone
the prize—but then, with most, the truth prevailed.
    Now if you are so amply privileged   127
that you will be admitted to the cloister
where Christ is abbot of the college, then
    pray say, for me, to Him, a Paternoster—   130
that is, as much of it as those in this
place need, since we have lost the power to sin."
    Then, to make place, perhaps, for those behind him,   133
he disappeared into the fire, just as
a fish, through water, plunges toward the bottom.
    Saying that my desire was making ready   136
a place of welcome for his name, I moved
ahead a little, toward the one who had
    been pointed out to me. And he spoke freely: 139
"So does your courteous request please me—
I neither could nor would conceal myself
    from you. I am Arnaut, who, going, weep   142
and sing; with grief, I see my former folly;
with joy, I see the hoped-for day draw near.
    Now, by the Power that conducts you to   145
the summit of the stairway, I pray you:
remember, at time opportune, my pain!"
    Then, in the fire that refines, he hid.   148

CANTO XXVII

Sì come quando i primi raggi vibra
    là dove il suo fattor lo sangue sparse,
cadendo Ibero sotto l'alta Libra,

    e l'onde in Gange da nona rïarse,   4
sì stava il sole; onde 'l giorno sen giva,
come l'angel di Dio lieto ci apparse.

    Fuor de la fiamma stava in su la riva,   7
e cantava *"Beati mundo corde!"*
in voce assai più che la nostra viva.

    Poscia "Più non si va, se pria non morde,   10
anime sante, il foco: intrate in esso,
e al cantar di là non siate sorde,"

    ci disse come noi li fummo presso;   13
per ch'io divenni tal, quando lo 'ntesi,
qual è colui che ne la fossa è messo.

    In su le man commesse mi protesi,   16
guardando il foco e imaginando forte
umani corpi già veduti accesi.

    Volsersi verso me le buone scorte;   19
e Virgilio mi disse: "Figliuol mio,
qui può esser tormento, ma non morte.

    Ricorditi, ricorditi! E se io   22
sovresso Gerïon ti guidai salvo,
che farò ora presso più a Dio?

    Credi per certo che se dentro a l'alvo   25
di questa fiamma stessi ben mille anni,
non ti potrebbe far d'un capel calvo.

    E se tu forse credi ch'io t'inganni,   28
fatti ver' lei, e fatti far credenza
con le tue mani al lembo d'i tuoi panni.

From the Seventh Terrace to the threshold of the Earthly Paradise. Sunset. The angel of chastity. The Sixth Beatitude. Dante's fear of entering the flames. Virgil's exhortation. The passage through fire. Dante's sleep and dream of Leah, exemplar of the active life, and Rachel, exemplar of the contemplative life. Dante's waking. Virgil's last words to him.

Just as, there where its Maker shed His blood,
the sun shed its first rays, and Ebro lay
beneath high Libra, and the ninth hour's rays

were scorching Ganges' waves; so here, the sun   4
stood at the point of day's departure when
God's angel—happy—showed himself to us.

He stood along the edge, beyond the flames,   7
singing *"Beati mundo corde"* in
a voice that had more life than ours can claim.

Then: "Holy souls, you cannot move ahead   10
unless the fire has stung you first: enter
the flames, and don't be deaf to song you'll hear

beyond," he said when we were close to him;   13
and when I heard him say this, I became
like one who has been laid within the grave.

I joined my hands and stretched them out to fend   16
the flames, watching the fire, imagining
clearly the human bodies I'd once seen

burning. My gentle escorts turned to me,   19
and Virgil said: "My son, though there may be
suffering here, there is no death. Remember,

remember! If I guided you to safety   22
even upon the back of Geryon,
then now, closer to God, what shall I do?

Be sure: although you were to spend a full   25
one thousand years within this fire's center,
your head would not be balder by one hair.

And if you think I am deceiving you,   28
draw closer to the flames, let your own hands
try out, within the fire, your clothing's hem—

Pon giù omai, pon giù ogne temenza;   31
volgiti in qua e vieni: entra sicuro!"
E io pur fermo e contra coscïenza.

Quando mi vide star pur fermo e duro,   34
turbato un poco disse: "Or vedi, figlio:
tra Bëatrice e te è questo muro."

Come al nome di Tisbe aperse il ciglio   37
Piramo in su la morte, e riguardolla,
allor che 'l gelso diventò vermiglio;

così, la mia durezza fatta solla,   40
mi volsi al savio duca, udendo il nome
che ne la mente sempre mi rampolla.

Ond' ei crollò la fronte e disse: "Come!   43
volenci star di qua?"; indi sorrise
come al fanciul si fa ch'è vinto al pome.

Poi dentro al foco innanzi mi si mise,   46
pregando Stazio che venisse retro,
che pria per lunga strada ci divise.

Sì com' fui dentro, in un bogliente vetro   49
gittato mi sarei per rinfrescarmi,
tant' era ivi lo 'ncendio sanza metro.

Lo dolce padre mio, per confortarmi,   52
pur di Beatrice ragionando andava,
dicendo: "Li occhi suoi già veder parmi."

Guidavaci una voce che cantava   55
di là; e noi, attenti pur a lei,
venimmo fuor là ove si montava.

"Venite, benedicti Patris mei,"   58
sonò dentro a un lume che lì era,
tal che mi vinse e guardar nol potei.

"Lo sol sen va," soggiunse, "e vien la sera;   61
non v'arrestate, ma studiate il passo,
mentre che l'occidente non si annera."

Dritta salia la via per entro 'l sasso   64
verso tal parte ch'io toglieva i raggi
dinanzi a me del sol ch'era già basso.

E di pochi scaglion levammo i saggi,   67
che 'l sol corcar, per l'ombra che si spense,
sentimmo dietro e io e li miei saggi.

    put down, by now put down, your every fear;   31
turn toward the fire, and enter, confident!"
But I was stubborn, set against my conscience.

    When he saw me still halting, obstinate,   34
he said, somewhat perplexed: "Now see, son: this
wall stands between you and your Beatrice."

    As, at the name of Thisbe, Pyramus,   37
about to die, opened his eyes, and saw her
(when then the mulberry became bloodred),

    so, when my stubbornness had softened, I,   40
hearing the name that's always flowering
within my mind, turned to my knowing guide.

    At which he shook his head and said: "And would   43
you have us stay along this side?"—then smiled
as one smiles at a child fruit has beguiled.

    Then he, ahead of me, entered the fire;   46
and he asked Statius, who had walked between us
before, diving us, to go behind.

    No sooner was I in that fire than I'd   49
have thrown myself in molten glass to find
coolness—because those flames were so intense.

    My gentle father, who would comfort me,   52
kept talking, as we walked, of Beatrice,
saying: "I seem to see her eyes already."

    A voice that sang beyond us was our guide;   55
and we, attentive to that voice, emerged
just at the point where it began to climb.

    "Venite, benedicti Patris mei,"   58
it sang within a light that overcame me:
I could not look at such intensity.

    "The sun departs," it added; "evening comes;   61
don't stay your steps, but hurry on before
the west grows dark." The path we took climbed straight

    within the rock, and its direction was   64
such that, in front of me, my body blocked
the rays of sun, already low behind us.

    And we had only tried a few steps when   67
I and my sages sensed the sun had set
because the shadow I had cast was spent.

E pria che 'n tutte le sue parti immense   70
fosse orizzonte fatto d'uno aspetto,
e notte avesse tutte sue dispense,

ciascun di noi d'un grado fece letto;   73
ché la natura del monte ci affranse
la possa del salir più e 'l diletto.

Quali si stanno ruminando manse   76
le capre, state rapide e proterve
sovra le cime avante che sien pranse,

tacite a l'ombra, mentre che 'l sol ferve,   79
guardate dal pastor, che 'n su la verga
poggiato s'è e lor di posa serve;

e quale il mandrïan che fori alberga,   82
lungo il peculio suo queto pernotta,
guardando perché fiera non lo sperga;

tali eravamo tutti e tre allotta,   85
io come capra, ed ei come pastori,
fasciati quinci e quindi d'alta grotta.

Poco parer potea lì del di fori;   88
ma, per quel poco, vedea io le stelle
di lor solere e più chiare e maggiori.

Sì ruminando e sì mirando in quelle,   91
mi prese il sonno; il sonno che sovente,
anzi che 'l fatto sia, sa le novelle.

Ne l'ora, credo, che de l'orïente   94
prima raggiò nel monte Citerea,
che di foco d'amor par sempre ardente,

giovane e bella in sogno mi parea   97
donna vedere andar per una landa
cogliendo fiori; e cantando dicea:

"Sappia qualunque il mio nome dimanda   100
ch'i' mi son Lia, e vo movendo intorno
le belle mani a farmi una ghirlanda.

Per piacermi a lo specchio, qui m'addorno;   103
ma mia suora Rachel mai non si smaga
dal suo miraglio, e siede tutto giorno.

Ell' è d'i suoi belli occhi veder vaga   106
com' io de l'addornarmi con le mani;
lei lo vedere, e me l'ovrare appaga."

Before one color came to occupy 70
that sky in all of its immensity
and night was free to summon all its darkness,

each of us made one of those stairs his bed: 73
the nature of the mountain had so weakened
our power and desire to climb ahead.

Like goats that, when they grazed, were swift and tameless
along the mountain peaks, but now are sated,
and rest and ruminate—while the sun blazes—

untroubled, in the shadows, silently, 79
watched over by the herdsman as he leans
upon his staff and oversees their peace;

or like the herdsman in the open fields, 82
spending the night beside his quiet flock,
watching to see that no beast drives them off;

such were all three of us at that point—they 85
were like the herdsmen, I was like the goat;
upon each side of us, high rock walls rose.

From there, one saw but little of the sky, 88
but in that little, I could see the stars
brighter and larger than they usually are.

But while I watched the stars, in reverie, 91
sleep overcame me—sleep, which often sees,
before it happens, what is yet to be.

It was the hour, I think, when Cytherea, 94
who always seems aflame with fires of love,
first shines upon the mountains from the east,

that, in my dream, I seemed to see a woman 97
both young and fair; along a plain she gathered
flowers, and even as she sang, she said:

"Whoever asks my name, know that I'm Leah, 100
and I apply my lovely hands to fashion
a garland of the flowers I have gathered.

To find delight within this mirror I 103
adorn myself; whereas my sister Rachel
never deserts her mirror; there she sits

all day; she longs to see her fair eyes gazing, 106
as I, to see my hands adorning, long:
she is content with seeing, I with labor."

E già per li splendori antelucani,   109
che tanto a' pellegrin surgon più grati,
quanto, tornando, albergan men lontani,

le tenebre fuggian da tutti lati,   112
e 'l sonno mio con esse; ond' io leva'mi,
veggendo i gran maestri già levati.

"Quel dolce pome che per tanti rami   115
cercando va la cura de' mortali,
oggi porrà in pace le tue fami."

Virgilio inverso me queste cotali   118
parole usò; e mai non furo strenne
che fosser di piacere a queste iguali.

Tanto voler sopra voler mi venne   121
de l'esser sù, ch'ad ogne passo poi
al volo mi sentia crescer le penne.

Come la scala tutta sotto noi   124
fu corsa e fummo in su 'l grado superno,
in me ficcò Virgilio li occhi suoi,

e disse: "Il temporal foco e l'etterno   127
veduto hai, figlio; e se' venuto in parte
dov' io per me più oltre non discerno.

Tratto t'ho qui con ingegno e con arte;   130
lo tuo piacere omai prendi per duce;
fuor se' de l'erte vie, fuor se' de l'arte.

Vedi lo sol che 'n fronte ti riluce;   133
vedi l'erbette, i fiori e li arbuscelli
che qui la terra sol da sé produce.

Mentre che vegnan lieti li occhi belli   136
che, lagrimando, a te venir mi fenno,
seder ti puoi e puoi andar tra elli.

Non aspettar mio dir più né mio cenno;   139
libero, dritto e sano è tuo arbitrio,
e fallo fora non fare a suo senno:

per ch'io te sovra te corono e mitrio."   142

And now, with the reflected lights that glow   109
before the dawn and, rising, are most welcome
to pilgrims as, returning, they near home,

the shadows fled upon all sides; my sleep   112
fled with them; and at this, I woke and saw
that the great teachers had already risen.

"Today your hungerings will find their peace   115
through that sweet fruit the care of mortals seeks
among so many branches." This, the speech,

the solemn words, that Virgil spoke to me;   118
and there were never tidings to compare,
in offering delight to me, with these.

My will on will to climb above was such   121
that at each step I took I felt the force
within my wings was growing for the flight.

When all the staircase lay beneath us and   124
we'd reached the highest step, then Virgil set
his eyes insistently on me and said:

"My son, you've seen the temporary fire   127
and the eternal fire; you have reached
the place past which my powers cannot see.

I've brought you here through intellect and art;   130
from now on, let your pleasure be your guide;
you're past the steep and past the narrow paths.

Look at the sun that shines upon your brow;   133
look at the grasses, flowers, and the shrubs
born here, spontaneously, of the earth.

Among them, you can rest or walk until   136
the coming of the glad and lovely eyes—
those eyes that, weeping, sent me to your side.

Await no further word or sign from me: 139
your will is free, erect, and whole—to act
against that will would be to err: therefore

I crown and miter you over yourself."   142

XXVII·51

CANTO XXVIII

Vago già di cercar dentro e dintorno
    la divina foresta spessa e viva,
ch'a li occhi temperava il novo giorno,

    sanza più aspettar, lasciai la riva,   4
prendendo la campagna lento lento
su per lo suol che d'ogne parte auliva.

    Un'aura dolce, sanza mutamento   7
avere in sé, mi feria per la fronte
non di più colpo che soave vento;

    per cui le fronde, tremolando, pronte   10
tutte quante piegavano a la parte
u' la prim' ombra gitta il santo monte;

    non però dal loro esser dritto sparte   13
tanto, che li augelletti per le cime
lasciasser d'operare ogne lor arte;

    ma con piena letizia l'ore prime,   16
cantando, ricevieno intra le foglie,
che tenevan bordone a le sue rime,

    tal qual di ramo in ramo si raccoglie   19
per la pineta in su 'l lito di Chiassi,
quand' Eolo scilocco fuor discioglie.

    Già m'avean trasportato i lenti passi   22
dentro a la selva antica tanto, ch'io
non potea rivedere ond' io mi 'ntrassi;

    ed ecco più andar mi tolse un rio,   25
che 'nver' sinistra con sue picciole onde
piegava l'erba che 'n sua ripa uscìo.

    Tutte l'acque che son di qua più monde,   28
parrieno avere in sé mistura alcuna
verso di quella, che nulla nasconde,

Now keen to search within, to search around
    that forest—dense, alive with green, divine—
which tempered the new day before my eyes,

    without delay, I left behind the rise   4
and took the plain, advancing slowly, slowly
across the ground where every part was fragrant.

    A gentle breeze, which did not seem to vary   7
within itself, was striking at my brow
but with no greater force than a kind wind's,

    a wind that made the trembling boughs—they all   10
bent eagerly—incline in the direction
of morning shadows from the holy mountain;

    but they were not deflected with such force   13
as to disturb the little birds upon
the branches in the practice of their arts;

    for to the leaves, with song, birds welcomed those   16
first hours of the morning joyously,
and leaves supplied the burden to their rhymes—

    just like the wind that sounds from branch to branch   19
along the shore of Classe, through the pines
when Aeolus has set Sirocco loose.

    Now, though my steps were slow, I'd gone so far   22
into the ancient forest that I could
no longer see where I had made my entry;

    and there I came upon a stream that blocked   25
the path of my advance; its little waves
bent to the left the grass along its banks.

    All of the purest waters here on earth,   28
when matched against that stream, would seem to be
touched by impurity; it hides no thing—

avvegna che si mova bruna bruna   31
sotto l'ombra perpetüa, che mai
raggiar non lascia sole ivi né luna.

Coi piè ristetti e con li occhi passai   34
di là dal fiumicello, per mirare
la gran varïazion d'i freschi mai;

e là m'apparve, sì com' elli appare   37
subitamente cosa che disvia
per maraviglia tutto altro pensare,

una donna soletta che si gia   40
e cantando e scegliendo fior da fiore
ond' era pinta tutta la sua via.

"Deh, bella donna, che a' raggi d'amore   43
ti scaldi, s'i' vo' credere a' sembianti
che soglion esser testimon del core,

vegnati in voglia di trarreti avanti,"   46
diss' io a lei, "verso questa rivera,
tanto ch'io possa intender che tu canti.

Tu mi fai rimembrar dove e qual era   49
Proserpina nel tempo che perdette
la madre lei, ed ella primavera."

Come si volge, con le piante strette   52
a terra e intra sé, donna che balli,
e piede innanzi piede a pena mette,

volsesi in su i vermigli e in su i gialli   55
fioretti verso me, non altrimenti
che vergine che li occhi onesti avvalli;

e fece i prieghi miei esser contenti,   58
sì appressando sé, che 'l dolce suono
veniva a me co' suoi intendimenti.

Tosto che fu là dove l'erbe sono   61
bagnate già da l'onde del bel fiume,
di levar li occhi suoi mi fece dono.

Non credo che splendesse tanto lume   64
sotto le ciglia a Venere, trafitta
dal figlio fuor di tutto suo costume.

Ella ridea da l'altra riva dritta,   67
trattando più color con le sue mani,
che l'alta terra sanza seme gitta.

that stream—although it moves, dark, dark, beneath   31
the never-ending shadows, which allow
no ray of sun or moon to reach those waters.

I halted, and I set my eyes upon   34
the farther bank, to look at the abundant
variety of newly-flowered boughs;

and there, just like a thing that, in appearing   37
most suddenly, repels all other thoughts,
so great is the astonishment it brings,

I saw a solitary woman moving,   40
singing, and gathering up flower on flower—
the flowers that colored all of her pathway.

"I pray you, lovely lady, you who warm   43
yourself with rays of love, if I may trust
your looks—which often evidence the heart—

may it please you," I asked of her, "to move   46
ahead and closer to this river, so
that I may understand what you are singing.

You have reminded me of where and what—   49
just when her mother was deprived of her
and she deprived of spring—Proserpina was."

As, when she turns, a woman, dancing, keeps   52
her soles close to the ground and to each other
and scarcely lets one foot precede the other,

so did she turn, upon the little red   55
and yellow flowers, to me, no differently
than would a virgin, lowering chaste eyes.

I had beseeched, and I was satisfied,   58
for she approached so close that the sweet sound
that reached me then became intelligible.

No sooner had she reached the point where that   61
fair river's waves could barely bathe the grass,
than she gave me this gift: lifting her eyes.

I do not think a light so bright had shone   64
beneath the lids of Venus when her son
pierced her in extraordinary fashion.

Erect, along the farther bank, she smiled,   67
her hands entwining varicolored flowers,
which that high land, needing no seed, engenders.

Tre passi ci facea il fiume lontani;   70
ma Elesponto, là 've passò Serse,
ancora freno a tutti orgogli umani,

più odio da Leandro non sofferse   73
per mareggiare intra Sesto e Abido,
che quel da me perch' allor non s'aperse.

"Voi siete nuovi, e forse perch' io rido,"   76
cominciò ella, "in questo luogo eletto
a l'umana natura per suo nido,

maravigliando tienvi alcun sospetto;   79
ma luce rende il salmo *Delectasti*,
che puote disnebbiar vostro intelletto.

E tu che se' dinanzi e mi pregasti,   82
dì s'altro vuoli udir; ch'i' venni presta
ad ogne tua question tanto che basti."

"L'acqua," diss' io, "e 'l suon de la foresta   85
impugnan dentro a me novella fede
di cosa ch'io udi' contraria a questa."

Ond' ella: "Io dicerò come procede   88
per sua cagion ciò ch'ammirar ti face,
e purgherò la nebbia che ti fiede.

Lo sommo Ben, che solo esso a sé piace,   91
fé l'uom buono e a bene, e questo loco
diede per arr' a lui d'etterna pace.

Per sua difalta qui dimorò poco;   94
per sua difalta in pianto e in affanno
cambiò onesto riso e dolce gioco.

Perché 'l turbar che sotto da sé fanno   97
l'essalazion de l'acqua e de la terra,
che quanto posson dietro al calor vanno,

a l'uomo non facesse alcuna guerra,   100
questo monte salìo verso 'l ciel tanto,
e libero n'è d'indi ove si serra.

Or perché in circuito tutto quanto   103
l'aere si volge con la prima volta,
se non li è rotto il cerchio d'alcun canto,

in questa altezza ch'è tutta disciolta   106
ne l'aere vivo, tal moto percuote,
e fa sonar la selva perch' è folta;

The river kept us just three steps apart;   70
but even Hellespont, where Xerxes crossed—
a case that still curbs all men's arrogance—

did not provoke more hatred in Leander   73
when rough seas ran from Abydos to Sestos,
than hatred I bestowed upon that river

when it refused to open. She began: 76
"You are new here and may—because I smile
in this place, chosen to be mankind's nest—

wonder, perplexed, unable to detect   79
the cause; but light to clear your intellect
is in the psalm beginning '*Delectasti*.'

And you, who have stepped forward, who beseeched me,
tell me if you'd hear more; I have come ready
for all your questions till you're satisfied."

I said: "The water and the murmuring forest   85
contend, in me, against the recent credence
I gave to words denying their existence."

At this, she said: "I'll tell you how the source   88
of your amazement has its special cause;
I'll clear the cloud that's left you so distraught.

The Highest Good, whose sole joy is Himself,   91
made man to be—and to enact—good; He
gave man this place as pledge of endless peace.

Man's fault made brief his stay here; and man's fault   94
made him exchange frank laughter and sweet sport
for lamentation and for anxiousness.

Below this mountain, land and water vapors,   97
which follow heat as far as they are able,
produce their perturbations; to prevent

them from molesting man placed here, this mountain   100
rose up this close to Heaven; from the point
where its gate locks, it's free of such disturbance.

Now, since all of the atmosphere revolves   103
within a circle, moved by the first circling,
unless its round is broken at some point,

against this height, which stands completely free   106
within the living air, that motion strikes;
and since these woods are dense, they echo it.

e la percossa pianta tanto puote,   109
che de la sua virtute l'aura impregna
e quella poi, girando, intorno scuote;

e l'altra terra, secondo ch'è degna   112
per sé e per suo ciel, concepe e figlia
di diverse virtù diverse legna.

Non parrebbe di là poi maraviglia,   115
udito questo, quando alcuna pianta
sanza seme palese vi s'appiglia.

E saper dei che la campagna santa   118
dove tu se', d'ogne semenza è piena,
e frutto ha in sé che di là non si schianta.

L'acqua che vedi non surge di vena   121
che ristori vapor che gel converta,
come fiume ch'acquista e perde lena;

ma esce di fontana salda e certa,   124
che tanto dal voler di Dio riprende,
quant' ella versa da due parti aperta.

Da questa parte con virtù discende   127
che toglie altrui memoria del peccato;
da l'altra d'ogne ben fatto la rende.

Quinci Letè; così da l'altro lato   130
Eünoè si chiama, e non adopra
se quinci e quindi pria non è gustato:

a tutti altri sapori esto è di sopra.   133
E avvegna ch'assai possa esser sazia
la sete tua perch' io più non ti scuopra,

darotti un corollario ancor per grazia;   136
né credo che 'l mio dir ti sia men caro,
se oltre promession teco si spazia.

Quelli ch'anticamente poetaro   139
l'età de l'oro e suo stato felice,
forse in Parnaso esto loco sognaro.

Qui fu innocente l'umana radice;   142
qui primavera sempre e ogne frutto;
nettare è questo di che ciascun dice."

Io mi rivolsi 'n dietro allora tutto   145
a' miei poeti, e vidi che con riso
udito avèan l'ultimo costrutto;

poi a la bella donna torna' il viso.   148

And when a plant is struck, its power is such 109
that it impregnates air with seeding force;
the air, revolving, casts this seed abroad;

the other hemisphere, depending on 112
the nature of its land and sky, conceives
and bears, from diverse powers, diverse trees.

If what I've said were known, you would not need 115
to be amazed on earth when growing things
take root but have no seed that can be seen.

And you must know: the holy plain on which 118
you find yourself is full of every seed;
and it has fruit that—there—cannot be gathered.

The water that you see does not spring from 121
a vein that vapor—cold-condensed—restores,
like rivers that acquire or lose their force;

it issues from a pure and changeless fountain, 124
which by the will of God regains as much
as, on two sides, it pours and it divides.

On this side it descends with power to end 127
one's memory of sin; and on the other,
it can restore recall of each good deed.

To one side, it is Lethe; on the other, 130
Eunoe; neither stream is efficacious
unless the other's waters have been tasted:

their savor is above all other sweetness. 133
Although your thirst might well be satisfied
even if I revealed no more to you,

I'll give you freely, too, a corollary; 136
nor do I think my words will be less welcome
to you if they extend beyond my promise.

Those ancients who in poetry presented 139
the golden age, who sang its happy state,
perhaps, in their Parnassus, dreamt this place.

Here, mankind's root was innocent; and here 142
were every fruit and never-ending spring;
these streams—the nectar of which poets sing."

Then I turned round completely, and I faced 145
my poets; I could see that they had heard
with smiles this final corollary spoken;

that done, my eyes returned to the fair woman. 148

CANTO XXIX

C antando come donna innamorata,
  continüò col fin di sue parole:
"Beati quorum tecta sunt peccata!"

E come ninfe che si givan sole   4
per le salvatiche ombre, disïando
qual di veder, qual di fuggir lo sole,

allor si mosse contra 'l fiume, andando   7
su per la riva; e io pari di lei,
picciol passo con picciol seguitando.

Non eran cento tra ' suoi passi e ' miei,   10
quando le ripe igualmente dier volta,
per modo ch'a levante mi rendei.

Né ancor fu così nostra via molta,   13
quando la donna tutta a me si torse,
dicendo: "Frate mio, guarda e ascolta."

Ed ecco un lustro sùbito trascorse   16
da tutte parti per la gran foresta,
tal che di balenar mi mise in forse.

Ma perché 'l balenar, come vien, resta,   19
e quel, durando, più e più splendeva,
nel mio pensier dicea: "Che cosa è questa?"

E una melodia dolce correva   22
per l'aere luminoso; onde buon zelo
mi fé riprender l'ardimento d'Eva,

che là dove ubidia la terra e 'l cielo,   25
femmina, sola e pur testé formata,
non sofferse di star sotto alcun velo;

sotto 'l qual se divota fosse stata,   28
avrei quelle ineffabili delizie
sentite prima e più lunga fïate.

The Earthly Paradise. The banks of the Lethe. Sudden light and melody.
Invocation to the Muses. The extraordinary procession. The seven can-
delabra. The seven pennants. The twenty-four elders. The four animals.
The chariot drawn by a griffin. The seven women. Seven more elders.
The sudden halt.

Her words were done, but without interruption
she sang—like an enamored woman—thus:
"Beati quorum tecta sunt peccata!"

And just as nymphs who used to walk alone   4
among the woodland shadows, some desiring
to see and some to flee the sun, so she

moved countercurrent as she walked along   7
the riverbank; and following her short
footsteps with my own steps, I matched her pace.

Her steps and mine together did not sum   10
one hundred when the banks, still parallel,
so curved about that I was facing east.

Nor had we gone much farther on that path   13
when she turned fully round toward me and said:
"My brother, look and listen"; and I saw

a sudden radiance that swept across   16
the mighty forest on all sides—and I
was wondering if lightning had not struck.

But since, when lightning strikes, it stops at once,   19
while that light, lingering, increased its force,
within my mind I asked: "What thing is this?"

And through the incandescent air there ran   22
sweet melody; at which, just indignation
made me rebuke the arrogance of Eve

because, where earth and heaven were obedient,   25
a solitary woman, just created,
found any veil at all beyond endurance;

if she had been devout beneath her veil,   28
I should have savored those ineffable
delights before, and for a longer time.

Mentr' io m'andava tra tante primizie   31
de l'etterno piacer tutto sospeso,
e disïoso ancora a più letizie,

    dinanzi a noi, tal quale un foco acceso,   34
ci si fé l'aere sotto i verdi rami;
e 'l dolce suòn per canti era già inteso.

    O sacrosante Vergini, se fami,   37
freddi o vigilie mai per voi soffersi,
cagion mi sprona ch'io mercé vi chiami.

    Or convien che Elicona per me versi,   40
e Uranìe m'aiuti col suo coro
forti cose a pensar mettere in versi.

    Poco più oltre, sette alberi d'oro   43
falsava nel parere il lungo tratto
del mezzo ch'era ancor tra noi e loro;

    ma quand' i' fui sì presso di lor fatto,   46
che l'obietto comun, che 'l senso inganna,
non perdea per distanza alcun suo atto,

    la virtù ch'a ragion discorso ammanna,   49
sì com' elli eran candelabri apprese,
e ne le voci del cantare *"Osanna."*

    Di sopra fiammeggiava il bello arnese   52
più chiaro assai che luna per sereno
di mezza notte nel suo mezzo mese.

    Io mi rivolsi d'ammirazion pieno   55
al buon Virgilio, ed esso mi rispuose
con vista carca di stupor non meno.

    Indi rendei l'aspetto a l'alte cose   58
che si movieno incontr' a noi sì tardi,
che foran vinte da novelle spose.

    La donna mi sgridò: "Perché pur ardi   61
sì ne l'affetto de le vive luci,
e ciò che vien di retro a lor non guardi?"

    Genti vid' io allor, come a lor duci,   64
venire appresso, vestite di bianco;
e tal candor di qua già mai non fuci.

    L'acqua imprendëa dal sinistro fianco,   67
e rendea me la mia sinistra costa,
s'io riguardava in lei, come specchio anco.

While I moved on, completely rapt, among   31
so many first fruits of eternal pleasure,
and longing for still greater joys, the air

before us altered underneath the green   34
branches, becoming like an ardent fire,
and now the sweet sound was distinctly song.

O Virgins, sacrosanct, if I have ever,   37
for your sake, suffered vigils, cold, and hunger,
great need makes me entreat my recompense.

Now Helicon must pour its fountains for me,   40
Urania must help me with her choir
to put in verses things hard to conceive.

Not far beyond, we made out seven trees   43
of gold, though the long stretch of air between
those trees and us had falsified their semblance;

but when I'd drawn so close that things perceived   46
through mingled senses, which delude, did not,
now they were nearer, lose their real features,

the power that offers reason matter judged   49
those trees to be—what they were—candelabra,
and what those voices sang to be "Hosanna."

The upper part of those fair candles flamed   52
more radiantly than the midmonth moon
shines at midnight in an untroubled sky.

Full of astonishment, I turned to my   55
good Virgil; but he only answered me
with eyes that were no less amazed than mine.

Then I looked at the extraordinary   58
things that were moving toward us—but so slowly
that even brides just wed would move more quickly.

The woman chided me: "Why are you only   61
so eager to behold the living lights
and not in seeing what comes after them?"

Then I saw people following those candles,   64
as if behind their guides, and they wore white—
whiteness that, in this world, has never been.

The water, to my left, reflected flames,   67
and it reflected, too, my left-hand side
if I gazed into it, as in a mirror.

Quand' io da la mia riva ebbi tal posta,　　70
che solo il fiume mi facea distante,
per veder meglio ai passi diedi sosta,

　e vidi le fiammelle andar davante,　　73
lasciando dietro a sé l'aere dipinto,
e di tratti pennelli avean sembiante;

　sì che lì sopra rimanea distinto　　76
di sette liste, tutte in quei colori
onde fa l'arco il Sole e Delia il cinto.

　Questi ostendali in dietro eran maggiori　　79
che la mia vista; e, quanto a mio avviso,
diece passi distavan quei di fori.

　Sotto così bel ciel com' io diviso　　82
ventiquattro seniori, a due a due,
coronati venien di fiordaliso.

　Tutti cantavan: "Benedicta tue　　85
ne le figlie d'Adamo, e benedette
sieno in etterno le bellezze tue!"

　Poscia che i fiori e l'altre fresche erbette　　88
a rimpetto di me da l'altra sponda
libere fuor da quelle genti elette,

　sì come luce luce in ciel seconda,　　91
vennero appresso lor quattro animali,
coronati ciascun di verde fronda.

　Ognuno era pennuto di sei ali;　　94
le penne piene d'occhi; e li occhi d'Argo,
se fosser vivi, sarebber cotali.

　A descriver lor forme più non spargo　　97
rime, lettor; ch'altra spesa mi strigne,
tanto ch'a questa non posso esser largo;

　ma leggi Ezechïel, che li dipigne　　100
come li vide da la fredda parte
venir con vento e con nube e con igne;

　e quali i troverai ne le sue carte,　　103
tali eran quivi, salvo ch'a le penne
Giovanni è meco e da lui si diparte.

　Lo spazio dentro a lor quattro contenne　　106
un carro, in su due rote, trïunfale,
ch'al collo d'un grifon tirato venne.

When I was at a point along my shore 70
where all that sundered me from them was water,
I stayed my steps in order to see better,

and I could see the candle flames move forward, 73
leaving the air behind them colored like
the strokes a painter's brush might have described,

so that the air above that retinue 76
was streaked with seven bands in every hue
of which the rainbow's made and Delia's girdle.

These pennants stretched far back, beyond my vision; 79
as for the width they filled, I judged the distance
between the outer ones to be ten paces.

Beneath the handsome sky I have described, 82
twenty-four elders moved on, two by two,
and they had wreaths of lilies on their heads.

And all were singing: "You, among the daughters 85
of Adam, *benedicta* are; and may
your beauties blessed be eternally."

After the flowers and the other fresh 88
plants facing me, along the farther shore,
had seen those chosen people disappear,

then—as in heaven, star will follow star— 91
the elders gone, four animals came on;
and each of them had green leaves as his crown;

each had six wings as plumage, and those plumes 94
were full of eyes; they would be very like
the eyes of Argus, were his eyes alive.

Reader, I am not squandering more rhymes 97
in order to describe their forms; since I
must spend elsewhere, I can't be lavish here;

but read Ezekiel, for he has drawn 100
those animals approaching from the north;
with wings and cloud and fire, he painted them.

And just as you will find them in his pages, 103
such were they here, except that John's with me
as to their wings; with him, John disagrees.

The space between the four of them contained 106
a chariot—triumphal—on two wheels,
tied to a griffin's neck and drawn by him.

Esso tendeva in sù l'una e l'altra ale   109
tra la mezzana e le tre e tre liste,
sì ch'a nulla, fendendo, facea male.

Tanto salivan che non eran viste;   112
le membra d'oro avea quant' era uccello,
e bianche l'altre, di vermiglio miste.

Non che Roma di carro così bello   115
rallegrasse Affricano, o vero Augusto,
ma quel del Sol saria pover con ello;

quel del Sol che, svïando, fu combusto   118
per l'orazion de la Terra devota,
quando fu Giove arcanamente giusto.

Tre donne in giro da la destra rota   121
venian danzando; l'una tanto rossa
ch'a pena fora dentro al foco nota;

l'altr' era come se le carni e l'ossa   124
fossero state di smeraldo fatte;
la terza parea neve testé mossa;

e or parëan da la bianca tratte,   127
or da la rossa; e dal canto di questa
l'altre toglien l'andare e tarde e ratte.

Da la sinistra quattro facean festa,   130
in porpore vestite, dietro al modo
d'una di lor ch'avea tre occhi in testa.

Appresso tutto il pertrattato nodo   133
vidi due vecchi in abito dispari,
ma pari in atto e onesto e sodo.

L'un si mostrava alcun de' famigliari   136
di quel sommo Ipocràte che natura
a li animali fé ch'ell' ha più cari;

mostrava l'altro la contraria cura   139
con una spada lucida e aguta,
tal che di qua dal rio mi fé paura.

Poi vidi quattro in umile paruta;   142
e di retro da tutti un vecchio solo
venir, dormendo, con la faccia arguta.

E questi sette col primaio stuolo   145
erano abitüati, ma di gigli
dintorno al capo non facëan brolo,

His wings, stretched upward, framed the middle band 109
with three bands on each outer side, so that,
though he cleaved air, he left the bands intact.

His wings—so high that they were lost to sight; 112
his limbs were gold as far as he was bird;
the rest of him was white mixed with bloodred.

Not only did no chariot so handsome 115
gladden Rome's Africanus or Augustus
himself—even the Sun's own cannot match it;

the Sun's—which, gone astray, was burnt to cinders 118
because Earth offered up her pious prayers,
when Jove, in ways not known to us, was just.

Three circling women, then advancing, danced 121
at the right wheel; the first of them, so red
that even in a flame she'd not be noted;

the second seemed as if her flesh and bone 124
were fashioned out of emerald; the third
seemed to be newly fallen snow. And now

the white one seemed to lead them, now the red; 127
and from the way in which the leader chanted,
the others took their pace, now slow, now rapid.

Upon the left, four other women, dressed 130
in crimson, danced, depending on the cadence
of one of them, with three eyes in her head.

Behind all of the group I have described 133
I saw two elders, different in their dress
but like in manner—grave and decorous.

The first seemed to be one of the disciples 136
of great Hippocrates, whom nature made
for those who are her dearest living beings;

the other showed an opposite concern— 139
his sword was bright and sharp, and even on
this near side of the river, I felt fear.

Then I saw four of humble aspect; and, 142
when all the rest had passed, a lone old man,
his features keen, advanced, as if in sleep.

The clothes these seven wore were like the elders' 145
in the first file, except that these had no
garlands of lilies round their brow; instead,

    anzi di rose e d'altri fior vermigli;   148
giurato avria poco lontano aspetto
che tutti ardesser di sopra da' cigli.

    E quando il carro a me fu a rimpetto,   151
un tuon s'udì, e quelle genti degne
parvero aver l'andar più interdetto,

    fermandosi ivi con le prime insegne.   154

roses and other red flowers wreathed their heads;   148
one seeing them less closely would have sworn
that all of them had flames above their eyebrows.

And when the chariot stood facing me,   151
I heard a bolt of thunder; and it seemed
to block the path of that good company,

which halted there, its emblems in the lead.   154

XXIX

106-154

CANTO XXX

Quando il settentrïon del primo cielo,
    che né occaso mai seppe né orto
né d'altra nebbia che di colpa velo,

    e che faceva lì ciascuno accorto   4
di suo dover, come 'l più basso face
qual temon gira per venire a porto,

    fermo s'affisse: la gente verace,   7
venuta prima tra 'l grifone ed esso,
al carro volse sé come a sua pace;

    e un di loro, quasi da ciel messo,   10
"Veni, sponsa, de Libano" cantando
gridò tre volte, e tutti li altri appresso.

    Quali i beati al novissimo bando   13
surgeran presti ognun di sua caverna,
la revestita voce alleluiando,

    cotali in su la divina basterna   16
si levar cento, *ad vocem tanti senis,*
ministri e messaggier di vita etterna.

    Tutti dicean: *"Benedictus qui venis!"*   19
e fior gittando e di sopra e dintorno,
"Manibus, oh, *date lilïa plenis!"*

    Io vidi già nel comínciar del giorno   22
la parte orïental tutta rosata,
e l'altro ciel di bel sereno addorno;

    e la faccia del sol nascere ombrata,   25
sì che per temperanza di vapori
l'occhio la sostenea lunga fiata:

    così dentro una nuvola di fiori   28
che da le mani angeliche saliva
e ricadeva in giù dentro e di fori,

The Earthly Paradise. The seven candelabra likened to seven stars (as if a Great Bear) of the Empyrean. The disappearance of Virgil. Beatrice's rebuke of Dante. The angels' compassion for Dante. Beatrice's accusations.

When the first heaven's Seven-Stars had halted
(those stars that never rise or set, that are
not veiled except when sin beclouds our vision;

those stars that, there, made everyone aware   4
of what his duty was, just as the Bear
below brings helmsmen home to harbor), then

the truthful band that had come first between   7
the griffin and the Seven-Stars turned toward
that chariot as toward their peace, and one

of them, as if sent down from Heaven, hymned   10
aloud, *"Veni, sponsa, de Libano,"*
three times, and all the others echoed him.

Just as the blessed, at the Final Summons,   13
will rise up—ready—each out of his grave,
singing, with new-clothed voices, Alleluia,

so, from the godly chariot, eternal   16
life's messengers and ministers arose:
one hundred stood *ad vocem tanti senis.*

All of them cried: *"Benedictus qui venis,"*   19
and, scattering flowers upward and around,
"Manibus, oh, date lilia plenis."

I have at times seen all the eastern sky   22
becoming rose as day began and seen,
adorned in lovely blue, the rest of heaven;

and seen the sun's face rise so veiled that it   25
was tempered by the mist and could permit
the eye to look at length upon it; so,

within a cloud of flowers that were cast   28
by the angelic hands and then rose up
and then fell back, outside and in the chariot,

sovra candido vel cinta d'uliva   31
donna m'apparve, sotto verde manto
vestita di color di fiamma viva.

E lo spirito mio, che già cotanto   34
tempo era stato ch'a la sua presenza
non era di stupor, tremando, affranto,

sanza de li occhi aver più conoscenza,   37
per occulta virtù che da lei mosse,
d'antico amor sentì la gran potenza.

Tosto che ne la vista mi percosse   40
l'alta virtù che già m'avea trafitto
prima ch'io fuor di püerizia fosse,

volsimi a la sinistra col respitto   43
col quale il fantolin corre a la mamma
quando ha paura o quando elli è afflitto,

per dicere a Virgilio: "Men che dramma   46
di sangue m'è rimaso che non tremi:
conosco i segni de l'antica fiamma."

Ma Virgilio n'avea lasciati scemi   49
di sé, Virgilio dolcissimo patre,
Virgilio a cui per mia salute die'mi;

né quantunque perdeo l'antica matre,   52
valse a le guance nette di rugiada
che, lagrimando, non tornasser atre.

"Dante, perché Virgilio se ne vada,   55
non pianger anco, non piangere ancora;
ché pianger ti conven per altra spada."

Quasi ammiraglio che in poppa e in prora   58
viene a veder la gente che ministra
per li altri legni, e a ben far l'incora;

in su la sponda del carro sinistra,   61
quando mi volsi al suon del nome mio,
che di necessità qui si registra,

vidi la donna che pria m'appario   64
velata sotto l'angelica festa,
drizzar li occhi ver' me di qua dal rio.

Tutto che 'l vel che le scendea di testa,   67
cerchiato de le fronde di Minerva,
non la lasciasse parer manifesta,

    a woman showed herself to me; above   31
a white veil, she was crowned with olive boughs;
her cape was green; her dress beneath, flame-red.

    Within her presence, I had once been used   34
to feeling—trembling—wonder, dissolution;
but that was long ago. Still, though my soul,

    now she was veiled, could not see her directly,   37
by way of hidden force that she could move,
I felt the mighty power of old love.

    As soon as that deep force had struck my vision   40
(the power that, when I had not yet left
my boyhood, had already transfixed me),

    I turned around and to my left—just as   43
a little child, afraid or in distress,
will hurry to his mother—anxiously,

    to say to Virgil: "I am left with less   46
than one drop of my blood that does not tremble:
I recognize the signs of the old flame."

    But Virgil had deprived us of himself,   49
Virgil, the gentlest father, Virgil, he
to whom I gave my self for my salvation;

    and even all our ancient mother lost   52
was not enough to keep my cheeks, though washed
with dew, from darkening again with tears.

    "Dante, though Virgil's leaving you, do not   55
yet weep, do not weep yet; you'll need your tears
for what another sword must yet inflict."

    Just like an admiral who goes to stern   58
and prow to see the officers who guide
the other ships, encouraging their tasks;

    so, on the left side of the chariot   61
(I'd turned around when I had heard my name—
which, of necessity, I transcribe here),

    I saw the lady who had first appeared   64
to me beneath the veils of the angelic
flowers look at me across the stream.

    Although the veil she wore—down from her head,   67
which was encircled by Minerva's leaves—
did not allow her to be seen distinctly,

regalmente ne l'atto ancor proterva   70
continüò come colui che dice
e 'l più caldo parlar dietro reserva:

"Guardaci ben! Ben son, ben son Beatrice.   73
Come degnasti d'accedere al monte?
non sapei tu che qui è l'uom felice?"

Li occhi mi cadder giù nel chiaro fonte;   76
ma veggendomi in esso, i trassi a l'erba,
tanta vergogna mi gravò la fronte.

Così la madre al figlio par superba,   79
com' ella parve a me; perché d'amaro
sente il sapor de la pietade acerba.

Ella si tacque; e li angeli cantaro   82
di sùbito *"In te, Domine, speravi";*
ma oltre *"pedes meos"* non passaro.

Sì come neve tra le vive travi   85
per lo dosso d'Italia si congela,
soffiata e stretta da li venti schiavi,

poi, liquefatta, in sé stessa trapela,   88
pur che la terra che perde ombra spiri,
sì che par foco fonder la candela;

così fui sanza lagrime e sospiri   91
anzi 'l cantar di quei che notan sempre
dietro a le note de li etterni giri;

ma poi che 'ntesi ne le dolci tempre   94
lor compartire a me, par che se detto
avesser: "Donna, perché sì lo stempre?"

lo gel che m'era intorno al cor ristretto,   97
spirito e acqua fessi, e con angoscia
de la bocca e de li occhi uscì del petto.

Ella, pur ferma in su la detta coscia   100
del carro stando, a le sustanze pie
volse le sue parole così poscia:

"Voi vigilate ne l'etterno die,   103
sì che notte né sonno a voi non fura
passo che faccia il secol per sue vie;

onde la mia risposta è con più cura   106
che m'intenda colui che di là piagne,
perché sia colpa e duol d'una misura.

her stance still regal and disdainful, she　　　　70
continued, just as one who speaks but keeps
until the end the fiercest parts of speech:

"Look here! For I am Beatrice, I am!　　　　73
How were you able to ascend the mountain?
Did you not know that man is happy here?"

My lowered eyes caught sight of the clear stream,　　　　76
but when I saw myself reflected there,
such shame weighed on my brow, my eyes drew back

and toward the grass; just as a mother seems　　　　79
harsh to her child, so did she seem to me—
how bitter is the savor of stern pity!

Her words were done. The angels—suddenly—　　　　82
sang, *"In te, Domine, speravi";* but
their singing did not go past *"pedes meos."*

Even as snow among the sap-filled trees　　　　85
along the spine of Italy will freeze
when gripped by gusts of the Slavonian winds,

then, as it melts, will trickle through itself—　　　　88
that is, if winds breathe north from shade-less lands—
just as, beneath the flame, the candle melts;

so I, before I'd heard the song of those　　　　91
whose notes always accompany the notes
of the eternal spheres, was without tears

and sighs; but when I heard the sympathy　　　　94
for me within their gentle harmonies,
as if they'd said: "Lady, why shame him so?"—

then did the ice that had restrained my heart　　　　97
become water and breath; and from my breast
and through my lips and eyes they issued—anguished.

Still standing motionless upon the left　　　　100
side of the chariot, she then addressed
the angels who had been compassionate:

"You are awake in never-ending day,　　　　103
and neither night nor sleep can steal from you
one step the world would take along its way;

therefore, I'm more concerned that my reply　　　　106
be understood by him who weeps beyond,
so that his sorrow's measure match his sin.

Non pur per ovra de le rote magne,   109
che drizzan ciascun seme ad alcun fine
secondo che le stelle son compagne,

  ma per larghezza di grazie divine,   112
che sì alti vapori hanno a lor piova,
che nostre viste là non van vicine,

  questi fu tal ne la sua vita nova   115
virtüalmente, ch'ogne abito destro
fatto averebbe in lui mirabil prova.

  Ma tanto più maligno e più silvestro   118
si fa 'l terren col mal seme e non cólto,
quant' elli ha più di buon vigor terrestro.

  Alcun tempo il sostenni col mio volto: 121
mostrando li occhi giovanetti a lui,
meco il menava in dritta parte vòlto.

  Sì tosto come in su la soglia fui   124
di mia seconda etade e mutai vita,
questi si tolse a me, e diessi altrui.

  Quando di carne a spirto era salita,   127
e bellezza e virtù cresciuta m'era,
fu' io a lui men cara e men gradita;

  e volse i passi suoi per via non vera,   130
imagini di ben seguendo false,
che nulla promession rendono intera.

  Né l'impetrare ispirazion mi valse,   133
con le quali e in sogno e altrimenti
lo rivocai: sì poco a lui ne calse!

  Tanto giù cadde, che tutti argomenti   136
a la salute sua eran già corti,
fuor che mostrarli le perdute genti.

  Per questo visitai l'uscio d'i morti,   139
e a colui che l'ha qua sù condotto,
li preghi miei, piangendo, furon porti.

  Alto fato di Dio sarebbe rotto,   142
se Letè si passasse e tal vivanda
fosse gustata sanza alcuno scotto

  di pentimento che lagrime spanda."   145

Not only through the work of the great spheres—   109
which guide each seed to a determined end,
depending on what stars are its companions—

but through the bounty of the godly graces,   112
which shower down from clouds so high that we
cannot approach them with our vision, he,

when young, was such—potentially—that any   115
propensity innate in him would have
prodigiously succeeded, had he acted.

But where the soil has finer vigor, there   118
precisely—when untilled or badly seeded—
will that terrain grow wilder and more noxious.

My countenance sustained him for a while;   121
showing my youthful eyes to him, I led
him with me toward the way of righteousness.

As soon as I, upon the threshold of   124
my second age, had changed my life, he took
himself away from me and followed after

another; when, from flesh to spirit, I   127
had risen, and my goodness and my beauty
had grown, I was less dear to him, less welcome:

he turned his footsteps toward an untrue path;   130
he followed counterfeits of goodness, which
will never pay in full what they have promised.

Nor did the inspirations I received—   133
with which, in dream and otherwise, I called
him back—help me; he paid so little heed!

He fell so far there were no other means   136
to lead him to salvation, except this:
to let him see the people who were lost.

For this I visited the gateway of   139
the dead; to him who guided him above
my prayers were offered even as I wept.

The deep design of God would have been broken   142
if Lethe had been crossed and he had drunk
such waters but had not discharged the debt

of penitence that's paid when tears are shed."   145

CANTO XXXI

O tu che se' di là dal fiume sacro,"
    volgendo suo parlare a me per punta,
che pur per taglio m'era paruto acro,

    ricominciò, seguendo sanza cunta,   4
"dì, dì se questo è vero; a tanta accusa
tua confession conviene esser congiunta."

    Era la mia virtù tanto confusa,   7
che la voce si mosse, e pria si spense
che da li organi suoi fosse dischiusa.

    Poco sofferse; poi disse: "Che pense?   10
Rispondi a me; ché le memorie triste
in te non sono ancor da l'acqua offense."

    Confusione e paura insieme miste   13
mi pinsero un tal "sì" fuor de la bocca,
al quale intender fuor mestier le viste.

    Come balestro frange, quando scocca   16
da troppa tesa, la sua corda e l'arco,
e con men foga l'asta il segno tocca,

    sì scoppia' io sottesso grave carco,   19
fuori sgorgando lagrime e sospiri,
e la voce allentò per lo suo varco.

    Ond' ella a me: "Per entro i mie' disiri,   22
che ti menavano ad amar lo bene
di là dal qual non è a che s'aspiri,

    quai fossi attraversati o quai catene   25
trovasti, per che del passare innanzi
dovessiti così spogliar la spene?

    E quali agevolezze o quali avanzi   28
ne la fronte de li altri si mostraro,
per che dovessi lor passeggiare anzi?"

The Earthly Paradise. Dante's confession and new rebukes by Beatrice. Dante's repentance and loss of his senses. Matilda's immersion of Dante in Lethe. The four handmaids of Beatrice. The mystery of the griffin. The other three women beseeching Beatrice. Beatrice unveiled.

O you upon the holy stream's far shore,"
so she, turning her speech's point against me—
even its edge had seemed too sharp—began

again, without allowing interruption,   4
"tell, tell if this is true; for your confession
must be entwined with such self-accusation."

My power of speech was so confounded that   7
my voice would move and yet was spent before
its organs had released it. She forbore

a moment, then she said: "What are you thinking?   10
Reply to me, the water has not yet
obliterated your sad memories."

Confusion mixed with fear compelled a *Yes*   13
out of my mouth, and yet that *Yes* was such—
one needed eyes to make out what it was.

Just as a crossbow that is drawn too taut   16
snaps both its cord and bow when it is shot,
and arrow meets its mark with feeble force,

so, caught beneath that heavy weight, I burst;   19
and I let tears and sighs pour forth; my voice
had lost its life along its passage out.

At this she said: "In the desire for me   22
that was directing you to love the Good
beyond which there's no thing to draw our longing,

what chains were strung, what ditches dug across   25
your path that, once you'd come upon them, caused
your loss of any hope of moving forward?"

What benefits and what allurements were   28
so evident upon the brow of others
that you had need to promenade before them?"

Dopo la tratta d'un sospiro amaro,   31
a pena ebbi la voce che rispuose,
e le labbra a fatica la formaro.

Piangendo dissi: "Le presenti cose   34
col falso lor piacer volser miei passi,
tosto che 'l vostro viso si nascose."

Ed ella: "Se tacessi o se negassi   37
ciò che confessi, non fora men nota
la colpa tua: da tal giudice sassi!

Ma quando scoppia de la propria gota   40
l'accusa del peccato, in nostra corte
rivolge sé contra 'l taglio la rota.

Tuttavia, perché mo vergogna porte   43
del tuo errore, e perché altra volta,
udendo le serene, sie più forte,

pon giù il seme del piangere e ascolta: 46
sì udirai come in contraria parte
mover dovieti mia carne sepolta.

Mai non t'appresentò natura o arte   49
piacer, quanto le belle membra in ch'io
rinchiusa fui, e che so' 'n terra sparte;

e se 'l sommo piacer sì ti fallio   52
per la mia morte, qual cosa mortale
dovea poi trarre te nel suo disio?

Ben ti dovevi, per lo primo strale   55
de le cose fallaci, levar suso
di retro a me che non era più tale.

Non ti dovea gravar le penne in giuso,   58
ad aspettar più colpo, o pargoletta
o altra novità con sì breve uso.

Novo augelletto due o tre aspetta;   61
ma dinanzi da li occhi d'i pennuti
rete si spiega indarno o si saetta."

Quali fanciulli, vergognando, muti   64
con li occhi a terra stannosi, ascoltando
e sé riconoscendo e ripentuti,

tal mi stav' io; ed ella disse: "Quando   67
per udir se' dolente, alza la barba,
e prenderai più doglia riguardando."

After I had withheld a bitter sigh,   31
I scarcely had the voice for my reply,
but, laboring, my lips gave my words form.

 Weeping, I answered: "Mere appearances   34
turned me aside with their false loveliness,
as soon as I had lost your countenance."

 And she: "Had you been silent or denied   37
what you confess, your guilt would not be less
in evidence: it's known by such a Judge!

 But when the charge of sinfulness has burst   40
from one's own cheek, then in our court the whet-
stone turns and blunts our blade's own cutting edge.

 Nevertheless, that you may feel more shame   43
for your mistake, and that—in time to come—
hearing the Sirens, you may be more strong,

 have done with all the tears you sowed, and listen: 46
so shall you hear how, unto other ends,
my buried flesh should have directed you.

 Nature or art had never showed you any   49
beauty that matched the lovely limbs in which
I was enclosed—limbs scattered now in dust;

 and if the highest beauty failed you through   52
my death, what mortal thing could then induce
you to desire it? For when the first

 arrow of things deceptive struck you, then   55
you surely should have lifted up your wings
to follow me, no longer such a thing.

 No green young girl or other novelty—   58
such brief delight—should have weighed down your wings,
awaiting further shafts. The fledgling bird

 must meet two or three blows before he learns,   61
but any full-fledged bird is proof against
the net that has been spread or arrow, aimed."

 As children, when ashamed, will stand, their eyes   64
upon the ground—they listen, silently,
acknowledging their fault repentantly—

 so did I stand; and she enjoined me: "Since   67
hearing alone makes you grieve so, lift up
your beard, and sight will bring you greater tears."

Con men di resistenza si dibarba   70
robusto cerro, o vero al nostral vento
o vero a quel de la terra di Iarba,

ch'io non levai al suo comando il mento;   73
e quando per la barba il viso chiese,
ben conobbi il velen de l'argomento.

E come la mia faccia si distese,   76
posarsi quelle prime creature
da loro aspersïon l'occhio comprese;

e le mie luci, ancor poco sicure,   79
vider Beatrice volta in su la fiera
ch'è sola una persona in due nature.

Sotto 'l suo velo e oltre la rivera   82
vincer pariemi più sé stessa antica,
vincer che l'altre qui, quand' ella c'era.

Di penter sì mi punse ivi l'ortica,   85
che di tutte altre cose qual mi torse
più nel suo amor, più mi si fé nemica.

Tanta riconoscenza il cor mi morse,   88
ch'io caddi vinto; e quale allora femmi,
salsi colei che la cagion mi porse.

Poi, quando il cor virtù di fuor rendemmi,   91
la donna ch'io avea trovata sola
sopra me vidi, e dicea: "Tiemmi, tiemmi!"

Tratto m'avea nel fiume infin la gola,   94
e tirandosi me dietro sen giva
sovresso l'acqua lieve come scola.

Quando fui presso a la beata riva,   97
"Asperges me" sì dolcemente udissi,
che nol so rimembrar, non ch'io lo scriva.

La bella donna ne le braccia aprissi;   100
abbracciommi la testa e mi sommerse
ove convenne ch'io l'acqua inghiottissi.

Indi mi tolse, e bagnato m'offerse   103
dentro a la danza de le quattro belle;
e ciascuna del braccio mi coperse.

"Noi siam qui ninfe e nel ciel siamo stelle;   106
pria che Beatrice discendesse al mondo,
fummo ordinate a lei per sue ancelle.

There's less resistance in the sturdy oak   70
to its uprooting by a wind from lands
of ours or lands of Iarbas than I showed

in lifting up my chin at her command;   73
I knew quite well—when she said "beard" but meant
my face—the poison in her argument.

When I had raised my face upright, my eyes   76
were able to perceive that the first creatures
had paused and were no longer scattering flowers;

and still uncertain of itself, my vision   79
saw Beatrice turned toward the animal
that is, with its two natures, but one person.

Beneath her veil, beyond the stream, she seemed   82
so to surpass her former self in beauty
as, here on earth, she had surpassed all others.

The nettle of remorse so stung me then,   85
that those—among all other—things that once
most lured my love, became most hateful to me.

Such self-indictment seized my heart that I   88
collapsed, my senses slack; what I became
is known to her who was the cause of it.

Then, when my heart restored my outer sense,   91
I saw the woman whom I'd found alone,
standing above me, saying: "Hold, hold me!"

She'd plunged me, up to my throat, in the river,   94
and, drawing me behind her, she now crossed,
light as a gondola, along the surface.

When I was near the blessed shore, I heard   97
"Asperges me" so sweetly sung that I
cannot remember or, much less, transcribe it.

The lovely woman opened wide her arms;   100
she clasped my head, and then she thrust me under
to that point where I had to swallow water.

That done, she drew me out and led me, bathed,   103
into the dance of the four lovely women;
and each one placed her arm above my head.

"Here we are nymphs; in heaven, stars; before   106
she had descended to the world, we were
assigned, as her handmaids, to Beatrice;

Merrenti a li occhi suoi; ma nel giocondo   109
lume ch'è dentro aguzzeranno i tuoi
le tre di là, che miran più profondo."

Così cantando cominciaro; e poi   112
al petto del grifon seco menarmi,
ove Beatrice stava volta a noi.

Disser: "Fa che le viste non risparmi;   115
posto t'avem dinanzi a li smeraldi
ond' Amor già ti trasse le sue armi."

Mille disiri più che fiamma caldi   118
strinsermi li occhi a li occhi rilucenti,
che pur sopra 'l grifone stavan saldi.

Come in lo specchio il sol, non altrimenti   121
la doppia fiera dentro vi raggiava,
or con altri, or con altri reggimenti.

Pensa, lettor, s'io mi maravigliava,   124
quando vedea la cosa in sé star queta,
e ne l'idolo suo si trasmutava.

Mentre che piena di stupore e lieta   127
l'anima mia gustava di quel cibo
che, saziando di sé, di sé asseta,

sé dimostrando di più alto tribo   130
ne li atti, l'altre tre si fero avanti,
danzando al loro angelico caribo.

"Volgi, Beatrice, volgi li occhi santi,"   133
era la sua canzone, "al tuo fedele
che, per vederti, ha mossi passi tanti!

Per grazia fa noi grazia che disvele   136
a lui la bocca tua, sì che discerna
la seconda bellezza che tu cele."

O isplendor di viva luce etterna,   139
chi palido si fece sotto l'ombra
sì di Parnaso, o bevve in sua cisterna,

che non paresse aver la mente ingombra,   142
tentando a render te qual tu paresti
là dove armonizzando il ciel t'adombra,

quando ne l'aere aperto ti solvesti?   145

we'll be your guides unto her eyes; but it   109
will be the three beyond, who see more deeply,
who'll help you penetrate her joyous light."

So, singing, they began; then, leading me   112
together with them to the griffin's breast,
where Beatrice, turned toward us, stood, they said:

"See that you are not sparing of your gaze: 115
before you we have set those emeralds
from which Love once had aimed his shafts at you."

A thousand longings burning more than flames   118
compelled my eyes to watch the radiant eyes
that, motionless, were still fixed on the griffin.

Just like the sun within a mirror, so   121
the double-natured creature gleamed within,
now showing one, and now the other guise.

Consider, reader, if I did not wonder   124
when I saw something that displayed no movement
though its reflected image kept on changing.

And while, full of astonishment and gladness,   127
my soul tasted that food which, even as
it quenches hunger, spurs the appetite,

the other three, whose stance showed them to be   130
the members of a higher troop, advanced—
and, to their chant, they danced angelically.

"Turn, Beatrice, o turn your holy eyes   133
upon your faithful one," their song beseeched,
"who, that he might see you, has come so far.

Out of your grace, do us this grace; unveil   136
your lips to him, so that he may discern
the second beauty you have kept concealed."

O splendor of eternal living light,   139
who's ever grown so pale beneath Parnassus'
shade or has drunk so deeply from its fountain,

that he'd not seem to have his mind confounded,   142
trying to render you as you appeared
where heaven's harmony was your pale likeness—

your face, seen through the air, unveiled completely?   145

XXXII · 148~160

BEATRICE

CANTO XXXII

Tant' eran li occhi miei fissi e attenti
   a disbramarsi la decenne sete,
che li altri sensi m'eran tutti spenti.

   Ed essi quinci e quindi avien parete   4
di non caler—così lo santo riso
a sé traéli con l'antica rete!—

   quando per forza mi fu vòlto il viso   7
ver' la sinistra mia da quelle dee,
perch' io udì da loro un "Troppo fiso!"

   e la disposizion ch'a veder èe   10
ne li occhi pur testé dal sol percossi,
sanza la vista alquanto esser mi fée.

   Ma poi ch'al poco il viso riformossi   13
(e dico "al poco" per rispetto al molto
sensibile onde a forza mi rimossi),

   vidi 'n sul braccio destro esser rivolto   16
lo glorïoso essercito, e tornarsi
col sole e con le sette fiamme al volto.

   Come sotto li scudi per salvarsi   19
volgesi schiera, e sé gira col segno,
prima che possa tutta in sé mutarsi;

   quella milizia del celeste regno   22
che procedeva, tutta trapassonne
pria che piegasse il carro il primo legno.

   Indi a le rote si tornar le donne,   25
e 'l grifon mosse il benedetto carco
sì, che però nulla penna crollonne.

   La bella donna che mi trasse al varco   28
e Stazio e io seguitavam la rota
che fé l'orbita sua con minore arco.

The Earthly Paradise. The eastward path of the procession. Adam's tree.
The griffin, the chariot, and the reflowering tree. The sleep and waking
of Dante. Beatrice's words on Dante's mission. The eagle, the fox, the
dragon, and the transfigured chariot. The giant and the whore.

M y eyes were so insistent, so intent
on finding satisfaction for their ten-year
thirst that every other sense was spent.

And to each side, my eyes were walled in by   4
indifference to all else (with its old net,
the holy smile so drew them to itself),

when I was forced to turn my eyes leftward   7
by those three goddesses because I heard
them warning me: "You stare too fixedly."

And the condition that afflicts the sight   10
when eyes have just been struck by the sun's force
left me without my vision for a time.

But when my sight became accustomed to   13
lesser sensations (that is, lesser than
the mighty force that made my eyes retreat),

I saw the glorious army: it had wheeled   16
around and to the right; it had turned east;
it faced the seven flames and faced the sun.

Just as, protected by its shields, a squadron   19
will wheel, to save itself, around its standard
until all of its men have changed direction;

so here all troops of the celestial kingdom   22
within the vanguard passed in front of us
before the chariot swung around the pole-shaft.

Back to the wheels the ladies then returned;   25
and though the griffin moved the blessed burden,
when he did that, none of his feathers stirred.

The lovely lady who'd helped me ford Lethe,   28
and I and Statius, following the wheel
that turned right, round the inner, smaller arc,

Sì passeggiando l'alta selva vòta,   31
colpa di quella ch'al serpente crese,
temprava i passi un'angelica nota.

Forse in tre voli tanto spazio prese   34
disfrenata saetta, quanto eramo
rimossi, quando Bëatrice scese.

Io senti' mormorare a tutti "Adamo";   37
poi cerchiaro una pianta dispogliata
di foglie e d'altra fronda in ciascun ramo.

La coma sua, che tanto si dilata   40
più quanto più è sù, fora da l'Indi
ne' boschi lor per altezza ammirata.

"Beato se', grifon, che non discindi   43
col becco d'esto legno dolce al gusto,
poscia che mal si torce il ventre quindi."

Così dintorno a l'albero robusto   46
gridaron li altri; e l'animal binato:
"Sì si conserva il seme d'ogne giusto."

E vòlto al temo ch'elli avea tirato,   49
trasselo al piè de la vedova frasca,
e quel di lei a lei lasciò legato.

Come le nostre piante, quando casca   52
giù la gran luce mischiata con quella
che raggia dietro a la celeste lasca,

turgide fansi, e poi si rinovella   55
di suo color ciascuna, pria che 'l sole
giunga li suoi corsier sotto altra stella;

men che di rose e più che di vïole   58
colore aprendo, s'innovò la pianta,
che prima avea le ramora sì sole.

Io non lo 'ntesi, né qui non si canta   61
l'inno che quella gente allor cantaro,
né la nota soffersi tutta quanta.

S'io potessi ritrar come assonnaro   64
li occhi spietati udendo di Siringa,
li occhi a cui pur vegghiar costò sì caro;

come pintor che con essempro pinga,   67
disegnerei com' io m'addormentai;
ma qual vuol sia che l'assonnar ben finga.

were slowly passing through the tall woods—empty   31
because of one who had believed the serpent;
our pace was measured by angelic song.

The space we covered could be matched perhaps   34
by three flights of an unleashed arrow's shafts,
when Beatrice descended from the chariot.

"Adam," I heard all of them murmuring,   37
and then they drew around a tree whose every
branch had been stripped of flowers and of leaves.

As it grows higher, so its branches spread   40
wider; it reached a height that even in
their forests would amaze the Indians.

"Blessed are you, whose beak does not, o griffin,   43
pluck the sweet-tasting fruit that is forbidden
and then afflicts the belly that has eaten!"

So, round the robust tree, the others shouted;   46
and the two-natured animal: "Thus is
the seed of every righteous man preserved."

And turning to the pole-shaft he had pulled,   49
he drew it to the foot of the stripped tree
and, with a branch of that tree, tied the two.

Just like our plants that, when the great light falls   52
on earth, mixed with the light that shines behind
the stars of the celestial Fishes, swell

with buds—each plant renews its coloring   55
before the sun has yoked its steeds beneath
another constellation: so the tree,

whose boughs—before—had been so solitary,   58
was now renewed, showing a tint that was
less than the rose, more than the violet.

I did not understand the hymn that they   61
then sang—it is not sung here on this earth—
nor, drowsy, did I listen to the end.

Could I describe just how the ruthless eyes   64
(eyes whose long wakefulness cost them so dear),
hearing the tale of Syrinx, fell asleep,

then like a painter painting from a model,   67
I'd draw the way in which I fell asleep;
but I refrain—let one more skillful paint.

Però trascorro a quando mi svegliai,   70
e dico ch'un splendor mi squarciò 'l velo
del sonno, e un chiamar: "Surgi: che fai?"

Quali a veder de' fioretti del melo   73
che del suo pome lì angeli fa ghiotti
e perpetüe nozze fa nel cielo,

Pietro e Giovanni e Iacopo condotti   76
e vinti, ritornaro a la parola
da la qual furon maggior sonni rotti,

e videro scemata loro scuola   79
così di Moïsè come d'Elia,
e al maestro suo cangiata stola;

tal torna' io, e vidi quella pia   82
sovra me starsi che conducitrice
fu de' miei passi lungo 'l fiume pria.

E tutto in dubbio dissi: "Ov' è Beatrice?"   85
Ond' ella: "Vedi lei sotto la fronda
nova sedere in su la sua radice.

Vedi la compagnia che la circonda: 88
li altri dopo 'l grifon sen vanno suso
con più dolce canzone e più profonda."

E se più fu lo suo parlar diffuso,   91
non so, però che già ne li occhi m'era
quella ch'ad altro intender m'avea chiuso.

Sola sedeasi in su la terra mera,   94
come guardia lasciata lì del plaustro
che legar vidi a la biforme fera.

In cerchio le facevan di sé claustro   97
le sette ninfe, con quei lumi in mano
che son sicuri d'Aquilone e d'Austro.

"Qui sarai tu poco tempo silvano;   100
e sarai meco sanza fine cive
di quella Roma onde Cristo è romano.

Però, in pro del mondo che mal vive,   103
al carro tieni or li occhi, e quel che vedi,
ritornato di là, fa che tu scrive."

Così Beatrice; e io, che tutto ai piedi   106
d'i suoi comandamenti era divoto,
la mente e li occhi ov' ella volle diedi.

I move, therefore, straight to my waking time;   70
I say that radiance rent the veil of sleep,
as did a voice: "Rise up: what are you doing?"

Even as Peter, John, and James, when brought   73
to see the blossoms of the apple tree—
whose fruit abets the angels' hungering,

providing endless wedding-feasts in Heaven—   76
were overwhelmed by what they saw, but then,
hearing the word that shattered deeper sleeps,

arose and saw their fellowship was smaller—   79
since Moses and Elijah now had left—
and saw a difference in their Teacher's dress;

so I awoke and saw, standing above me,   82
she who before—compassionate—had guided
my steps along the riverbank. Completely

bewildered, I asked: "Where is Beatrice?"   85
And she: "Beneath the boughs that were renewed,
she's seated on the root of that tree; see

the company surrounding her; the rest   88
have left; behind the griffin they have climbed
on high with song that is more sweet, more deep."

I do not know if she said more than that,   91
because, by now, I had in sight one who
excluded all things other from my view.

She sat alone upon the simple ground,   94
left there as guardian of the chariot
I'd seen the two-form animal tie fast.

The seven nymphs encircled her as garland,   97
and in their hands they held the lamps that can
not be extinguished by the north or south winds.

"Here you shall be—awhile—a visitor;   100
but you shall be with me—and without end—
Rome's citizen, the Rome in which Christ is

Roman; and thus, to profit that world which   103
lives badly, watch the chariot steadfastly
and, when you have returned beyond, transcribe

what you have seen." Thus, Beatrice; and I,   106
devoutly, at the feet of her commandments,
set mind and eyes where she had wished me to.

Non scese mai con sì veloce moto   109
foco di spessa nube, quando piove
da quel confine che più va remoto,

   com' io vidi calar l'uccel di Giove   112
per l'alber giù, rompendo de la scorza,
non che d'i fiori e de le foglie nove;

   e ferì 'l carro di tutta sua forza;   115
ond' el piegò come nave in fortuna,
vinta da l'onda, or da poggia, or da orza.

Poscia vidi avventarsi ne la cuna   118
del trïunfal veiculo una volpe
che d'ogne pasto buon parea digiuna;

   ma, riprendendo lei di laide colpe,   121
la donna mia la volse in tanta futa
quanto sofferser l'ossa sanza polpe.

Poscia per indi ond' era pria venuta,   124
l'aguglia vidi scender giù ne l'arca
del carro e lasciar lei di sé pennuta;

   e qual esce di cuor che si rammarca,   127
tal voce uscì del cielo e cotal disse:
"O navicella mia, com' mal se' carca!"

Poi parve a me che la terra s'aprisse   130
tr'ambo le ruote, e vidi uscirne un drago
che per lo carro sù la coda fisse;

   e come vespa che ritragge l'ago,   133
a sé traendo la coda maligna,
trasse del fondo, e gissen vago vago.

Quel che rimase, come da gramigna   136
vivace terra, da la piuma, offerta
forse con intenzion sana e benigna,

   si ricoperse, e funne ricoperta   139
e l'una e l'altra rota e 'l temo, in tanto
che più tiene un sospir la bocca aperta.

Trasformato così 'l dificio santo   142
mise fuor teste per le parti sue,
tre sovra 'l temo e una in ciascun canto.

Le prime eran cornute come bue,   145
ma le quattro un sol corno avean per fronte:
simile mostro visto ancor non fue.

Never has lightning fallen with such swift   109
motion from a thick cloud, when it descends
from the most distant limit in the heavens,

as did the bird of Jove that I saw swoop   112
down through the tree, tearing the bark as well
as the new leaves and the new flowering.

It struck the chariot with all its force;   115
the chariot twisted, like a ship that's crossed
by seas that now storm starboard and now port.

I then saw, as it leaped into the body   118
of that triumphal chariot, a fox
that seemed to lack all honest nourishment:

but, as she railed against its squalid sins,   121
my lady forced that fox to flight as quick
as, stripped of flesh, its bones permitted it.

Then I could see the eagle plunge—again   124
down through the tree—into the chariot
and leave it feathered with its plumage; and,

just like a voice from an embittered heart,   127
a voice issued from Heaven, saying this:
"O my small bark, your freight is wickedness!"

Then did the ground between the two wheels seem   130
to me to open; from the earth, a dragon
emerged; it drove its tail up through the chariot;

and like a wasp when it retracts its sting,   133
drawing its venomed tail back to itself,
it dragged part of the bottom off, and went

its way, undulating. And what was left   136
was covered with the eagle's plumes—perhaps
offered with sound and kind intent—much as

grass covers fertile ground; and the pole-shaft   139
and both wheels were re-covered in less time
than mouth must be kept open when one sighs.

Transfigured so, the saintly instrument   142
grew heads, which sprouted from its parts; three grew
upon the pole-shaft, and one at each corner.

The three were horned like oxen, but the four   145
had just a single horn upon their foreheads:
such monsters never have been seen before.

Sicura, quasi rocca in alto monte,   148
seder sovresso una puttana sciolta
m'apparve con le ciglia intorno pronte;
    e come perché non li fosse tolta,   151
vidi di costa a lei dritto un gigante;
e basciavansi insieme alcuna volta.
    Ma perché l'occhio cupido e vagante   154
a me rivolse, quel feroce drudo
la flagellò dal capo infin le piante;
    poi, di sospetto pieno e d'ira crudo,   157
disciolse il mostro, e trassel per la selva,
tanto che sol di lei mi fece scudo
    a la puttana e a la nova belva.   160

Just like a fortress set on a steep slope,   148
securely seated there, ungirt, a whore,
whose eyes were quick to rove, appeared to me;
    and I saw at her side, erect, a giant   151
who seemed to serve as her custodian:
and they—again, again—embraced each other.
    But when she turned her wandering, wanton eyes   154
to me, then that ferocious amador
beat her from head to foot; then, swollen with
    suspicion, fierce with anger, he untied   157
the chariot-made-monster, dragging it
into the wood, so that I could not see
    either the whore or the strange chariot-beast.   160

CANTO XXXIII

*D*eus, venerunt gentes,"* alternando
  or tre or quattro dolce salmodia,
le donne incominciaro, e lagrimando;
    e Bëatrice, sospirosa e pia,   4
quelle ascoltava sì fatta, che poco
più a la croce si cambiò Maria.
    Ma poi che l'altre vergini dier loco   7
a lei di dir, levata dritta in pè,
rispuose, colorata come foco:
    "Modicum, et non videbitis me;   10
et iterum, sorelle mie dilette,
modicum, et vos videbitis me."
    Poi le si mise innanzi tutte e sette,   13
e dopo sé, solo accennando, mosse
me e la donna e 'l savio che ristette.
    Così sen giva; e non credo che fosse   16
lo decimo suo passo in terra posto,
quando con li occhi li occhi mi percosse;
    e con tranquillo aspetto "Vien più tosto,"   19
mi disse, "tanto che, s'io parlo teco,
ad ascoltarmi tu sie ben disposto."
    Sì com' io fui, com' io dovëa, seco,   22
dissemi: "Frate, perché non t'attenti
a domandarmi omai venendo meco?"
    Come a color che troppo reverenti   25
dinanzi a suo maggior parlando sono,
che non traggon la voce viva ai denti,
    avvenne a me, che sanza intero suono   28
incominciai: "Madonna, mia bisogna
voi conoscete, e ciò ch'ad essa è buono."

The Earthly Paradise. The lament of the seven women and the compassion of Beatrice. Beatrice's prophecy: God's vengeance against the dragon, the whore, and the giant. Her words on Adam's tree. Her last rebuke of Dante. Dante led to Eunoe by Matilda. The sweet draught. Readiness for Paradise.

Weeping, the women then began—now three,
   now four, alternately—to psalm gently,
"Deus venerunt gentes"; and at this,

   sighing and full of pity, Beatrice   4
was changed; she listened, grieving little less
than Mary when, beneath the Cross, she wept.

   But when the seven virgins had completed   7
their psalm, and she was free to speak, erect,
her coloring like ardent fire, she answered:

   "*Modicum, et non videbitis me*   10
et iterum, sisters delightful to me,
modicum, et vos videbitis me."

   Then she set all the seven nymphs in front   13
of her and signaled me, the lady, and
the sage who had remained, to move behind her.

   So she advanced; and I do not believe   16
that she had taken her tenth step upon
the ground before her eyes had struck my eyes;

   and gazing tranquilly, "Pray come more quickly,"   19
she said to me, "so that you are more ready
to listen to me should I speak to you."

   As soon as I, responding to my duty,   22
had joined her, she said: "Brother, why not try,
since now you're at my side, to query me?"

   Like those who, speaking to superiors   25
too reverently do not speak distinctly,
not drawing their clear voice up to their teeth—

   so did I speak with sound too incomplete   28
when I began: "Lady, you know my need
to know, and know how it can be appeased."

Ed ella a me: "Da tema e da vergogna   31
voglio che tu omai ti disviluppe,
sì che non parli più com' om che sogna.

Sappi che 'l vaso che 'l serpente ruppe,   34
fu e non è; ma chi n'ha colpa, creda
che vendetta di Dio non teme suppe.

Non sarà tutto tempo sanza reda   37
l'aguglia che lasciò le penne al carro,
per che divenne mostro e poscia preda;

ch'io veggio certamente, e però il narro,   40
a darne tempo già stelle propinque,
secure d'ogn' 'ntoppo e d'ogne sbarro,

nel quale un cinquecento diece e cinque,   43
messo di Dio, anciderà la fuia
con quel gigante che con lei delinque.

E forse che la mia narrazion buia,   46
qual Temi e Sfinge, men ti persuade,
perch' a lor modo lo 'ntelletto attuia;

ma tosto fier li fatti le Naiade,   49
che solveranno questo enigma forte
sanza danno di pecore o di biade.

Tu nota; e sì come da me son porte,   52
così queste parole segna a' vivi
del viver ch'è un correre a la morte.

E aggi a mente, quando tu le scrivi,   55
di non celar qual hai vista la pianta
ch'è or due volte dirubata quivi.

Qualunque ruba quella o quella schianta,   58
con bestemmia di fatto offende a Dio,
che solo a l'uso suo la creò santa.

Per morder quella, in pena e in disio   61
cinquemilia anni e più l'anima prima
bramò colui che 'l morso in sé punio.

Dorme lo 'ngegno tuo, se non estima   64
per singular cagione essere eccelsa
lei tanto e sì travolta ne la cima.

E se stati non fossero acqua d'Elsa   67
li pensier vani intorno a la tua mente,
e 'l piacer loro un Piramo a la gelsa,

And she to me: "I'd have you disentangle   31
yourself, from this point on, from fear and shame,
that you no longer speak like one who dreams.

Know that the vessel which the serpent broke   34
was and is not; but he whose fault it is
may rest assured—God's vengeance fears no hindrance.

The eagle that had left its plumes within   37
the chariot, which then became a monster
and then a prey, will not forever be

without an heir; for I can plainly see,   40
and thus I tell it: stars already close
at hand, which can't be blocked or checked, will bring

a time in which, dispatched by God, a Five   43
Hundred and Ten and Five will slay the whore
together with that giant who sins with her.

And what I tell, as dark as Sphinx and Themis,   46
may leave you less convinced because—like these—
it tires the intellect with quandaries;

but soon events themselves will be the Naiads   49
that clarify this obstinate enigma—
but without injury to grain or herds.

Take note; and even as I speak these words,   52
do you transmit them in your turn to those
who live the life that is a race to death.

And when you write them, keep in mind that you   55
must not conceal what you've seen of the tree
that now has been despoiled twice over here.

Whoever robs or rends that tree offends,   58
with his blaspheming action, God; for He
created it for His sole use—holy.

For tasting of that tree, the first soul waited 61
five thousand years and more in grief and longing
for Him who on Himself avenged that taste.

Your intellect's asleep if it can't see   64
how singular's the cause that makes that tree
so tall and makes it grow invertedly.

And if, like waters of the Elsa, your   67
vain thoughts did not encrust your mind; if your
delight in them were not like Pyramus

    per tante circostanze solamente   70
la giustizia di Dio, ne l'interdetto,
conosceresti a l'arbor moralmente.

    Ma perch' io veggio te ne lo 'ntelletto   73
fatto di pietra e, impetrato, tinto,
sì che t'abbaglia il lume del mio detto,

    voglio anco, e se non scritto, almen dipinto, 76
che 'l te ne porti dentro a te per quello
che si reca il bordon di palma cinto."

    E io: "Sì come cera da suggello,   79
che la figura impressa non trasmuta,
segnato è or da voi lo mio cervello.

    Ma perchè tanto sovra mia veduta   82
vostra parola disïata vola,
che più la perde quanto più s'aiuta?"

    "Perché conoschi," disse, "quella scuola   85
c'hai seguitata, e veggi sua dottrina
come può seguitar la mia parola;

    e veggi vostra via da la divina   88
distar cotanto, quanto si discorda
da terra il ciel che più alto festina."

    Ond' io rispuosi lei: "Non mi ricorda   91
ch'i' stranïasse me già mai da voi,
né honne coscïenza che rimorda."

    "E se tu ricordar non te ne puoi,"   94
sorridendo rispuose, "or ti rammenta
come bevesti di Letè ancoi;

    e se dal fummo foco s'argomenta,   97
cotesta oblivïon chiaro conchiude
colpa ne la tua voglia altrove attenta.

    Veramente oramai saranno nude   100
le mie parole, quanto converrassi
quelle scovrire a la tua vista rude."

    E più corusco e con più lenti passi   103
teneva il sole il cerchio di meriggie,
che qua e là, come li aspetti, fassi,

    quando s'affisser, sì come s'affigge   106
chi va dinanzi a gente per iscorta
se trova novitate o sue vestigge,

staining the mulberry, you'd recognize   70
in that tree's form and height the moral sense
God's justice had when He forbade trespass.

But since I see your intellect is made   73
of stone and, petrified, grown so opaque—
the light of what I say has left you dazed—

I'd also have you bear my words within you—   76
if not inscribed, at least outlined—just as
the pilgrim's staff is brought back wreathed with palm."

And I: "Even as wax the seal's impressed,   79
where there's no alteration in the form,
so does my brain now bear what you have stamped."

But why does your desired word ascend   82
so high above my understanding that
the more I try, the more am I denied?"

"That you may recognize," she said, "the school   85
that you have followed and may see if what
it taught can comprehend what I have said—

and see that, as the earth is distant from   88
the highest and the swiftest of the heavens,
so distant is your way from the divine."

And I replied to her: "I don't remember   91
making myself a stranger to you, nor
does conscience gnaw at me because of that."

"And if you can't remember that," she answered,   94
smiling, "then call to mind how you—today—
have drunk of Lethe; and if smoke is proof

of fire, then it is clear: we can conclude   97
from this forgetfulness, that in your will
there was a fault—your will had turned elsewhere.

But from now on the words I speak will be   100
naked; that is appropriate if they
would be laid bare before your still-crude sight."

More incandescent now, with slower steps,   103
the sun was pacing the meridian,
which alters with the place from which it's seen,

when, just as one who serves as escort for   106
a group will halt if he has come upon
things strange or even traces of strangeness,

le sette donne al fin d'un'ombra smorta,   109
qual sotto foglie verdi e rami nigri
sovra suoi freddi rivi l'alpe porta.

Dinanzi ad esse Eufratès e Tigri   112
veder mi parve uscir d'una fontana,
e, quasi amici, dipartirsi pigri.

"O luce, o gloria de la gente umana,   115
che acqua è questa che qui si dispiega
da un principio e sé da sé lontana?"

Per cotal priego detto mi fu: "Priega   118
Matelda che 'l ti dica." E qui rispuose,
come fa chi da colpa si dislega,

la bella donna: "Questo e altre cose   121
dette li son per me; e son sicura
che l'acqua di Letè non gliel nascose."

E Bëatrice: "Forse maggior cura,   124
che spesse volte la memoria priva,
fatt' ha la mente sua ne li occhi oscura.

Ma vedi Eünoè che là diriva: 127
menalo ad esso, e come tu se' usa,
la tramortita sua virtù ravviva."

Come anima gentil, che non fa scusa,   130
ma fa sua voglia de la voglia altrui
tosto che è per segno fuor dischiusa;

così poi che da essa preso fui,   133
la bella donna mossesi, e a Stazio
donnescamente disse: "Vien con lui."

S'io avessi, lettor, più lungo spazio   136
da scrivere, i' pur cantere' in parte
lo dolce ber che mai non m'avria sazio;

ma perché piene son tutte le carte   139
ordite a questa cantica seconda,
non mi lascia più ir lo fren de l'arte.

Io ritornai da la santissima onda   142
rifatto sì come piante novelle
rinovellate di novella fronda,

puro e disposto a salire a le stelle.   145

the seven ladies halted at the edge   109
of a dense shadow such as mountains cast,
beneath green leaves and black boughs, on cold banks.

In front of them I seemed to see Euphrates   112
and Tigris issuing from one same spring
and then, as friends do, separating slowly.

"O light, o glory of the human race,   115
what water is this, flowing from one source
and then becoming distant from itself?"

Her answer to what I had asked was: "Ask   118
Matilda to explain this"; and the lovely
lady, as one who frees herself from blame,

replied: "He's heard of this and other matters   121
from me; and I am sure that Lethe's waters
have not obscured his memory of this."

And Beatrice: "Perhaps some greater care,   124
which often weakens memory, has made
his mind, in things regarding sight, grow dark.

But see Eunoe as it flows from there: 127
lead him to it and, as you're used to doing,
revive the power that is faint in him."

As would the noble soul, which offers no   130
excuse, but makes another's will its own
as soon as signs reveal that will; just so,

when she had taken me, the lovely lady   133
moved forward; and she said with womanly
courtesy to Statius: "Come with him."

If, reader, I had ampler space in which   136
to write, I'd sing—though incompletely—that
sweet draught for which my thirst was limitless;

but since all of the pages pre-disposed   139
for this, the second canticle, are full,
the curb of art will not let me continue.

From that most holy wave I now returned   142
to Beatrice; remade, as new trees are
renewed when they bring forth new boughs, I was

pure and prepared to climb unto the stars.   145

THE UNIVERSE OF DANTE

The Earthly Paradise (summit)

Excessive Love of Earthly Goods

The Lustful — Terrace VII

The Gluttonous — Terrace VI

The Avaricious & The Prodigal — Terrace V

Insufficient Love — The Slothful — Terrace IV

Perverted Love

The Wrathful — Terrace III

The Envious — Terrace II

The Prideful — Terrace I

Purgatory

The Late-Repentant

The Valley of The Rulers — The Gate

Those Who Died By Violence — Without Last Rites

The Indolent

The Excommunicates

ANTE-PURGATORY

THE ISLAND

NOTES

The following annotations are meant to serve as a very basic apparatus; they do not substitute for the three volumes-in-progress, one devoted to each *cantica* of the *Comedy,* of the California Lectura Dantis. From its own century until today, the *Comedy* has given rise to many commentaries. Chronologies of Dante's life and works and interpretations of vexed points in the *Comedy* are various and, at times, more conflicting than complementary. Much that is said bears the implicit qualifications, "possibly," "probably," and "perhaps." But some assertions do have more cogency than others, and this modest guide has garnered reasonable, helpful opinion in addition to a fair sum of certainties.

The notes are supplemented by two drawings-diagrams by Barry Moser, showing the topology of Purgatory and the spatial organization of Dante's cosmos.

In the following notes, the *Aeneid* is cited with the English line numbers of the Bantam Classics edition (that edition carries Latin line numbers at the top of each page). Other works by Virgil carry the Latin line numbers of the Loeb Classical Library editions, as do all works of Ovid, Lucan, and Statius. Ovid's *Metamorphoses* is abbreviated as *Met.;* Lucan's *Pharsalia* as *Phars.;* and the *Thebaid* of Statius as *Theb.*

The *Summa theologica* of St. Thomas Aquinas is abbreviated as *Summa theol.* These notes use the standard mode of referring to the *Summa.* The Roman numeral I refers to Part I of the work; I–II refers to the *Prima Secundae,* or first portion of Part II; and II–II refers to the *Secunda Secundae,* or second portion of Part II. The Roman numeral is followed by the Arabic numeral of the question ("q.") considered and then by the Arabic numeral of the article ("a.") under that question.

A.M.

CANTO I

1–22 The first four tercets of *Purgatorio* echo the openings of classical epic, with the definition of the subject and the invocation to one or more of the Muses (with Dante's narrative being taken up again in line 13). The opening of *Inferno* is more abruptly narrative: "When I had journeyed half of our life's way," with Dante delaying his "proper" prologue, protasis, or exordium to the *Inferno* to the opening of Canto II. In Canto I of the *Inferno,* a prologue to all of the *Comedy,* Dante invoked no Muse; instead, he found as guide the chief protagonist of poetry in the language that had fathered Dante's own—Virgil, the "light and honor of all other poets." For this finding, Dante had no epic precedent.

2 The metaphor of the poem or intellectual task as ship has many antecedents. Dante himself had already used it in his *Convivio* (II, i, 1), "Time calls, summoning my ship to leave its harbor," and will use it again in *Paradiso* II, 3.

3 "a sea so cruel": the sea of Hell, as opposed to the "more kindly waters" of "that second kingdom," the realm of Purgatory.

4–6 "that second kingdom": Dante's vision of Purgatory as a separate place enlarges the afterworld. In imaging a "second kingdom" between the realms of Heaven and Hell, he inherits and crowns the growing emphasis in Catholic thought, belief, and legend of the 12th and 13th centuries on an intermediate domain—a domain, however, that, unlike Heaven and Hell, would disappear at the Last Judgment (see *Purg.* XXVII, 127–128 and note). (The Greek Orthodox Church was always reluctant to alter the afterworld of Heaven and Hell; and later, almost all Protestants were to reject Purgatory.) This growth in emphasis stretches over centuries before it reaches a crescendo in the 13th century; writ small, it can be traced in the evolution of the adjective "purgatorial," as in "purgatorial fires," to the full-fledged noun, Purgatory, a place, a space, to which Dante gave enduring specificity. For a rich description of this process, see: Jacques Le Goff, *La Naissance du Purgatoire,* Paris, 1981.

8 "May this poem rise again": Release from sin and death, renewal, resurrection, and rebirth are central to the *Purgatorio* and to the Easter day on which Dante sets his arrival in Purgatory. And though Dante meets the souls in Purgatory in specific places, those souls, too, are in upward motion. Behind Dante lies the journey through—and poem of—"Hell's dead realm," where souls were fixed in their allotted circles and Dante encountered "the air of death."

9 "Calliope": the Muse of epic poetry. Dante asks Calliope to rise "somewhat," because only in *Paradiso* will his song rise to its full height (Buti).

10–12 The "Pierides" were the daughters of Pierus. They had challenged the Muses to a singing contest and, having lost to Calliope (selected to represent the Muses in the contest), were changed into magpies (see Ovid, *Met.* v, 294–340, 662–678, and the tale in which those lines are embedded, 194–678).

At the opening of his *Thebaid,* Statius (a central figure in *Purgatorio*) refers to "Pierian fire" (*Theb.* I, 13). But where Statius sees his own spirit as touched by that "Pierian fire," Dante invokes Calliope, "who struck the poor Pierides." (Virgil's Calliope is invoked late in the *Aeneid,* IX, 696).

13–27   On this passage, see the Introduction, p. XI.

19–21   The "lovely planet" is Venus, and the time is about two hours before sunrise on Easter morning, 1300. Dante has Venus rising on that day in conjunction with the constellation Pisces, "the Fishes," which Venus, with her brightness, is "veiling in the train she led." The sun itself will rise in the constellation Aries (II, 1–6 and note).

23   The "other pole": the southern pole.

23–27   The "four stars": Dante is suggesting that Adam and Eve in their innocence were able to view them—but only before their transgression was punished by expulsion from Eden and removal to the "northern hemisphere," from which those stars cannot be seen.

29–30   This is the second use of "other pole" (see 23, note); Dante is turning his eyes back to the north, where he now sees that the Wain, or Ursa Major, has already sunk below the horizon, "disappeared."

31   The "solitary patriarch" is Cato, Marcus Porcius Cato Uticensis (see Intro., pp. xix–xx), famed among Romans and in Dante's world for his resolute character and moral independence. Defeated in his republican opposition to Caesar during the civil war, he committed suicide at Utica to avoid yielding to Caesar his liberty, "—so precious, / as he who gives his life for it must know" (70–74, note).

The use of "patriarch" for *veglio* in this translation is indebted to Ezio Raimondi's reading of this canto, where he sees the image of Cato as "drawing together the traits of the Roman hero and the more remote traits of the Biblical patriarch." And the sense of him as "patriarch" can only be reinforced by our awareness that Cato was freed from Limbo at the same time as the Old Testament worthies, in Christ's Harrowing of Hell (see 88–90 and note, and *Inf.* IV, 52–61 and note). It is some measure of Dante's careful strategies in reinforcing credibility that in his catalog of those "carried off" from Limbo by Christ, he does not mention Cato, adding only the nameless "many others" (*Inf.* IV, 61). Dante does, however, mention Cato's wife as one who is still in Limbo (*Inf.* IV, 128, and *Purg.* I, 78–79). With Virgil taken from antiquity in the prelude to *Inferno,* Dante omits the name of Cato in Limbo, preparing us (and himself?) for Cato's role in Purgatory with the mention of Marcia in Limbo and a fleeting allusion to Cato in *Inferno* XIV, 15.

As Donald Nicholl notes, "The importance in Dante's eyes of Cato's love for liberty may be gauged from the fact that Dante . . . gives him the office of custodian of Purgatory. And this in spite of Cato's being a pagan, an enemy of Julius Caesar, and a suicide—characteristics which are normally apt to land people in Dante's Hell."

If the Introduction sees Dante as a daring appropriator in placing Cato here (see Intro., pp. xix–xx), that daring is only abetted by our awareness that the only two speakers in this canto, at this entry-point to a Christian Purgatory, are drawn from pagan antiquity—an act of assimiliation but also of rejuvenation, allowing the past, too, to "rise again" (8).

34–36 Dante's description of Cato is indebted to Lucan (*Phars.* II, 373–374).

40–41 The "hidden river" is probably Lethe, referred to at the end of the *Inferno* (XXXIV, 130–132), whose runoff descends from Purgatory and carries down to Hell the sins that have been washed away (see also *Purg.* XXVIII, 130).

53 A lady: Beatrice (see *Inf.* II, 53ff.).

61–69 In these three tercets, Virgil summarizes the action of the *Inferno*.

73–75 See 31, note.

76–77 Minos is the judge who assigns sinners to places within or below the Second Circle of Hell (*Inf.* V, 4ff.). Minos has no power over Virgil, whose place is in Limbo.

78–79 Marcia was Cato's second wife. Lucan tells us that Cato, after Marcia had had three children by him, ceded her to his friend Hortensius, but that on Hortensius' death Marcia's prayers to Cato to remarry her were granted (*Phars.* II, 326–349).

88–90 Marcia "dwells beyond the evil river," Acheron, with many other virtuous pagans in Limbo. "The law decreed when [Cato] was freed"— that is, during Christ's Harrowing of Hell (see *Inf.* IV, 52–61, note)—made the saved impassive to the entreaties of the damned; thus, Marcia "has no power to move [Cato] any longer." Cato's mention of this law reminds us that Virgil has only *temporarily* ascended to Purgatory from his assigned place in Limbo.

94–105 The "smooth rush," which Cato instructs Virgil to wind around Dante's waist, symbolizes humility. The poets must return to the "very base" of the island, to begin properly their ascent to Purgatory. "There where the breakers pound" (101), the rush is the only plant that can survive, since it remains pliable, humbly yielding "beneath the waves' harsh blows" (105); so too, the souls in Purgatory will humbly yield to the punishments that make them "worthy of ascent to Heaven." (See also 134–136, note.) The "smooth rush" also contrasts with the cord Dante took from his waist and "knotted and coiled" for Virgil to throw down to Geryon (see *Inf.* XVI, 106–114).

98–99 Cato is probably referring to the first "custodian angel," who guards the gate of Purgatory.

115–117 The *ora mattutina* here is not the morning hour, but matins, the first of the seven canonical hours (see XV, 6, note), and the last canonical hour of night—"the dark's last hour."

121–129 As the sun gets stronger the dew would normally have to contend with it, but here the dew is protected from evaporation by moist "sea winds" and "shade." Dew is a symbol of God's grace and is used here, appropriately, to wash Hell's stains from Dante's cheeks.

130–133 This passage recalls the first simile in the *Inferno* (see *Inf.* I, 22–27). There, Dante's momentary relief from terror is to give way to even greater terror as he journeys to the depths of Hell. But here, the fact that "the deserted shore" of Purgatory "never yet had seen its waters coursed / by any man who journeyed back again" is no cause for terror.

This passage also recalls and echoes Ulysses' tale of his last voyage, in *Inferno* XXVI. Ulysses' hunger for experience led him to venture beyond the boundary of the known world (the "Pillars of Hercules" at the western end of the Mediterranean), sailing until there rose before him in the distance "the highest mountain [he] had ever seen," undoubtedly the very mountain of Purgatory. Ulysses relates that his destruction took place "as pleased an Other"; Dante, standing on the shore Ulysses could not reach, is girt with the smooth rush "just as pleased another" (133), i.e., Cato, in accordance with God's will.

134–136 The plant that "sprang up again" recalls the golden bough of the *Aeneid* (VI, 190–200). Like the rushes here, which do not harden (103–106), the golden bough had a "pliant stem"; and like the rushes, the golden bough is quickly renewed ("when the first / bough is torn off, a second grows again"). In this springing up again of the rushes, Buti sees "virtue as inconsumable."

CANTO II

1–6 These opening lines, which once again remind us of the global dimensions of Dante's journey, depend on his envisioning Jerusalem, in the northern hemisphere, as directly opposite the island mountain of Purgatory in the southern hemisphere—exactly twelve hours apart from it in time (see diagram, p. 314, and Intro., p. ix). Thus, Jerusalem's sunset coincides with sunrise in Purgatory. In relation to Jerusalem, the Ganges River in India marks the eastern horizon, the easternmost point of the inhabited world, while the westernmost horizon is marked by the Straits of Gibraltar (the "boundary stones of Hercules," *Inf.* XXVI, 108) between Spain and Morocco—though Dante will sometimes refer to that westernmost point as the Ebro River (*Purg.* XXVII, 2) or Cadiz (*Par.* XXVIII, 82) or Morocco (*Purg.* IV, 139). His Earth clock thus has four principal stations: Jerusalem, the Ganges River, Purgatory, the Straits of Gibraltar. With Jerusalem at 6 P.M., it is midnight at the Ganges, 6 A.M. in Purgatory, and noon over the Straits of Gibraltar. (At times, Dante will also use Italy as a reference point, three hours earlier than Jerusalem, three hours later than the Straits of Gibraltar. See III, 25 and note and XV, 6 and note.)

After the spring equinox, during the time of Dante's journey, the sun is in the constellation Aries, and night, opposite the sun, is in the constellation Libra, the Scales. Dante distracts us somewhat from springtime, identifying Libra in line 6 as the constellation that, after the *autumn* equinox ("when the length of dark defeats" or exceeds the length of day), "deserts night's hands," remaining below the horizon at night. After the autumn equinox, it is the sun, not night, that is in the constellation Libra.

8–10   The fair Aurora is dawn, which in advancing moves from the white of the sky's first light to the "scarlet" red of dawn proper and then, with full sunrise, to orange-red. Aurora will again be personified in the memorable opening lines of Canto IX.

13–14   In the *Convivio* (II, xiii, 21) Dante, citing Aristotle's *Meteorics* (perhaps at second hand), sees Mars as enveloped by vapors subject to self-ignition. These vapors are the "invading mists of dawn," inciting Mars to glow with more intensity.

33   This angel, moving so fast that he first appears as a white blur, is "sailing" over the wide waters "between such distant shores"—that is, between the shore at Ostia near Rome at the mouth of the Tiber, where the souls of the newly dead wait to be transported, and the shore of the island mountain of Purgatory.

37   In Hell, Lucifer is called a bird, *uccello* (*Inf.* XXXIV, 47).

46   *"In exitu Isräel de Aegypto":* "When Israel went out of Egypt" is the first line of Psalm 114 (113 in the Vulgate), a hymn of thanksgiving to God for Israel's liberation from bondage. It is quite appropriately sung here by souls who have been saved from the bondage of their own sinfulness. Dante glosses this Psalm in both his *Convivio* (II, i, 6–7) and in (what is probably) his Epistle to Cangrande.

56–57   As time has advanced, the sun, with its "arrows," has chased Capricorn (the Goat) beyond the meridian.

64   "Another path" is the path Virgil and Dante have taken through Hell, a path described here by Virgil as "difficult and dense," the same words that describe the "shadowed forest" in *Inferno* I, 5.

70   The olive branch is the traditional symbol for peace and, by extension, good tidings in general.

76   The spirit Dante sees "moving forward / in order to embrace" him is Casella, a musician and an affectionate friend of Dante's about whom very little is known to us except that he may have set lyrics to music. (See 112, note.)

80–81   "three times...chest": In the same way, Aeneas tries to clasp his father in the world of the shades. "Three times / he tried to throw his arms around Anchises' / neck: and three times the Shade escaped from that / vain clasp—like light winds, or most like swift dreams (*Aen.* VI, 924–927).

91   "to return again to where I am": Dante seems to relate his remembered journeying through Purgatory to his present spiritual state of penitence. Here Dante—hopefully—predicts, as Charon had in Hell (*Inf.* III, 91–93), that he will be going to Purgatory after his death.

92–97   "why...were you deprived of so much time?": Dante's amazement that Casella is only just now arriving at the shore of Purgatory implies that Casella died sometime before 1300, the year of Dante's journey.

Casella's first remark concerning his delayed arrival (94–97) suggests that the helmsman angel (see 33, note)—like Charon in the *Inferno* and in the *Aeneid*—is able to exercise discretion in his ferrying: he "takes up whom—and when—he pleases" (95). Casella goes on to explain the circumstances of his eventual passage to Purgatory (see 98–105, and 98, 100–101, notes). Nothing in his explanation, however, explains clearly why—once the angel, "for three months now" (98), has allowed free passage—Casella has had to wait until the day of Dante's arrival for his (Casella's) journey from Ostia to Purgatory.

98 "For three months now" the helmsman angel has accepted all those who wish to cross, because in the year 1300 Pope Boniface VIII proclaimed a Jubilee, or Holy Year, that granted indulgences (reductions of penance set for sin) to those visiting certain Roman churches (see *Inf.* XVIII, 28–33 and note). Dante, following popular belief and theological thought (but not the literal text of the papal bull), implies that these indulgences applied even to the souls of the deceased waiting to undergo their purgation.

100–101 "the shore / at which the Tiber's waters mix with salt": the shore of Ostia, near Rome, at the mouth of the Tiber, where souls depart for Purgatory (see Intro., p. ix, and 33, note). This point of departure emphasizes the role of the Roman Church in launching souls on their voyage toward redemption.

112 "Love that discourses to me in my mind" opens the second canzone of Dante's *Convivio,* commented on by Dante in Book III of that work—a canzone of which the whole or part may, in life, have been set to music by Casella.

119 "the grave old man" is Cato (see Intro., p. xx, and I, 31, note).

CANTO III

3 This translation follows Bosco-Reggio's suggestion in glossing *ragion* as *a ragion,* "rightfully," and follows many who read *frugare* as "to punish." Others would translate: "where justice probes us" (Singleton), or "where our conscience goads us."

7–9 Virgil's having lingered to listen is a testimony to the sweetness of Casella's music, for in *Inferno,* Virgil had at times chastened Dante for delaying (see especially, *Inf.* XXX, 130–148).

10–15 Until now, Dante's mind had been so "focused"—on Casella's song and Cato's rebuke—that he had not yet directed his "widened...attention" to the full span of the steep slope.

16–22 The sun, whose rays never reached Hell, has risen high enough over Purgatory to make it apparent that Dante—because he is still corporeal—casts a shadow, while Virgil, a shade, casts none. Virgil will explain this to Dante in lines 25–30, quelling Dante's fear that he "had been abandoned" (21).

25–28 "The body...now belongs to Naples." Though Virgil died at

Brindisi, his body was brought to Naples by order of the emperor Augustus. Virgil also reminds us here that the sun has set in Italy ("The body...is buried where it now is evening").

30 The heavens do not "impede each other's rays" because the nine concentric spheres that make up the heavens beneath the Empyrean are transparent. They are material bodies, but their matter is not one of the four substances—earth, water, fire, air—but a fifth substance: they are quintessential. (For the heavens, see diagram, p. 314).

31–33 "how this is done": a problem to which Virgil returns in Canto XXV, 88–108.

34–37 Virgil, embodiment of pagan, pre-Christian human reason, is most appropriate to voice the admonition contained in this and the next two tercets; as one of those deprived of salvation for lack of Divine Grace, he is acutely aware of the limitations of reason in penetrating divine mysteries. The *"quia"* to which humans ought to confine themselves is *what* exists rather than why it exists. (See Intro., p. xvi.)

40–45 Dante had seen "the fruitless longing of those men" in Limbo *(Inf.* IV), where he encountered the "great-hearted" contemplative spirits, whose punishment is spiritual rather than physical: their strong desire to see God will never be satisfied. (See *Inf.* IV, 25–42, 131–141, and notes.)

Virgil himself is one of those "whose desire eternally laments": he seems conscious of the temporariness of his presence here in Purgatory and of the tragic irony of his position. Even in death, as in life, Virgil is (in Statius' words, XXII, 67–69) "as he who goes by night and carries / the lamp behind him—he is of no help / to his own self but teaches those who follow."

50 Turbia is a village in southeastern France, the present-day La Turbie near Nice; and Lerici, a seaport on the Gulf of La Spezia in Liguria. The coastal area between these two points is defined by steep, jagged mountains that fall abruptly to the sea.

73 " 'O chosen souls, you who have ended well' ": Virgil's first words to these souls, shortly after he bent his head in sorrow at the thought of his own exclusion from salvation, emphasize again the absolute gulf separating Virgil from these souls—all the more poignant since these are the souls of the excommunicates who, despite having been cast out of the Church, won salvation by repenting at the very last moment.

89 The "gap in the sun's light" arises, of course, from its being blocked by Dante's body.

103 The "one" who begins speaking is Manfred, king of Apulia and Sicily, the illegitimate son of Frederick II. Manfred's defeat and death in the Battle of Benevento in 1266 ended the last great hope of the Imperial forces against the Papacy (allied with Charles of Anjou) in the 13th century (see *Inf.* XXVIII, 16, note and "Dante in His Age," in the Bantam Classics *Inferno,* pp. 322–323).

113 Manfred prefers to identify himself not as the illegitimate son of

Frederick II (one of the damned—see *Inf.* X, 119), but as the grandson of Frederick's mother, "the Empress Constance" (one of the blessed—see *Par.* III, 118). Manfred named his daughter (referred to in 115 and note) after her.

115 Manfred's "lovely daughter, mother / of kings of Sicily and Aragon," is Constance, who married Pedro III of Aragon and gave birth to Alfonso (king of Aragon from 1285 to 1291), James (king of Sicily from 1285 to 1295 and of Aragon from 1291 to 1327), and Frederick (king of Sicily from 1296 to 1337).

117 "The truth": namely, that Manfred is in Purgatory, not Hell.

124–129 Cosenza is in northern Calabria, near the Tyrrhenian Sea. Its "pastor" is identified by most as Bartolomeo Pignatelli, cardinal and archbishop, and by some as his successor, Tommaso d'Agni. It is hard to unravel the dependence of the chroniclers (Villani and Malispini) on Dante from the dependence of all of them on events. The tale that Dante tells, supplemented by the chroniclers, would have us see that sometime after the Battle of Benevento—following the orders of Pope Clement IV—this "pastor" disinterred Manfred's body from its original resting place at Benevento and placed it on the banks of the Verde River, where it would be outside papal territory. Originally, Manfred's body had been buried "near Benevento, at the bridgehead" (129) by Charles of Anjou. Charles would have liked to bury the body in consecrated ground but could not, since Clement IV had excommunicated Manfred. Before his disinterment, Manfred's gravesite had been marked by a "great heap of stones" (128) thrown in tribute by the men of Charles's army. The body was transported "with tapers spent"—the treatment reserved for heretics and excommunicates.

131 The Verde is usually identified with the river that runs from the Sambruini Mountains to the Gulf of Gaeta; this river is now called the Liri for three-fourths of its course and the Garigliano for its final seaward reach.

137 "In contumacy of the Holy Church": in willful refusal to submit to the authority of the Church.

CANTO IV

1–16 There is no precise array of sources from Plato, Aristotle, Averroes, Albertus Magnus, and Aquinas that all exegetes agree to be the direct or mediated founts of Dante's discourse in this passage of *Purgatorio*. Nor are the classifications of the powers of the soul, powers to which Dante refers, fully chartable. But his purport is clear: The "error" of line 6 is Plato's, whom Dante held to believe in a plurality of souls in man, a doctrine refuted by Aristotle in the *De Anima* III, 9. (Dante, in his *Convivio* III, ii, 11–16, refers to Book II of the *De Anima* for the principal "powers" of the soul: life, sensation, intellection, though Dante includes the Aristotelian category of locomotion in that of sensation.) If the "powers" of the soul were not subordinate to *one* soul but were separate, autonomized, unsubordinated souls, each with its separate presence in the body of an individual human, then while one soul was bent on something, it would not absorb *all* of a man's attention: he would still be free to notice something else. But if the soul is one, then when one of its subordinate powers is fully engaged (as Dante's power of sensation-perception is by Manfred), all the other powers of the soul would be immobilized (and the intellective power of Dante's soul, whose judgment would note the passage of time, would be inoperative). In sum, the fact of undivided attention is proof that, despite its multiple powers, the soul is indivisible: when a part of us is engaged, we are *fully* engaged.

14 "that spirit": Manfred.

15–16 "The sun had fully climbed fifty / degrees" from its starting point at about 6 A.M. With the sun completing 15° each hour, 50° would bring us to 9:20 A.M. at this point.

18 "Those souls" form the "worthy band" with whom Dante and Virgil have been moving (see III, 100). "Here's what you want," i.e., the point at which the slope of the mountain could begin to be climbed.

19–23 "The gap through which" Dante and Virgil are climbing is so narrow that "the farmer" can seal up a wider opening in the wall of hedges surrounding his vineyard (to protect the ripening grapes from theft) "with just a little forkful of his thorns."

25–27 San Leo is a fortress town on the summit of a rugged mountain in the north part of the Marches region. Noli, on the Gulf of Genoa, could be reached by land, in Dante's time, only by descending the sheer cliffs that rise behind it. Cacume is a steep mountain near Frosinone between Rome and Naples; Bismantova, a sheer, semicircular, flat-topped mountain in the region of Emilia.

41–45 The "line drawn / from middle-quadrant to the center point" of a circle would make an angle of 45°—quite a climb.

47 This "somewhat higher terrace" is the First Spur of Ante-Purgatory, occupied by the souls of those who, though not excommunicates like the "company of souls" (24) that Dante and Virgil have left behind, did, like those souls, delay their repentance until the moment of death.

56–57 Dante is accustomed to doing his celestial observation from the northern hemisphere, where the sun would rise to his right in the southeast portion of the sky. Since the mountain of Purgatory is in the southern hemisphere, Dante sees—to his amazement—the sun to his left, in the northeastern sky.

61–66 "Castor and Pollux," the Twins, are stars in Gemini. Virgil means that if Gemini were moving with ("in conjunction with") the sun ("that mirror there"), Dante would see the zodiac tinted by the sun (therefore, "reddish") along a path even farther northward ("still closer" to the constellation of "the Bears"). In other words, the path of the sun would be even farther to the north than it is now.

69–71 Mount Zion in Jerusalem, in the northern hemisphere, and the mountain of Purgatory, in the southern hemisphere, are directly opposite one another on the globe, and therefore "share one horizon," from opposite directions.

73–75 "That same path which Phaethon drove so poorly" is the path of the sun. Phaethon, son of Apollo, pleaded to be allowed to drive the chariot of the sun, normally guided by his father; granted permission, he then proved unable to control its horses, and they ran violently off course, threatening to set the earth on fire. Therefore, Zeus had to kill him with a thunderbolt. (See Ovid, *Met.* II, 47–328, the same reference needed for *Inf.* XVII, 107.)

83–84 "the site from which the Hebrews . . . saw it": Jerusalem.

98–99 See 119–120, note.

115 "Then I knew who he was": Dante recognizes this indolent shade as a friend of his, and will address him by name in line 123 (see note).

119–120 "And have you fathomed how . . ." is in the same sardonic vein as "Perhaps you will / have need to sit before you reach that point!" (98–99).

123 We know very little about the historical figure of Dante's friend Belacqua. He seems to have been a character witness by profession, and perhaps a player of musical instruments—and was, it is fair to assume, rather indolent.

128 "God's angel," who refuses Belacqua permission to enter, will allow Dante and Virgil passage in Canto IX.

130–134 Like Manfred, Belacqua delayed his repentance until the moment of death. But while Manfred, as an excommunicate, must wait on the shore of the island for thirty times as long as he delayed repentance (III, 136–141), Belacqua, as an "ordinary" Late-Repentant, need only wait on this First Spur of Ante-Purgatory the same number of years he delayed his repentance. Like any soul in Purgatory, Belacqua would be speeded on his way "by prayer / that rises from a heart that lives in grace." For the compatibility between the effectiveness of prayer and the immutability of God's justice, see Canto VI, 34–39.

137 The "meridian touched by the sun" indicates the noon hour, some two and a half hours later than Dante's encounter with Manfred. The reference to "elsewhere," i.e., Morocco, where night is just beginning, reminds us of the relation of Jerusalem and Purgatory (see 69–71, note), for Morocco is midway between them, directly opposite the Ganges River.

CANTO V

5 The "sun seems not to shine on his left side" because he is facing west and the sun is striking him from the north.

20–21 The "hue that makes one sometimes merit grace" is the red blush of shame, which sometimes—but not always—is sufficient repentance for sin.

22–23 "Slightly ahead of us, people approached," moving to the right, counterclockwise (for someone facing the mountain). This will be the normal direction of movement in Purgatory, whereas movement in Hell was (with two exceptions) to the left. (See *Inf.* IX, 132, note.)

23 "The Miserere" is Psalm 51 (50 in the Vulgate), a prayer for God's mercy and for the cleansing of guilt. It is especially appropriate for these souls, who, as we shall learn in line 52, "were done to death by violence" and therefore must have received no last rites.

36 Welcoming Dante graciously "may profit them," since Dante is still living and may return to the world to ask the living to pray for these souls.

50 "that you may carry word of him beyond": This suggests that "these people pressing in on" Dante share something of the desire expressed by shades in Hell—the desire for worldly fame—but the chief desire of these shades is for the "profit" mentioned by Virgil in line 36 (see note and 71–72).

60 "Spirits born to goodness" are contrasted with the "spirits born to evil" in *Inferno.*

64 "And one began": This shade is Jacopo del Cassero (c1260–1298), a distinguished warrior and politician, whose death at the hands of Azzo d'Este's killers was so well known to Dante's contemporaries that Dante does not even need to name him here.

68–71 "The land / that lies between Romagna and the realm / of Charles": i.e., Fano, between Romagna and the kingdom of Naples, ruled by Charles of Anjou.

73–84 Jacopo, formerly *podestà,* or chief magistrate, of Bologna, opposed Azzo VIII d'Este, who wished to rule Bologna. Azzo had him killed later while he journeyed to Milan to assume a new office as *podestà.* He was killed near Padua, a city supposedly founded by Antenor, the Trojan warrior who betrayed his city to the Greeks. This allusion suggests the Paduans' perfidious complicity in the crime. "Mira" and "Oriaco" are both small villages between Padua and Venice. Jacopo implies that he would have found help if he had fled toward Mira instead of toward Oriaco.

85–129 "another shade": This other shade is Buonconte da Montefeltro, son of the renowned Ghibelline leader, Guido da Montefeltro (see *Inf.* XXVII, 29). Buonconte fought as captain of the Aretines when they were routed by the Guelphs of Florence at the Battle of Campaldino in 1289, but Buonconte's body could not be found on the battlefield. In telling his story now, he clears up the mystery surrounding his death—and his salvation contrasts with the damnation of his father.

94 "the Casentino": The Casentino region is the valley formed by the upper course of the Arno.

95–97 "a stream called Archiano": This stream starts high up in the Apennines near the Camaldoli monastery, known as the "Hermitage." At a point close to Campaldino, the Archiano flows into the Arno and becomes "lost."

106   "For just one tear": i.e., for even the smallest sign of contrition.

112–113   "His evil will...conjoined with intellect." These are considered separate faculties. (See *Inf.* XXXI, 55–57.)

115–116   "Pratomagno" is a mountain on the southwest border of the Casentino; to the east the Casentino is bordered by "the great ridge," the highest ridge in the northeastern Apennines.

122   "The royal river" is the Arno.

124   "The angry Archiano...thrust it in the Arno": see 95–97, note.

130–136   The initially unidentified shade who suddenly begins speaking is La Pia, possibly of the Tolomei family of Siena, who was hurled down from the balcony of her house in Maremma by her husband, Nello, chief magistrate of Volterra and Lucca. As noted in the Introduction (p. xxi), "she concentrates her tragedy in three lines, but not before she has voiced her own compassion for the weariness of any living body undertaking a journey as arduous as Dante's."

CANTO VI

1   The dice game referred to in the Italian as *zara* was of Arabic origin, but then spread to Byzantium and the West. Our word "hazard" has its ultimate origin in that Arabic word.

13–24   All of those mentioned in these lines are 13th-century figures.

13–14   The "Aretine" is the jurist Benincasa da Laterina, who may have taught law in Bologna. As a judge in Siena, he condemned to death one or two relatives of the notorious nobleman turned bandit Ghino di Tacco. When Benincasa moved to Rome as judge, the avenging Ghino barbarously decapitated Benincasa and carried off his head. Ghino's own death—later—was by assassination. He is the protagonist of a well-known novella in Boccaccio's *Decameron* (X, 2).

15   Most commentators are agreed that the "one who drowned" is Guccio de' Tarlati of Pietramala (a stronghold of the Ghibellines in the Aretine region). Guccio drowned either in pursuit of Guelph exiles from Arezzo or, according to other commentators, in escaping from the Guelphs after the battle of Campaldino. (In the Italian, *correndo in caccia* can mean either "in pursuit" or "in flight.")

16–17   Federigo Novello, son of Guido Novello, fell at the hands of the Guelphs of Arezzo as he aided the Tarlati of Pietramala against them.

17–18   The "Pisan" is Gano (or Farinata), the son of Marzucco degli Scornigiani. The son was killed by Count Ugolino (see *Inf.* XXIII) in Pisa's civil strife, around 1287. The father was a worthy judge in Pisa and later became a Franciscan friar in Florence. He probably showed "his fortitude" in calmly urging his family to forgo violent retaliation after the killing of his son.

19   Count Orso, son of Count Napoleone degli Alberti, was violently murdered in 1286 by his cousin Alberto, son of Alessandro degli Alberti, in continuation of a blood feud between their fathers, who lie buried in ice in Hell for having killed each other. (See *Inf.* XXXII, 56–57, note.)

19–24 Pier de la Brosse, physician, chamberlain, and favorite of Philip III of France, was arrested quite suddenly and for mysterious reasons in 1278, two years after he was involved in accusing Philip's second wife, Marie of Brabant, of poisoning the heir to the throne, Philip's son by his first marriage, in order to establish her own son as Philip's successor. The "Lady of Brabant" may have accused Pier of treachery with Alfonso X of Castile (or—others say—of trying to seduce her). Pier, whom Dante sees as innocent, was hanged. Dante warns Marie (still alive—she died in 1321) against her ending up in Hell, "among a sadder flock."

28 "O my light" recalls the reference in Canto IV to "the guide who gave me hope and was my light."

29 "In one passage you deny...": The "one passage" where Virgil denies "that prayer can bend the rule of Heaven" is in *Aeneid* VI (492–496), where the shade of Aeneas' fallen helmsman Palinurus—who, since his body is unburied, is forbidden to cross Styx—begs Aeneas to take him across Styx anyway, so "that at least in death" he might "find a place of rest." Palinurus' plea is answered by the Sibyl, "How can you, unburied, / look at the waves of Styx, upon the Furies' / stern river, and approach its shore, unasked?"

42 These "prayers without a passageway to God" are such because they are uttered by pagan souls, who lived before the redeeming sacrifice of Christ. However, others' prayers could also be denied a passageway if the petitioner, through sin or stubbornness, stood outside of God's grace.

43–48 Here Virgil foreshadows the necessary separation of himself and Dante, as Dante will need then to be guided by one (Beatrice) who can illuminate the Truth, standing as she does—unlike Virgil—in God's grace.

51 "The slope now casts a shadow" because it is afternoon (about 3 P.M.) and they are on the eastern side of the mountain in the southern hemisphere.

52–54 "Our climb won't be as rapid as you thought," and, as Virgil hints here, it will in fact take them two more days to reach the peak. In the next canto we find out that there can be no climbing by night.

58 The "soul who is completely apart" identifies himself in line 74 (see note).

74 Sordello (1200–d. after 1269), the most famous of the Italian troubadours, was, like Virgil, born in the region of Mantua. He wrote in Provençal and served as courtier in Italy, Provence, and then again—under Charles of Anjou—in Italy. Sordello's considerable achievements in political and didactic poetry make him an ideal figure to spur on Dante's long invective against Italy and Florence.

88–89 Under the emperor Justinian, who ruled the Eastern Roman Empire from A.D. 527 to 565, Roman law was codified in a form that served as the chief vehicle for the transmission of that law to Europe.

Justinian was thus responsible for "mending [Italy's] bridle," but Dante laments the present lack of an emperor who would fill "the saddle." All of Canto VI of *Paradiso* is devoted to an uninterrupted discourse by Justinian, a central presence in Dante's pantheon.

91–96 "Ah you" is addressed to those holding Church office. For Dante they, instead of usurping temporal power and laying their hands "upon the bit," should allow an emperor to sit "in the saddle." "What God ordained" is, in Christ's words, "Render therefore unto Caesar the things which are Caesar's; and unto God the things that are God's" (Matt. 22:21). For Dante's view of the just relation between temporal and spiritual power, see his *Monarchy* and the essay "Dante in His Age" in the Bantam Classics *Inferno*. (For a translation of Dante's *Monarchia—Monarchy—*see the entry under Nicholl in the bibliographical note at the end of these canto notes, or see the translation by H. W. Schneider, under the title *On World-Government,* New York, 1957.)

97–105 "German Albert" is Albert I of Austria. In 1298 he succeeded his father Rudolf I of Hapsburg, as emperor: both father and son bore the additional title "King of the Romans," but because the son, like the father, was more concerned for the consolidation and extension of his German patrimony, he neglected Italy, the "garden of the Empire." For Albert's failure to exercise his authority, which might have quelled the internal strife tearing Italy apart, Dante calls down on him "the just judgment of the stars." This may allude to the fact that in 1308—eight years after the time in which Dante is supposed to be encountering him here in Purgatory—Albert was violently assassinated at the hands of his nephew. Of course, since Dante is writing from the perspective of 1300, he is careful to avoid jumping ahead of that time, but his knowledge of events between 1300 and the time when he is writing allows him to exploit the resources of prophecy. (See *Inf.* I, 1–3, note.)

106–111 These two tercets lament the sad fate of the Imperial feudal nobility in an Italy now ruled by local overlords. In this lament Dante includes both pro-Imperial Ghibellines and anti-Imperial Guelphs—all nobles whose warring has led to Italy's decline, warring to which they and a proper emperor should have put an end. The Montecchi were Ghibellines of Verona; the Cappelletti the Guelph faction of Cremona. Both the Guelph Monaldi and Ghibelline Filippeschi were factions in Orvieto. Santafior (or Santafiora) was an Aldobrandeschi feudal domain near Siena, which had occupied much of that territory by Dante's time.

125–126 Some three Marcelluses fill the role of Dante's Marcellus if we see the line as a sarcastic reference to every anti-Imperial upstart who mimes the anti-Caesarism of G. Claudius Marcellus, consul in 50 B.C., or of G. Claudius' cousins, M. Claudius Marcellus, consul in 51 B.C., and another G. Claudius Marcellus, consul in 49 B.C. Moore (like Benvenuto) identifies him with the "talkative Marcellus" of Lucan's *Pharsalia* (I, 313), but does not specify Lucan's *own* referent, identified by Singleton with the second of the above Marcelluses; by J. D. Duff, editor of the Loeb Library Lucan, with the third; and by Casini-Barbi with the first.

Another gloss would see the line as meaning: "Every townsman who reaches prominence in factional disputes pretends to be the savior of his country"—referring to M. Claudius Marcellus, victor over Syracuse in 212 B.C., known as the Sword of Rome.

127–151 The reasons for Florence's "exemption" from "this lament" turn out, ironically, to be even more baleful than the reasons for its condemnation; Dante is scarcely about to let his native city off the hook. Dante contrasts the civic behavior of other countries and towns with that of Florence, in a tone of ironic invective that recalls the opening lines of *Inferno* XXVI.

139 Athens and Lacedaemon (Sparta) were noted as the chief lawgiving cities of ancient Greece.

149 Singleton notes that St. Augustine, at one point in his *Confessions*, conveys the sick state of his soul by speaking of it as a restless woman who tossed and turned on her bed (*Confessions*, VI, 16).

There is a glancing return, in this final simile, to the opening simile of this canto. In the Italian, the two are linked by *volte*, the throws and tosses of the dice player, and *dar volta*, the turning and tossing of the sick woman. And the dice player is *dolente*, disconsolate, grieving, while the woman is in *dolore*, pain.

CANTO VII

3 "Who are you?": Though the "you" of Sordello's question in the Italian is plural, his amazement on learning that it is Virgil he has just met distracts him from inquiring further about Dante. Since Dante is standing behind Virgil, the shadow he casts goes unnoticed by Sordello, who, in Canto VIII, will be astonished to learn that Dante is alive.

4–7 "Before...Octavian.": Virgil died in 19 B.C. during the reign of the first Roman emperor, Augustus (Gaius Julius Caesar Octavianus, hence "Octavian"), roughly fifty years before Christ's descent into Limbo (after his death in A.D. 33) known as the Harrowing of Hell, in which he liberated "the spirits worthy of ascent to God." (See *Inf.* IV, 52–61, note.)

15 "Where the lesser presence clasps" is possibly the waist, the knees, the feet, or under Virgil's arms.

17 "You through whom our tongue revealed its power...": The phrase assumes the continuity of Latin and its Romance heirs. Virgil's power lay in Latin, Sordello's in Provençal, and Dante's lies in Italian.

18 Virgil and Sordello were both born in the region around Mantua; it was this that prompted their first embrace (see VI, 71–75).

20 "Tell me if you're from Hell and from what cloister.": Since Virgil has just told Sordello that he is "deprived of Heaven," Sordello draws this inference.

25–27 "Not for the having—but not having—done": Here Virgil stresses that he was "deprived of Heaven" (7) not for any sinfulness but rather for the guiltless fact of his ignorance of Christ.

28   This "place below" is Limbo.

31   "The infant innocents" are those who died before baptism could cleanse them of original sin.

34–35   "Those souls" are the virtuous pagans, whom we encountered in *Inferno* IV. The "three holy virtues" are, of course, faith, hope, and charity.

39   Virgil's request for "the true entry point of Purgatory" underscores the fact that they are still in Ante-Purgatory.

40–41   "He answered: 'No fixed place has been assigned to us'": The souls in Ante-Purgatory seem free to wander. As for the category to which Sordello ("completely apart" in *Purg.* VI, 58–59) belongs—that seems uncertain or nonexistent.

83   *"Salve, Regina"* is an 11th-12th-century hymn to the blessed Virgin, recited after vespers, asking her to pity those *"in hac lacrimarum valle,"* "in this valley of tears"—appropriate to this moment and place of rest for Dante and Virgil.

84   "not visible from the outside": i.e., from the outside of the valley, since its depth is sufficient to hide them.

85   "before the meager sun seeks out its nest"—reminding us again that ascent at night is not possible in Purgatory.

91–96   "He who is seated highest" is Rudolf I of Hapsburg, emperor from 1273 to 1291, who, like his son—the "German Albert" of the previous canto—was guilty of neglecting his imperial duties in Italy. (See VI, 97–105, note.) "Another" (96) refers again to Dante's hope, first voiced in *Inferno* I, 106, that a redeemer will come to "restore low-lying Italy."

97–100   "His neighbor, whose appearance comforts him" is Ottokar II, who from 1253 to 1278 was king of Bohemia, the land described here (98–100) by the rivers that flow through it. Ottokar had refused to acknowledge Rudolf as emperor, for which Rudolf waged war against him, finally slaying him in battle in 1278. The fact that, in Purgatory, Ottokar's appearance "comforts" Rudolf (97) is in sharp contrast to the vehement curses that souls in Hell continue to lavish on their earthly enemies.

102–103   "his son, the bearded Wenceslaus": After his father was slain, Wenceslaus (1271–1305) refused to fight Rudolf and instead begged for his mercy. (That—and more—warrant Dante's description of him as feeding "on wantonness and ease.") Later, the two were reconciled; Rudolf gave Wenceslaus his daughter in marriage and restored his kingdom. Thus, Wenceslaus ruled Bohemia from 1278 to 1305.

103–105   "That small-nosed man" is Philip III (the Bold) of France, who reigned from 1270 to 1285. He waged war on Pedro III of Aragon, but suffered a calamitous and disgraceful defeat, thus "deflowering the lily," symbol of France. He is introduced as the "father . . . of the pest of France" (109–110), Philip IV (the Fair).

104 "His kindly friend" is Henry I (the Fat), king of Navarre from 1270 to 1274 and father-in-law of Philip the Fair (see 109–112, note).

109–112 "The pest of France," Philip IV (the Fair), was largely responsible for the succession of Clement V to the papal throne. It was Clement who, in 1309, transferred the Papacy to Avignon and began what is usually referred to as the Babylonian Captivity, which lasted until 1377. (See *Inf.* XIX, 82–88, note.) Dante has nothing but scorn for Philip in the *Comedy*, denouncing him in *Inferno* XIX, *Purgatorio* XX and XXXII, and later, in *Paradiso* XIX.

112–114 "That other, who seems so robust" is Pedro III, king of Aragon from 1276 to 1285. In 1282, Pedro wrested the crown of Sicily from Charles of Anjou, who strove in vain to win it back, even to the extent of challenging Pedro to a duel. Here Pedro and his former enemy Charles, described as having "a nose so manly," sing together in harmonious accord.

Charles of Anjou, born in 1226, died in 1285, the same year in which Pedro III died. Called by the pope to battle Manfred (*Purg.* III), Charles won the kingdom of Naples after victories at Benevento (*Purg.* III, 124–129, note) and Tagliacozzo (*Inf.* XXVIII, 17–18, note).

115 "The young man seated there" probably refers to Pedro III's last-born son, Pedro, who predeceased his father. Unlike his two brothers, James and Frederick, Pedro had inherited his father's virtue and might have proved a vessel of his father's valor had he lived to reign.

119–120 James II was king of Sicily from 1285 to 1295 and succeeded to the throne of Aragon after the death of his elder brother Alfonso III of Aragon in 1291, leaving the governance of Sicily in the hands of his younger brother, Frederick II. Later, however, James ceded Aragon to his fiancée's father, Charles II of Naples. This led to war between the brothers. Pedro III's sons James and Frederick "do not possess his best bequest" (120), i.e., his noble virtue.

124–129 Neither "the large-nosed one," Charles, nor Pedro is exempted from Dante's maxim (121–123), as both have had inferior sons. The reign of Charles II (the Lame) over Puglia (Naples) and Provence was lamented by those regions; the inferiority of Charles II ("the plant") to Charles I ("its seed") is as great as the inferiority of Charles I (wedded first to Beatrice, then to Margaret) to Pedro III (wedded to Constance).

130–132 "The king who led the simple life" is Henry III, king of England from 1216 to 1272, who had "better fortune with his progeny": his son Edward I was noted for the extensive legal reforms he instituted during his long reign.

133–136 "He who is seated lowest on the ground" is Guiglielmo, the marquis of Monferrato from 1254 to 1292. After subjugating several cities in Lombardy, Guiglielmo formed an alliance with Charles of Anjou, but turned against him when Charles himself tried to gain power in Lombardy. In 1290, while attempting to quell a rebellion in Alexandria, one of the cities under his control, Guiglielmo was captured by the Alexandrians; he was caged like a wild beast and exhibited to the public for seventeen months until his death in 1292. Guiglielmo's son Giovanni I led Monferrato and Canavese in a war of vengeance against Alexandria, which resulted, however, in the invasion of Monferrato, and the occupation of several of its towns, by the Alexandrians.

CANTO VIII

1–6 These lines have tempted many translators (see Intro., p. xii). They refer to the hour of dusk, when evening prayers are said, and when "the bell" of Compline sounds, marking the last of the day's seven canonical hours. (For the hours, see XV, 6, note.)

13 *"Te lucis ante,"* a Compline hymn, known in English as "Before the ending of the day," is a prayer asking God the Creator to defend us from evil and troubling dreams, and from any pollution that might come to us once we have dropped the guard of consciousness. Since in this canto we meet those who were too preoccupied with worldly affairs, their singing of this hymn may signify a redoubled vigilance that would guard against the entry of even the least willful kind of sin. But the souls in Ante-Purgatory are saved and essentially beyond temptation. Thus, they may be singing this hymn not for themselves but, out of compassion, for the living (see XI, 19–24).

26 The "two angels bearing flaming swords" recall the angels who were placed before Eden after Adam and Eve's expulsion "to keep the way" to "the tree of life" (Gen. 3:24).

27 "the blades were broken off, without the tips" For Singleton, "swords can be as token swords where He guides." For Bosco-Reggio the demons have already been "defeated once and for all: the angels need only present themselves with the weapons of their victory, but now broken-off because they are needless: mementos of an old victory." And there are still other glosses. (For Singleton, see "In exitu Israel de Aegypto," in *Dante: A Collection of Critical Essays,* ed. John Freccero, Englewood Cliffs, 1965, p. 117.)

28–29 The garments and wings of these angels are green, the color symbolizing hope.

47 The "one who watched" will soon be identified (53).

53 Nino Visconti was, through his mother, a grandson of Count Ugolino (see *Inf.* XXXIII, 13–75, note). Nino was a judge of the district of Gallura in Sardinia; he had his deputy, Fra Gomita, hanged for accepting bribes to let some prisoners escape. Fra Gomita is denounced for this and for "other matters," in *Inferno* XXII, 81–87. Between 1288 and 1293 Nino was often in Florence, encouraging the Guelphs against Ghibelline Pisa. Dante would have had ample opportunity to become his friend.

61–63 "When they had heard my answer, / Sordello and Judge Nino...": This informs us that, until this point, Sordello had not realized that Dante is not a shade.

64 The "one" is Sordello, and "the other" who speaks to Dante (67) is Nino.

65 "Currado" is Currado Malaspina, about whom we shall hear more. (See 109ff. and note.)

71–75 "My own Giovanna" is Nino's daughter; "her mother" (73) is Beatrice d'Este. After Nino's death, Beatrice "gave up her white veils" (74)—worn by widows in Dante's time as a sign of mourning—and married Galeazzo Visconti of Milan for political reasons. Nino predicts that Beatrice "will wish them [her white veils] back again" (75), that is, that she will regret her marriage to Galeazzo—alluding to the fact that two years after his marriage to Beatrice (just under two years after the time in which Nino is supposed to be speaking) Galeazzo Visconti would be expelled from Milan. Galeazzo's consequent hard times were shared by Beatrice. (Though ultimately widowed a second time, in 1328, she did find ease when her son became lord of Milan.)

79–81 "The serpent that assigns the Milanese their camping place" is the serpent depicted on the Visconti coat of arms, which was emblazoned on the banner around which the Milanese forces would camp. Nino's own coat of arms bore "Gallura's rooster" (81). Since the tomb of a lady traditionally bore her husband's coat of arms, in these lines Nino is reproaching Beatrice for her marriage to Galeazzo, and alluding to Galeazzo's poverty following his expulsion from Milan (see 71–75, note).

86 "that portion of the sky where stars are slower" (in their seeming revolution): the South Pole.

89–93 "Those three torches," or three stars, which now—as Dante nears Purgatory itself—burn in place of "the four bright stars" that Dante saw that morning from the shore of Ante Purgatory (see I, 23), are emblemantic of the three theological virtues of faith, hope, and charity, which supersede the four cardinal virtues (prudence, justice, fortitude, and temperance).

95 "Our adversary": the Devil in serpent form.

104 "The hawks of heaven," as the next lines make clear, are the angels.

109ff. "The shade who . . . had drawn closer to him" and who had been called by Nino in line 65 is Currado II of the powerful Ghibelline Malaspina family, a grandson of "the old Currado" (119). Currado II died c1294. After Dante's exile from Florence, in 1306, another of the old Currado's grandsons, Franceschino, hosted Dante in Lunigiana, site of the "Val di Magra" (116), which, at least in part, accounts for Dante's praise of the Malaspina family.

131 "the evil head": Probably Satan is meant, though the phrase may refer to the corrupt Papacy, or more specifically, to Pope Boniface VIII.

134–139 "The sun will not have rested . . .": Currado predicts that before the sun returns seven times to the Ram (Aries)—that is, before seven years have passed—Dante will take refuge with the Malaspina (which he did in 1306).

CANTO IX

1–9 This translation accords with those who gloss these somewhat vexed lines thus:

In the first two tercets, Aurora, concubine ("she who shares the bed") of old Tithonus, was now rising in the northern hemisphere, in Italy, with the constellation Scorpio facing her as she rose. Thus, in Italy, it was about 5 A.M.; in Jerusalem it was about 8:30–9 A.M.; and in Purgatory it was about 8:30–9 P.M. The third tercet tells the time in Purgatory ("where we were"). Night is divided into twelve hours, six before midnight, six after. Two of these hours or "steps" (8) had already passed, and the third was about to complete its passage, which brought the time close to 9 P.M.

For a defense of this composite gloss, especially for the reading of *la sua fronte* not as "her [Aurora's] forehead" but as "facing her," and for seeing Dante as using two places—the northern and the southern hemispheres—to tell us the time (but with Scorpio and not Pisces involved) see Bosco-Reggio.

10 "something of Adam," i.e., the flesh, which needs rest.

12 "all five": Virgil, Sordello, Nino, Currado Malaspina, and Dante.

13–15 The reference here is to the myth of Philomela, best known through Ovid (*Met.* VI, 412–674; but also see Virgil, *Eclogues* VI, 78–81, and *Georgics* IV, 15 and 511–515). Philomela was raped by her brother-in-law Tereus, who cut out her tongue to prevent her telling what had happened. Philomela, however, managed to convey the story to her sister, Procne, by weaving it into a piece of cloth. The two took revenge on Tereus by serving up his son's flesh for Tereus to eat. After realizing what he had fed on, Tereus tried to murder the two, but as he pursued them, Philomela was changed into a nightingale, Procne into a swallow, and Tereus into a hoopoe. But here Dante seems to have Philomela as the swallow, and in XVII, 19–21, Procne as the nightingale. His deviance from tradition is very possibly the result of ambiguity in his sources.

16–18 "when … our intellect's envisionings become almost divine": "Divine" here means "divinatory"; medieval opinion often held that early-morning dreams were prophetic. In expounding this idea here, Dante is preparing to relate the first of three early-morning dreams he will have while in Purgatory. As will become clear, each of Dante's dreams has, indeed, something of truth to it.

19–20 On the "eagle … with golden pinions," Casini-Barbi comments: "This eagle is nothing other than the form that, in Dante's dream, the real figure of Lucia takes (55), and the actions Dante attributes to the eagle are those of the divine woman: both figures are thus symbols of the same idea—both signify illuminating Grace."

22 Ganymede, son of a king of Troy, was so extraordinarily beautiful that the enamored Jove sent down (or transformed himself into) an eagle to bear Ganymede up to Olympus, there to serve as Jove's cupbearer (see *Aen.* V, 332–339, and *Met.* X, 155–161).

30 "the fire's orbit": the sphere of fire, which in Dante's time was believed to surround the air and extend up to the moon (see diagram, p. 314).

34–39 "The waking of Achilles, when...": The youthful Achilles' mother, hoping to keep him out of the Trojan War (in which it had been prophesied he would die), stole him away while he slept, from his tutor, the centaur Chiron, and carried him to the island of Skyros, where, dressed in women's clothing, he remained in hiding in the court of King Lycomedes. Later, Ulysses discovered Achilles' identity and persuaded him to join the Greeks, then on their way to the Trojan War. (See Statius, *Achilleid,* I, 104–241).

42 "cold as ice": cf. *Inferno* XXXIV, 22–25.

44 "the sun was more than two hours high": This would make it after eight in the morning on Easter Monday—and make Dante's predawn dream rather prolonged.

49 The rampart wall with its gate marks the entryway to Purgatory proper.

55 St. Lucia, patron saint of those who suffer defects of sight, and symbol of illuminating Grace, intercedes here, as she did once before (as Beatrice informs Virgil, in *Inf.* II, 100–108), to further the progress of Dante's journey.

78 "A custodian": Here the narrow gate is guarded, in contrast to the untended, wide open gate of Hell. The symbolic contrast recalls Matthew 7:13–14: "Enter ye in at the strait gate: for wide is the gate, and broad is the way, that leadeth to destruction, and many there be which go in thereat: Because strait is the gate, and narrow is the way, which leadeth unto life, and few there be that find it."

82–85 The "naked sword" is one traditional symbol of a judge. Like the "two angels" of Canto VIII (26 and note), this custodian with a naked sword—whose dazzling reflections Dante is unable to sustain—also recalls the cherubim of Genesis 3:24.

86 "Where is your escort? / Take care lest you be harmed by climbing here" implies that the guardian wishes to be sure that these approaching souls are armed with the warrant of Grace; once informed that they are, he is most gracious in his welcome. Again, this guardian contrasts with Minos, in *Inferno* V, 19, who uses similar words ("be careful how you enter, whom you trust"), but lapses into brute silence when informed that the poets' passage "has been willed above."

94–102 "the first step was white marble": This first of the three steps corresponds to the first of the three parts of the sacrament of penance-confession—contrition of the heart. The clear polish of the marble reflects the sinner's true image, so that he can recognize his sinfulness. The second, made out of dark crumbling rock, corresponds to the emotional upheaval that comes with confession by the lips, the second part of penance;

and the third step of "porphyry, / as flaming red as blood that spurts from veins" corresponds to satisfaction by works, the third stage of penance. The bloodred color suggests both the blood Christ shed to redeem the sins of mankind and the zeal needed to shun future sins.

103–105 In Matthew 16:18–19 Christ says: "And I say also unto thee, That thou art Peter, and upon this rock I will build my church, and the gates of hell shall not prevail against it. And I will give unto thee the keys of the kingdom of heaven: and whatsoever thou shalt bind on earth shall be bound in heaven: and whatsoever thou shalt loose on earth shall be loosed in heaven." That text rests, of course, on the meaning of the word *petrus,* "rock." Dante crystallizes this meaning in his conception of Purgatory, for the threshold of Purgatory, on which the custodian angel sits, is made of adamant—the firmest of foundations.

112–114 "Upon my forehead, he traced seven *P*'s with his sword's point...": The *P*'s stand for *peccatum,* i.e., sin, or moral "wounds." Once engraved on the forehead they can only be "washed away" through the completion of the expiation that follows the three parts of the sacrament of penance. Thus, the angel imposes another journeying on Dante—that of the penitent, who must move through the seven terraces of Purgatory to cleanse himself successively of the seven sins.

115–116 "Ashes...would share one color with his robe," this color symbolizing humility and contrition.

116–117 "from beneath that robe he drew two keys". As the custodian angel will shortly tell Dante (127), he received these two keys from Peter. See 103–105, note.

118–126 In *Inferno* XXVII, 104–105, the two keys the pope holds are the keys of condemnation and absolution, but here the two "keys of the kingdom of heaven" (Matt. 16:18–19), entrusted by Christ to St. Peter and, thus, to the priest-confessor, are the silver key that allows the *science* of judging both the nature of the sinner's sin and the appropriate absolution that can "undo the knot" and the golden key that sanctions the priest's *authority* to absolve.

127 "These I received from Peter": another link between the custodian angel and Peter, whom he prefigures, and whom Dante will actually encounter in Paradise.

131–132 "Enter; but I warn you...": These words are reminiscent of the story of Lot, who was similarly warned not to look back at the destruction of Sodom lest that be a sign of his attachment to its wickedness. Similarly, the true penitent must not look back with any sense of loss to the old life but must keep his will turned toward the new life on which he is embarking.

133–138 The simile for the opening of the gate emphasizes its rustiness from lack of use (see also X, 1–3). Metellus, a Roman tribune, attempted to protect the Roman treasury, situated on the Tarpeian Rock, from seizure by Julius Caesar. Lucan describes the thunderous echoes of the rock once Metellus had been overthrown (*Phars.* III, 153–168).

141   *"Te Deum Laudamus,"* "We Praise Thee, O God" is the famous hymn celebrating the Trinity. It is especially linked to occasions of thanksgiving.

144–145   This translation follows R. Monterosso (entry in *E.D.* under *"organo"),* who sees the use of the organ in churches as established well before Dante's time (others see *organi* as meaning polyphonic chanting). both the English and the Italian for line 145 allow the possibility that Dante is referring to chant and instrument that do not sound together but alternately. But such an "alternate" presence of chant and organ need not invite us to see the "words" and "music" of 140–141 as other than the simultaneous presence, in chant, of word and song, where, too, words may be sometimes "clear" and sometimes "lost."

CANTO X

4   "The soul's aberrant love" is the love of sinfulness and evil ways, because of which the gate to Purgatory is so seldom used. As Virgil will later explain (in Canto XVII), love is the seed "of all acts deserving punishment" as well as "of every virtue."

5–6   "If I'd turned toward it, how could my fault have found a fit excuse?" i.e., since I had been warned of the consequences in no uncertain terms (see IX, 131–133).

7–16   The difficulty of passage between these cracked, veering rocks leading to the First Terrace contrasts with the easy access through the wide entryway to Hell (see IX, 78, note). This narrow passageway likened to a "needle's eye" (16) recalls Christ's words to his disciples: "And again I say unto you, It is easier for a camel to go through the eye of a needle, than for a rich man to enter into the kingdom of God" (Matt. 19:24).

13   "the declining moon had reached its bed . . . ," i.e. had set. Since it is four days after the full moon (mentioned in *Inf.* XX, 127), the moon would be setting over three hours after sunrise. Since "the sun was more than two hours high" (IX, 44) when the poets approached the gate of Purgatory, and the moon has set before they emerge from the "needle's eye," their difficult passage must have taken well over an hour.

18   "This place at which the slope retreats" is the First Terrace of Purgatory, occupied by the prideful.

29–31   "the bordering bank / . . . was of white marble and adorned with carvings": At the entrance to each of the seven terraces of Purgatory, Dante will encounter examples (usually three in number) correcting the sin being purged. His first encounter with these corrective examples takes the pictorial form of carvings, though usually the corrective examples will be called out by voices. Here, as on all the other terraces, the first of the corrective examples is taken from the life of Mary (see 34–37, note).

32–33   "Not only Polycletus / but even Nature, there, would feel defeated": Polycletus (c452–421 B.C.) was a Greek sculptor renowned for the accuracy and beauty of his portraiture. Since, as Virgil instructed

Dante (in *Inf.* XI, 97–105), "nature follows...the Divine Intellect and Divine Art," and man's art, "when it can,...would follow nature," Dante means that these carvings, as direct examples of "Divine Art," are superior both to Polycletus' art and to Nature itself.

34–37 "The angel..." is Gabriel, who announced to the Virgin Mary her election as mother of Christ, which Mary accepted with great humility (see 44, note). The "long interdict" is the time between the closing of Heaven's gates following Adam's sin and the Annunciation to Mary, which ultimately led to Christ's sacrifice and "the peace that opened Heaven" (36).

40–43 "'Ave'; / for...one who turned the key that had unlocked / the highest love": "Ave" ("Hail") is the first word of the angel Gabriel's annunciation of the Incarnation to Mary, "Hail, thou that art highly favoured, the Lord is with thee" (Luke 1:28). In becoming the mother of Christ—who is referred to in Revelation 3:7 as "the key of David"—Mary "turned the key that...unlocked the highest love."

44 *"Ecce ancilla Dei"*: "Behold the handmaid of the Lord" (Luke 1:38) are the words with which Mary humbly accepted the Annunciation.

56–69 The "sacred ark which makes men now fear tasks not in their charge" is the ark of the covenant—the sign of God's presence—which Uzzah grasped at to prevent it from falling, whereupon he was struck dead (see II Sam. 6:6–7). When the ark was finally drawn into Jerusalem, King David danced before it: "And David danced before the Lord with all his might; and David was girded with a linen ephod. So David and all the house of Israel brought up the ark of the Lord with shouting, and with the sound of the trumpet. And as the ark of the Lord came into the city of David, Michal Saul's daughter looked through a window and saw king David leaping and dancing before the Lord; and she despised him in her heart" (II Sam. 6:14–16).

73–93 "He whose worth had urged on Gregory to his great victory" is Trajan, Roman emperor from A.D. 98 to 117. Trajan's actions on behalf of a poor widow inspired St. Gregory (pope from A.D. 590 to 604) to weep and pray that Trajan, a pagan, be brought back to life, that he might have a chance to repent and receive the Grace of God. An angel informed Gregory that his prayer had been granted—Gregory's "great victory"—but told him never to make a prayer of that sort again.

94–95 "One within whose sight no thing is new": For God, whose wisdom is eternal, no thing can be new. Dante will avow (103–104) that his own eyes "had been satisfied in seeking / new sights—a thing for which they long."

108 "the debt we owe": the debt of purgation that we, as sinners, owe to God.

109–111 "Don't dwell upon the form of punishment": Dante's admonition prepares us for his account of the first of the punishments of Purgatory—the punishment of the prideful; but he also reminds us that Paradise "comes after" the expiation. Furthermore, however harsh the punishments of Purgatory, they cannot last beyond the Judgment Day, when Purgatory will disappear, and each soul, reunited with its body, will be consigned to Heaven or to Hell. All those in Purgatory will, presumably, find a place in Heaven.

112–120 These are the prideful, whom we will meet more fully in the next canto; they are bent beneath their stone weights in atonement for the arrogance of their posture in life.

123 "in backward steps": steps that are morally retrograde.

125 "the angelic butterfly": the soul passing through purgation and mounting to eventual beatitude is said to emerge from the "worm"—as in Augustine (*In Ioan.* I, 13): "All men who are born of the flesh, what are they if not worms? And from worms He makes angels."

130–132 "A corbel" is a stone or wooden bracket that projects from the face of a wall and is most often used to support a cornice or arch. The corbel Dante refers to is, of course, in the form of a man.

CANTO XI

1–24 Dante's paraphrase of the Lord's Prayer, the Pater Noster (Matt. 6:9–13 and Luke 11:2–4) has, with its seven tercets (the eighth is not part of the paraphrase), been linked numerologically to "the seven terraces of Purgatory, to the seven sins that are purged thereon, and to the seven virtues that oppose those sins" (Singleton). But the content of this paraphrase is most centered on humility, the virtue that opposes, not seven sins, but the principal sin, pride. It is that remarkable concentration on humility that redeems what might otherwise have seemed a somewhat overingenious, advanced artificer's expansion on a prayer that is already indelible in itself. That concentration on humility and Dante's addition of "longed for peace" (7) by a proud, and very restless, man serve to personalize this paraphrase of the Lord's Prayer.

1–3 God, being limitless, is not contained or bounded by the heavens, but chooses to dwell there out of his love for his "first works," the heavens and the angels.

4–6 "Name," "omnipotence," and "effluence" may be seen as aspects of the Trinity or as attributes of the Father alone.

7–9 Dante adds both "peace" and the insufficiency of man—unaided— to reach God's grace.

13–15 The "bread" of the Pater Noster is already (also) spiritual bread, a meaning that Dante's "manna" can only accent more.

20 The "ancient foe" is the Devil. (Also see VIII, 95, and XIV, 146.)

22 Those in Purgatory cannot be tempted to sin and thus have no need to pray for their own deliverance from the Devil's temptations; the last part of their prayer (19–21) is for souls on earth. (See also 31–35, note.)

31–35 "If there they pray on our behalf...": Just as these souls pray for the sake of those who are living (see 22–24 and note), so "those whose wills are rooted in true worth"—souls living in God's grace—should pray for these souls, to "help them wash away / the stains they carried from this world." The need of these souls to "wash away the stains" recalls the admonition of the custodian angel to Dante (see IX, 113–114).

36 "The starry wheels": the spheres of the fixed stars and planets, by way of which the penitent ascend to abide with God in beatitude in the Empyrean (see diagram, "The Universe of Dante," p. 314).

52–54 "were I not impeded by this stone": The speaker's punishment weighs so heavily on him that he cannot even lift his eyes.

58 Guiglielmo Aldobrandesco, proud count of Santafiora, a domain near Siena, so hated the Sienese that he allied himself with the Guelphs of Florence.

61–69 "The ancient blood and splendid deeds of my forefathers": The Aldobrandeschi were powerful lords who were continually warring with the Sienese. In 1259 Omberto, the speaker of these lines, was slain, although we are not sure if he died in battle near Campagnatico or was killed in bed by assassins hired by the Sienese. His death led to the decline of the Aldobrandeschi. In lines 64–65 Dante implies that all this was common knowledge.

74–77 "one of those souls...twisted himself...fixing his eyes on me..."—which may imply that his stone is not as heavy as that of Guiglielmo (see 52–54, note).

78 On three of the seven terraces—those where the sins of which Dante considers himself most guilty (pride, wrath, and lust) are punished—Dante will participate in, or empathize especially strongly with, the punishment of the sinners. Here, as he walks along "completely hunched," side by side with the burdened souls of those being punished for pride—the sin he considers his own worst failing, as we shall learn in Canto XIII—Dante already begins, as he will later admit, to "feel the heavy weights of the first terrace" (XIII, 137–138). And even when he later rises from the posture of the punished prideful, Dante's thoughts will be "still submissive, bent" (XII, 9–11).

79–81 The artist Oderisi of Gubbio (c1240–1299) was a famous miniaturist (an illuminator of manuscripts) known for his pride as well as his work. Though Dante addresses him as the "glory of Gubbio," Oderisi concedes the glory to Franco Bolognese, who was, however, Oderisi's pupil as well as, later, his rival—thus, although "all the glory" now is Franco's, Oderisi perhaps means that as Franco's teacher, he shares "a part" of that glory.

83 We know very little about Franco Bolognese except that he was a pupil of Oderisi and probably, like Oderisi, received commissions from Pope Boniface VIII. (See 79–81, note.)

92–93 The "green" of fame, or renown, endures very briefly upon "the peak" of an artist's accomplishment, unless the historical age that follows is so dull that nothing new surpasses his accomplishment and eclipses his fame.

94–95 Giovanni Cimabue (c1240–1302), the renowned Florentine painter who began the break with the Byzantine tradition, was the master of the great Florentine artist Giotto di Bondone (1266–1337), who is cred-ited with the astonishing renewal and extension of the art of painting from nature. Giotto may have been a friend of Dante, whose portrait in the Bargello in Florence was attributed by some to Giotto's hand (though now it is attributed to the school of Giotto).

97–98 Here Dante moves closer to the vanity of his own kind of earthly artistry, with references to the Florentine poet—and Dante's close friend—Guido Cavalcanti, whose father Dante met in Hell (see *Inf.* X, 52–60 and note) and to Guido Guinizzelli, whose excellence Cavalcanti is here said to have surpassed. Guinizzelli, who was exiled from Bologna in 1274 and died by 1276, and whom we shall meet in Canto XXVI, was ad-mired by Dante as a poetic predecessor (see Intro., p. xxiv).

103–108 "Before a thousand years have passed...would you find greater glory...?": The question is clearly rhetorical, for accomplishment in the living world is as "an eyeblink for the slowest sphere in heaven." The eighth sphere of Heaven, the sphere of the fixed stars, was believed to take a century to move one degree eastward, so that its complete revolu-tion around the earth would take 36,000 years. Lines 103–105 recall Psalm 90: "For a thousand years in thy sight are but as yesterday when it is past, and as a watch in the night" (Ps. 90:4 [89:4 in the Vulgate]).

109–111 "All Tuscany acclaimed his name..., and now they scarcely whisper of him": Fittingly, Dante will have to ask this shade's name, in lines 120–121. (See 121–123, note.)

115–117 As did lines 103–105 (see 103–108, note), these lines recall Psalm 90: "...in the morning they are like grass which groweth up. In the morning it flourisheth, and groweth up; in the evening it is cut down, and withereth." (Ps. 90:5–6 [89:5–6 in the Vulgate].) Cf. also Isaiah 40:6–8.

121–123 Provenzan Salvani (c1220–1269), leader of Siena, acquired tremendous power after the Ghibelline victory at the Battle of Montaperti (1260) and urged the total destruction of Florence, opposed by Farinata degli Uberti (see *Inf.* X, 91–93). His power diminished after the Battle of Benevento in 1266, and in 1269, battling at Colle di Val d'Elsa (see *Purg.* XIII, 115–120), he was killed by the Florentine Guelphs.

136–138 In an effort to raise the 10,000 florins demanded by Charles of Anjou as ransom for the release of Provenzan's friend (whom Charles threatened otherwise to execute), Provenzan seated himself on a bench in the square of Siena and humbly—and successfully—begged the money of the Sienese.

139–141 Oderisi's prophecy concerns the exile that will be inflicted on Dante and the indigence he will experience. Dante, as Oderisi suggests in the "obscure" style appropriate to prophecy, will know what it is to beg and, thus, in humiliation, to tremble "in each vein" as did Salvani.

142   "those confines": the bounds of Ante-Purgatory.

CANTO XII

25–63   In this sequence of thirteen tercets, each with its example of punished pride, there are three sets of four tercets each. In each set, the four tercets begins with the same words: respectively, "I saw," "O [followed by a proper name]," and "it showed." In the thirteenth tercet each of its three lines begins with one of the aforementioned onset-words. This much can be, and is, carried over into the English. To this, Dante's Italian adds the acrostic formed by the initial letters of the three onset-words: *V O M,* meaning "man," since, in the orthography of the time, *v* and *u* were written identically. This bravura display by Dante is indebted to medieval Latin and to Romance emphasis on elaborate anaphora. It is very un-Virgilian and, for the poet who joins antiquity in the Limbo of *Inferno* IV, something of a relapse but, as such, is a perfect example of the sort of bravura that, in the poet, bolsters pride—the sin punished here on the First Terrace.

25–27   "one who / had been created nobler than all other beings": Lucifer, whom God cast down from heaven for his prideful disobedience.

28–30   Briareus (whom we encountered in *Inf.* XXXI, 98 and note) was one of the giants who fought against the Olympian gods; Jupiter consequently struck him with a thunderbolt.

31–33   "Thymbraeus," another name for Apollo (see *Aen.* III, 1·12, and *Georgics* IV, 323), and "Pallas" (Athena) are gazing at the fallen bodies of the giants who had attacked Olympus and tried to overthrow Jove and the gods. With the aid of Hercules, the gods had defeated the giants and scattered their limbs about the earth. (See *Theb.* II, 597ff., and *Met.* X, 150–151.)

34–36   According to the Bible, Nimrod built the Tower of Babel in Shinar to reach the sky. To thwart such pride and presumption, God decreed that man would ever after speak in many languages. (See *Inf.* XXXI, 67–81, note.)

37   The legendary Niobe was the wife of Amphion, the king of Thebes. She had boasted that as mother of seven sons and seven daughters she was better than the goddess Latona, who bore only Apollo and Diana; for this, Latona slew all of Niobe's children. Niobe's ceaseless tears continued to flow—even after she was turned into stone. Here, her being represented in "effigy," in stone, and Dante's tears on seeing the story represented play on that legend. (See *Met.* VI, 182–312.)

40–41   Saul, first king of Israel, whose pride led him to disobey God, killed himself on Mount Gilboa after defeat in battle. In lamenting Saul's death, David cried out that Gilboa should know neither the dew nor the rain (II Sam. 1:17–21).

43   Arachne, proud of her skills as a weaver, challenged Minerva to a weaving contest; the goddess, enraged at the perfection of her artistry, tore Arachne's cloth to shreds and kept striking her with her shuttle, whereupon Arachne, in despair, hanged herself. Minerva changed the hang-rope into a cobweb and Arachne into a spider (see *Met.* VI, 5–145).

46   Rehoboam, son of Solomon and king of Israel, whose tyrannous and arrogant treatment of Israel caused a revolt, had to flee from his own people (I Kings 12:18).

50–51   Eriphyle, wife of Amphiaraüs (see *Inf.* XX, 31–33, note), betrayed her husband's hiding place to his enemies, being bribed by the allure of a necklace, "the ill-omened ornament." Her son Alcmaeon slew her in revenge. (See Statius, *Theb.* II, 265–305.)

52   Sennacherib, tyrannical king of Assyria, from 705 to 681 B.C., launched expeditions against Judah and was assassinated by his own sons as they fled from defeat in battle (II Kings 19:37).

55–57   Cyrus of Persia (560–529 B.C.) slew the son of Queen Tomyris of Scythia. To revenge this bloodthirstiness of Cyrus, she had his head cut off and plunged into a basin of blood, speaking the words that Dante cites (57) almost literally from the account in Orosius (*Hist.* II, vii, 6), which derives, via Justin, from Herodotus.

58–60   Holofernes, general of the army of King Nebuchadnezzar of Assyria, set up his king as the only God; thereupon, Israel prayed for his pride to be punished. At his siege of Bethulia the beautiful Judith came to his tent and while he slept, cut off his head. Without their leader the Assyrians panicked and fled (Judith 6–15).

61–62   In the *Aeneid,* Troy ("Ilium") is often referred to as the "proud city"; its downfall is the classic example of pride brought low.

79   "an angel": the Angel of Humility.

80   "the sixth of the handmaidens...": The hours are often represented as handmaidens of the sun, so Virgil is telling Dante that six hours have passed since day began at 6 A.M. Therefore, it is noon on Easter Monday.

98   "then he struck my forehead with his wing": erasing the first *P*—that of pride (see IX, 112–114 and note).

101   "Rubaconte's bridge" was a bridge named after the chief magistrate of Florence in 1237. Its modern name is the Ponte alle Grazie (destroyed by the Germans in 1944, but now reconstructed).

102   "the church": San Miniato al Monte, the Romanesque masterpiece built between the 11th and 13th centuries that, from its height, dominates Florence.

105   The ironically termed "well-ruled city" (102) is here seen by Dante in the light of two scandals of his own time, involving nefarious tampering with judicial records and tampering with the size of the salt-measure by officials of Florence. Against this degraded present, Dante nostalgically sets a time when "record books and measures could be trusted."

110   *"Beati pauperes spiritu":* "blessed are the poor in spirit," the First

Beatitude of the Sermon on the Mount (Matt. 5:3). As Dante and Virgil prepare to leave the First Terrace, the terrace of the proud, this benediction comes as a reminder of Christ's blessing of the humble.

112–114 "How different...": Cf. *Inferno* III, 22.

133 This translation follows most modern commentators in seeing *scempie* as an adjective meaning "outspread" and modifying "fingers." Porena, too, sees it as an adjective, but meaning "diminished" (in number) and modifying "letters." Bosco-Reggio opt for *scempie* as an adjective serving as adverb and meaning "simply."

CANTO XIII

6 "except that it describes a sharper arc": As the wayfarers ascend, the terraces circling the conical mountain of Purgatory become smaller.

7–9 "No effigy...and no outline...only the livid color of raw rock": Whereas the terrace of the prideful had been elaborately ornamented, the terrace of the envious reflects the meanness of their sin; the "livid," blue-black color of its "raw rock" suggests the bruised hearts of those who have been wounded by the sight of the good fortune of others.

14–15 The time is now past noon, and the sun striking from the north-west is on Virgil's right as the poets reach the Second Terrace. In wheeling "his left around," Virgil turns to face the sun, whose guidance he will implore, as he and Dante begin circling the terrace toward the sun. Thus their movement will be counterclockwise—the proper direction in Purgatory (see V, 22–23, note).

25–27 The "courteous invitations" called out by invisible spirits are incitements to fraternal love—examples of charity, correcting the sin of envy.

29 The first example of charity called out by the flying voices is that of Mary, who, concerned about the celebrants at the marriage feast in Cana, told her son, "They have no wine," thus spurring Christ's first miracle (see John 2:1–11).

33 Orestes' act of charity was in refusing to allow his devoted friend Pylades to lay down his life for him. Orestes had slain his mother, Clytemnestra (who had murdered Orestes' father, Agamemnon). Pylades tried to impersonate the condemned Orestes so as to die in his stead, but Orestes, persistently identifying himself, would not let Pylades make such a sacrifice. Thus the allusion suggests a double act of charity. (Dante's probable sources here are Cicero's *De amicitia* VIII, 24, and *De finibus* V, xxii, 63.)

36 To love one's enemies and those by whom one has been hurt is one of Christ's central teachings (see Matt. 5:43–48 and Luke 6:27–36).

38–39 "the cords that form the scourging lash": This "lash" consists of the voices Dante hears, which scourge the blind souls of the envious by calling out examples of charity, the love of others.

47–48 "shades / with cloaks that shared their color with the rocks": i.e., "the livid color of raw rock" (see 7–9, note).

50–51 The souls are chanting the Litany of All Saints, invoking the prayers of those most free from the sin of envy.

62 "pardon days": feast days when—and places where—indulgences were sold.

71–72 "as untamed hawks / are handled": Captured wild falcons, indeed, had their eyes stitched closed with a thread to quiet them down so that they could be trained.

89–90 This stream probably alludes to Lethe (*Purg.* XXXI, 91–102, and XXXIII, 99), which will erase the memory of past sins.

94–95 "citizen of one true city": the city of God.

109 Sapia, of Siena, the aunt and enemy of Provenzan Salvani of Canto XI, exulted in the defeat at Colle di Val d'Elsa of the Sienese Ghibellines, including her own nephew (see XI, 121–123, note), whose rise to power she had envied. The translation anglicizes the pronunciation of her name; instead of the trisyllabic Sapìa, with penultimate accent, it invites to a bi-syllable with terminal diphthong and stress on the first syllable. The rhetorical figure employed in this line involves a play on the correspondence—or lack thereof—between a proper name and a thing, quality, or attribute.

117 "that which He had willed": the defeat of her "fellow citizens," the Sienese.

122 "the blackbird after brief fair weather": According to popular fable, a blackbird, seeing some sunlit days, was fooled into thinking that spring had arrived. Emerging from hiding, it sang out, "I fear thee no more, O Lord, for the winter is over."

128–129 Pier Pettinaio (the comb-merchant—possibly the carding combs used in textile manufacture) lived in Siena and ended his days with a reputation for saintliness. His prayers have lessened Sapia's punishment. (This translation, in its binding of line-end sounds, links "Pettin(a)io" and "petition(s)" as near-anagrams.)

136–138 Dante considers his own worst sin to be that of pride. (See XI, 78, note.)

149 Sapia wishes "to see [her] name restored among [her] kin" by having Dante tell them that, in spite of her sins, she is in Purgatory, not in Hell.

152 Talamone was a small Tuscan seaport. The Sienese, hoping to compete for some of Genoa's sea trade, bought it in 1303 and tried to convert it into a working harbor. The expense of the constant dredging required to prevent the port from choking with silt, as well as the malaria that made Talamone practically uninhabitable, doomed the venture to failure.

153 Diana was a phantom subterranean river that the Sienese believed flowed beneath their city. They spent large sums searching for it.

154 "the admirals will lose the most": Those superintending the project at Talamone will lose not merely their money but "the most"—their lives—from malaria. (This may be the most cogent gloss of a line variously interpreted.)

CANTO XIV

7 These "two spirits" will be named in lines 81 and 88 (also see notes).

16–17 The "little stream" spreading through central Tuscany is the Arno (as we learn in line 24), which flows from Mount Falterona in the Apennines. In the subsequent lines, Dante follows the course of the Arno to structure his condemnation of cities on its banks.

31–33 "Its source" on Mount Falterona (see 16–17, note) is part of the "rugged chain" of the Apennine Mountains. Stretching through Italy, this chain is cut off from Pelorus, a promontory in northeastern Sicily. The implication here is that the Apennines can be viewed as a single range "interrupted" by the Straits of Messina, which separate Sicily from the rest of Italy.

34 "its end point": the mouth of the Arno, not far from Pisa.

42 The enchantress Circe transformed men into beasts *(Aen.* VII, 12–25). The spirit speaking to Dante is about to catalog similar transformations of his countrymen.

43–44 The Arno starts in the Casentino region, whose people—being "foul hogs"—were "more fit for acorns" (a common food of hogs) than for men's food.

46 "As that stream descends," it flows into Arezzo, a Ghibelline city, whose motto was, *"A cano non magno saepe tenetur Aper,"* "a boar is often caught by a small cur."

48 "it swerves its snout away": Near Arezzo, the Arno veers to the northwest.

51 These "wolves" are the avaricious Florentines.

52 "Descending... through... dark ravines, it comes on foxes...": The Arno, after descending through the gorge of Pietra Golfolina, passes through Pisa, whose inhabitants are as crafty as "foxes."

55–57 "my comrade": The speaker here is Guido del Duca (who identifies himself in line 81), and his "comrade" is Rinieri da Calboli. Guido's speech "will serve" Dante (who has identified himself only as being from Tuscany) since it will deal with the future of Florence, and Dante (as Guido is aware) is to return to the world of the living. This translation has Rinieri as "my comrade" and Dante as the "you" in the parentheses.

58 Guido's prophecy concerns Rinieri da Calboli's grandson Fulcieri da Calboli, the chief magistrate of Florence in 1303, who came to rule through the influence of the Black Party and whose barbarous punishment of accused enemies inspired deep hatred and fear in faction-torn Florence. The "wolves," again as in line 51, are the Florentines.

81-126 Both the speaker and his comrade, as we are to learn, are from the Romagna (91–92). In lines 15–66 the speaker presented a long cadenza on the corruption of Tuscany, using the course of the Arno to chart his lament and concluding with the grandson of his comrade, with Fulcieri, a Romagnole who served as hateful chief magistrate of Florence. After Tuscany, it is the turn of Romagna. But now the attack on the present is launched through praise of those worthy Romagnoles who, earlier in the 13th century, embodied values now lost, values with which Dante nostalgically—and polemically—sympathizes. The Romagnoles of the present, who have "returned to bastardy" (99), are measured against those worthy Romagnoles.

81 At last the speaker introduces himself. He is Guido del Duca, a Ghibelline of Bretinoro (see 112 and note). He was related to the Traversari and Mainardi (97–98), and served as judge in several cities of central Italy in the first half of the 13th century.

88-90 The speaker introduces his "comrade" (55). He is Rinieri, an illustrious member of the Guelph Paolucci family of Forlì, chief magistrate in various cities and prominent protagonist of struggles between pro-Imperial and pro-Papal forces. At the end of a long career, he was expelled from Forlì in 1294. Though he returned in 1296, he was not able to establish firm control; and in that year, with his castle of Calboli besieged by Ghibellines, he was killed in action.

91-96 Now the speaker defines the boundaries of Romagna: the "Po" to the north, the Apennine "mountains" to the south, the river "Reno" to the west, and the Adriatic "coast" to the east.

97-111 For *ubi sunt,* "where are they?"—a formula for evoking the worthies of the past—see Canto XXII, 97–99 and note, where the same formula reappears (and at exactly the same point in the canto, line 97).

97-99 Lizio da Valbona was a Guelph who helped Rinieri against the Ghibellines. Arrigo Mainardi was a friend of the Ghibelline speaker, Guido del Duca. Pier Traversaro, Ghibelline lord of Ravenna early in the 13th century, died in 1225. Guido da Carpigna, Guelph chief magistrate of Ravenna in 1251, died c1283. All were seen in their time as magnanimous presences. Like Guido del Duca and Rinieri, respectively Ghibelline and Guelph, the pair in each of these two lines matches Ghibelline and Guelph, transcending internecine wars and the past envy of which the speaker has now been purged and offering us Dante's own embracing compassion and admiration—free, however briefly, from polemic. The return to excoriation in the next line (99) can only remind us how fragile is that sympathetic stance when the prophet has to confront both past and present in the light of a utopian future.

100-102 Again a pairing of Ghibelline and Guelph: Fabbro dei Lambertazzi, Ghibelline chief of Bologna and Romagna and chief magistrate in several cities, died in 1259. Bernardin di Fosco, of lowly origin ("a humble plant"), became a leading citizen of Faenza, where he fought against Frederick II. Around the middle of the century, he served as chief magistrate of Pisa and Siena.

102–104   Just as Rinieri's Romagnole grandson served to link present-day Tuscany and Romagna in iniquity, so a Tuscan of the past perhaps serves at this point to link the Tuscany and Romagna of the past in worthiness—"perhaps," because we do not have much support for a definite identification of Ugolino d'Azzo. But some have seen him as a Tuscan of the Ubaldini family who distinguished himself in Romagna, where he "lived among us." (Others of the Ubaldini family are distributed in Hell and Purgatory—see *Inf.* X, 120, and XXXIII, 14, and notes; *Purg.* XXIV, 28–30 and note.) Guido da Prata—Prata is a town near Faenza—seems to have been present in Ravenna in 1228.

106–107   The "house of Traversara" had Pier Traversaro as a leading member (see 97–98, note). The Anastagi were noble Ghibellines of Ravenna and close allies of the Traversara. For a time both these houses were very powerful in the region, but as Guido says, they both were "without heirs."

107–108   "Federigo Tignoso and his gracious company": Federigo was a hospitable nobleman of Rimini, of whom little else is known.

112   Bretinoro (modern Bertinoro), a small town southeast of Forlì, was once noted for its hospitality and was the home of the spirit who speaks here, Guido del Duca.

115   Bagnacaval, or Bagnacavallo, a town in Romagna between Imola and Ravenna, was used by the Ghibellines as a seat of power after they expelled the Guelphs from Ravenna (see 81, note). The family then in control of Bagnacavallo, the Malvicini, was becoming extinct around 1300 (the year in which Dante's journey to Purgatory is set); thus Guido says of the town, that it "breeds no more."

116   Castrocuro, a village near Forlì, and Conio, near Imola, were both small fortress towns in Romagna.

118–121   The Pagani were a powerful family of Faenza. In Dante's time, the head of this family was the infamous Maghinardo Pagano da Susinana, whose cruelty and cunning political opportunism earned him his surname, "the Demon"; he is mentioned by reference to his coat of arms, in *Inferno* (see *Inf.* XXVII, 49–51 and note).

121   Ugolino dei Fantolini died c1278. He was—as Guido says—left without heirs (since both his sons died childless), and therefore his good name and worthy works in the region of Faenza would leave their mark undefiled by degenerate progeny.

127–129   Although these "gentle souls" cannot see, they can hear—and would presumably have spoken up if they had heard Dante and Virgil set off on the wrong path.

130–139   The voices that strike like lightning and thunder are from invisible presences calling out examples of punished envy.

133   "Whoever captures me will slaughter me": the fear expressed by
Cain after he had slain Abel (Gen. 4:13–14).

139   "I am Aglauros, who was turned to stone": Aglauros, princess of
Athens, was envious of her sister Herse, who was loved by Mercury.
Because she tried to prevent their trysts, Aglauros was petrified—literally
changed into stone. (See Ovid. *Met.* II, 708–832.)

146   The "old adversary" is, like the adversary of VIII, 95, and the "ancient foe" of XI, 20, the Devil.

CANTO XV

1–5   "The sphere that's always playing like a child": the sun. Dante may
be characterizing it so because "the sun rises now under one zodiacal sun
and now under another, and now approaches the Tropic of Capricorn, now
the Tropic of Cancer" (Bruno Nardi).

   To tell us that it is three hours before sunset (i.e., 3 P.M.), Dante measures the first three hours after sunrise. (This kind of mirroring will be central to the images and ideas of this canto.)

6   "Where we are" is Italy, and midnight in Italy would make it 3 A.M. in
Jerusalem and 3 P.M., the beginning of vespers, "there"—in Purgatory.

   "Vespers" is one of the four three-hour periods, each named for the
hour with which it *finished,* into which it was customary to divide the day
from dawn to sunset: *tierce,* from the third hour (i.e., from 6 to 9 A.M.);
sext, from the fourth to the sixth (i.e., from 9 A.M. to noon); *none,* from the
seventh to the ninth (i.e., from noon to 3 P.M.); and *vespers,* from the ninth
to the twelfth (i.e., from 3 to 6 P.M.). (The shift of meaning of *none* or
nones from 3 P.M. to midday is institutionalized in the English language,
for the word *noon* was originally simply an alternative spelling of the
same word.)

   As Dante notes (*Conv.* III, vi, 2–3), there are two modes of measuring
the hours: the "temporal hours...used by the Church" are hours that divide day and night into twelve hours each, hours that increase or diminish
in length as the length of day and night, respectively, diminishes or in-
creases with changing seasons; the other mode measures "equal hours,"
dividing the sum of day and night, whatever the respective length of day
and night, into twenty-four equal hours. For the Church, the four daytime
hours listed above *(tierce, sext, none,* and *vespers)* would be supplemented
by three additional predaylight or postdaylight hours: *matins* with *lauds*
(see *Purg.* I, 115–117, note); *prime,* the hour of sunrise; and *compline* (see
Purg. VIII, 1–6 and 13, note). Together, these formed the seven canonical
hours, times of day canonically appointed for offices of devotion. Since
Dante places his journey so close to the vernal equinox, the discrepancy
between "temporal hours" and "equal hours" is of little account in the
Comedy.

16–21   This technical simile paraphrases a fundamental law of optics,
namely, that the angle of incidence of a ray of light is equal to its angle of

reflection. Dante also refers to the laws of optics in his *Convivio* (II, xiii, 26).

38   *"Beati misericordes"* is the Fifth Beatitude of the Sermon on the Mount: "Blessed are the merciful: for they shall obtain mercy" (Matt. 5:7).

47   "his worst vice": envy.

52   The "Highest Sphere": the Empyrean.

55–57   As incisive as any of the other sources (Gregory the Great, Fra Giordano) for the quality of love present in "that cloister," the Empyrean of the blessed, is St. Augustine: "For the possession of goodness is not lessened by being shared: nay, it is increased when it has many possessing it in one link and league of charity" (*The City of God* XV, 5).

67   "That Good . . . directs Itself toward love . . .": God's good is directed toward those prepared to receive it—those who love. (See *Conv.* IV, 20.)

75   "mirror-like, each soul reflects the other": cf. 16–23 and note.

79–81   Only five of the seven *P*'s that were inscribed on Dante's forehead remain (see IX, 112). Virgil is informing Dante that the *P* representing the sin of envy has been removed by the Angel of Charity.

83   "another circle": the Third Terrace, occupied by the wrathful.

85–117   In his "ecstatic vision" (86) Dante will see, as on each terrace, three examples of the virtue contrary to the sin being punished. Here, on the terrace of the wrathful, the examples are of gentleness; as on all the terraces, the first positive example is taken from the life of Mary.

87–93   This "woman at the threshold" is Mary. She and Joseph had discovered Jesus missing from the company as they returned home from the Passover feast in Jerusalem. After returning to Jerusalem, they searched for three days, and finally found the young Jesus in the temple, questioning and disputing with the learned men. Not wrathfully, but mildly, Mary asked him why he had caused them such sorrow by disappearing. (See Luke 2:41–48.)

94–105   The speaker in this second part of Dante's "ecstatic vision" is the wife of Pisistratus, ruler of Athens ("that proud city" that Athena and Poseidon once "vied" to name [*Met.* VI, 70–82]). Her daughter had been embraced by an amorous youth, and she had urged her husband to kill him, which prompted Pisistratus' kind reply (104–105).

106–114   This is the martyrdom of St. Stephen, who was accused of blasphemy and stoned to death; as he was dying, he prayed for the souls of his killers. (See Acts 7:54–59.)

115–117   The three parts of Dante's vision are "errors," in that they are not "real"; but they are "not false," because they reflect divine truth. Indeed, these visionings may mime Dante's sense of his larger vision, the "not false" fiction of his poem as a whole.

118–138   This exchange between Dante and Virgil indicates that, although Virgil has not seen Dante's vision, he has been able to "read" it from Dante's face (as he earlier "read" his thoughts, in *Inf.* XVI, 118–123, and XXIII, 25–28).

139–141 "until the end of vespers": until 6 P.M. These lines reflect the opening of the canto (4–6) and tell us that in the three hours Dante and Virgil have spent on this terrace, they have continued to face the sun—moving in the same direction.

142 "Smoke black as night" is, as we shall see in the next canto, part of the punishment of the wrathful.

CANTO XVI

13 While the word *sozzo*, "filthy," is frequently used in *Inferno*, this is its only appearance in *Purgatorio* (Bosco-Reggio).

16–21 These voices of the wrathful sing the *"Agnus Dei"* from the liturgy of the Mass. This prayer, emphasizing the gentle and benevolent aspect of Christ, asks the "Lamb of God, who takest away the sins of the world" (a line based on John 1:29), to "have mercy on us" and to "grant us peace." Here the wrathful sing this prayer in "fullest concord"—as against the discord engendered by their wrath on earth. *"Agnus Dei"* is a repeated "exordium" (19) because it appears three times, at the beginning of each of the three sentences of the prayer.

27 "a man who uses months to measure time": i.e., a living man—one not yet in the timeless realm of the dead. (Though, in fact, the population of Purgatory is not free from concern with time—or with the prayers of the living, which shorten the stay of the shades on this mountain.)

28 "A voice...": See 46, note.

37 The "swaddling bands / that death unwinds" are the flesh.

40 "a manner most unusual for moderns": See the essay "Dante as Ancient and Modern" in the Bantam Classics *Inferno*.

46 Marco Lombardo is not one about whom we have much certain word before he figures in the *Comedy*. If we think of Lombardy as northern Italy (see *Inf.* I, 68 and note; *Inf.* XXVII, 20), then Marco is best seen as a noble from the region of Treviso, a worthy courtier.

47–48 "I loved those goods / for which the bows of all men now grow slack": Marco's "bow" was aimed at moral virtues that men no longer strive to cultivate.

57 Marco's words on human corruption are at one with those of "another." Guido del Duca on the previous terrace (see XIV, 37–40).

70–72 "then your free will would be / destroyed, and there would be no equity / in joy for doing good, in grief for evil.": If man had no free will with which to choose his actions, it would not be fair, or equitable, to punish those who had done evil and to reward those who had done good.

73 According to Aquinas, the will and the intellect are exempt from the direct influence of the celestial bodies, the "heavens," but these bodies can affect the body's sensitive "appetites." But in spite of the resulting *indirect* influence of the heavenly bodies on intellect and will, since man has "received both light / on good and evil, and free will," it would be a mistake "to assign / to heaven every cause" (67–68)—i.e., man can still choose. (See *Summa theol.* I–II, q. 95, a. 5: "Nothing prevents man's resisting his passions by his free will.")

79–81 Man is not engendered by the heavens; he is directly created by and "depend(s)" on God, whose "power" and "nature" are "greater" than those of the heavens. And God created man "free" to choose between good and evil, "outside the heavens' sway."

88–93 "that soul is simple, unaware"—possessing the capacity to understand, but not yet understanding. The soul is naturally inclined to seek the Highest Good, but the understanding, undeveloped at first, does not know where to turn to find that Good; thus, "at first it savors trivial goods." To lead the soul to the Highest Good, a "guide or rein" is needed "to rule its love." Bosco-Reggio see in these lines, with their insistence on God's direct and *continuous* creation of "simple" individual souls, a polemical repudiation both of "the teaching of Origen and others, who sustained the once-and-for-all creation of souls, and of the Platonic doctrine of innate ideas."

95–96 Dante again chimes on the need for a "ruler" or emperor, whose rule over the city of man can at least allow us to glimpse the "tower of the true city," the City of God.

98–99 "the shepherd who precedes his flock can chew the cud but does not have cleft hooves": This corrupt shepherd of his flock is Pope Boniface VIII, anathematized by Dante throughout the *Comedy*. Since Leviticus (11:3) tells us that an animal must not only chew its cud in order to be deemed edible but also must have the distinguishing feature of the cloven hoof, these lines may be interpreted as follows: Pope Boniface may ruminate, allegorically "chew the cud" of the Scriptures and God's law, but he does not recognize the need for "cloven hooves," the separation or cleft between spiritual and temporal powers.

103 "misrule": bad ecclesiastical guidance.

106–109 Rome, in applying good civil rule under Emperor Augustus, paved the way for the City of God and thus "made the world good." (See *Inf.* II, 13–24.) However, the Church, subject to a higher law, must be completely above and independent of temporal concerns, for where it allows itself to be economically or politically "interested," it is capable of being corrupted. Under Pope Boniface's politically grasping "misrule," each (state and church) "has eclipsed the other," for Boniface has refused to "render unto Caesar the things that are Caesar's." For Dante's image, in his *Monarchy* (III, iv), of church and state not as sun and moon, but as two suns, see "Dante in His Age," in the Bantam Classics *Inferno*, pp. 327–328.

114 "Every plant is known by what it seeds"; and since the result or seed of this mixture of temporal and spiritual power has resulted in evil, the "plant" or principle of such a mixture must be suspect.

115–116 The "territory watered by the Adige and Po" rivers is Lombardy, from which Marco comes (but see 46, note).

118 "The Emperor Frederick" is Frederick II, king of Naples and Sicily from 1215 to 1250, whom Dante regarded as "the last emperor of the Romans," and who was locked in a struggle with the three popes, Honorius III, Gregory IX, and Innocent IV. (See *Inf.* x, 119, and, especially, "Dante in His Age," in the Bantam Classics *Inferno,* pp. 322–323, 326.)

121 The "three old men" of Lombardy, whom Dante identifies next, stand as models of bygone virtue in a Lombardy now grown corrupt.

124 Currado da Palazzo, a Guelph from Brescia, chief magistrate of Florence in 1276 and of Piacenza in 1288, was famous for his civil manners and mode of governance. The "good Gherardo," Gherardo da Cammino (1240–1306) was captain-general of Treviso from 1283 until his death. Dante seems not to know that he may have been an accomplice in the death of Jacopo del Cassero (*Purg.* v, 67–84). A patron of the arts, Gherardo is praised in the *Convivio* (IV, xvi, 12) just as Guido da Castello "the candid Lombard" is (IV, xvi, 6). The latter, born of the Guelph Roberti family of Reggio Emilia, was said by some to have been an exile at Verona, where Dante may have met him (but the Guelphism of the Roberti makes that uncertain). Guido is singled out for his candor and liberality, which distinguishes him from other Lombards, whom the French considered avaricious. For even the French to call him "the candid Lombard" is, therefore, quite a tribute.

131 "Levi's sons," the sons of the tribe of Levi, were ministers of the temple and sometimes regarded as priests. In Numbers (18:20–24) they are specifically excluded from receiving any monetary inheritance, so as to avoid any corrupting admixture of spiritual and temporal concerns.

136–140 Marco's answer registers incredulity at Dante's not having heard of Gherardo, and referring to him as "Gaia's father" may imply that Dante belongs to a later and more dissolute age, for some say "Gaia"— who died in 1311—was reputed to be a loose woman.

142–143 "the rays . . . already whitening": the rays of the sun, which is "almost at the point at which it sets" (see XVII, 4–9).

CANTO XVII

3 "as moles see through their skin": The mole is proverbially dim-sighted, just barely able to see through the protective membrane that covers its tiny eyes.

6 For "imagination" see 13–18, note.

8–9 It is about 6 P.M.

10 Now free from the dark smoke, Dante no longer relies on Virgil's shoulder (see XVI, 9).

13–18 The Italian text has *"imagine"* in line 6, *"imaginativa"* in line 13, *"fantasia"* in line 19, *"imagine"* again in line 31, and *"imaginar"* in line 43. This translation follows those who would see the first three instances (in lines 6, 13, and 19) as words equivalent for Dante—words designating that internal sense or power that retains sensible forms drawn from external things through the "outer" senses. Thus the English uses "imagination" in lines 6 and 13, and "fantasy" in line 19, as interchangeable terms. (For the last two instances, *"imagine"* in line 31 and *"imaginar"* in line 43, see 31 and 43, notes.)

Dante's query (13–16) asks for the source of sensible forms in the imagination or fantasy when *no* external thing is present. His answer (17–18)—a heavenly force may be at work, in one of two ways: 1) *per sé,* "of itself," through the influence of the light of the heavenly spheres—not, however, through the effect of the spheres on any of the "outer" senses, but through the direct influence of the stars on the internal sense, those stars whose light, having found "its form in Heaven," reflects God's power; or 2) through a light that may be specially "led downward" by God's will, as is the case—for Dante—with the three images of punished wrath that now arise in his fantasy (19–39). The text Bosco-Reggio cite for this second way is Aquinas: "Sometimes also the images in the imagination are divinely formed, so as to express divine things better than those which we receive naturally from sensible things, as appears in prophetic visions" (*Summa theol.* I, q. 12, a. 13). But while Aquinas would hardly have qualified poetic fictions (or fictions within a fiction—as Dante's are here) as "prophetic visions," Dante does conjure that possibility both here and, implicitly, in the fiction of which these fictions are a part.

19–21 The first of the three examples of punished wrath that appear in Dante's fantasy is the "one who then, transformed / became the bird that most delights in song," namely, Procne. For the story of Procne's "savagery," and for Dante's dealings with her and Philomela's metamorphoses, see Canto IX, 13–15, note.

26–30 This second example of punished wrath is taken from the Book of Esther. After Mordecai, a Jew, refused to bow down to Haman, counselor of King Ahasuerus of Persia, Haman tried to murder all the Jews. Through the intervention of Mordecai's cousin Esther (whom Ahasuerus, unaware that she was Jewish, had selected to replace his recalcitrant queen), the Jews of Persia were saved, and the king ordered Haman hanged on the gallows he had prepared for Mordecai. To the representation of Haman as "crucified," Dante was led by the Latin word *cruci* for "gallows" in the Vulgate (Esther 8:7, and see G. Sarolli in *E.D.* entry under *"Estèr."*)

31 This *"imagine,"* unlike the *"imagine"* of line 6, seems to be the "image"—or vision—seen, rather than the power of imagination.

34–39 The "girl who wept most bitterly" is Lavinia, daughter of Queen Amata and King Latinus of Latium. Amata, seeing her city attacked and in flames, mistakenly concluded that Turnus, Lavinia's betrothed, had been killed. Overcome by grief and rage at the thought that the match proposed by Latinus between Lavinia and Aeneas would take place—a match she bitterly opposed—Amata hanged herself with a piece of her torn robe. (See *Aen.* XII, 796–819.)

43 Here *"imaginar,"* still another form of the words in this lexical set, may be closer to the *"imagine"* of line 31 than to the *"imagine"* of line 6, but the translation seems to work well with "imagination"—yet this time with some metonymic admixture in its meaning, as in one of the *Oxford English Dictionary*'s definitions of "imagination": "the result of this, a mental image."

55 For the full prosodic significance of Dante's enjambing across this line in the Italian, which has a definite article at line-end, see the Introduction to Bantam Classics *Inferno,* pp. xix–xxi.

67–68 "a wing, and wind / that beat against my face": Another *P* is erased from Dante's forehead by the angel's wing.

68–69 *"Beati pacifici"* are the first words of the Seventh Beatitude from the Sermon on the Mount, "Blessed are the peacemakers: for they shall be called the children of God" (Matt. 5:9).

70–72 "The final rays . . . were raised to such a height": As the sun drops below the horizon, its last rays strike the uppermost reaches of the mountain. In the darkening sky, the poets, only midway up the mountain, already "see the stars on every side."

73 As we have learned (VII, 43–61), there is no climbing the mountain at night, so it is not surprising that Dante's strength has melted away.

76 "the upward stairs / no longer climbed": They have arrived at the top of the stairs, just at the edge of the Fourth Terrace.

91–92 See I John 4:8 and 16: "God is love." For the love that the Creator's creatures have, see Dante's *Convivio* III, iii, 25, where he expands on the love in earth, fire, minerals, magnets, plants, animals, and men.

92–96 "natural or mental": Natural love is the love each thing has for that toward which it is inclined by nature. This natural inclination is implanted in all things by God; therefore, "the natural is always without error" (94). Furthermore, as Aquinas says, "God, in so far as He is the universal good, from Whom every natural good depends, is loved by everything with natural love" (*Summa theol.* I, q. 60, a. 5).

But the mode in which each thing loves is in accord with its own nature; therefore, creatures with a nature that includes *"animo"* (mind, soul, will), creatures with free will (namely, men and angels), have not only a natural love, but also a mental love—a love that can choose its object. And as Virgil says here, "Mental love may choose an evil object / or err through too much or too little vigor" (95–96). This translation accords *animo* as "mind" in "mental love" in line 93 with *animo* as "mind" in line 128, in both cases with a will-ful component in "mind."

97 The "First Good" is, of course, God, while "secondary goods" are lesser (but still proper) objects of love, such as friends, food, and material wealth, which, if loved "with measure, . . . cannot be the cause of evil pleasure." The chosen object of mental love always appears to it as good, but if it mistakenly chooses an evil object—and so "twists toward evil" (100)—or if it attends to a genuinely good object "with more or less care than it should," then the creature sins by working against God.

103–105   Love, if properly directed, "is the seed ... of every virtue," and if improperly directed (with respect to its objects or its degree) "is the seed ... of all acts deserving punishment."

106–108   Even when love is directed toward others as objects, the subject (he who loves) is never without concern for his own well-being. (The personal subjects in the Italian are not called "persons" but *cose,* "things.") Thus, all are "surely free from hatred of themselves." For an objection that may occur to many, Aquinas is appropriate: "Even those who kill themselves apprehend death as a good, insofar as it puts an end to some misery or pain" (*Summa theol.* I–II, q. 29, a. 2).

109–111   Since each being must love itself, it must love that Being to whom it owes its existence: and thus no being can hate God—such is Virgil's (that is, Dante's) conclusion. Bosco-Reggio cite Dante's own Capaneus and Lucifer as counterproofs against this argument. Singleton, who omits Lucifer, remembers Capaneus and Vanni Fucci, but says that the argument "has it that creatures *in this life* do not hate Him." Those whom the inscrutable bewilders will share Bosco-Reggio's doubts.

114   "this love's born in three ways in your clay": Virgil is about to outline the three ways in which "ill love" can come about in man. These three forms of ill love correspond, as we shall see, to the sins that he and Dante have seen punished on the first three terraces of Purgatory: pride, envy, and wrath.

115   "He who, through abasement of another, / hopes for supremacy" is guilty of the sin of pride, punished on the First Terrace of Purgatory.

118–119   "One who, when he is outdone, / fears his own loss of fame, power, honor, favor," is guilty of envy, punished on the Second Terrace of Purgatory.

121–123   He "who, over injury / received, ... seeks out another's harm" is guilty of wrath, punished on the Third Terrace.

124–125   "here / below": i.e., on the first three terraces.

126   "The love that seeks the good distortedly" is the love that, as Virgil explained earlier, "attends / to good with more or less care than it should" (100–101).

127–132   According to Aquinas, the knowledge that God exists "is implanted in us by nature," though for the most part we have this knowledge "in a general and confused way" (*Summa theol.* I, q. 2, a. 1, ad 1). "All strive to reach" the "Good / in which the mind may rest," i.e., God, and although God, as the Highest Good, can never be loved sufficiently, He certainly can be loved with a love that "is lax"—and "this [fourth] terrace, after / a just repentance, punishes for that" (131–132).

133 "a different good": i.e., a "secondary good" (see 97–102, note).

136 Virgil leaves it to Dante to discover for himself the three sins involving "the love that—profligately—yields" to a secondary good. Virgil has thus outlined the threefold division of Purgatory: On the lower three terraces love of an evil object and of harm to others is expiated. On the central (fourth) terrace, "lax" love of the Good is expiated. On the upper three terraces, immoderate love of a secondary good is expiated. This threefold division corresponds to the threefold division of Hell's eternal punishments, which Virgil outlined for Dante during a pause in their descent (see *Inf.* XI, 16–89).

CANTO XVIII

14–15 Dante is referring to Virgil's statement in the previous canto (XVII, 104–105).

17 "Let the error of the blind / who'd serve as guides be evident to you": an echo of "the blind leading the blind" (Matt. 15:14).

19–21 This backtracks to the argument in Canto XVI, where Marco Lombardo explained that the "simple soul," just created, "turns willingly to things that bring delight" (XVI, 85–93).

22–33 The Italian *intenzione* in line 23 is the Scholastic term, *intentio,* the image or representation of a "real object." Once our apprehension has seized upon an object and "expands" upon it, it is natural for the soul, if the object has beauty (the Italian *piacer,* as in *Inf.* V, 104), to tend toward that object with love, even as the "form"—or essential nature—of fire tends to seek its natural end. This progression follows Aquinas closely, with the latter perhaps more metaphorically rich in detailing the end that love seeks (see Introduction to the Bantam Classics *Inferno,* p. xvi). As for the only uncertain point in this passage: "anew" in line 27 may well mean that "nature" joins "the soul"—again and again, "anew"—each time that beauty urges love to move from the potential to the actual.

35–39 Those who insist that "every love is, in itself, praiseworthy" are "the blind" of line 17. They very probably include those poets and untheological analysts of love who formed the consciousness of the young Dante. Contrary to this view, Dante now asserts that the propensity to love, good in itself (like "the wax"), can be misdirected toward unworthy objects ("not each seal is fine").

45 "soul—going straight or crooked—has no merit": i.e., the soul would be passive if it merely responded to what it is offered, good or bad.

49 "every substantial form": the quintessence of something—that which, though distinct from matter, imparts to a given thing its individuality and the actuality of its existence, in man, this is his soul *(Summa theol.* I, q. 76, a. 4).

52 Part of man's "substantial form" is his "free will" (74), a power—like other powers inborn in man (55–59)—"unknown to us until it acts." We know of this power only by virtue of witnessing it in operation, as the "green boughs" testify to the life belonging to the plants (54).

55 Man cannot consciously explain *how* he has the power to act freely—not, at any rate, by means of unaided intellect; such power is simply *there* and, as such, is neither praiseworthy nor blameworthy. In the same way, man cannot account for his inborn intelligence of "primal notions," the categories and axioms of reason, or for his tending toward the "primal objects" of desire, those goods toward which man moves naturally *(Summa theol.* I–II, q. 10, a. 1).

67–70 "those reasoners": especially Aristotle. For the indispensable link, in Dante's ideology, between "free will" and "ethics" see again *Purgatorio* XVI, 70–72.

76–78 The revised version of this translation, changing "delayed almost to midnight" to "with midnight now behind us," removes a nagging thorn plucked out by Bosco-Reggio: if it is the waning moon whose rising is delayed until midnight, can such a moon obscure the stars? Reading *tarda* as modifying "midnight" rather than moon removes the problem. A ewer-shaped moon rising between 9 and 10 P.M. would have mustered enough light past midnight to obscure the fainter stars. (Reading *tarda* in the earlier fashion led to much perplexity and irresolvable difficulty.)

82 Pietola: Virgil's birthplace, a small village near Mantua.

91 Ismenus and Asopus: two rivers in Boeotia, running through and near Thebes, that were the sites of Bacchic orgies (see Statius, *Theb.* 434–449).

99 "Mary / made haste to reach the mountain" to share with Elizabeth the joy of the Annunciation and of the coming motherhood of the aged Elizabeth, who had been barren until now (Luke 1:39–44). And Caesar, in the civil war against Pompey, showed the zeal of a conqueror by leaving his men behind to complete his successful attack on Marseilles and hurrying to meet his enemy in Lérida (Catalonia). These two corrective examples illustrating zeal (shouted by rushing spirits) are counterposed against the tardy will of those souls in the Fourth Terrace.

116–117 "and do forgive us, should / you take our penance for discourtesy": their punishment—their being forced to rush about constantly—should not be taken for unwillingness to talk.

118 This anonymous abbot of St. Zeno has not been satisfactorily identified.

119–120 "valiant Barbarossa / of whom Milan speaks with so much sorrow": the emperor Frederick Barbarossa, who in his quarrels with the pope, destroyed Milan in 1162.

121 "One with one foot in the grave" is Alberto della Scala, a lord of Verona. Alberto sired Giuseppe, whose illegitimacy, notorious depravity, and malicious violence scarcely fitted him to hold the abbacy of San Zeno, which he did from 1291 to 1314. (Alberto, however, also fathered Cangrande, who was Dante's host and patron at Verona.)

133–135 After the Red Sea had parted to let the Israelites pass through, those who sluggishly refused to follow Moses to the Promised Land died in the desert (Exod. 14:10–20).

136–138 "those who did not suffer...with Anchises' son": Aeneas left behind in Sicily those of his comrades who were too weary to follow him to Latium (*Aen.* v, 923–993).

CANTO XIX

1–3 "that hour": i.e., somewhat before dawn, when the sun-brought heat of the preceding day has been dissipated from earth, and the influence of the moon and Saturn (both considered "cold planets") has left the earth cold. Like Dante's other two purgatorial dreams, this one takes place predawn (see Intro., p. x).

3 "geomancers": diviners who told the future from the patterns formed by lines traced between random patterns of points marked on sand. They correlated these patterns with various configurations of the stars, and one of these patterns was called *Fortuna Major.* It was like the form of the con- stellation Pisces (six stars in the form of a trapezoid, with a two-star tail) and was supposed to bring good fortune with it.

7–33 Dante's second dream is the dream of the siren. In Homer (*Odyssey* XII, 39–54 and 158–200) Ulysses is a potential victim of the sirens, who lured men from their sea-paths and sang them to enraptured death. But Ulysses is forewarned by Circe. Nearing the island of the sirens, he stuffs the ears of his men with beeswax and has himself (his ears are left open) firmly lashed to the mast. He also orders his crew to ignore any sign he gives asking to be released. With those elaborate precautions, Ulysses steers free of the sirens. Dante, however, did not know Homer's tale directly, and Dante's siren (one, not several) claims that she had "turned aside" (22) Ulysses. If Dante knew Cicero's *De officiis* (v, xviii), which includes a translation into Latin of the sirens' song but omits any unambiguous word on the success or failure of their temptation of Ulysses, then Cicero's account could have led Dante astray. However, the ancient myth was widely and variously transmitted down to Dante's time, and on so long a journey, confusions may easily have arisen. Also, there is some cogency in Bosco-Reggio's observation that Dante's siren claims, not to have thwarted Ulysses' journey, but to have turned him "aside," to have diverted him to listening to her song—and, even in Homer, Ulysses did listen. (For other sources, other views, see G. Padoan, entry under *sirena* in *E.D.)*

The astronomical information of lines 1–6 tells us that this dream must be a prophetic one, since dreamed close to dawn (as was the dream in Canto IX). With this information and with the distinctions between defi- ciencies and excesses of love drawn by Virgil in the previous canto, the reader can better grasp the meaning of the dream. Both a goal and a pro- jection of man's own sinful lusts—his excesses of love—the siren seems at first contorted and crippled to Dante. As Dante gazes, however, his own desire—his "love" directed toward an unworthy object—is fanned, and his "eyes transformed the wanness of her features." This arousal to desire parallels the movement from the lethargy of the Fourth Terrace (the deficiency of love of the slothful) to the overextended, excessive love of the avaricious and the prodigal, the gluttonous, and the lustful on the three terraces above (see 58–59).

Just as we have learned of these perversions of love in the previous canto, we have learned of the rational "power that counsels, keeper of the threshold / of your assent" (XVIII, 63–64), a power that seems to be summonable even in the depths of dream. This seems to be the function of the "saintly" woman who unmasks the siren for the foul and stinking hag that she really is. This saintly woman (variously identified by many, but conclusively identified by none) would seem to be an emblem of enlightenment, a "keeper of the threshold" against the seductions of unregulated desire. However one regards her, it should be noted how quick she is to summon Virgil to help Dante move out of the siren's sphere of influence. Likewise, Virgil continues in his association with the intellect, which can help us discern good from evil love.

35   "At least three times I've called": Virgil calling "three times" mirrors Virgil called upon twice (28) as the moment just before and just after waking are telescoped, reality breaking in upon dream.

37   With "new sun" at their back, the poets are journeying westward.

42   "The semiarch" is the diagonal rib that in Gothic architecture formed the vault. This likeness for being weighted down conveys Dante's sluggishness, which will change dramatically after the angel removes the fourth *P* from Dante's forehead (as implied in 49–51). Bosco-Reggio contest the use of such arches in medieval bridges and would opt for a "fragment of an arch of a broken bridge," with its impression of "a partial curve."

46   "He who addressed us" is the Angel of Zeal of the Fourth Terrace, whose "open wings" are emblematic of his zeal.

50   "those *'Qui-lugent'* ": "those who mourn," from the Fourth Beatitude of the Sermon on the Mount (Matt. 5:5, and Luke 6:21), is addressed to those who have mournfully acknowledged their sinfulness and have thus been purged of the sin of sloth, from which Dante, too, has just been released (46).

58–59   "that ancient witch": the siren. On the three terraces "above" them, man atones for his sins of excessive love.

62–63   "the lure that's spun / by the eternal King with His great spheres": The lure of Heaven is counterposed against the allure of the "ancient witch."

64–65   Dante compares God to a falconer luring the falcon to him by offer of reward—and tempting him to look up instead of looking down.

69–70   "the circle," i.e., the Fifth Terrace. The "people there who wept" are the avaricious and the prodigal, who have hoarded or wasted material goods.

70–73 *"Adhaesit pavimento anima mea":* "My soul cleaves to the dust" (Ps. 119:25 [118:25 in the Vulgate]), the prayer of the covetous in penitent, prostrate position, face down upon the ground.

76–81 Dante in his new zeal seems to ignore the prostrate position of those to whom he addresses his question, and the answerer, being himself prostrate, cannot see that Dante is alive; he thinks that Dante and Virgil are purgatorial spirits.

84 "What was hidden" has been variously interpreted. But it may simply mean that Dante was now able to see the face of the prostrate penitent.

92 "that without which there's no return to God": penitence.

99 *"scias quod ego fui successor Petri":* "know that I was successor to Peter." It is a pope who speaks.

100–102 The speaker is Pope Adrian V, who was elected in 1276 and died later in that same year; we have no historical evidence of his avarice or of his "conversion" mentioned in line 106. (But Bosco suggests, for the conversion, a confusion in Dante between Adrian IV, pope from 1154 to 1159, and Adrian V. From or derived from John of Salisbury's *Policraticus,* there was a tradition identifying Adrian IV as a pope deluded at the summit of his career.)

133–135 Just as Adrian is a "fellow-servant," so was the angel at whose feet St. John had cast himself: "And I fell at his feet to worship him. And he said unto me, See thou do it not: I am thy fellow servant, and of thy brethren that have the testimony of Jesus: worship God: for the testimony of Jesus is the spirit of prophecy" (Rev. 19:10).

137 According to Matthew 22:23–30, the Sadducees, who did not believe in the Resurrection, presented Jesus with the example of a woman who was widowed many times, each time marrying another of seven brothers. Jesus was then asked the question, "In the resurrection, whose wife shall she be of the seven?" Jesus answered, "In the resurrection, they neither marry nor are given in marriage [*neque nubent*] but are as the angels of God in Heaven." Pope Adrian is extrapolating from the parable. His own wedding to the Church is such a marriage, and like all earthly ties, it is dissolved upon death, where a higher bond is forged.

142 Alagia was the wife of Moroello Malaspina (see *Inf.* XXIV, 145 and note) and the daughter of Niccolò dei Fieschi, brother of Adrian V. (For Dante's stay with the Malaspina, see VIII, 109ff., note.) Evidently, most of the women of "our house" were less than virtuous, but the exceptional Alagia was reputed to be both devout and generous to the poor.

CANTO XX

1–3 Dante's desire to hear more from Pope Adrian is likened to a sponge—a sponge that has been withdrawn from water before it has sopped up its full capacity. But Adrian would continue his penance, and "to please him," Dante must forgo his own desire for more speech.

4–7 "unencumbered space": whatever space was not occupied by the many souls guilty of avarice who crowd the terrace.

10 The "ancient wolf" recalls the lean and hungry she-wolf of *Inferno* I, 50, who "seemed / to carry every craving in her leanness."

13–14 "heavens, through whose revolutions many / think things on earth are changed": This view of planetary causation is implicitly corrected by the lines' implication; it is, of course, God who moves the spheres. (This takes up the theme of XIX, 63.)

14–15 "when will he come— / the one whose works will drive that wolf away?": This, too, recalls the outcry of *Inferno* I, Dante's hope for "the Greyhound," a temporal liberator, perhaps a secular political figure, a Holy Roman Emperor, who will "restore low-lying Italy" (see *Inf.* I, 101–106 and notes).

19–24 He who cries out "Sweet Mary" is a penitent undergoing the pain of purgation for avarice. The reference to Christ's birth in the humble manger is the first of the three corrective examples to this sin. As in the case of all the series of corrective examples, Mary is cited in the first example.

25 "good Fabricius": Gaius Fabricius, Roman consul in 282 B.C. and censor in 275. His refusal to accept gifts from the Samnites (with whom he negotiated peace) and substantial bribes from Pyrrhus, king of Epirus, during negotiations for an exchange of prisoners, testifies to his indifference to worldly goods, as did his work as censor to correct and curb the luxury of the Romans.

31–32 "the largesse of Nicholas" (whom we call "Saint Nick"): Bishop of Myra in the 4th century A.D., Nicholas was said to have thrown bags of gold into his neighbor's window one night so that the poor man could provide dowries for his three daughters.

43 "the root of the obnoxious plant": Dante has conflated two figures, Hugh Capet the Great (d. 956) and his son, also Hugh, who ruled France from 987 to 996. The composite figure is, in Dante's mind at any rate, the one from whom the long and powerful line of the Capetian kings of France was descended. Hugh's condemnation of his own progeny carries a special weight.

46 The four cities mentioned here were the four major cities of Flanders, where Philip the Fair and his ally, Charles of Valois, in 1299 staged a particularly ugly episode of the Flemish wars. The French had offered Count Guy of Flanders very honorable and seemingly favorable terms of surrender: upon his acceptance, Flanders was cruelly besieged by its conquerors and Guy and his sons imprisoned. The "vengeance" referred to in line 47 was taken with the staggering defeat of the French at the Battle of Courtrai in 1302.

50 Eight of the kings of the Capetian dynasty were named either Louis or Philip.

52 History seems to indicate that Hugh's origins were noble, but Dante seems to have his own reasons for preferring the account of popular legend: it supports his diatribes against upstarts in search of power and wealth.

53–54 "the line of ancient kings": the Carolingian dynasty. However, the "monk in gray" whom Dante sees as having survived that dynasty is a mystery, since there were no churchmen in the Carolingian line. Dante may have had in mind the "last survivor" of the Merovingians—Childeric III, who became a monk after being deposed in 752. It is also possible that the confused reference alludes to Charles of Lorraine, uncle of Louis V (see 58, note) and the "last survivor" of the Carolingians. Charles was a vassal of the German emperor and, therefore, unacceptable to the French as a ruler; because of that. Hugh Capet was able to win election and power.

58 "the widowed crown": the crown of the Carolingians, widowed by Louis V, who left no progeny at his death.

61 "the giant dowry of Provence": Hugh is probably referring to the marriage of Charles of Anjou (see *Purg.* VII, 128) to Beatrice, daughter of Raymond Berenger, the count of Provence, in 1245. This marriage enabled the Capetians to gain power in Provence.

66 Philip IV (the Fair) seized Ponthieu and Gascony from England in 1295. Philip II seized Normandy in 1204—a date somewhat out of line with the progression of this discourse.

67 "Charles came to Italy": We have heard before about the exploits of Charles of Anjou against Manfred (III, 112); in 1268, Manfred's nephew Conradin was also defeated by Charles.

68–69 Charles was also (unjustly) rumored to have had Thomas Aquinas poisoned in 1276.

70–75 "another Charles": Charles of Valois, who, as we have learned in *Inferno* VI, was in league with Pope Boniface VIII. Boniface sent Charles to "make peace" in Florence in 1301—a time "not too far off." Instead, Charles recalled and empowered the exiled Black party, who plundered the city and expelled the Whites. His coming as ostensible peacemaker, carrying only the "lance that Judas tilted," is a commentary on Charles's treachery.

76 Charles's unsuccessful attempts, through various intrigues and expeditions, to take over several kingdoms made him the subject of much mockery.

79 "The other," i.e., another Charles: Charles II (the Lame) of Anjou (1248–1301), who suffered a naval defeat by Peter III of Aragon in 1264 and was taken prisoner. He married his youngest daughter, Beatrice, to the elderly Azzo VIII of Este for a large dowry.

86–87 The town of Anagni in Lazio was the birthplace and family domain of Pope Boniface VIII. Boniface excommunicated Philip the Fair because the latter imposed a tax on the clergy. Thereupon, Philip's confederates captured and tormented Boniface at Anagni, in that manner renewing the "gall and vinegar" given to Christ to drink by his tormentors (Matt. 27:34). Despite Dante's detestation of Pope Boniface, he takes a firm and harsh view of those enemies of Boniface who dared to lay hands on God's anointed and, through him, to crucify Christ once again.

91 The "new Pilate" is Philip, who "crucified" Boniface but disclaimed responsibility (see 86–87, note).

93 The "greedy sails" suggest a pirate ship attacking the vessel of the Church. The "Temple": the Knights Templar, whom Philip persecuted cruelly, unjustly, and illegitimately, from 1307 on.

94–96 The "vengeance" that Hugh prophesies—and prays for—here came when Philip's troops were driven out of Flanders in 1302. "Your secrecy": God's inscrutability.

97–103 These lines directly answer Dante's question, voiced many lines earlier (34–36), as to the speaker's identity and the reason for his praises of Mary and of Fabricius. "The only bride the Holy Ghost has known" is, of course, Mary. As Hugh tells him, these praises are sung in daylight, but alternate, once night falls, with the recitation of counterexamples of the "lust for gold," of which seven are mentioned in subsequent lines.

103 Pygmalion, the brother of Queen Dido, murdered Dido's husband Sychaeus for his wealth *(Aen.* I, 484–516). The reason he is called a parricide is that Sychaeus was also his uncle.

106 King Midas of Phrygia's lust for gold led him to ask the god Bacchus to turn everything that he (Midas) touched into gold. Finding that he could no longer eat, however, he asked the gods to take back their gift *(Met.* XI, 85–145).

109 Achan, a biblical figure, seized a part of the booty from the Battle of Jericho against Joshua's orders that it be consecrated to God. Thereupon, Joshua had Achan stoned to death (Josh. 6:19 and 7:1–26).

112 Sapphira and her husband secretly withheld from the Apostles some of the proceeds from the sale of their property (see Acts 4:32–37, 5:1–2).

113 The king of Syria sent Heliodorus to rob the temple at Jerusalem, but the Lord then sent a horse with an angelic rider and a golden harness. When Heliodorus ran up to seize the bridle, the horse trampled him with its hooves (II Macc. 3:25).

114 Priam's son Polydorus was sent with a huge sum of gold to give for safekeeping to King Polymnestor of Thrace, who instead seized the gold and had Polydorus killed. (See *Aen.* III, 47–74, and *Met.* XIII, 429–438; and *Inf.* XXX, 13–21.)

116–117 M. Licinius Crassus (c115–53 B.C.), notorious for his lust for gold, was one of the triumvirate with Caesar and Pompey in 59 B.C. He was defeated and slain in battle against King Hyrodes, the king of the

Parthians, who had molten gold poured down the throat of Crassus' decapitated head—or so it has been said.

130 Delos, an island in the Greek Archipelago, was supposedly a floating island before Jupiter anchored it in place so that Latona, fleeing from the jealous wrath of Juno, might give birth there to the twins Apollo and Diana (*Met.* VI, 186–91, and *Aen.* II, 73–77).

136–138 *"Gloria in excelsis Deo,"* "glory to God in the highest," is the hymn of the angels in announcing to the shepherds the birth of Christ (see Luke 2:8–14).

CANTO XXI

1 "The natural thirst" is the thirst for knowledge, which can never be quenched by reason alone, but only through God's grace or revelation.

2–3 At the well of Jacob in the city of Sychar in Samaria, Jesus told the woman who had come to draw water, "Whosoever drinketh of this water shall thirst again: but whosoever drinketh of the water that I shall give him shall never thirst; but the water that I shall give him shall be in him a well of water springing up into everlasting life"; and the woman said to Jesus, "Sir, give me this water, that I thirst not, neither come hither to draw." (See John 4:5–15.)

7–9 Two disciples of Jesus on their way to Emmaus, absorbed in thought and talk, did not realize that they were being accompanied by "Christ, new-risen from his burial cave," until He spoke to them. (See Luke 24:13–17.)

16–21 With the word "exile," Dante summons, perhaps more indelibly than anywhere else in the *Comedy,* the pain of Virgil's exclusion from the company of the blessed and the tragic irony of his presence here in Purgatory. Virgil's situation is made that much more poignant by the fact that he is addressing Statius, a "redeemed" Latin author who is about to do elaborate homage to Virgil. The word "exile" also echoes later in this canto, when Statius declares that, could he have set his eyes on Virgil, he would have willingly paid the price of an additional year in Purgatory, in "exile"—of a very different kind—from Heaven (see 101–102). Of course, "exile" also reverberates as an emblematic word for Dante's own life situation.

25–27 "She who spins night and day" is Lachesis, one of the three Fates. "Clotho" prepares and holds "the spool" of a man's life. Lachesis spins the thread, and Atropos, with her scissors, cuts it at the appropriate moment. The many sources in which these Fates appear attest to their role as staples of ancient and medieval mythography.

40–60 The gate of Purgatory (at "the top of the three steps...where Peter's vicar plants his feet" [53–54]) is also, in a sense, the gate of Heaven, since any soul who enters Purgatory—with the remarkable exception of Virgil—is already assured of ultimate beatitude. As part of the heavenly realm, Purgatory proper is free from the natural atmospheric and geologic perturbations (cataloged in lines 46–58) that affect the earth, including the lower slopes of the mountain, i.e., Ante-Purgatory.

50–51 "Thaumas' daughter": Iris, goddess of the rainbow. (See *Aen.* IV, 964–966.)

52 In Dante's time, earthquakes were thought to be caused by the violent escape of pent-up "dry vapor" from underground.

58 "It only trembles here"—i.e., in Purgatory—when a soul feels itself cleansed of the sins it has committed and is ready to ascend the mountain.

60 "that shout": the cry of *"Gloria in excelsis Deo"* (see XX, 136 and note).

61–63 There is no edict, no guard (as there were guards in *Inferno*), no one to say when the soul's expiation is complete. The moment when the soul not only wishes to ascend but—cleansed—is ready to do so, it will become aware of that readiness. The purity of the will will "surprise" the soul; it will come unexpectedly.

64–66 As long as penance and atonement are necessary, the will wills penance and atonement. This will for suffering is proof that the soul is on the way to salvation. The same principle (converted) that led the unregenerate soul to sin on earth leads it to want to make up for sin in Purgatory.

67–69 "And I, who have lain in this suffering / five hundred years...": This just-liberated shade will identify himself at length in lines 82–93.

82–84 The capture and destruction of Jerusalem in A.D. 70 by "the worthy Titus" (who was later to be Roman Emperor from A.D. 79 to 81) was held by Christians to be God's vengeance upon the Jews for the death of Christ.

85–93 Statius (A.D. 45–96), author of the *Thebaid,* died before finishing his "last labor," the *Achilleid.* In introducing himself here, Statius emphasizes that although he "bore the name that lasts the longest / and honors most," i.e., the name of *poet,* this mattered little as long as "faith was not yet" his. For more on Statius (and on Toulouse), see Introduction, pp. xxiii–xiv.

101–102 "for that I would extend by one more year / the time I owe before my exile's end.": In these remarkable lines, Statius, who has just experienced the exultation of release from his "exile" from Heaven, declares that to have lived when Virgil lived, he would willingly endure the torments of Purgatory for another full year. This praise of Virgil recalls and echoes the conclusion of Statius' *Thebaid,* where he apostrophises his own poem, exhorting it with, "Live, I pray, / and do not rival the divine *Aeneid,* / but following afar, adore its footsteps" (*Theb.* XII, 810–819).

115 "held by one side and the other," i.e., by Virgil, whose "face, through silence, said: 'Be still' " (104) and by Statius, who wants to know why Dante smiled.

131–132 " 'Brother, there's no need— / you are a shade, a shade is what you see.' " Contrast this response with Virgil's response to Sordello in

Canto VII (13–15). And note the likeness between Virgil's response and the response of Adrian V (see XIX, 127–135 and note).

CANTO XXII

6 The angel stops at the Latin word *sitiunt,* meaning "thirst." In full, this Fourth Beatitude from the Sermon on the Mount (Matt. 5:6) reads in Latin: *"Beati qui esurient et sitiunt iustitiam, quoniam ipsi saturabantur."* ("Blessed are they which do hunger and thirst after righteousness: for they shall be filled.") Here the angel mentions only "thirst," correcting the sins of avarice and prodigality, while "hunger" is mentioned later, in the final line of Canto XXIV, as correcting another sin of excess, gluttony. Putting together these two halves of Dante's use of the Fourth Beatitude, one sees that a Beatitude centering on justice or righteousness has been somewhat shifted to emphasize moderation. Instead of hearing of hungering for righteousness—or justice, *iustitiam*—we shall hear of hungering "in just measure" (XXIV, 154—but see note there for an alternative reading).

10–12 Virgil's words recall those of Francesca da Rimini (*Inf.* V, 103), "Love that releases no beloved from loving," but here the added phrase, "that is kindled by virtue," qualifies and corrects Francesca's formulation.

13 Juvenal, the Roman satirist (A.D. c60–c140), was a younger contemporary of Statius. Since he admired Statius and outlived him by more than forty years, there must have been some talk in Limbo when Juvenal arrived—talk to which Virgil would have been a witness—concerning the whereabouts of Juvenal's admired predecessor, Statius.

40–41 Statius is translating, or rather, mistranslating, Virgil's *Aeneid*. The lines in question, in the original, are, *"Quid non mortalia pectora cogis, / auri sacra fames?"* III, 56–57 ("To what, accursed lust for gold, do you / not drive the hearts of men?" III, 73–74). Dante's wrenching of the meaning of the Latin *sacer,* which here in Virgil means "accursed," "detestable," is in keeping with the slant that Dante gives to the Fourth Beatitude; it implies that for Virgil, too—that is, not only for a Christian but for a pagan moralist—a just and moderate ("holy") hunger for gold can exist. The Italian lines and their meaning are a minor crux of Dante criticism; much ingenuity has been spent in an effort to exonerate Dante from the charge of being an imperfect Latinist, since it is he who puts the words into Statius' mouth.

42 This line refers to the punishment of the avaricious and the prodigal in the Fourth Circle of Hell: "wheeling weights, they used their chests to push" (*Inf.* VII, 27).

46–47 Cropped heads were the distinguishing feature of the unrepentant prodigals, in *Inferno* VII, 57.

56 The twin sorrows of Jocasta were the two sons of her incestuous union with Oedipus, Eteocles and Polynices, who eventually killed each other in single combat beneath the walls of Thebes. In *Inferno* XXVI, 54, the forked flame containing Ulysses and Diomedes is compared to the

twinned forked flame rising from the funeral pyre of Eteocles and
Polynices, graphically illustrating the survival of their enmity even beyond death. Their "savage wars" are the subject of Statius' epic *Thebaid*.

56–57 Virgil's bucolic poems, *Eclogues,* will shortly be quoted by
Statius in lines 70–73.

58–63 Clio is the Muse of History, invoked by Statius in the *Thebaid,*
which purports to be a historical poem. Virgil means simply that that
poem contained no indication that Statius was a convert to Christianity,
the religion of Peter the fisherman.

65 This is the first of three references to Parnassus in these poet-
populated cantos of *Purgatorio* (for the other instances, see XXVIII, 141,
and XXXI, 141). Dante and others may—or may not—have confused
Parnassus and Helicon, also mentioned in these cantos (XXIX, 37–42 and
note). Parnassus was a massive mountain in Phocis, along the Gulf of
Corinth, overlooking Delphi. For the two peaks of Parnassus, see *Paradiso*
I, 36. Here, in this canto of *Purgatorio,* Dante—with many sources behind
him—sees Parnassus as the seat of the Muses, and drinking "within
Parnassus' caves," or at the Castalian spring, as a metaphor for writing poetry.

70–72 Statius' quote is a translation and a paraphrase of lines 5–7 of
Virgil's Fourth Eclogue: "The centuries' great line begins anew. Now the
Virgin returns, the rule of Saturn returns; now new progeny descends from
heaven on high." From early Christian times, these lines, probably written
by the Augustan Virgil as a flattering salute to the birth of a son to the
Roman consul Gaius Asinius Pollio, were seen as prophesying the birth of
Christ—the "new progeny" who descends "from Heaven" (72) to restore
mankind. "Man's first time on earth," in this interpretation, is Adam's existence in Eden, a paradisal age that Christ will "renew." The pagan Virgil
was, in fact, referring to the reign of Saturn, or the so-called Age of Gold,
the classical equivalent of Eden. The connection between the two myths is
made explicit in Matilda's words to Dante in the final lines of Canto XXVIII
(139–144). For another commentary by Dante on line 6 of Virgil's
eclogue, see the *Monarchy* (I, xi).

76–77 "messengers": the Apostles.

83 Domitian, who succeeded his father, Vespasian, and his brother,
Titus, as emperor of Rome (A.D. 81–96), is accused by early Christian historians of persecuting the adherents of the new religion, though modern
researchers have failed to come up with convincing historical evidence of
this.

88–89 The lines probably mean nothing more precise than "before I finished composing the *Thebaid.*"

97–114 "Where are they now?" is the formulaic opening of a typical
medieval lament, often in the form of a catalog or litany of names, for
those whom time has taken from us (of which one of the best known examples is François Villon's *Ballade des dames du temps jadis*). Statius'

"where are they?" and Virgil's answer amplify the list of dwellers in Limbo, the First Circle of Hell, given in *Inferno* IV. Terence, Caecilius, Plautus, Varius Rufus, and Persius Flaccus were Roman dramatists and poets. It should not, however, be assumed that their works formed part of the medieval canon, since it is likely that Dante knew most of them only by name. This is certainly the case with the Greek poets mentioned as being in the company of Homer ("that Greek to whom / the Muses gave their gifts in greatest measure"). Even today, while we have many of the works of Euripides and Simonides, only a few fragments by Antiphon survive and nothing by Agathon.

109–113 "Your own people" refers to characters in Statius' *Thebaid*. Antigone and Ismene were the daughters of Oedipus and Jocasta and the sisters of Eteocles and Polynices. Deiphyle and Argia were the daughters of Adrastus, king of Argos. Argia married Polynices and became the mother of Diomedes, Ulysses' companion among the False Counselors, thus establishing a family connection between the "twinned flame" of *Inferno* XXVI, 52, and the funeral flame of the rival sons of Oedipus (see 56, note).

112 The woman who showed the spring of Langia near Nemea to the army of the Seven as they marched against Thebes was Hypsipyle. Tiresias' daughter can only be Manto. Dante appears to have forgotten that he placed her not in Limbo, but in the Fourth Pouch of Malebolge with the Diviners (*Inf.* XX, 53ff.).

113–114 Thetis and Deidamia are characters from Statius' *Achilleid*. Thetis was the mother of Achilles by Peleus; Deidamia was one of the daughters of Lycomedes, king of Skyros, among whom Thetis, in a vain attempt to avert his fated death at Troy, tried to hide the young Achilles, dressing him up as a girl. The disguise did not survive the birth to Deidamia of Achilles' son Neoptolemus.

117–119 Day's handmaidens, here as in *Purgatorio* XII, 80, are the Hours. If the fifth handmaiden is guiding the chariot-pole of the sun's chariot, by our modern clock it is between 10 A.M. and 11 A.M. on Easter Tuesday, and Dante and Virgil have been on the Sixth Terrace for about four hours.

131–138 The branches of this strange fruit tree become longer the higher up they are; the tree comes to a point, so to speak, at the bottom, rendering its tempting fruit inaccessible. Its leaves, moreover, absorb the cool water that falls upon them, denying the passerby the opportunity to quench his thirst.

141 Here, as in the case of the other tree in Canto XXIV, 103–117, there is an echo of the prohibition in Genesis 2:17: "But of the tree of the knowledge of good and evil, thou shalt not eat of it."

142–154 We are entering the Sixth Terrace, that of the gluttonous, and the examples cited are illustrative of the contrary virtue of temperance.

142–144 The example of Mary at the marriage-feast of Cana was used previously, in Canto XIII, 29, where her observation, *"Vinum non habent"* ("They have no wine"), signified her charity. Here the fact that her concern for her guests took precedence over her own appetite for eating and drinking makes her an example of temperance.

145–146   Valerius Maximus, a 1st-century A.D. compiler of moral examples, is Thomas Aquinas' authority for his assertion that the women of ancient Rome drank no wine, and Thomas Aquinas is Dante's *(Summa theol.* I–II, q. 149, a. 4).

146–147   The reference is to Daniel 1:8: "But Daniel purposed in his heart that he would not defile himself with the portion of the King's meat, nor with the wine he drank ..."

148–150   The classical myth of the Age of Gold parallels, as we have seen, the biblical story of Eden.

151–154   In Matthew 3:4 we learn that John the Baptist's "meat was locusts and wild honey." In Matthew 11:11 Christ declares, "Verily I say unto you, among them that are born of women there hath not risen a greater than John the Baptist ..."—words which are repeated almost identically in Luke 7:28.

CANTO XXIII

10   *"Labia mea, Domine":* These words begin verse 15 of the *Miserere* (Psalm 50 [51 in the Vulgate]), "O Lord, open thou my lips; and my mouth shall shew forth thy praise," and are appropriately sung here by the gluttonous, who once opened their lips only in self-indulgence.

12   The intertwining of "delight and sorrow," weeping and singing, is a leitmotif of this canto (see also 64–66, 71, and 87) and of much of the life of the penitents in Purgatory.

25–27   Erysichthon, a Thessalian prince, was punished by the goddess Ceres for presuming to fell an oak within a grove sacred to her. He was afflicted with an insatiable hunger and, after exhausting his ancestral riches, sold his own daughter in order to purchase more food. Since she, like Proteus, had the power to change her shape at will, her father was able to sell her and get her back in an endless series of different forms. Finally, however, "when his fast made him fear most," his hunger became so uncontrollable that he turned on his own body and devoured himself. (See *Met.* VIII, 725–884.)

28–30   The first-century historian Flavius Josephus is the ultimate source of this gruesome incident, which occurred during the terrible siege of Jerusalem by the Romans in A.D. 70. Mary, daughter of Eleazar, mad with rage and hunger, killed her infant son at her breast, roasted him, and ate half, offering the remaining half to the marauding partisans. Hardened, famished, and accustomed though they were to eating anything they could lay their hands on, the scavengers were nonetheless appalled, and drew back in horror. (See Josephus, *The Jewish War* VI, 3.)

32–33   A common medieval tradition saw man's Latin name *homo* (or rather *omo*, without the initial *"h"*) inscribed upon his face—the two *O*'s formed by the eye sockets enclosed epigraphically within the large *M* described by the cheekbones, eyebrows, and nose. Of course, the more emaciated the face, the more prominently would this inscription appear.

35 "longing born from odor of a tree," i.e., from the fragrance of the fruit on this tree. Doubtless, the idea that this longing "could reduce souls so" echoes the story of man's first disobedience (see 61–75, note).

40–48 The shade whom Dante recognizes is a dear friend of his youth, Forese Donati, who died in 1296 ("less than five years" [78] before the supposed date of Dante's journey, he says; in fact, it is even less than four years). Forese was the son of Simone Donati (see *Inf.* XXX, 32–45, note), and brother of the fair Piccarda (see *Purg.* XXIV, 10–16, note) and of Corso Donati (see XXIV, 82–87, note); he was also a distant relative of Dante's wife, Gemma Donati. Among his other talents, Forese seems to have been an accomplished amateur poet, judging from the spiritedness of three vituperative sonnets he wrote in reply to three Dante addressed to him. (For the importance of Forese's poetic exchange with Dante, see Intro., p. xxv. For a look at these vilifying sonnets, see Kenelm Foster and Patrick Boyde, *Dante's Lyric Poetry,* Oxford, 1976, vol. I). The ongoing poetic *tenzone,* "quarrel," in epistolary poems, sometimes containing scurrilous insults, was a traditional late medieval genre. In spite of their stylization, such poetic exchanges, when vulgarly realistic (as in the case of Dante and Forese), would be more consonant with the quarrelsome divisiveness of the Infernal Malebolge (see Virgil's reproof to Dante for listening to the reciprocal vilification of Master Adam and Sinon, in *Inf.* XXX, 148: "to want to hear such bickering is base") than with the affectionate fellowship of Purgatory.

61–75 Forese suggests that he knows it is God's wisdom, "His eternal counsel," that has filled the tree with such "fragrance" that the souls "waste away" (63) with longing for its fruits, thereby correcting the excess of their overindulgence in life. (The purgatorial tree they have encountered is linked to two other trees that we shall be hearing about—the Tree of Knowledge, in Canto XXIV, and the tree of the Earthly Paradise, in Canto XXXII.) The penitents endure pain but welcome it as "solace" (71), even as Christ on the Cross, when He cried out, *"Eli, Eli, lama sabachthani? that is to say, My God, My God, why hast thou forsaken me?"* (Matt. 27:46), welcomed his agony and death with "joyousness."

83–90 Knowing that Forese had put off repentance until the end, Dante had expected to find his friend in Ante-Purgatory with the late-repentant. Finding Forese already so far advanced on his journey of atonement gives the poet another opportunity to underscore the efficacy of prayer (see especially VI, 28–42).

85–93 Nella was Forese's wife, whose reputation suffered greatly from the innuendo of Dante's poetic attacks on her and her husband in the *tenzone.* The emphasis here on her exemplary virtue might well be taken as a retraction of the disparaging remarks applied to her there.

94–96   The women of Barbagia, a remote region of Sardinia, were, perhaps because of the sound of their name, proverbial for their barbarity. They are cited here as exemplars of modest Christian behavior, in contrast to the shameless women of Florence, who think themselves so civilized.

106–109   Forese's prophecies, of course, had already been borne out by the time Dante wrote this canto. Between the years 1301 and 1315 ("before the cheeks of those / whom lullabies can now appease grow beards") Florence saw the onslaught of Charles of Valois (see XX, 70–73 and note), Rinieri da Calboli (see XIV, 88–90 and note), and various natural disasters.

115–117   These lines are the most explicit palinode of the dissolute, unregenerate life that Forese and Dante shared and of its literary emblem, the *tenzone* previously alluded to (see 40–48, note).

119–120   "The sister" of Apollo, the sun, is Diana, the moon goddess. Dante's efforts to escape from the "shadowed forest" of sin began in daylight, while here at the antipodes it was night. The reminder of the allegories of *Inferno* I and the brief recapitulation of the journey thus far are appropriate here as Dante approaches the summit of the mountain of Purgatory.

CANTO XXIV

8–9   He who "is more slow" is Statius, whose name Dante chooses not to mention to Forese. Statius' purgation was complete on the Fifth Terrace, leaving him free to mount unimpeded to the summit of Purgatory, but in order to remain in the company of Virgil, he is willing to moderate his pace. His slowed ascent, particularly if we bear in mind the eager desire that spurs the souls in Purgatory onward, more than confirms Statius' earlier protestation that, to have lived on earth when Virgil lived, he would have been willing to extend his stay in Purgatory for "one more year" (see XXI, 100–102).

10–16   Piccarda Donati, Forese's sister, was a nun of the order of St. Clare. She was forced to leave the order by her other brother, Corso, who had arranged for her to marry a Florentine named Rossellino della Tosa for Corso's political advantage. Dante will encounter Piccarda in Paradise, where, as Forese tells us, "she / rejoices in her crown already" (see *Par.* III, 34–123). Forese will shortly prophesy the imminent death and certain damnation of Corso (see 82–90 and note).

17–19   The faces of the gluttonous are so emaciated as to defy recognition.

20   Ser Bonagiunta Orbicciani degli Overardi from the city of Lucca, a notary, as well as an important poet, may have been born in 1220, though next to nothing is known about his life. He would seem to have known Dante personally, since he starts to predict Dante's future without having to be told who he is (see 37–48). Bonagiunta, whose style is condemned by Dante in the *De vulgari eloquentia* (I, xiii) as being too "municipal" or local, not attaining the ideal of a *vulgare illustre* ("illustrious vernacular")—a literary language common to the entire peninsula and without provincial and dialectal scoriae—is nonetheless acknowledged to have had a key role in the development of 13th-century Italian poetry. He was an important intermediary, instrumental in introducing the mode of the Sicilian poets to central Italy.

21–24 The one "even more emaciated than the rest" is Simon de Brion, a former treasurer of the cathedral of St. Martin in Tours and pope under the name of Martin IV from 1281 to 1285. His addiction to the pleasures of the table was proverbial. He is said to have died of a surfeit of lampreys or eels fished from the lake of Bolsena and boiled alive in white wine from Vernaccia (the modern Vernazza) in the Cinque Terre region of Liguria.

26 The satisfaction of these shades at being named is in strong contrast to the reluctance of many of the shades of lower Hell to have their identities revealed. Here, the shades hope that, by having their presence in Purgatory made known to their surviving friends and relatives, their purgation may be speeded by "prayer / that rises from a heart that lives in grace" (see IV, 133–134, note).

28–30 The Ghibelline nobleman Ubaldin da la Pila was the brother of Cardinal Ottaviano degli Ubaldini (punished in Hell along with the emperor Frederick II and other heretics—*Inf.* X, 120) and the father of the bloody persecutor of Count Ugolino, Archbishop Ruggieri (see *Inf.* XXXIII, 13–75, note). The Boniface "who shepherded so many" is Bonifazio Fieschi, archbishop of Ravenna from 1274 to 1295. The Fieschi family also produced two popes, Adrian V (see XIX, 79–145) and Innocent IV.

31 Messer Marchese degli Arguliosi, from the town of Forlì in Romagna, was chief magistrate of nearby Faenza in 1296.

37 Bonagiunta's parched mouth ("the place where he could feel / the wound of justice that denudes them so") utters a word that has been variously explained by commentators. But "Gentucca" is probably the name of the "woman" (44) whose kindness in Dante's years of exile after 1302 will, Bonagiunta predicts, make Dante find Bonagiunta's city, Lucca, "pleasing" (45)—in spite of the poor opinion of Lucca that Dante placed in the mouths of the demons in Hell (see *Inf.* XXI, 38, 41, and notes). At the time of Dante's meeting with Bonagiunta, Gentucca "wears no [marriage] veil / as yet," though presumably she will by the time of her friendship with Dante.

49–51 "Ladies who have intelligence of love" is the opening line of the first canzone in Dante's *Vita Nuova*—a line given to him, he says there, directly by inspiration, with his tongue speaking "as if by itself" *(Vita Nuova,* XIX). With the *Vita Nuova,* Dante "brought the new rhymes forth," beginning the "sweet new manner" (57) whose mode he is now about to explain most briefly.

52–54 For Bonagiunta's "he who" (50), Dante modestly substitutes "one who." Parallels to Dante's declaration in these lines have been found in the writings of the medieval mystics. A text once attributed to Richard of Saint Victor and now to a Brother Ivo, the *Epistola ad Severinum De Caritate,* asks on its first page: "What man can speak of love who does not know love, who does not feel love's force?" And replies: "Only he then can speak fittingly of love who, accordingly as his heart dictates within, sets forth his words without." (For this antecedent, see M. Casella.) Dante, in a traditional metaphor derived from the medieval scriptorium (continued by Bonagiunta in his reply below), affirms that he is Love's scribe, that his poems are a faithful register of what Love dictates.

55–63 Dante's explanation of what makes his poetry new (which has vexed critics for the last century and a half at least, anxious to prove or disprove the medieval Dante's allegiance to a Romantic poetic) is quite enough for Bonagiunta, who contents himself in his reply with rephrasing Dante's self-exegesis.

56 The "Notary" by definition is Giacomo da Lentini, poet and notary at the southern Italian court of the emperor Frederick II in the first half of the 13th century. Here he stands in for the whole "Sicilian" school of poetry to which he belongs. Guittone del Viva from Arezzo, who died in Florence around 1294, was the head of the Tuscan school of imitators of the more blatantly ingenious of the Provençal modes; his verses were less harmonious and subtle than those of Guido Cavalcanti, the younger Dante, and their friends.

　　The words "sweet new manner" (*dolce stil novo* in Italian) have been taken from this context and used to identify a "school" of poets by Italian literary historians. Insofar as such a school existed, its "father" was the Bolognese poet Guido Guinizzelli (the "other Guido" of XI, 97), whom Dante will meet in Canto XXVI and salute as his poetic father in XXVI, 97. Since Bonagiunta had attacked the Guinizzellian manner publicly in a well-known sonnet, it is fitting that he should be allowed to retract that opinion here.

64 The migratory "birds that winter on the Nile": cranes, birds that also appear in a simile in *Inferno* V, 46–47.

82–90 For the prophesied death of the "guiltiest of all" (83), Forese's brother, Corso, see Introduction, pp. xxv–xxvi. Each of the three Donati siblings is associated with a different realm of the afterworld, as if to underscore once again the evenhandedness of divine justice.

99 "two . . . marshals"—or guides: Virgil and Statius.

103 The second tree presumably has the same upside-down form as the first tree in XXII, 131.

115–119 The voice emanating from the tree warns passersby not to draw near, reminding them—as the first of three examples of punished gluttony—of the baleful consequences of Eve's apple picking. This tree sprang from a seed taken from the Tree of Knowledge of Good and Evil, which Dante will encounter in the Earthly Paradise (XXXII, 37–42 and note, and XXXIII, 55–56 and note).

119–120 In order to avoid the forbidden tree, Dante and his two guides stay as close as they can to the mountain wall on the inside of the ledge.

121–123 In the second example of punished gluttony, "those with double chests" are the centaurs, half man and half horse, joined at the chest. They were the offspring of the incorrigible Ixion and a cloud formed by Zeus into the shape of Hera to foil Ixion's lust for Hera. The centaurs were invited to the wedding of their half-brother—Ixion's son Pirithous, king of the Lapiths—to Hippodamia, the daughter of Adrastus of Argos. At the wedding feast, excited by lust and encouraged by wine, the centaurs proceeded to make off with the bride, whereupon Theseus, Pirithous' sworn friend, rescued Hippodamia and helped the Lapiths drive the centaurs off. (See *Met.* XII, 210–235.) The incident is one of those narrated on the famous Elgin Marbles in the British Museum.

124–126 The final example of punished gluttony spoken by the voice emanating from the tree is taken from the Book of Judges. There it is told how the Lord, who wished to give Israel the victory over the Midianites in a way that would allow the Jews to recognize it as *His* miracle, instructed Gideon to lead his army of 10,000 down to the water, and to eliminate all those whose impatience to drink made them go down on all fours and lap the water with their tongues like dogs. Those who lifted the water to their mouths and lapped it from their cupped hands numbered only 300, and with these alone, the Lord delivered Midian into Gideon's hands (see Judges 7:2–7).

139 "one I saw": the blindingly bright Angel of Temperance.

148–149 "the movement of his wings"—erasing the penultimate *P* from Dante's forehead.

151–154 This translation sees the canto's final line, a paraphrase of part of the same Fourth Beatitude spoken by the angel in the opening lines of Canto XXII, as adapting that Beatitude to emphasize moderation (see XXII, 6 and note). But an alternative gloss is also cogent and might read in English: "whose only hungering is after justice."

CANTO XXV

1–3 At noon in this season the sun is over Purgatory in Aries. It enters Taurus two hours later. In the northern hemisphere the sign opposed to Aries, namely, Libra, gives way to Scorpio at the same time. This astronomical circumlocution means that it is approximately 2 P.M. on the afternoon of Easter Tuesday here in Purgatory, while at Jerusalem it is 2 A.M. There can be no pausing, for the day is two-thirds of the way toward its end; only four hours of daylight are left.

17–18 Virgil, who on other occasions has shown that he is aware of the inner workings of Dante's mind, encourages him with the metaphor of the stretched bow to fire off his question.

19–21 Dante asks Virgil how it is that the disembodied spirits of the gluttonous, who no longer have any need for material sustenance, can become thin. Earlier, Dante had been amazed at the fact that although his own body cast a shadow, Virgil's body did not. Virgil took advantage of that amazement to reflect on God's inscrutability ("The Power has disposed such bodiless / bodies to suffer torments, heat and cold; / how this is done, He would not have us know" [III, 31–33]). Speaking to Dante much as Christ did to Thomas Didymus, he urged the need for unquestioning faith ("Confine yourselves, o humans, to the *quia,*" III, 37). But now he will attempt an explanation.

22–24 One of the most celebrated of Greek heroes, Meleager was the son of Oeneus, king of Calydon, and his wife, Althaea. When Althaea learned from the Fates that Meleager would live only until a log that they had thrown onto the fire was consumed, she quickly removed the burning brand, doused it, and hid the charred remains in a chest. Many years and many adventures later, Meleager killed two of his maternal uncles for contesting his right to dispose as he chose to of the spoils of the Calydonian Boar. His mother, in her grief and anger at the loss of her brothers, threw the log into the flames, and as it burned away Meleager died (*Met.* VIII, 260–525). The idea of a person's life being dependent on some external object or event is a common theme in folklore (see Stith Thompson, *Motif-Index of Folk Literature,* Bloomington, 1955–1958, III, 513, E765 *et seq.*).

25–28 Virgil's example of Meleager and that of the mirror image that keeps pace with the person reflected no matter how fast he moves are little more than casual analogies—certainly unsatisfactory as causal explanations of *how* the spirits can waste away (the phenomenon that interests Dante). The full explanation, we shall see, calls for expertise that goes well beyond the merely physiological. In fact, Statius' demonstration leads to a theological disquisition of considerable subtlety on the controversial topic of the soul's linkage to the body. It is one of the first examples in the poem of Dante's more properly philosophical mode, a mode that will culminate in the pages of *Paradiso.* Vittorio Russo ably elucidates Dante's psychophysiology.

34–48 In order to get to Dante's doubt, Statius begins his explanation of what happens to the soul after death, examining the nature of the link between the immortal soul and the mortal body, and how that link is formed. The questions he deals with had been discussed at length by medieval scientists, philosophers, and theologians (Avicenna, Thomas Aquinas, Albertus Magnus, and Siger of Brabant, among others). Their conclusions had frequently been contradictory, tentative, and uncertain, because of the difficulties they encountered in reconciling rational and scientific considerations with questions of theology and faith. Through Statius, Dante is taking sides here in an ongoing argument (though much of the first part of Statius' explanation was not considered controversial).

The physiological notions alluded to (37–48), though foreign to the ear of a modern reader, were thought of in Dante's day as received scientific truth. They were given their classic statement by Aristotle in his *Generation of Animals.* Fundamental to the argument is the theory—current in Dante's time—of the four "digestions" governing the nutritional cycle of the organism. The food we ingest passes successively through various organs—the stomach, the liver, the heart—and at each stage the

organ draws off what it can use, discarding the waste and sending the re-
fined residue on for the next "digestion." In the heart, the "perfect place,"
it is finally transformed into "perfect" (or "perfected") blood. At this point
it is ready to be transmitted to and assimilated by the various limbs. This
process constitutes the fourth "digestion." It takes place through the operation in the heart of the "formative power," a kind of built-in physiological
program, that perfects the blood. Not all of the perfect blood, however, is
absorbed by the veins or assimilated by the limbs. A portion of it is left,
like "leavings that are taken from the table," and is transformed, by still
one more process, into the active male sperm, or semen. It descends to the
genital organs ("what is best not named"). Now it is ready, thanks to the
"formative power" it, too, acquired in the heart, to generate another organism, when introduced into the proper place, the womb ("the natural receptacle"). There it can find the proper matter, the passive menstrual blood
of the female ("another's blood").

49–51   The semen of the father, joined with the blood of the mother, begins to act, first of all "coagulating" the matter with which it has been
brought into contact, and then giving life, through its own "active virtue"
(or "power"), to what it has coagulated—to that nucleus of matter, that is,
"to the matter it has made more dense."

52–57   The "formative power" transmitted by the heart of the begetter to
the perfect blood and to the semen, which has acted on the menstrual
blood, causing it to coagulate, becomes the soul. This soul gives life to the
coagulated material—to the organism about to develop in the mother's
womb. At first the soul is comparable to the soul of a plant, in that its function is merely vegetative—limited, that is, to nourishing and stimulating
growth. However, this soul is quite different from the life-principle of a
plant. For the plant, the vegetative or nutritive phase is the highest point of
its development, whereas for the human embryo, this is simply a momentary stage in its evolutionary process.

56–60   The "formative power," continuing its action, goes on to unfold
more complex functions such as movement and reactions to stimuli—
functions beyond the vegetative or nutritive—sensory functions.

61–66   These lines, which appear to constitute an aside in the ongoing argument, actually mark the passage from the physiological to the theological level. They are directed against the Spanish-Arabian philosopher
Averroes (*Inf.* IV, 42–44, note), who, because he could find no organ for
it, defined the "possible intellect" as separate from the individual soul. For
Averroes, the "possible intellect," man's capacity to reach the knowledge of universals, was only present to each man during his lifetime; only
during that lifetime do we share in the universal, unique, and separated
mind of the human species as a whole. That intellect was eternal, but trans-
individual. It was immortal, but the individual soul was not. Dante's dealings with the "possible intellect," a staple of 13th-century philosophy, are
many and various. But certainly here, in his ardent desire to see the intact-
ness of each individual in the summative soul—where life, sense, and reason are joined by God's *direct* intervention in the wake of the formative

power—he would set aside anything that might threaten the specificity and immortality of the person.

67 With the complete development, first of the vegetative, then of the sensory functions, the role and action of the "formative power" is over. Its place is taken, as a result of the direct intervention of God Himself, by the rational soul, which distinguishes man from the other living beings of creation, the plants and the animals, conferring upon him the superior powers of understanding and speech, will and memory. This "new spirit," breathed by God into the human embryo does not, however, remain detached and separate from the vegetative-sensitive soul already present. Instead it "draws" that soul into its own "substance." In other words, it transforms and then assumes the functions of the soul in its two preceding phases, forming in the end a *single* soul, which unites in itself all three "powers"—vegetative, sensitive, and rational.

76–78 How all this happens, Dante does not, and could not, really explain. This is the divine mystery of the Christian myth of the human soul. Statius' argument at this point ceases to be logical and falls back on the poetic device of analogy. If the sun coupled with the juice of the grape produces wine in the natural world, this will offer you a clue as to how the three souls can coalesce in one in the spiritual.

79–84 At the moment of death (when "Lachesis," the Fate who spins out our mortal life, "lacks more thread") the soul is freed from the body. It carries with it *both* the human part (the "formative power" that became the vegetative-sensitive soul) and the divine part (the new spirit infused by God). Once the soul is separated from the body, the divine powers (memory, understanding, and will) become more acute and active than before, while the human powers (vegetative and sensitive), though not entirely extinguished, suspend their activity, since they are now deprived of their organs.

85–111 When the soul discovers its fate in the next world and finds itself either on the shore of Acheron or at the mouth of the Tiber, the same "formative power" becomes active once again and radiates into the surrounding air the shape that its former body had. In like manner, the sun, shining through the air saturated with water vapor, imprints on the air the colors of the rainbow. This new form, which, since it has acquired a visible shape, is called a "shade," follows the soul wherever it goes, just as flame follows fire. Little by little, the shade develops again the various sensory faculties: touch, taste, smell, hearing, and even the more complex sense of sight. This is how what so amazed Dante can come about—this is how the souls are able to speak and to be glad, to weep and to suffer, and how their appearance can be influenced, as the appearance of the gluttonous was, by their longings and desires.

122 The hymn sung by the lustful in the flames, *"Summae Deus clementiae"* (in the modern Breviary, *"Summae parens clementiae"*), was sung at Matins on Saturdays. The third stanza invokes God's aid in combatting the temptations of the flesh. Singleton quotes the following somewhat free rhymed translation: "Our reins and hearts in pity heal, / And with Thy chastening fires anneal; / Gird Thou our loins, each passion quell, / and every harmful lust expel."

127–128 The first example of chastity shouted aloud by the lustful is taken from Holy Scripture. *"Virum non cognosco"* ("I know not a man") is from the reply of the Virgin Mary to the angel of the Annunciation: "How shall this be, seeing I know not a man?" (Luke 1:34.)

130–132 The second example is from classical mythology. The chaste Diana dismissed the nymph Helice (or Calisto) from her retinue after she discovered that Helice had been seduced by Jove (see *Met.* II, 401–530).

CANTO XXVI

1–6 As Virgil, Dante, and Statius move cautiously in single file along the outer rim of the ledge, with the purifying fire between them and the mountain wall, Dante becomes aware, from the angle at which its rays strike his right shoulder, that the sun has already sunk quite low in the western sky. Though the rest of the sky is blue and cloudless, the sun makes the sky immediately surrounding it seem white. The position of the sun indicates that it is between 4 and 5 P.M. Only a couple of hours remain until nightfall.

7–12 The sun behind him throws Dante's shadow onto the flames, making them look redder (and more threatening). The shadow on the flames draws the attention of the shades once again to the fact that Dante has a real flesh-and-blood body that breaks the sun's rays, and not "a fictive body" like those of the shades.

15 Even in their curiosity to know why Dante obstructs the light, the shades are concerned not to emerge for an instant from the welcome torment of the purging fire.

16–24 The shade who voices the urgent perplexity of all the others, and who will introduce himself in line 92, is the Bolognese poet Guido Guinizzelli, a poet much admired by Dante, but about whose life little is known for certain, other than that he must have died before the year 1276. For Guinizzelli as forerunner of Cavalcanti and Dante, see Introduction, p. xxiv.

28–30 Movement to the left, usual in Hell, is exceptional here in Purgatory.

31–33 The embrace of these shades of the lustful is unlingering and unerotic, a kiss of peace in the same fraternal spirit that characterizes the canticle as a whole. One tends to forget, incidentally, that although Dante talks to and mentions mostly men, there must be a number of women on this and the other terraces.

34–36 The simile of the ants has its antecedents in Virgil (*Aen.* IV, 551–560, where the Latin poet's *"nigrum agmen"* is the probable source of the "dark company" of line 34) and Ovid (*Met.* VII, 624–626).

40 The shades cry out examples chastening the sin of lust. The first ex-

ample is of the two vice-ridden biblical cities, Sodom and Gomorrah,
which were destroyed by God with fire and brimstone (see Gen. 19:1–28).

41–42 The second example of chastened lust is of Pasiphaë, the wife of
Minos, king of Crete. Pasiphaë became enamored of a handsome bull and
had Daedalus the master craftsman build her a lifelike model of a cow, in
which she hid, allowing the bull to mount her. She subsequently gave birth
to the Minotaur, half bull and half man. (See *Inf.* XII, 11–20, note.)
Logically enough, most commentators tend to view this as an instance of
"natural"—that is, heterosexual—if excessive, sexual appetite.

43–45 The simile of the cranes, birds associated by Dante with the lustful in *Inferno* V, 46–47 as well, seems somewhat contrived and improba-
ble. Migrating birds would normally all fly in the same direction. Perhaps
the unnatural direction taken by one segment of the flock is meant to underscore the unnaturalness of one of the groups of sinners. The Riphean
Mountains are a chain mentioned by ancient geographers as lying far to
the north of the known world.

76–78 According to the Roman historian Suetonius, Julius Caesar was
greeted with the title of "Queen" by a certain Octavius at a public gathering. He also reports another incident in which the troops who followed his
triumphant entry joshed him, as soldiers will, about his relations with the
Bithynian king Nicomedes. It is not clear whether Dante's mention of this
means that he, too, imputed homosexual practices to Caesar. The fact that
Caesar is among the "great-hearted souls" in the exalted castle in Limbo
(*Inf.* IV, 119) and not in the circle of Brunetto Latini, is hardly a cogent argument against it, since Caesar was not a Christian. The pagans in Hell
tend to be prominently representative of their sins.

82 Guinizzelli is with the heterosexual lovers (Dante uses the Italian
term *ermafrodito,* "hermaphroditic"). Like Arnaut Daniel, the famous
troubadour poet he is about to introduce to Dante, Guinizzelli is here, presumably because he was an author of love poetry.

94 Dante, in order to convey the intensity of his filial desire to embrace
his poetic "father," Guinizzelli, compares his situation to a poignant scene
from Statius' *Thebaid* (V, 720ff.). Lycurgus, king of Nemea, left his infant
son in the care of the Lemnian slavewoman Hypsipyle. She left the child
alone briefly in order to conduct the seven heroes to the spring of Langia
(see *Purg.* XXII, 112), but when she returned she found he had been killed
by the bite of a serpent. Sad and enraged, Lycurgus condemned her to
death forthwith. She was about to be executed when her twin sons, Thoas
and Euneus, arrived in the nick of time to save her. Dante puts himself in
the place of the two sons embracing their mother, whom they had given up
for dead. The implication may be that Dante had feared that his revered
predecessor might have been condemned to the "second death" of Hell,
even though Dante had not encountered him personally in the Second
Circle.

114–121 Guinizzelli's presentation of Arnaut Daniel begins in the same
key of modesty in which Oderisi of Gubbio, on being praised by Dante,

defers to Franco Bolognese (XI, 82–83), and it leads to the same kind of polemical statement. (For more on Arnaut, see 140–147, note.)

120 Limoges, or more precisely Excideuil in nearby Périgord, was the birthplace of the Provençal poet Giraut de Bornelh (c1150–c1220), a contemporary of Arnaut. (And some favored him over Arnaut.) In the *De vulgari eloquentia* (II, ii) three of the poets of Provence mentioned in the *Comedy* are cited as outstanding exemplars, each of a different kind of poetry. There, Giraut was placed first as the poet of "rectitude"; Arnaut Daniel was the poet of love; and Bertran de Born (*Inf.,* XXVIII, 134), the poet of arms. The present apparent reassessment of their relative stature seems to be based on formal and stylistic considerations, rather than on content.

124 For Guittone d'Arezzo, see Introduction, p. xxiv, and XXIV, 56, note.

128–129 "The cloister / where Christ is abbot of the college" is a turn of phrase remarkably similar to Beatrice's "Rome in which Christ is Roman" in XXXII, 102–103, though the emphasis here is religious rather than political. Perhaps it is significant that the monastic metaphor is used here in the circle of the lustful. The lustful now aspire to a life of chastity and brotherly devotion.

140–147 Arnaut Daniel, active at the end of the 12th century and the beginning of the 13th, was a poet much admired by Dante. A difficult and hermetic poet who wrote for a circle of initiates, he was a dedicated craftsman, a master of the challenging manner of composition known as *"trobar clus."* Modern poets and critics—one thinks of T. S. Eliot, who cites Guinizzelli's characterization of Arnaut as a *miglior fabbro del parlar materno* ("a better artisan of the mother tongue") in his dedication of *The Waste Land* to Ezra Pound—concur with Dante's high assessment.

Arnaut does not address Dante in Italian but in his "mother tongue." Provençal (in the italic type in the text). He is in fact the only character in the poem who goes against the convention according to which everyone, no matter what place or period he belongs to, is made to speak the language Dante spoke. The reason for this exception is not clear, but see Introduction, p. xxv. His speech contains several turns of phrase reminiscent of lines from extant Provençal poems by Arnaut and others. Above all, his Provençal *"leu sui Arnaut,"* "I am Arnaut," is a direct quotation from one of his poems; and with its use of the first person pronoun, the present-tense copula, and the proper name, a sequence so incisively used in *Purgatorio,* it epitomizes the movement from the indefinite, shadowed, nameless pronoun into the light of individuality. That emphasis here may, too, be a factor in his holding fast to his *own* language.

CANTO XXVII

1–6 Dante takes note of the time by referring to all four principal stations on his Earth clock (see II, 1–6, note). At Jerusalem, where Christ died ("where its Maker shed His blood"), it is dawn; the river Ebro in southern Spain lies directly beneath the constellation Libra (that is to say, it is midnight at the Strait of Gibraltar, between Spain and Morocco); the midday sun was beating down on the Ganges, at the point opposite the Ebro; in Purgatory, it is close to sunset when Dante and his two companions encounter the seventh and last sentinel angel, the Angel of Chastity.

7–9   The angel who will show them the stairway up to the next level stands on the terrace's outer edge, out of reach of the wall of flames that encircles the whole mountain at this point. He intones in Latin the Sixth Beatitude: "Blessed are the pure in heart: for they shall see God" (Matt. 5:8). This Beatitude is appropriate here, at the exit from the Seventh Terrace, first, because the ascending souls have just expiated the sin of lust, and secondly, because this is the final terrace—they (that is, all those who pass here "normally," as Statius does, and extraordinarily, as Dante does—but not Virgil) will indeed soon see God.

12–13   For the "song you'll hear / beyond," see lines 58–59.

18–19   The "human bodies" Dante had "seen burning"—perhaps in executions at the stake, which he presumably had witnessed.

23   "upon the back of Geryon": See *Inferno* XVII, 79–134.

34–45   When all else fails to draw Dante to cross the wall of fire, Virgil invokes Beatrice. The mention of her at this juncture might, on another, more autobiographical level, point to the fact that the passage through the flames represents the ultimate step in the process of purification of his love for her, a process of which the *Vita Nuova (New Life)* recounts the initial stages.

37–39   Ovid's tale of Pyramus and Thisbe appears in burlesque version in *A Midsummer Night's Dream.* And this tale of two young lovers from Babylon whose union is opposed by their parents also has links to the plot of *Romeo and Juliet.* In Ovid the lovers agreed to meet at the tomb of Ninus, where Thisbe, arriving first, saw a lioness and dropped her veil as she fled in terror. Pyramus, seeing the shredded veil in the claws of the lioness and believing Thisbe dead, stabbed himself in despair and fell at the foot of a mulberry bush, whose white berries, stained with his blood, "became bloodred." Thisbe, on returning and seeing her dying lover, killed herself in turn, and flinging her body on his, prayed that the mulberry might always remain "bloodred." (See *Met.* IV, 55–166.) Dante will again allude to this tale in Canto XXXIII, 69–70.

55–58   Emerging from the flames at the foot of the stairway leading to the next level, the three poets are greeted by a dazzlingly bright angel who chants the words that Christ will address to the just at the Last Judgment after he has separated, as the pastoral metaphor has it, the sheep from the goats. "Then shall the King say unto them on his right hand, Come, ye blessed of my Father, inherit the Kingdom prepared for you from the foundation of the world" (Matt. 25:34).

74   Virgil's fellow Mantuan, the poet Sordello, explained "the nature of the mountain" in VII, 52–61, as Dante prepared to spend his first night in Purgatory. Without the sun's light, progress is impossible.

90   On the literal level, the stars appear brighter because the air is thin and pure and free from all atmospheric disturbances (see XXI, 43–54). They appear larger because here, close to the summit of the mountain, they are appreciably nearer. But the literal accuracy of the narrative reinforces the moral significance. As the 15th-century commentator Cristoforo Landino observed, "heavenly things seem greater, the higher we raise our minds to contemplate them."

91–96   Gazing upward at the stars, Dante falls off to sleep; and as he sleeps he dreams his third dream. Like the others, in Cantos IX and XIX, it occurs just before dawn, when Cytherea, or Venus, ("the lovely planet that is patroness of love," I, 19–20) rises bright over the horizon. Dreams that came in the early morning hours, the reader will recall, were traditionally regarded as divinatory (IX, 16–19 and note).

100–108   The patriarch Jacob, son of Isaac and Rebekah, loved Rachel and served her father, Laban, for seven years in order to win Rachel as his wife. On Jacob's wedding night, however, Laban substituted his firstborn daughter Leah, and Jacob had to work seven more years before Laban would give him Rachel also. The slighted Leah bore Jacob seven children, while her sister Rachel, for a long time cursed with barrenness, bore him only two. In Christian exegesis of the Bible, Leah is often interpreted as a symbol of the active life, the life dedicated to good works (the "labor" of line 108), and Rachel as a symbol of the contemplative and speculative life ("seeing"). Some see in Rachel's mirror a symbol of God, others an image of her own conscience. Singleton cites a passage from Dante's *Convivio* (IV, ii, 18) in which Dante says that philosophy is not only the contemplation of truth but also the contemplation of that contemplation itself. Aside from the symbolism alluded to within it, the dream of Leah may, like Dante's earlier dreams, foretell an event about to take place in the fiction—in this case, the appearance of Matilda in the next canto.

111   If our true home is Paradise, then Dante is truly a pilgrim nearing home.

127–128   The "eternal fire" is the fire of Hell. The "temporary fire" is the fire of Purgatory, for Purgatory will last only until the Last Judgment.

133   The sun, which set at Dante's back, now rises in front of him, illuminating his brow as the stars of Canto I had lit the face of Cato. Like the stars, the sun has a symbolic meaning; the light of God's illuminating grace. And Dante's brow is now free of the seven *P*'s.

136   Another allusion to the active and contemplative versions of the just life. Dante may rest in contemplation or move about through the garden as Leah did in her dream.

137–138   "the glad and lovely eyes...that, weeping, sent me to your side": the eyes of Beatrice (see *Inf.* II, 55–74).

139–142   Dante has completed the education of his will, which now is no longer inclined toward evil. His will and desire are again at one with reason. With a solemn metaphor, taken from the formulaic language of investiture, Virgil declares Dante to be judge and master of his own actions.

CANTO XXVIII

1–2 Dante's keenness "to search within" and "around that forest" is so great that he does not respond to Virgil's last words.

3 "The new day" is the fourth day on the mountain of Purgatory, the Wednesday after Easter Sunday, and the last day of Dante's entire pilgrimage.

10–12 The soft breeze bends the trees' branches toward the west, "in the direction / of morning shadows from the holy mountain."

19–21 Aeolus, the king of the Winds, was supposed to keep them prisoner in a cave, releasing one or more of them at will. The Sirocco is a hot, dry wind that blows from North Africa. The magnificent and cool pine forest of the simile still stretches along the Adriatic shore near Ravenna (where Dante is buried) and the abandoned Roman port of Classe.

25 "a stream that blocked / the path of my advance": see 121–132 and note.

40–41 The lovely woman who sings and gathers flowers reminds us of Leah in Dante's last dream. She will only be named once—in the final canto of *Purgatorio* (XXXIII, 119), where we learn from Beatrice that her name is Matilda. Despite the efforts of the commentators to identify her, it is unlikely that her name refers to any specific historical figure. She is usually interpreted allegorically as a figure of earthly felicity, the *beatitudo huius vitae* ("the happiness of this life") of which Dante speaks in the *Monarchy* (III, xvi), "which consists in the [perfect] exercise of [man's] own powers, and which is typified by the Earthly Paradise."

43 The love whose rays warm Matilda is a sacred love, though the tone of Dante's words and the mood of the whole episode are reminiscent of the modes of the profane love lyrics of the poet's youth. This is possible because, at least for his own poetry, Dante had already, in the *Vita Nuova (New Life)*, performed a radical act of reinterpretation—in a spiritual direction—of his earlier production. (See the essay "Dante as Ancient and Modern," Bantam Classics *Inferno*.)

49–51 Ovid *(Met.* v, 385–408) sets the scene for the tale of Ceres and Proserpina at Enna in Sicily. There the maiden Proserpina was gathering abundant flowers in a landscape of perpetual spring by a cool shade of a wood, when Pluto, god of Hades, carried her off to be his queen. Proserpina's mother, the earth goddess Ceres, longed for her daughter and interceded with Jupiter to send Hermes to retrieve her from Hades. But Proserpina had already eaten part of a pomegranate, which committed her to remaining in Hades. The story ends in a compromise between the claims of Pluto and Ceres: ever after, Proserpina could stay above ground with her mother but had to return to Hades for half of the year. Thus, through the winter, the earth, "deprived of spring" (51), goes into mourning until Proserpina can again be restored to her mother. The perpetual springtime of earth before Proserpina was carried off clearly parallels the Edenic state of Adam and Eve, just as earth's deprivation in winter mimes man's loss of Paradise.

64–66 Ovid recounts the accidental wounding of Venus by one of her son Cupid's arrows, a wound which caused her to fall in love with Adonis (*Met.* X, 525–533).

69 "land, needing no seed, engenders": This echoes the flowers that grow without having been planted—"without seeds"—in Ovid's description of the Golden Age (*Met.* I, 108).

70–75 The situation of a man and a woman on opposite sides of a narrow body of water reminds Dante of the story of the priestess Hero and her lover Leander, which he probably knew from Ovid's allusion to it in Book XVIII of the *Heroides.* Whenever the waters were calm, Leander used to swim from Abydos, where he lived, to meet his beloved Hero in her city of Sestos, across the Hellespont. (That narrow strait, uniting the Sea of Marmara with the Aegean and separating Europe from Asia, is now called the Dardenelles.) One night his longing for her was so great that, even though the strait was storm-tossed, he tried to swim over, and drowned. The reference to the Hellespont reminds Dante of an unrelated historical incident, the crossing of the same strait by the Persian king Xerxes in 480 B.C. to wage war upon the Greeks. The defeat of Xerxes' vast army at Salamis and his ignominious flight are for Dante an exemplary warning against arrogance and overweening pride.

77 Matilda uses the plural pronoun *voi:* her answer to Dante's question is also addressed to Statius and Virgil, who accompany Dante and are no less new here than he is. Apparently, Matilda explains the nature of the Earthly Paradise to all the souls who arrive there and guides them on this final phase of their journey. She also has, as we shall eventually see, certain ministerial functions in the final rites of purification.

77–80 The divine forest was chosen to be "mankind's nest" by the Creator when he planted the garden of Eden and placed Adam there (see Gen. 2:8). The fact that Matilda sings and smiles here must be confusing to newcomers, who would naturally associate the garden with the dire consequences of the Fall. Evidently, they do not yet realize that the journey through Purgatory restores the Christian to the joyful state of Adam and Eve *before* the Fall. The word *"delectasti"* (80) is taken from the Latin text of Psalm 93:4 (92:4 in the Vulgate), "For thou, Lord, hast *made me glad* through Thy work; I will triumph in the work of Thy hands." Matilda's rejoicing in the Earthly Paradise, the work of God's hands, is a function of her knowledge.

85–89 Dante is "contending" with an apparent contradiction: on the one hand, the evidence of his senses tells him that the running stream and the wafting wind point to shifting natural phenomena; on the other, Statius has already explained (XXI, 43–54) that, above the entrance to Purgatory proper, no atmospheric changes could occur. Bosco-Reggio point out that the stream would seem to "presuppose a source fed by rains or snow."

88–108 Matilda confirms the truth of Statius' explanation, clarifying the supranatural nature of the place. This is indeed Eden, which Adam lost by his fault. The wind that Dante feels and hears does not proceed from earthly causes but from the circling of the heavenly spheres around the earth. The mountain is raised so high that the effects of the heavens are perceptible at its summit, and so the sounds of this wind in the branches of the forest of peace and justice are a distant echo of the Pythagorean music of the spheres.

103–117 As the heavens and the atmosphere below them revolve they empower the air to impregnate the hemisphere of land. This explains the apparently spontaneous generation in our hemisphere of new plants and new varieties of plants that spring up when there is no parent plant visible to have provided the seed. Though the plants of the Earthly Paradise were engendered "without seed" (see 69 and note), they do produce seeds that then engender plants in the northern hemisphere.

118–120 The flora of Eden, since it is not dependent on atmospheric conditions, is richer than our earthly flora.

124–133 We shall encounter this "pure and changeless," self-replenishing spring, the source of the two rivers of the Earthly Paradise, in Canto XXXIII, 112–114. The river that separates Dante and Matilda is Lethe, descended from Virgil's river of oblivion (*Aen.* VI, 930 and 990–991), whose waters had the power to make anyone who drank of them forget his former existence. In *Inferno* XIV, 131, Dante had inquired about the whereabouts of Lethe when Virgil was explaining the common source of the rivers of Hell and had been told he would find it in Purgatory. Here in Purgatory, the classical river of Lethe has been Christianized, functioning in a kind of baptismal rite that brings with it forgetfulness of the sins we committed on earth. For Eunoe, the stream that descends "on the other side" of the fountain, whose waters must be tasted *after* one has been immersed in Lethe, see XXXIII, 127 and note.

136–144 Typical of Dante's syncretism, of his desire to reconcile his sacred and profane sources, is his coupling of the Judeo-Christian Eden with the classical myth of the Golden Age, most familiar to Dante from Ovid's description (*Met.* I, 89–112). Perhaps on Mount Parnassus (home of the Muses and of poetic inspiration) the ancient poets were granted a faint inkling of this place. Such a reading of the pagan poets was, of course, common practice in the Middle Ages, as we saw, for instance, in Statius' Christian reading of Virgil's Fourth Eclogue, in Canto XXII, 70–72.

142–144 Adam and Eve were "mankind's root," innocent in Eden before the Fall. These lines align and adapt verses from Ovid, weaving pagan antiquity into a Christian fabric. For "mankind's root" as "innocent," see *Met.* I, 89–90: "That first age was a golden age: with no one who counselled, and with no laws, spontaneously, loyalty and righteousness were honored."

(For "never-ending spring," see *Met.* I, 107; and see the "streams of nectar" in *Met.* I, 111.)

145–148 At the mention of the ancient poets, Dante turns around to catch the reactions of Virgil and Statius. They are smiling, pleased that poets are "perhaps" (141) numbered among those who perceived the truth. That perception may be seen as faint or—if we allow those who "dreamt this place" some of the weight that dream, vision, and imagination bear in the *Purgatorio*—as penetrating.

CANTO XXIX

1–3 Matilda returns to her singing with the opening verse of Psalm 32 (31 in the Vulgate), "Blessed is he whose transgression is forgiven, whose sin is covered," appropriate to the properties of Lethe, which cancels and covers all memory of sin. The words of line 2 of the English text (line 1 of the Italian original), "She sang—like an enamoured woman," are an almost verbatim quotation from a pastoral ballad by Dante's "first friend," Guido Cavalcanti, but the profane love in Cavalcanti acquires other overtones in Matilda's song.

10 Dante had been facing east when he first ventured into the forest, before he encountered the obstacle of the river. He had turned south with Matilda along the bank, against the course of the stream. Now, after less than fifty paces, the river itself makes a right angle, so, in following it upstream, Dante is once again facing east, toward the rising sun, the symbolic direction from which God's grace and justice proceed.

15 Matilda's affectionate vocative ("My brother") and her injunction to look and listen herald a remarkable development in the action of these cantos.

21 Dante's astonished question is phrased in the language of biblical rhetoric (see, for example, Mark 1:27)—a part of Dante's attempt once again to "lift his matter" so as to render in words the miraculous events that follow.

22–30 The radiant light and "sweet melody" Dante sees and hears are the source of ineffable delight, which causes Dante to regret even more bitterly the sin of our first parents and the consequent exile from Eden. Lines 26–27 note that Eve, the "solitary woman," found the "veil" (27) of ignorance or obedience "beyond endurance."

37–42 For his difficult task, Dante must now invoke the special aid of the virgin Muses, the nine sister divinities, daughters of Zeus and Mnemosyne, who presided over poetry, science, and the arts. One of the localities sacred to the Muses (as in *Met.* I, 219) was their grove on Helicon (40), a mountain chain in Boetia and Phocis, where Pegasus, the winged horse, had struck the ground with his hoof, causing two springs, Hippocrene and Aganippe—with their powers of inspiring poetry—to gush forth. Urania was the muse of astronomy, of matters celestial. Dante probably knew the Greek etymon of Urania's name, *"ouranos,"* "sky."

43–51   At first, because of the distortion brought about by its great distance from the viewers, the source of the unusual light that fills the forest
is wrongly identified as seven golden trees. The sense of lines 46–47 is
clearer if we recall that Dante subscribed to a theory of perception that
distinguished brightness and color, the "proper objects" of sight, about
which it cannot err, from such secondary features as size, shape, number,
movement and motionlessness, etc., which were considered the "common
objects" of perception—common, that is, to several "mingled senses"
(47). As they approach, and as Dante and Matilda advance toward them,
the outlines of the bright objects become clearer, and Dante's power of
perception—the power that presents sense impressions to the brain, "the
power that offers reason matter" (49)—judged them correctly to be seven
lighted candelabra. (Though he earlier took them for trees, other details of
the vision suggest that Dante may have had in mind not seven branching
candelabra, but seven candlesticks, each with a single lit candle. The Latin
version of the Book of Revelation, which could be said to contain the seed
of his invention, has the word *candelabra,* which is translated in the King
James version as "candlesticks": "And I turned to see the voice that spake
within me. And being turned, I saw seven golden candlesticks" [Rev.
1:12].) At the same time as the form of the candelabra becomes unmistak-
able, and for the same reason, what had seemed at first a melody (23) and
then distinctly a song (36) becomes to Dante's ear an intelligible sequence
of syllables forming the Hebrew word "Hosanna," the cry with which the
multitude greeted Christ as he entered Jerusalem on the occasion com-
memorated on Palm Sunday (see Matt. 21:9).

52–54   A "midmonth moon," i.e., a full moon, would shine radiantly at
midnight, against a dark, "untroubled sky." These candlesticks, like the
seven lamps of fire burning before the throne in Revelation 4:5, may represent the sevenfold spirit of God (but also see Intro., p. xxvii–xxviii).

61–63   The "woman": Matilda.

70–81   The candlesticks are followed by a procession; above them the
candles leave seven bands, or streamers, of light where they have passed,
in an image which seems to anticipate time-lapse photography. Each
streamer is of a separate color (or each of all the colors) of the rainbow or
the moon's halo, "Delia's girdle" (Diana, goddess of the moon, was from
Delos). Since the procession that will follow is emblematic of the provi-
dential history of God's Church before and after the Redemption, the
blaze of these pennants of light heralds the coming illumination of Church
history. The radiant pennants or streamers extending into the distance over
the whole of the procession probably represent the seven gifts of the Holy
Spirit (wisdom, understanding, counsel, might, knowledge, piety, and the
fear of the Lord) that derive from the sevenfold spirit of God. For a quick
overview of the symbolism of this pageant, see Introduction, p. xxviii.

83–87   The twenty-four elders, clothed in white raiment and wreathed
with lilies (the white color of garments and lilies symbolizing righteousness; the lilies themselves, faith in the coming Messiah) recall the twenty-
four elders of Revelation 4:4, and, like them, are usually taken to stand for

or to "be" the twenty-four books of the Old Testament. They sing a paraphrase of the words of the angel to Christ's mother Mary: "Blessed *(benedicta)* art thou among women." In the Bible, this is later echoed by Mary's
cousin Elizabeth, with the addition "and blessed is the fruit of thy womb"
(see Luke 1:28 and 42).

91–105 The four animals are the four Beasts of the Apocalypse (Rev.
4:6–8, and Ezek. 1:4–14—the passage referred to in line 100), who traditionally symbolized the four Evangelists. They wear crowns of green, the
color of hope. "Each had six wings" (as in John, though Ezekiel gives
each four), which signify their knowledge of the past and the future; these
wings are "full of eyes" as vigilant as the eyes of the monster Argus (96),
a shepherd assigned by Jove to watch over Io, the nymph Jove had transformed into a heifer. Argus had a hundred eyes all over his body, at least
two of which were always awake, but his vigilance ended when he was
killed by Mercury, who lulled all his eyes to sleep by singing songs and
stories, accompanying himself on the syrinx, or reed pipe. (See *Met.* I,
568–746.)

106–108 In the center of the square formed by the four animals is a
chariot similar to those used in ancient Roman triumphal processions,
drawn by a griffin, a fabulous animal with the head and wings of an eagle
and the body and hind quarters of a lion. The griffin is traditionally a symbol of Christ, who possessed both a human and a divine nature. The chariot will soon become the focal point of the pageant and is interpreted
almost unanimously by commentators as symbolizing the Church.

109–111 The griffin's wings "stretched upward" on either side of the
middle one of the seven streamers or bands, leaving three bands on either
side and not interfering with or interrupting any of them. Apart, however,
from the general notion of the unbroken continuity of the divine inspiration of the Church, the precise symbolism is uncertain.

112–114 The upper part of the griffin's body, in the form of an eagle, is
gold in color because it corresponds to Christ's divine nature. The lower,
lionlike portion is "white mixed with bloodred," white symbolizing the
purity of Christ's human nature; bloodred, his passion.

115–116 Both Scipio the Elder (236–143 B.C.) and his adopted grandson Scipio the Younger (c185–129 B.C.) were famous generals honored by
triumphal processions in Rome and the honorary title of Africanus
("Conqueror of Africa")—the Elder for defeating Hannibal at Zama in
North Africa in 202 B.C., the Younger for his successful siege of Carthage,
which he captured in 146 B.C. For the triumphal procession of Augustus
Caesar, see *Aeneid* VIII, 929–950.

118–120 Phaethon, the son of Apollo, drove his father's chariot (the
chariot of the sun) off course and was in danger of setting the earth on fire,
but when "Earth offered up her pious prayers," Jove killed the rash chario-
teer with a thunderbolt (see *Inf.* XVII, 107, note, *Purg.* IV, 73–75, note, and
Met. II, 47–328). There may be a suggestion here, anticipating the revela-

tions of Cantos XXXII and XXXIII, that God, "in ways not known to us," will punish the erring occupants of His chariot in the same way.

121–129 The three women are the three Theological Virtues. Flame red symbolizes Charity; emerald green, Hope; and snow white, Faith.

130–132 The "four other women" are the four Cardinal Virtues, clothed in crimson because they cannot exist without Charity. The one with three eyes is Prudence; the others are Justice, Fortitude, and Temperance.

133–141 Following the animals (representing the Gospels) and the chariot (representing the Church) come figures representing the remaining books of the New Testament. The first of these is the physician Luke (a disciple of "great Hippocrates," the Greek pioneer of medicine after whom the Hippocratic Oath is named); the second is St. Paul, who is seen brandishing the sword of the Spirit, that is, the word of God contained in his Epistles.

The next four marchers are humble because the books they represent are relatively short: the Epistles of James, Peter, John, and Jude. Bringing up the rear, venerable and alone (because his work is unique among the otherwise historical, narrative, and moralizing books of the New Testament), with a face paradoxically keen though apparently asleep (to indicate the veiled yet visionary character of his work), is John of the Book of Revelation.

145–150 Like the twenty-four elders who preceded the chariot, the seven who come after it are clothed in white, but instead of being crowned with white lilies they are crowned with "roses and other red flowers." Since red is the color of Charity, it fittingly completes the sequence of symbolic colors evident in the crowns of the successive groups in the procession: white, for the messianic faith of the Old Testament, green for the renewed hope for salvation promised by the Gospels, and red for the zealous spirit of Christian charity with which the apostles spread God's word.

CANTO XXX

1–12 The basic sense of these syntactically complex opening lines is simply this: "When the moving candelabra halted, the twenty-four elders who had gone before the chariot turned around to face it and, responding to one of them, their leader, burst into song." The syntax of the sentences of this canto will continue to be unusually intricate, sustained, and suspenseful.

1–3 The "Seven-Stars," a complex figurative reference to the "candelabra" of the previous canto, are described as pertaining to the "first" or outermost heaven, the Empyrean, which lies beyond the nine concentric spheres (see diagram, "The Universe of Dante," page 314). This is at first perplexing, since the "first heaven," the Empyrean, where the blessed dwell with God, is itself star*less,* being immobile and incorporeal, pure light and love. In line 2, Dante plays with this paradox by suggesting that these "stars" of the "first heaven" are quite different from material stars that "rise or set." The light of the Seven-Stars is never in itself dimmed or "veiled"; if those stars are lost from sight, the fault is in our sinfulness, which "beclouds" our spiritual "vision." Thus if, in a sense, they are stars, the candelabra can only be the stars of a starless Empyrean—not a material but a spiritual constellation. This figure complements what we have already learned about the candelabra: that they symbolize the sevenfold spirit of God.

4–6 The seven candelabra (metaphorically, the constellation of seven stars) teach the other members of the procession what they must do. They stop, and the remainder of the procession stops. In like manner, the helmsman of a ship takes his bearings from the constellation of the Bear and learns from the stars which way he must steer to reach home port.

7–9 The "truthful band" that came between the candlesticks and the chariot was composed of the twenty-four elders, the prophetic books of the Old Testament. They turn toward the chariot, Christ's Church, whose advent they had predicted and whose founding was all their desire ("their peace").

11–12 The hymn of the elders is from the Song of Solomon 4:8: "Come with me from Lebanon, my spouse" (repeated "three times" because the biblical lines repeat "come" three times). Christian exegesis often interprets the spouse as the Church, the bride of Christ—but here the Church is already present in the form of the chariot. Who or what is to come must be someone or something else. Another implication followed by Dante in the *Convivio* (II, xiv, 20) identifies the spouse as Divine Knowledge. In light of the imminent arrival of Beatrice and of Beatrice's role in the *Comedy* as Dante's guide to the divine mysteries, it seems quite reasonable for Divine Knowledge to be the meaning of *sponsa*, "spouse," here.

12–18 At the "Final Summons," on Judgment Day, the righteous will rise up from their graves, praising, with the voices they have recovered with their resurrected bodies, the advent of Christ, come in glory to judge all. So here, one hundred heavenly angels—"ministers and messengers"—rise up from the chariot that all are watching. The allusion to Christ's last coming and to the Universal Judgment prepares the reader for the advent of Beatrice and the judgment about to take place here.

16 The Latin phrase *ad vocem tanti senis* ("at the voice of so venerable an elder") is not a quotation. In the Italian text *senis* is at the end of the line, in rhyme with *venis* and *plenis,* words from Latin sentences that are quotations. (Though the poet may have introduced the phrase to provide a rhyme, it is quite in keeping with the solemnity and stylistic difficulty of the whole passage, and the reader does not have the sense that it is filler.)

19 The words *Benedictus qui venis* are, with a slight modification (*venis* instead of *venit),* the words with which the multitude greeted Christ's triumphal entry into Jerusalem: "Blessed is he that cometh [in the name of the Lord]" (Matt. 21:9). The grammatical change makes the sentence mean "Blessed art thou who comest." Since he took the trouble to introduce this change, Dante's failure to alter the masculine gender of *Benedictus* to the feminine *Benedicta* may be deliberate (or simply sanctioned by the liturgical formula or the use of a masculine adjective for one who is still nameless—whatever his or her sex). The reader may, thus, be invited to see the coming of Beatrice as analogous to the Second Coming of Christ. It is Singleton who has explored most satisfactorily the implications of the parallel in Dante's works between Beatrice and Christ, already present in his *Vita Nuova (New Life)*. (See Charles S. Singleton, *Journey to Beatrice*, Cambridge, MA, 1958, especially pp. 72–85.)

21 *"Manibus date lilia plenis"* ("With full hands, give me lilies," *Aen.* VI, 1179) are words spoken to Aeneas in the underworld by the shade of his father, Anchises. They mourn the premature death, in 23 B.C. (he was not yet twenty), of Marcus Claudius Marcellus, a favorite nephew of Virgil's patron, the emperor Augustus. This Virgilian reminiscence in a context so dense with references to the Scriptures heralds the cloud of flowers flung up by the angels. Some commentators have seen in the Virgilian quotation a final melancholy homage on the part of Dante the poet to his beloved guide, who is about to leave or who has already left him.

31–33 Beatrice's veil, cape, and dress repeat the liturgical colors that signify faith, hope, and charity. The crown of olive boughs—from the tree sacred to Minerva, goddess of wisdom (see 68)—is suited to Beatrice, who speaks for Divine Knowledge or Theology; this crown may also suggest peace.

36 Beatrice died in 1290, so it is ten years since Dante last trembled in her presence. (In Canto XXXII, 2–3, he will speak of his "ten-year thirst.")

41–42 The *Vita Nuova*, obviously an important subtext for this and the next canto, tells us that Dante saw Beatrice for the first time at the age of nine.

48 The line is a faithful translation of Virgil's *"Adgnosco veteris vestigia flammae"* (*Aen.* IV, 27—23 in the Latin), spoken by Dido to her sister and confidante, Anna. It is as if Dante, recognizing within himself an emotion he had read about, were turning for help to the author, who might know how to cope with it since he had described it so well.

52–54 Even the fact that he is in Eden ("all our ancient mother lost") cannot stay Dante's grief.

55 This is the first and only time that Dante's name is mentioned in the *Comedy*. (He will apologize in lines 62–63 for naming himself, but the effect is actually to underscore it.)

58 The likening of his lady to an admiral is somewhat surprising, but Dante's reunion with the longed-for Beatrice has already been set in "official" circumstances. The authority of Beatrice is reinforced by her distance from Dante (he is still on the other side of the stream), her elevation (she speaks down at him from the chariot), and her regal and disdainful stance.

82–84 The song of the angels speaks for the tongue-tied Dante, who is moved to tears of self-pity by what he interprets as this demonstration of their sympathy. They sing the opening verses of Psalm 31 (30 in the

Vulgate), which begins, "In thee, O Lord, do I put my trust; let me never be ashamed: deliver me in Thy righteousness." Later, the psalmist continues: "I will be glad and rejoice in Thy mercy: for Thou hast considered my trouble; Thou hast known my soul in adversities; and hast not shut me up in the hand of the enemy: Thou hast set my feet in a large room." (This is the verse that ends with *"pedes meos,"* "my feet," in the Latin Vulgate.)

91–93 Those "whose notes always accompany the notes / of the eternal spheres" are the choiring angels.

103–108 The angels' place is in the eternal light of the Empyrean, where they contemplate God everlastingly. Nothing that occurs in the universe eludes them. Beatrice's detailed indictment of Dante is not meant for them, but for Dante, "who weeps beyond the stream."

109–111 Not only because of the benign celestial influences—"the work of the great spheres"—that attended him, but also because of the "bounty of the godly graces" showered on him from on high (from God), Dante's potential as a youth was such that, "had he acted"—i.e., properly nurtured his natural aptitude or disposition—his nature would have borne prodigious fruit.

121–132 Beatrice sustained him with her countenance from 1274, when Dante was nine, until 1290, when she died, exchanging terrestrial for celestial life. The first of the four ages of life, adolescence, lasts until the age of twenty-five. The "second age" is youth, by which Dante meant the years from twenty-five to forty-five, the age that "can bring us to perfection" (see *Convivio* IV, xxiv, 1, 3, 4, 13).

125–132 In the *Vita Nuova* (XXXV–XXXVIII), Dante recounts how he was led temporarily to neglect Beatrice's memory by an otherwise unnamed *donna gentile* ("a gentle lady"). The entity (real or allegorical) and the identity (if real) of this lady have never been conclusively explained. The present lines can be read either or both ways. Certainly, Dante's own retrospective identification of the *donna gentile* as Philosophy in the *Convivio* does abet Beatrice's polemic against overreliance on reason in XXXIII, 85–90.

130 This "untrue path" recalls the situation at the beginning of the *Inferno,* where Dante "had lost the path that does not stray" (*Inf.* I, 3).

131–132 "counterfeits of goodness": earthly goods.

136–145 Dante was so far removed from goodness, so inured and obstinate in his error, that contrition and repentance, without which salvation is unthinkable, could only have been induced by the experience of Hell—by seeing "the people who were lost."

CANTO XXXI

2–3 Beatrice's speech at the end of Canto XXX had been ostensibly addressed not to Dante but to the angels who had prayed on his behalf for mercy. But even though he had felt only "its edge," her speech had still stung him sharply. Now Beatrice addresses Dante directly, turning the "point" of her speech's sword against him.

5 It is not enough for Dante to recognize his fault in the words of Beatrice. The culminating ritual demands that, as in the sacrament of confession, he confess his errors aloud (see IX, 94–102, note).

11–12 Dante has not yet been immersed in the stream of Lethe, whose waters obliterate the "sad memory" of sin. Thus, he can still recall and confess his sins.

13–21 "One needed eyes to make out what it was" because Dante is so distraught that the syllable is never actually voiced. Since his "Yes" cannot be heard, it is not acceptable as a confession.

34–36 Dante's reply is an index of his submission. It is nothing more than a dutiful repetition of Beatrice's accusation in XXX, 124–132.

37–42 Dante's confession does not reveal to God, Beatrice, or the angels anything they did not already know. His fulfillment of the ritual, however, causes the heavenly court to look upon him with mercy. It "blunts" the "cutting edge" of the sword of Divine Justice.

55–57 "The first / arrow of things deceptive" was Beatrice's own death, which should have revealed to Dante the deceptiveness of even the loveliest of mortal things, the highest earthly beauty, hers. At that point Dante ought to have turned away from the ephemeral to pursue the incorruptible spiritual blessings of the world to which Beatrice's soul had flown.

72 Iarbas, rejected suitor of Dido, was a North African king (*Aen.* IV, 262–286). From his lands, a hot wind would blow toward Italy.

74–75 The use of the term "beard" for Dante's face brings home forcefully that, in spite of his standing "as children stand when they're ashamed" (64), he is not a child.

77 "the first creatures": the angels.

80–81 The "animal / that is, with its two natures, but one person": the griffin (see XXIX, 106–108 and note).

88–96 Dante swoons and wakes to find himself almost totally immersed in Lethe, drawn across by Matilda (see XXVIII, 40–41 and note).

98 The angels sing a verse from one of the penitential Psalms, the *Miserere:* "Purge me with hyssop, and I shall be clean: wash me, and I shall be whiter than snow" (Psalm 51:7—50:9 in the Vulgate). The verse is sung in the liturgy when the priest sprinkles the congregation with holy water, symbolically washing away their sins.

103 On emerging from the purifying waters of Lethe, Dante is encircled by the four women representing the Cardinal Virtues, who hold their hands over his head and dance as they lead him to Beatrice.

106 In Canto I of *Purgatorio* these women had appeared in the predawn sky as stars—"four stars / not seen before except by the first people" (I, 23–24).

109–111 "the three beyond": The three women who dance on the other side of the chariot (the Theological Virtues, whose powers exceed the natural powers of the Cardinal Virtues) will enable Dante to penetrate more deeply Beatrice's "joyous light."

115–116 Gazing into the eyes of Beatrice—"those emeralds / from which Love once had aimed his shafts" at him—Dante sees the two natures of the griffin alternately reflected there. The changing shape of the griffin mirrored in the emerald mirrors of Beatrice's eyes may point to the inadequacy of our human understanding to fathom the mystery of the hypostatic union of the two natures in one person, God and man in Christ.

133–145 The Theological Virtues beseech Beatrice to turn her gaze directly upon Dante and also to unveil her second beauty, her lips. She does so, and Dante's poetic gift is overcome. No poet, Dante says, has "ever grown so pale"—i.e., spent so much time—in the inspirational groves of Mount Parnassus or has "drunk so deeply" from the Castalian Spring (see XXII, 65, note) that he would not still seem confused and tongue-tied and "have his mind confounded" if he attempted to put into words the beauty of God's light, reflected in the beauty of the face of Beatrice, "unveiled completely."

CANTO XXXII

7–9 In Canto XXXI, 115, the natural Cardinal Virtues, leading Dante to Beatrice's eyes, had instructed him, "See that you are not sparing of your gaze." Now the supernatural Theological Virtues warn him that he is staring "too fixedly." In fact, when he looks away, Dante finds that the splendor of Beatrice's beauty has dazzled him, leaving him, for a few moments, blind. Despite the autobiographical allusion to his ten-year thirst for the sight of Beatrice, this dazzlement may, perhaps, best be interpreted by stressing the continuing allegorical significance of Beatrice and by taking the three goddesses' words as a warning that the resplendent truth of the knowledge of things divine must be approached gradually, sipped not gulped—rather than by viewing these words as a reproof to Dante for concentrating too long on the lovely human form of his lady. In any case, this interruption signals a change of focus and a new turn of events.

16–18 The procession first approached from the east; now "the glorious army" wheels around, to return in the direction from which they came, still preceded by the candelabra, but now facing the morning sun.

19–24 The military imagery and vocabulary ("army," "squadron," "troops") stress that the emphasis in the events to come will be on the Church Militant—on the earthly historical vicissitudes of the Church.

27 The stillness of the feathers on the raised wings of the griffin is an allegorical detail that has been variously interpreted. It may signify that Christ guides by spiritual not material means, or that in the passage from the Old Testament to the New Testament divine justice and mercy remained unchanged, or that, though the Church may change, the Divinity remains unaltered.

31–32 The woods of the Earthly Paradise have been deserted since Adam and Eve were expelled after Eve "had believed the serpent."

37–42 The murmured name of Adam is an accusation and a sad reminder of that first transgression. It also informs us that the singular tree without leaves and flowers to which they all draw near is the Tree of the Knowledge of Good and Evil (Gen. 2:9, 16–17, and 3:1–6). The tree, which, like the legendary trees of the forests of India, grows to an amazing height, has the same form as the inaccessible trees we saw on the terrace of the gluttonous (XXII, 131–135, and XXIV, 103–117). In fact it provided the seeds from which those trees sprang (see XXIV, 115–119 and note). In the next canto (XXXIII, 70–72) Dante will point out that on the level of moral interpretation the tree signifies divine justice. Those commentators, many of them modern, who read the tree as an allegorical figure of the Empire, have to explain away the fact that, in the "dumb show" (Singleton) that is to follow, the Empire is represented by "the bird of Jove" (112), the imperial eagle.

43–45 The formula "Blessed are you" repeats in the vernacular the *"Benedictus"* of XXX, 19. The members of the procession, who a moment ago reproached Adam for his disobedience, praise the griffin, who refrains from plucking and eating the sweet-tasting but inauspicious fruit. Within the allegory, they praise Christ for his respect for divine justice, for his proverbial obedience to the Father.

48 The "seed" of the righteous is preserved by obedience to the Law.

49–60 When the chariot is attached to the barren tree, it is as if it were suddenly spring. The solitary branches burgeon, and the tree renews its leaves and flowers. The "great light" is the light of the sun. It is mixed with the light of the constellation that shines behind (i.e., after) that of Pisces, namely, Aries, from late March to late April. On the allegorical level the tying of the chariot to the tree blasted by the sin of the first Adam and the tree's reflowering presumably indicate the reconciliation of God and mankind through Christ's (the second Adam's) atonement and the restoration of the reign of justice and the promise of eternal life.

60 The tint between the red of the rose and the violet may signify the purple of Christ's blood, but as John Ruskin points out (*Modern Painters.* London: Smith, Elder & Co., 1843–1860, Vol. III, p. 226), this is a perfect description of the color of the apple blossom, which appears in early spring.

64–69 For the charming to sleep of the one-hundred-eyed Argus, see XXIX, 91–105, note.

70–84 Dante, who swooned at the ineffable beauty of the angel's hymn (61–63), is awakened by "a radiance," a bright light, accompanying the departure (to the Empyrean?) of the griffin and all of the company except Beatrice, the chariot, and the Virtues. The voice of Matilda bids him rise (72). The long simile that comes next is somewhat complex. Dante compares the moment with the moment of Christ's transfiguration, recounted in the gospels of Matthew, Mark, and Luke, and his state with that of

Christ's disciples. The account in Matthew is perhaps the most complete: "And after six days Jesus taketh Peter, James, and John his brother, and bringeth them up into an high moûntain apart, and was transfigured before them: and his face did shine as the sun, and his raiment was white as the light. And, behold, there appeared unto them Moses and Elias talking with him. Then answered Peter, and said unto Jesus, Lord, it is good for us to be here: if thou wilt, let us make here three tabernacles; one for thee, and one for Moses, and one for Elias. While he yet spake, behold, a bright cloud overshadowed them: and behold a voice out of the cloud, which said, This is my beloved Son, in whom I am well pleased; hear ye him. And when the disciples heard it, they fell on their face, and were sore afraid. And Jesus came and touched them, and said, Arise, and be not afraid. And when they had lifted up their eyes, they saw no man, save Jesus only" (Matt. 17:1–8).

74–76 The brief Transfiguration witnessed by the disciples was merely a sample of the eternal vision of Christ in all His splendor that will be granted to the blessed in Paradise—like the springtime blossoms of the apple tree that are a promise of fruit to come. The metaphor of the Messiah as apple tree is taken from biblical prophecy: "As the apple tree among the trees of the wood, so is my beloved among the sons. I sat down under his shadow with great delight, and his fruit was sweet to my taste" (Song of Sol. 2:3). This is the fruit for which the angels hunger and with which they are continuously regaled at the never-ending marriage-feast of Heaven.

78 The "word that shattered deeper sleeps" is the word *Surge* ("Rise up," "Arise"), which shattered the sleep of death in the miracles of the raising of the widow's son (Luke 7:14), the raising of Jairus' daughter (Luke 8:54), and the raising of Lazarus (John 11:43).

81 When the disciples came to, Jesus was no longer clothed in light.

101–103 The "Rome in which Christ is Roman" is of course the celestial not the terrestrial Rome, Augustine's City of God, Paradise, where, Beatrice prophesies, Dante will eventually share her own bliss for all eternity.

105–106 After the assurance from Beatrice that he is one of the elect, Dante is invested with his poetic and prophetic mission. Until now, his journey might have seemed to be directed to his personal salvation; now its universal, exemplary aspect becomes explicit. St. John, too, was instructed more than once to record the contents of his vision. (See, for example, Rev. 1:11: "What thou seest, write in a book.") Beatrice's words to Dante—her first since she instructed him to raise his downcast head and look upon her, midway through Canto XXXI (67–69)—mark the beginning of yet another "act" in the symbolic drama of sacred history. This final act traces the vicissitudes of the historical Church from the early persecutions to the present day.

109–117 The eagle ("the bird of Jove") that swoops down upon the chariot, damaging the tree (i.e., offending divine justice) in the process, repre-

sents the persecutions of the early Church by the Roman emperors, from
Nero to Diocletian, through the 3rd century A.D.

118–123   The ravening fox that insinuates itself into the chariot stands
for heresy, ably combatted and routed by Beatrice, with her true knowledge of things divine. She mimes the antiheretical force of the Fathers of
the Church.

124–129   The imperial eagle returns, this time to leave its feathers in the
chariot. The eagle's feathers signify earthly rule, the exclusive prerogative,
in Dante's conviction, of the Empire. The legendary 4th-century Donation
by the emperor Constantine of temporal dominion in the Western Empire
to Pope Sylvester and his successors, however well-meaning (line 138), is
continually deplored by Dante in his works. (The Donation was actually
an 8th-century forgery.) It is seen as contaminating two irreconcilable
spheres and interfering with the Church's purely spiritual mission, which
cannot be fulfilled outside of the rule of poverty practiced by the primitive
Christians. "Render to Caesar the things that are Caesar's, and to God the
things that are God's" (Mark 12:17). (See "Dante in His Age," Bantam
Classics *Inferno,* pp. 326–328.)

129   In vying with the emperors for temporal sway, the ship of the
Church (the bark of St. Peter) has taken on an illicit cargo that can only
lead to her foundering.

130–136   The dragon who comes up out of the ground (he is called a
"serpent" in XXXIII, 34) to plant his venomous tail in the chariot from below carries off a portion of it—an allusion to a depletion of the Church's
membership by a diabolically inspired schism. Among the many candidates for that role is Mohammed, punished with his son Alì as the arch-
schismatic in the Ninth Pouch of Malebolge in *Inferno* XXVIII, 22–33.

142–147   Finally, the chariot is hideously transformed into a beast with
seven heads and ten horns, modeled on the beast that rose from the sea,
described by John in Revelation 13:1. (See *Inf.* XIX, 106–111 and note.)

148   The brazen whore who sits upon the chariot-turned-monster is a figure of the corrupt Papal Curia, whose latest sovereign pontiffs were
Boniface VIII (1294–1303), Benedict XI (1303–1304), and the Gascon
Clement V (1304–1314), who was responsible for the removal of the papacy to Avignon. The reader may recall that a previous pope, Nicholas III
(1277–1280), had mistaken Dante for the simonist Boniface in *Inferno*
XIX, 52–53.

148–150   Like the deformed beast itself, the figure of the whore or scarlet woman who sits upon it, "with whom the kings of the earth have committed fornication," is inspired by Revelation 17:1–3.

151–156   The giant is generally seen as a symbol of the French monarchy, the hegemonic power in Europe in the late 13th and early 14th centuries, before whom the popes of that period were largely acquiescent.
Some would identify him specifically with the French king Philip the Fair.
The thrashing of the whore by the giant might then refer to Boniface's hu-

miliation by Philip's troops at Anagni in 1303 (see *Purg.* XX, 85–90 and note). But what Dante means by bringing himself into the picture is not quite clear. Since he is the only other male present, the whore's turning away from her paramour to him may simply reflect Boniface's valiant but unsuccessful attempt, toward the end of his reign, to stem French influence and break with Philip.

157–160   The detaching and sequestering of the chariot by the giant continues Dante's criticism of the high-handed behavior of the French crown. It may refer to the transfer of the Curia to Avignon in 1309 under Clement V, a French pope (see "Dante in His Age," Bantam Classics *Inferno,* pp. 326–328).

CANTO XXXIII

1–3   As they weep, the three women who represent the Theological Virtues and the four who represent the Cardinal Virtues alternate in singing the words of Psalm 79 (78 in the Vulgate), which begins: "O God, the heathen are come into thine inheritance; thy holy temple have they defiled; they have laid Jerusalem on heaps." In the present context, the Virtues are expressing their grief over the ruin and corruption brought upon Christ's Church by unworthy popes.

7–12   When the Psalm is over, Beatrice (who until now has been sitting on the roots of the tree) rises to her feet and addresses her sister Virtues with the words of Christ to his disciples in John 16:16, words that refer allusively to His imminent death and resurrection: "A little while, and ye shall not see me: and again, a little while, and ye shall see me..." Here Beatrice repeats Christ's words, in the person of His Church, as an assurance that Divine Providence will restore the Church from its present fallen state. Her words may, as some suggest, refer to the 14th-century transferral of the seat of the papacy from Rome to Avignon (the so-called Babylonian Captivity, still in the future in 1300, but begun before *Purgatorio* was composed) and its eventual return to Rome (see XXXII, 157–160, note). In John's Gospel, too, Christ's words are not immediately understood by his disciples, because, as He Himself admits, they are spoken in figurative language, in what He calls "proverbs" (though the precise meaning of this term is debated). This mode of biblical discourse will be imitated at length in Beatrice's hermetic oracular pronouncements in lines 31–78 of this canto.

14   The "lady": Matilda.

15   The "sage who had remained": Statius.

16–17   Beatrice's nine steps (the tenth is not taken) presumably have a specific allegorical meaning, though no convincing explanation emerges from the commentators. The mystic number nine was frequently associated with Beatrice in the *Vita Nuova.*

23–33   Though she uses the familiar *tu* form of address and calls him "brother," Dante, still entangled in the net of fear and shame, continues to

address Beatrice hesitantly (almost like "one who dreams," 33) with the
pronoun of reverence, *voi,* calling her *Madonna* ("Lady" or "Milady").

34–78 Beatrice's interpretation of the prophetically symbolic events of
the preceding canto, themselves imitative of the visionary mode of the
Book of Revelation, is allusive, dense, and cryptic. The English reader
will do well to bear in mind that, at points, the interpretation of Dante's
Italian text remains the subject of ongoing exegetical controversy. The ob-
scurity of the text is avowedly deliberate (see, for example, lines 46–50).
Modeled on the veiled discourse of the Apocalypse, the whole speech is
also a virtuoso poetic cadenza in the manner of the Provençal *trobar clus:*
a periphrastic, enigmatic prophecy. Attilio Momigliano and some other
modern readers may find the figure of the vatic Sybil—especially so soon
after the intensely personal and affecting moments of Cantos XXX and
XXXI—not one of Beatrice's more convincing roles. Still others may revel
in the travail of Dante's poetry as he seeks meaning in history and consciously struggles with the modes of conveying meaning.

34–36 The "vessel which the serpent broke" is the chariot pierced by the
dragon in XXXII, 132, which, the reader will recall, represented the
Church. The phrase "was and is not" echoes the Book of Revelation 17:8
("The beast that thou sawest was, and is not...") and signifies that at least
in the eyes of God, the Church, because of its corruption, has ceased to exist.

37–40 The eagle that left its plumes within the chariot (see XXXII,
124–126) symbolized the Empire, which, in Dante's view, was "without
an heir" since the death of the man he considered the last legitimate emperor, Frederick II of Hohenstaufen, in 1250. The Church became a "monster" with the Donation of Constantine (see XXXII, 124–129, note). In
recent times, the Church had further prostituted herself, becoming a
"prey" and a creature of the giant (the power of the French throne), with
whom the whorish 13th- and 14th-century papacy had dallied. (See XXXII,
148–160 and notes.)

40–45 The rapt Beatrice sees in the not-too-distant future a favorable
constellation approaching, heralding the advent of a divinely appointed
scourge and savior who will put to death the whore and her giant paramour, thereby ending the corrupt line of popes. These popes, abetted by
the French monarchy—especially by Philip IV (the Fair), king of France
from 1285 to 1314—have diverted the Church from the poverty essential
to her spiritual mission, toward her present hunger for temporal power. The
general lines of Beatrice's prophecy are clear. The enigma of the "Five /
Hundred and Ten and Five" has, however, like that of the Greyhound in *Inferno* I, 101, never been satisfactorily resolved. Most exegetes, starting
with the earliest, translate the numbers into their Roman letter equivalents
($500 = D$, $10 = X$, $5 = V$ or U) and then transpose them to produce the Latin
anagram *DVX* or *DUX,* meaning "guide," "leader," "chief," "commander,"
a term applied on occasion to the Roman emperors. But it is in identifying
the precise historical figure that Dante had in mind (if any) when he used
this extremely generic appellation that the exegetical carnival starts. The

candidates include just about everybody from Jesus Christ, to a future just pope, to Dante's Veronese protector Cangrande Della Scala (1291–1329), to Dante himself. In the context, the only clue is the apparent identification of the *DUX* as heir to the imperial eagle. The most persuasive explanation, then, identifies the *DUX* with the emperor Henry VII of Luxembourg (c1274–1313), whom Dante may have had in mind as he composed his *Monarchia (On World-Government,* trans. H. W. Schneider, New York, 1957). Henry's descent into Italy in 1310–1311 to claim his inheritance was hailed as heaven-sent by the poet in a series of Latin epistles (see "Dante in His Age," Bantam Classics *Inferno,* pp. 327–328).

Still other solutions to the riddle interpret the numbers as containing a veiled chronological reference. Among these, the most convincing case is made for adding Dante's 515 to the year 800, when, with the coronation of Charlemagne, the Western Empire was revived. This would situate the hoped-for palingenesis in the year 1315. Whether we read the enigma as referring to a person or as a chronological date, when we reflect that the *Purgatorio* was probably composed sometime between 1309 and 1313, we may conclude that Dante saw, or hoped for, an imminent redemption of the Church.

46–51 The riddle of the cruel Theban Sphinx, a winged monster with a girl's face and a lion's body, was solved by Oedipus, son of Laius. According to Ovid (*Met.,* VII, 759–765), the goddess Themis, herself a prophetic divinity who spoke through obscure oracles, then sent a second monstrous beast to ravage the crops and livestock of the Thebans (the "grain and herds" of line 51). Beatrice compares her riddle with that of the Sphinx but affirms that there will be no call for expert riddle solvers to explicate it. Time and historical events themselves—that is, the peaceful coming of the prophesied redeemer—will make its meaning plain. Why such expertise in the expounding of riddles was attributed by Dante to the Naiads, attractive but not especially intelligent female spirits who presided over freshwater streams and springs, calls for explanation. A certain family of manuscripts containing the Ovidian text contained a scribal error. In this manuscript tradition, Dante read, in the passing reference to the solution of the Sphinx's riddle by Oedipus, not his singular patronymic *Laiades* ("son of Laius"), followed by a singular verb, but the plural subject *Naiades* ("the Naiads"), with the dependent verb also in the plural. Thus, a purely accidental complication was added to a text (Dante's) already obscure enough in itself.

52–54 Dante is enjoined to commit Beatrice's prophecy to memory and to relay it, on his return to earth, to his fellow mortals. The characterization of our life on earth as "a race to death," elegiacally expressed in this aside, recalls the world view of St. Augustine. It is a theme that will be obsessively reiterated by Dante's lyric junior, Francesco Petrarca (1304–1374).

54–66 The "tree / that now has been despoiled twice over": the tree of the Knowledge of Good and Evil. That tree (XXXII, 37–42 and note) had long since been stripped of its leaves (as a consequence of the sin of

Adam) when Beatrice and the other members of the procession surrounded it. It burgeoned again when the pole-shaft of the chariot was tied
to it (XXXII, 49–60 and note). Later, the bird of Jove damaged the bark and
leaves of the tree in its swift descent (see XXXII, 109–117 and note).
Finally, the giant detached the life-restoring chariot from the tree and
dragged it off into the wood, presumably completing (though it is not
stated) the despoliation begun by the eagle (XXXII, 157–160 and note).

Those exegetes who would have Dante say exactly who and when
would do well to heed Angus Fletcher's distinction between prediction and
prophecy. Vagueness is an essential characteristic of the prophetic tradition. Dante the seer sees, like St. Paul, "through a glass darkly." (See
Angus Fletcher, *The Prophetic Moment: An Essay on Spenser,* Chicago,
1971, p. 4.)

61–63   Adam, the first soul, who trespassed beyond the limits assigned
to him by God and ate the fruit of the forbidden tree, lived on earth for 930
years (Gen. 5:5) and then spent 4302 years in Limbo waiting for the redeeming sacrifice of Christ ("for Him who on Himself avenged that
taste") and the Harrowing of Hell. This precise chronology—which is that
established by Eusebius of Caesarea (c260–c339) in his *Thesaurus
Temporum*—will be confirmed in person by Adam, whom Dante encounters in the Empyrean Heaven (*Par.* XXVI, 118–123).

64–72   If Dante's intellect were not still "asleep," he would already have
grasped the moral significance of the tree's form. In its tallness and in the
way its branches, like those of an inverted fir tree, spread wider and wider
the closer they are to the top, the Tree of Knowledge is a visible figure of
Divine Justice as it revealed itself in the injunction imposed upon Adam.
Its height and form discourage "trespass" (72) and transgression.

67–68   The waters of the Elsa, a tributary stream of the Arno River in
Tuscany, contain a high percentage of calcareous salts, which form a
stonelike encrustation around any object immersed in those waters. What
Dante was able to learn from purely human and rationalistic speculation
has had the same effect upon his mind. Such learning is not a help but an
obstacle to the understanding of eternal truths.

69–70   When Pyramus died on his sword, according to Ovid (*Met.* IV,
121–127) his blood spurted out over the branches of the mulberry tree,
"staining" its previously white berries purple. (For an earlier use of Ovid's
tale in *Purgatorio,* see XXVII, 37–39 and note.) And Dante's complacent
self-satisfaction with his learning is a stain obscuring the clarity of his vision, a further impediment to true understanding. The involved similes are
in keeping with Dante's attempt to enhance the formal prestige of these
prophetic pages.

73–78   Beatrice realizes that her words have been obscure to Dante's
"petrified," "opaque" mind. She tells him to try and carry with him, when
he goes back to earth, at least the gist of what she has said, just as a medieval "palmer" or pilgrim returning from the Holy Land would wreath
his staff with palm fronds as a reminder of where he had been.

79–84 Dante replies that he hears not merely the gist but Beatrice's every word. "But why," he asks, "does she persist in speaking in riddles that so far exceed my grasp?" The more he struggles to fathom her meaning, the more it eludes him. Dante's disappointment with the impenetrability of Beatrice's discourse is all the more comprehensible when we recall how many times in *Inferno* and *Purgatorio* Virgil had promised Dante that, when he came to Beatrice, all would be clarified.

85–90 Beatrice declares that she deliberately made her message mysterious in order to make Dante aware of the limitations of the philosophical learning he had pursued so avidly and pridefully. The distinction between the doctrine of the school Dante followed and heavenly knowledge, between his way and the divine, recalls St. Augustine's distinction between *scientia* and *sapientia* (scientific knowledge vs. wisdom). We may recall at this point the figure of Ulysses, in *Inferno* XXVI, who strove to become expert in "the vices and the worth of men," and was punished for pursuing an obstinately human ideal of knowledge even to within sight of the slopes of the sacred mountain of Purgatory.

89 The "highest and the swiftest of the heavens" is the Primum Mobile, the heaven that is closest to the Empyrean (see diagram, page 314).

96–99 All will note that Beatrice's argument is—from a logical point of view—fallacious. Chimenz pinpointed that fallaciousness succinctly: the relation of necessity that exists between "smoke" and "fire" does not exist between the absence of memory and "fault" or sin (whether or not the "forgetfulness" can be occasioned by supernatural Lethe or by the imperfections of human recall). However, Beatrice draws her conclusions not with scientific, logical knowledge but with divine wisdom.

100–102 Beatrice has finished her prophecy. From now on her speech will be straightforward, "naked," more within the reach of Dante's and the reader's "still-crude sight."

103–105 It is noon. The sun is at its brightest and, being directly overhead, appears to move more slowly. This is the last indication of time in the *Purgatorio*. It is into this full sun that Beatrice will gaze as the journey of *Paradiso* starts, while Dante, who is facing her, will gaze at the reflection of the sun in her eyes. We are reminded that ever since it first rose over the shoulders of the mountain in *Inferno* I, the sun has often served as a symbol of God and of the illumination of Divine Wisdom. It is appropriate that it should appear at its brightest as the journey toward purification approaches its end.

112–113 The Tigris and Euphrates are rivers in Asia Minor; in Dante's time they were believed to spring from the same source. The names of the two rivers are also mentioned in the account of Eden given in Genesis 2:14, where we learn that the river that watered the garden divided into four branches, two of which were the Hiddekel (in Greek, the Tigris) and the Euphrates.

115–118 Tigris and Euphrates offered Dante a likeness of and suggestion for a double rivering from one source; Isidore of Seville did refer to two fountains in Boetia, "one awakening memory, one bringing forgetfulness"; and Islamic sources have also been suggested. But the spring announced in Canto XXVIII (121–133) and encountered here is essentially a remarkable invention by Dante, serving his liturgical, ethical, and cultural fiction.

127–135 Matilda leads Dante and Statius to drink at the waters of Eunoe, the final step in the ritual of purification that began with Virgil's cleansing Dante's tear-stained cheeks with his dew-soaked hands in *Purgatorio* I, 124–129. Like Cato, who guards the threshold of Purgatory and initiates the arriving shades in the ways of this new realm, Matilda's role is to lead all of the redeemed shades through Lethe and Eunoe, thus preparing them for the final ascent to Paradise.

To complement Lethe, Dante derived the name "Eunoe" from random Greek gathered up in medieval glossaries, from *eu* as "good" and *nous* as "mind," to form the "memory of the good" (for "mind" as "memory," see *Inf.* II, 7–9, note).

136–141 At the close of the second canticle, as he has done at other crucial points, Dante speaks directly to the reader. He would have us see the "space" and symmetry of the work as passionately precise, its "pages predisposed"; and he would introduce the *topos* of untellability, the sense that even "ampler space" would still confine him to singing "incompletely." This *topos* will recur again and again in the final canticle as Dante attempts to recreate and create his vision of Paradise.

143–144 The rhetorical figure of repetition (*"new* trees," "renewed," *"new* boughs") underscores the theme of conversion and Christian *renovatio* (or renewal), a theme central to the *Comedy,* and indeed to all of Dante's works since the youthful *Vita Nuova (New Life).*

The foregoing translation and brief annotations are much indebted to the exegetes cited in the Introduction to the *Inferno,* as well as to many earlier commentators. Recent publications that have been consulted throughout are:

The *Enciclopedia Dantesca,* the six-volume work directed by Umberto Bosco, with Giorgio Petrocchi and (from Vol. IV on) Ignazio Baldelli as general editors. Rome, 1970–1978. The first five volumes are ordered alphabetically. The sixth volume includes: Petrocchi's biography of Dante: a unique collective series of essays on the language and style of Dante; a bibliography; and the texts of all of Dante's works—and works that may be Dante's. The *E.D.* is one of the finest examples of a collective scholarly-critical enterprise that our times have produced, but the special bibliographical section in Vol. VI is much less cogent and complete than many of the separate bibliographies at the end of the alphabetically ordered entries.

Francesco Mazzoni's edition of the commentaries of Tommasso Casini-Silvio Adrasto Barbi (the latter revising the former after Casini's death in 1917) and of Attilio Momigliano: Dante Alighieri, *La Divina Commedia: Purgatorio,* Florence, 1977, Mazzoni has careful bibliographical indications and brief but precious exegetical updates on each canto of the *Purgatorio.*

Essays on the individual cantos of the *Purgatorio* are to be found far beyond the range of the principal collective volumes—or pamphlet collections—of *Purgatorio* readings. But the following compilations (with their separate essays on each canto, in the Lectura Dantis format that the *California Lectura Dantis* volumes, now in progress, will follow) have been both convenient and particularly helpful.

Letture dantesche: Purgatorio, ed. Giovanni Getto, Florence, 1958 (now in the 1965 single-volume edition of the three *cantiche*); *Lectura Dantis Scaligera: Purgatorio,* ed. Mario Marcazzan, Florence, 1967; the separate pamphlets of the *Lectura Dantis Romana,* ed. Giovanni Fallani, Turin, 1959–1967; the third, fourth, and fifth volumes of the *Nuove letture dantesche* of the Casa di Dante di Roma, Florence, 1969–1972; *Letture del Purgatorio,* ed. Vittorio Vettori, Milan, 1965; and readings of *Purgatorio* cantos scattered through Vols. II–VI and VIII of the *Letture Classensi,* Ravenna, 1969–1979.

The notes themselves make full references to several exegetes. Other references are to the author alone. These references are here expanded to include the work referred to and, where the reference is not *ad locum* (to the same place in the *Purgatorio* at which the exegete is cited in these notes), page numbers.

Benvenuto: *Benvenuti de Rambaldis de Imola Comentum super Dantis Aldigherii Comoediam,* ed. G. F. Lacaita, 5 vols., Florence, 1887 (for *Purgatorio,* Vols. III and IV). The reference to Benvenuto is *ad loc.*

Bosco-Reggio: Umberto Bosco and Giovanni Reggio, eds., Dante Alighieri, *La Divina Commedia: Purgatorio,* Florence, 1979. Reference to Bosco-Reggio are *ad loc.*

Buti: *Commento di Francesco da Buti sopra la Divina Comedia di Dante Alighieri,* ed. Crescentino Giannini, 3 vols., Pisa, 1862 (for *Purgatorio,* Vol. II). References to Buti are *ad loc.*

Chimenz: Siro A. Chimenz, ed., Dante Alighieri, *La Divina Commedia: Purgatorio,* Turin, 1967. References to Chimenz are *ad loc.*

Moore: Edward Moore, *Studies in Dante: First Series, Scripture and Classical Authors in Dante,* Oxford, 1896 (reprinted, 1969); p. 231, for the reference in the note to Canto VI, 125–126.

Nardi: Bruno Nardi, *Il canto XV del Purgatorio,* Rome, 1953, then Turin, 1964 (one of the pamphlets in the *Lectura Dantis Romana*); p. 8, for the quotation in the note to Canto xv, 1–5.

Nicholl: Donald Nicholl, in a note, in *Dante, Monarchy and Three Political Letters,* Introduction by Donald Nicholl and a Note on the Chronology of Dante's Political Works by Colin Hardie, New York, 1954, p. 41 (for the quotation from Nicholl in our note to Canto I, 31). The translation of the *Monarchy* is by Nicholl; of the Epistles, by Hardie.

Porena: Manfredi Porena, ed., *La Divina Commedia di Dante Alighieri: Purgatorio,* Bologna, 1947. The reference to Porena is *ad loc.*

Raimondi: Ezio Raimondi, "Canto I del Purgatorio," in *Lectura Dantis Scaligera: Purgatorio,* Florence, 1967, pp. 3–37. (The quotation in our note to Canto I, 31 is on p. 18.)

Russo: Vittorio Russo, "A proposito del Canto XXV del Purgatorio," in *Studi di filologia romanza offerti a Silvio Pellegrini,* Padua, 1971; then in *Esperienze e / di letture dantesche* (tra il 1966 e il 1970), Naples, 1971, pp. 103–160. The notes to Canto XXV are much indebted to Russo's reading.

Singleton: Charles S. Singleton, translator and commentator, Dante Alighieri, *The Divine Comedy: Purgatorio. 2. Commentary,* Princeton, 1973. References to this volume are *ad loc.*

ALLEN MANDELBAUM's verse volumes are: *Chelmaxioms: The Savantasse of Montparnasse; Journeyman; Leaves of Absence;* and *A Lied of Letterpress.* His volumes of verse translation include *The Aeneid of Virgil,* a University of California Press volume for which he won a National Book Award; the *Inferno, Purgatorio,* and *Paradiso* volumes of the California Dante; the *Odyssey of Homer;* the *Metamorphoses of Ovid,* a finalist for the Pulitzer Prize in poetry; *Ovid in Sicily; Selected Poems of Giuseppe Ungaretti; Selected Writings of Salvatore Quasimodo; David Maria Turoldo;* and the forthcoming volumes of his *Convivio: From Twentieth-Century Italian Poetry.* Most recently he has co-edited, with Robert D. Richardson, Jr., the anthology *Three Centuries of American Poetry.* After his Ph.D. from Columbia University, Mandelbaum was in the Society of Fellows at Harvard and a Fulbright Research Scholar in Italy. Professor Emeritus of English and Comparative Literature at the Graduate Center of CUNY, he has been visiting professor at Washington University in St. Louis, the University of Houston, University of Denver, University of Colorado at Boulder, and Purdue University. His honorary degrees are from Purdue University, the University of Cassino, and the University of Torino (where he is Professor of the History of Literary Criticism). He is now the W. R. Kenan, Jr., Professor of Humanities at Wake Forest University.

Born in Chattanooga in 1940, BARRY MOSER was educated at Auburn University, the University of Tennessee at Chattanooga, and the University of Massachusetts, where he did his graduate studies. His work as illustrator, designer, and printer, which includes the books of Pennyroyal Press, is represented in numerous collections, museums, and libraries in the United States and abroad, among them the British Museum, the Library of Congress, the New York Public Library, the National Library of Australia, the London College of Printing, the Houghton Library at Harvard University, the Beinecke Library at Yale University, and the Firestone Library at Princeton University. Mr. Moser's illustrated books form a list of over sixty titles, including the Arion Press *Moby Dick,* the University of California Press edition of this translation of *The Divine Comedy,* and the Limited Editions Club of New York edition of Homer's *Odyssey.* The Pennyroyal *Alice's Adventures in Wonderland* was awarded the American Book Award for design/pictorial. An associate of the National Academy of Design, Mr. Moser frequently lectures and acts as visiting artist at universities and institutions across the country. His most ambitious work, the heralded Pennyroyal Caxton Bible in two volumes, with 231 engravings, published in October 1999.

ASK YOUR BOOKSELLER FOR THESE
BANTAM CLASSICS

ANNE FRANK'S TALES FROM THE SECRET ANNEX, Anne Frank, 0-553-58638-6

THE AUTOBIOGRAPHY AND OTHER WRITINGS, Benjamin Franklin, 0-553-21075-0

THE YELLOW WALLPAPER AND OTHER WRITINGS, Charlotte Perkins Gilman, 0-553-21375-X

FAUST: FIRST PART, Johann Wolfgang von Goethe, 0-553-21348-2

THE WIND IN THE WILLOWS, Kenneth Grahame, 0-553-21368-7

THE COMPLETE FAIRY TALES OF THE BROTHERS GRIMM, The Brothers Grimm, 0-553-38216-0

ROOTS, Alex Haley, 0-440-17464-3

FAR FROM THE MADDING CROWD, Thomas Hardy, 0-553-21331-8

JUDE THE OBSCURE, Thomas Hardy, 0-553-21191-9

THE MAYOR OF CASTERBRIDGE, Thomas Hardy, 0-553-21024-6

THE RETURN OF THE NATIVE, Thomas Hardy, 0-553-21269-9

TESS OF THE D'URBERVILLES, Thomas Hardy, 0-553-21168-4

THE HOUSE OF THE SEVEN GABLES, Nathaniel Hawthorne, 0-553-21270-2

THE SCARLET LETTER, Nathaniel Hawthorne, 0-553-21009-2

THE FAIRY TALES OF HERMANN HESSE, Hermann Hesse, 0-553-37776-0

SIDDHARTHA, Hermann Hesse, 0-553-20884-5

THE ODYSSEY OF HOMER, Homer, 0-553-21399-7

THE HUNCHBACK OF NOTRE DAME, Victor Hugo, 0-553-21370-9

FOUR GREAT PLAYS: A DOLL'S HOUSE, GHOSTS, AN ENEMY OF THE PEOPLE, and THE WILD DUCK, Henrik Ibsen, 0-553-21280-X

THE PORTRAIT OF A LADY, Henry James, 0-553-21127-7

THE TURN OF THE SCREW AND OTHER SHORT FICTION, Henry James, 0-553-21059-9

A COUNTRY DOCTOR, Sarah Orne Jewett, 0-553-21498-5

DUBLINERS, James Joyce, 0-553-21380-6

A PORTRAIT OF THE ARTIST AS A YOUNG MAN, James Joyce, 0-553-21404-7

THE METAMORPHOSIS, Franz Kafka, 0-553-21369-5

THE STORY OF MY LIFE, Helen Keller, 0-553-21387-3

CAPTAINS COURAGEOUS, Rudyard Kipling, 0-553-21190-0

THE JUNGLE BOOKS, Rudyard Kipling, 0-553-21199-4

KIM, Rudyard Kipling, 0-553-21332-6

LADY CHATTERLEY'S LOVER, D. H. Lawrence, 0-553-21262-1

SONS AND LOVERS, D. H. Lawrence, 0-553-21192-7

WOMEN IN LOVE, D. H. Lawrence, 0-553-21454-3

THE PHANTOM OF THE OPERA, Gaston Leroux, 0-553-21376-8

BABBITT, Sinclair Lewis, 0-553-21486-1

MAIN STREET, Sinclair Lewis, 0-553-21451-9

THE CALL OF THE WILD and WHITE FANG, Jack London, 0-553-21233-8